Also by Kitty Wilson

Every Day in December

THE LOVE EXPERIMENT

KITTY WILSON

One More Chapter
a division of HarperCollins*Publishers*
1 London Bridge Street
London SE1 9GF
www.harpercollins.co.uk

HarperCollins*Publishers*
1st Floor, Watermarque Building, Ringsend Road
Dublin 4, Ireland

This paperback edition 2022
First published in Great Britain in ebook format
by HarperCollins*Publishers* 2022

A catalogue record of this book is available from the British Library

ISBN: 978-0-00-840544-1

Printed and bound in the UK using 100% Renewable Electricity
by CPI Group (UK) Ltd
1

For Norma and for Matthew

Chapter One

Remember, people, the dating world is not that scary. When the time is right you will meet the perfect person. This is Dr Lily Galbraith signing off and reminding you of the four golden rules of dating – Be brave, have faith, be true to yourself and don't lick their faces!

I listen to my sign-off on the final version of this week's *Love Doctor* podcast. The subject matter is a little close to home but I'm done, I click upload and tap through to make sure all has gone smoothly before I close the lid of my laptop. As I do so I cast around the box room cum wardrobe where I record each week. This room is perfect with clothes on racks along each wall which absorb the sound and provide me with a little podcast-making cocoon, with just enough room for my teeny table.

Now I'm finished, I give a quick but firm nod to the polystyrene heads that adorn high shelves. I try not to be intimidated by them. Obviously, I'm aware they are inanimate objects and that we don't live in a *Toy Story* kind of world where these things come to life, but still, I don't trust them, not one iota.

With this room being the ideal recording space, we have to co-exist; but they seriously freak me out, especially late at night and home alone. All the wigs are displayed on lifeless heads that have been coloured in, badly, with felt-tips by Kevin and myself one drunken evening and further decorated with sequins, feathers and glitter in an attempt to hide the appalling ineptitude of our drunken colouring.

With each one now having a lurid face to match the wig's personality, they look even more horror-movie-esque than they did unadorned. Even with the lights on full, every time I sit in here I half expect them to suddenly come to life, manifest machetes and begin some sort of crazed spree that will ultimately end in high-pitched singing with Jinx's glorious Technicolor wardrobe shredded on the floor. Frankly, the thought of the music these creatures would produce scares me far more than the machetes.

I give them one more glare, just to remind them of their place, as I pick up my laptop and head on out. Maybe Kevin is right, maybe I need to work a little bit on my own head alongside my teaching and therapy work. A case of physician heal thyself. Although whilst I would want to work on why I'm spooked by shaped polystyrene, he is beginning to drop hints – again – that there are other things I should be concentrating on.

Kevin seems to have breathed fire into his determination to tell me where I'm going wrong in my life. I love him desperately – he appears wildly confident and more than a little bit bitchy but he is the sweetest, most considerate person I have ever known – however his views on my lifestyle can well and truly sod off. He cackled for a full ten minutes when he heard the topic of this week's podcast: *My friends all say my sexual behaviour is unhealthy but I'm happy with my choices. How do I get them to understand?*

I do date frequently and am very happy doing so regardless of what he has to say about it. There were years when I was younger that I despaired of ever being attractive and now that I am, I'm going to damn well enjoy myself. Not judging people on consensual relationship choices is important to me and it irks me, *really* irks me, that my best friend seems to think my refusal to want to be part of a couple is worthy of judgement.

I know Kevin is coming from a place of love and even if I do need to make some changes – I Very Definitely Don't – he needs to remember that people have to do things in their own time.

Looking up at the gap on the shelf I know that tonight Kevin will be working at our very favourite bar, Chrysalis, and doing so in full French revolutionary chic – the pink Marie Antoinette wig is missing – as he transforms himself into the beautiful, ever-talented, potty-mouthed cat that is High Jinx, Bristol's finest (I'm a little biased) Drag Queen.

Part of me is itching to join him. I could do with throwing my arms above my head and dancing until dawn but I need a slightly more, um … intimate Saturday night this week, especially after such a disappointing date last weekend. Mark was a lovely guy but he talked and talked and talked. And there is only so much any person can say about railways, specifically the disused Strawberry Line between Yatton and Cheddar, on a Saturday night. On *any* night.

Dating apps are meant to screen some of this stuff out. Mark had been savvy enough not to mention this slightly niche obsession in either his profile or our initial messages, but after an hour in his company I beat a polite retreat. I am open-minded, I love sex and cast a wide net but there are limits. I suspect he's the type of man that keeps his socks on.

Tonight, however, is looking promising. I have a new date lined up, am all sorts of excited and am heading there now. On the app he looks like a cross between Tom Hiddleston and Ryan Reynolds. There is very definitely a naughty twinkle and I do like a naughty twinkle; throw in beautifully groomed and I'm halfway there before any actual meeting takes place. And this guy claims to work largely overseas so will spend most of his time in far-away climes... perfect. I have a feeling that tonight is going to be very satisfying indeed.

I dress in one of my favourite date outfits – a slinky green jumpsuit that does more than hint at the hidden treasures on offer – touch up my make-up, pop some product on my hair, do a twirl and skip down the stairs and out of the door.

Just as I lock it behind me, I hear my ringtone. Pulling my phone from my bag I see that it's Angela, my newest client. Angela has a date tonight. An actual date. And she shouldn't be calling me now... this isn't a good sign at all. I have a sinking feeling that Angela may not have adhered to my advice, *any* of my advice. And whilst I'm all about finding someone who loves you for you, sometimes the 'you' bit can do with a smidge of refinement. And with most of my clients, that is quite a bit. With Angela, things are a little more ... um ... complex.

'I don't think I'll ever find someone who understands me,' Angela sobs down the phone before I even get a hello in. I take a deep breath and try to make my voice as gentle as can be. Having met Angela – and her life-size companions – for the first time last week I figure I already know the answer to the question I am obliged to ask.

'Angela, did you take the dolls on the date with you?'

'You said to be true to myself,' she retorts defensively, between sniffles.

'I did. I also told you to let this man get to know *you* first and that learning to love Fredrico, Paisley, Courtney and Robert may take time. Not everyone will be comfortable with life-sized dolls taking up four extra seats in the cinema. We did discuss this…'

'He wouldn't even buy them popcorn!' she sobs.

———————

Nearly two hours later and somewhat disheartened, I slide into Chrysalis. This evening has been a complete wash-out and by the time I escaped it was too late to swim out my frustrations but at least I can have a little bit of a boogie. As I push open the bar door, High Jinx catches my eye from behind the decks and pulls a what-are-you-doing-here? face. Seconds later she changes the music and Gloria Estefan floods the bar as she pages Doctor Beat.

I grin. She is naughty and I watch as she signals to Dan who is helping at the bar to take over on the decks before she comes bounding up to me and pulls me into a super-fast salsa. We dance as quickly as the music dictates, the two of us so used to each other that we feel fluid, as if we run into one another, my feet moving so fast as I keep up with the beat that I can picture them flying off. Our bodies mirror each other and even though she's my best friend, I can see, feel, that there is a sensuality to our movements. Highlighted as Dan shouts into the mic, 'Doctor Beat is in the house and on the floor, ladies. Look at those hips, we can see why she's the Luurrrve Doctor.'

Jinxy smirks as she hears Dan use that name, spins me fast and we seamlessly move into the cha-cha we learned to dance together at university. I drop into a half split and as Jinxy twirls me up and spins me around again she pulls me into her and our hips gyrate and then as the climax builds to the end of the song, I know Jinxy well enough to know exactly how she wants to finish this. As I suspect does Dan, who deliberately hasn't lined up a new track yet. I dance back into my own space and *kapow*, as the last note sounds, she death drops and everyone around us cheers. She gets to her feet, makes a swirly bow to me and I drop a curtsy. As put out as I feel by another catastrophic date, I can't help how the high energy of my friend brings the smile right back to my face.

Jinxy returns to the decks and I dance until her set is over and the lights are on. I am so out of breath, I may actually need an ambulance. I'm fit, super fit and my swimming means I have strong lungs but Dan had joined me on the floor and he is something else – as Phyllis so succinctly put it when she hired him, *That boy has hips that James Brown would covet* – and even he is panting as we drop onto one of the velour banquettes that line the back wall of the bar.

'What are you doing here tonight? You should be on your back, on his front, on someone any which way. It's Saturday night, are you losing your touch?' Jinx bounds over, her set finished for the evening, her wig slightly askew and her face flushed from jumping around like a lunatic for the last couple of hours. She has, however, stopped to grab a jug of water for us and some glasses from the bar. She's wearing one of her favourite dresses, one that she made herself with a little bit of help from Dan and which manages to encapsulate the luxury and hedonism of the French court with its corseted but very low top, poufy sleeve endings and full skirt, albeit one that is drastically shortened and far from floor-length.

'Maybe she's refining her touch,' Dan says to Jinx. 'Maybe she turned this one down.'

'This one had come-to-bed eyes and floppy hair, so I doubt it. What actually happened?'

'Dan's right,' I say, still a bit panty but my smugness manages to come through. Jinx clasps her bosom and draws in enough breath to intimidate the Big Bad Wolf before quirking her brow in query. 'Oh my God, okay, yes he was so gorgeous to look at and you know me—'

'Uh-huh, no shame and the sexual appetites of Casanova himself!' she interjects, quick as a flash.

'Charming. But not this evening. I'm not completely shameless and this evening the shame kicked in. I mean there was no denying it, he was beautiful, beau-ti-ful...' I draw out the word and my fingers curl into an 'o' shape to reiterate the intensity of that fact.

'Should the nationally renowned feminist Love Doctor be referring to men as if they are merely pieces of meat?' Jinxy queries.

'If you let the nationally renowned feminist Love Doctor finish what she was saying you would hear that she did not respond to this guy as if he were merely a piece of meat. I think it's fair to say I took a thoroughly holistic view and assessed him as an individual with opinions and emotions before deciding his very beautiful piece of meat wouldn't be allowed anywhere near me tonight. Or indeed ever.'

'Well done, girl, you are making progress.'

'Oh, do fuck off.'

Dan laughs. 'Come on then, what did he do? What could he have done that put you off your stride, that made him suddenly unbearable?'

'Honestly, his dating skills were strong. He was a gentleman – well-presented, smelt like heaven, asked me questions and actually listened to my answers, managed not to look at my boobs as he did so. All the old-fashioned chivalrous stuff, I was loving it. The Love Doctor would give him a strong ten on first impressions.'

'Don't keep referring to yourself in the third person. It smacks of sociopathy,' Jinx says.

'The Love Doctor likes it.'

'I knew I would regret coming up with that name in uni.'

'Regret it bad!'

'Still haven't told us what he did,' Dan pulls us back on topic.

'Oh right, well, his charming gentleman-of-yore persona was so deeply entrenched that I think he would happily have children up chimneys again and bring back the workhouse if only he could make it a bit less of a free ride. Honestly, once he relaxed with me enough to let his true self emerge –' Jinx wiggles her thickly painted brows at me and I raise mine in return '– no, not that bit, I told you we didn't get that far ... then it was pretty clear that he would like anyone with even vague pretensions of progressiveness to be hung, drawn and quartered and strongly believes that the welfare state merely keeps alive those that suck the soul from society. You thought that far-right woman was bad on *Question Time* the other night? Well, let me tell you, she was practically a communist compared to this guy.'

Jinx screws up her face and I know she understands. I do have a healthy ... um ... very high sex drive, but I do put the brakes on when I need to. I need to be attracted to a person's mind as much as their body, although the body can definitely help – I literally wink at myself in my mind and then grimace. But as much as I wanted to get laid tonight, I cannot engage with someone I think is a bit of a dick.

'So, sexually, you are drawing the line at Nazis?' Jinx gives me a look that indicates faux surprise at the fact I have a line, but I don't want to get into a squabble, not until I've got my breath back properly at least.

'Truth.' I smile back in return. 'Plus, he looked like he might quiz me on Latin, double-check my socio-economic status and then dip me in TCP, just to make sure I was suitable.'

'Now don't go kink-shaming.' Dan giggles. 'That's not what we do.'

'The kinks I don't mind, the arseholery I do.'

'Oh my God, if that girl doesn't get outta my bar soon I'm not going to be held responsible.' Phyllis – the owner of Chrysalis, mother hen and O.G. legend – joins us at the table. 'I'm all for letting her process but her misery has been battering us down for years and if she takes to the stage again, with the boys locking up in a minute, to sing "All By Myself", I am going to throttle her with a microphone lead.'

Phyllis is tiny, very wrinkled and terrifying. She's in her eighties now – we think – but she could take on anyone and win, merely with the force of her presence. She is one of those people you lean in to, to listen.

All eyes turn to Miss Havoc de Belle, who, true to form, is dressed in bridal wear – not much of it, more garter than dress – and is hunched over the bar, her hand clasping a glass of whisky, the grip of her fingers very much at odds with the looseness of her posture.

'Oh, you know she can't help it. It's just who she is. She loves love. Our very own Miss Havocsham,' Jinx says, her eyes softening as they alight on her fellow queen. Dan joins in Jinx's look and wordlessly – they have this freaky telepathic symmetry – gets up and walks towards the piano next to the stage as Jinx approaches Havoc at the bar.

Dan stands over the piano, his tongue slightly stuck out as he begins to play. And boy can he play, he's a younger, funkier version of Alicia Keys but male, with a broad Bristolian accent and a tendency to dress in anything with a skull printed on it. He strokes the keys and I instantly recognise the tune as 'We Are Family'. Jinx drops a kiss on Havoc's shoulder, gently takes the whisky from her hands and pulls her to her feet. The object of Jinx's attention is not looking like she wants to take part and I lean over and grab Phyllis's hand, pull her to her feet whilst she lightly growls at me – a growl is fine, it's silence that's terrifying with this octogenarian – and together we join the other two, motioning for Adore Vajayjay and Twinkibelle, who are also in tonight, to join us as we sing loud and dance like our feet are on fire until Miss Havocsome is buoyed up with our love and I realise that there is nowhere on earth, naughty twinkly eyes or not, that I would rather be than here with my chosen family.

Chapter Two

'Bye, Jay,' Jasmine singsongs at me as I smile at Cass, hating that I am leaving my baby sister with that steely-eyed raptor who radiates bonhomie and wellness vibes as if they are chemical weapons. One small jab at her defences and the whole thing is going to blow sky-high.

Halfway down the stairs, I pause and it takes all my self-control not to turn back to the flat, pick Cassie up, put her under my arm and carry her down the stairs. I picture myself transporting her out of the building and into my car, her little legs kicking and her mighty lungs alerting the whole of the neighbourhood just as they had the last time I had tried to carry her off, when she was six years old and refused to leave the swings. But to do so would be kidnap and the thing with kidnap is it doesn't really matter how much you love the person involved; it is *never* all right. Tempting but never all right. Besides, she is twenty-four and I really have to learn to respect the fact that she may be my baby sister but she is my *adult* baby sister.

What I do have in my arms instead is a kitten, a very cute kitten and one that Cassie had fallen desperately in love with. Last week my phone had been blown up by kitten videos, love heart eye emojis and my sister channelling Elmyra Fudd, *I love him, I love him, I'll hug him, I'll squeeze him.* Yet five minutes ago she handed him over to me saying he can't stay in the flat. So Darling Dimkins – what a name – is now sat in a cat box, his sad little face peering through the grille and summing up what I'm feeling now as I open the car door and know I must drive away.

I carefully place the box in the footwell, let myself in the driver's side and look down at him before I turn the key. 'Hey, little guy, don't look so sad. You can come and stay with me and we'll do the whole men together thing. You'll have your mum back soon.' I smile, hope it's true and reach through the grille to stroke the kitten, who draws back hesitantly. My heart goes out to the little grey ball of fluff. He has only met me today – I'm fairly sure Cass hasn't made him watch videos of *me* all week – and now he's here and I'm about to drive him away from his home. I stroke him, as much as I can with steel bars between us, to reassure him that I have his back.

'Ow!'

The little shit.

This little ball of fluff I was so worried about has taken a step back and then launched himself at my finger and clamped his teeth down as hard as he can. Which considering he has kitten teeth is pretty damn hard. I withdraw my finger sharply and shake it whilst the kitten holds eye contact with me as if issuing a challenge – Go on, come at me again and I'll take the damn thing off!

No shame and not so cute.

Seems I *have* got Cass back, just in kitten form.

When it comes to my sister and her relationship with Jasmine, I know all the theory. My day job, running community programmes at City Youth, means that I understand how people have to reach decisions themselves, they can't be pushed into doing things that they don't want to do, that sometimes people have to hit rock bottom before they can truly reach out. I've done endless training on this, both receiving and delivering. But what I have never truly understood before, other than on a theoretical level, is how hard it is to watch. I go around in circles trying to rationalise things. I know it could be worse. It's not as if Cassie is sat slumped in her flat freebasing, it's just that I really don't like her girlfriend.

No, it's more than not liking, much more. I don't trust her, there's something off there and it runs deep. She has me on my guard, my hackles up whenever I'm in a room with her. I can't name it but it's there, it is, and I don't understand how Cass can't sense it.

I feel guilty that when Cassie came out, I felt an overwhelming sense of relief, a belief that if she wasn't into men then she'd never have to put up with the bullshit I know many men mete out. Even today when we tell each other that men are better educated now, that this generation coming up have been weaned on issues like consent, I know – I see it at work – that some boys are still often driven by their ego and their cocks. *Obviously* not all, but enough. I thought if Cassie were gay, I wouldn't have to worry so much about control and bullshit. But control and bullshit aren't merely the preserve of heterosexuality. I had needed to learn that, yes, but I hadn't wanted to learn it this fast. And not with Cass.

'Meow.' Darling Dimkins' tone is as aggressive as his claws, but he has a point.

'Yep, you're right. We can't sit here all day, let's get you home. I'm happy to look after you –' I waggle my finger at him, the bitten one ,'but you'd best not test me.'

'Meow.'

'Chopsy as well as violent, huh?'

My phone beeps and I wriggle it out of my front pocket whilst casting a look up at the window of Cass's flat. Ever hopeful.

It is not a message from my sister begging me to free her from her tower. Instead, it's a notification about a podcast some of the girls from work made me add, something they're raving about and challenged me to listen to. *The Love Doctor* or some such nonsense. It'll do no harm to give it a listen and it's important to show the girls I respect their interests. You never know, it may feature a segment on non-violent confrontation for Darling Dimkins. I reckon he has an awful lot to learn if we're to live in harmony.

I press the notification and it leads me to the latest podcast so I hit play and then turn the ignition. The introduction bursts into life and immediately I can tell this woman is a professional.

As I drive away from the flat, I remember Chloe's words as she had been holding court at the Youth Centre, preaching that everyone should be forced to listen to this woman. *She's a Bristol gal and she don't talk shit. If it's consensual it's fine, if it's a no, it's a no, you understand? She ain't about the looks, she's not telling no female to lose weight or get BBL, nah, she's all about being true. I like her, you should give her a listen. Serious.*

I had left the room smirking at how forceful Chloe was

with her peers, confirming my belief that she would be an excellent ambassador in a wellbeing project I am currently working on. But as I let this woman's voice spill over me – discussing healthy sexual choices and how much input our friends should have – I realise I should have taken Chloe's advice earlier. This Love Doctor woman is practical, no-nonsense and professional with the advice she gives.

And that is exactly the sort of advice I need, to make sure I don't cock this up with Cassie. I know I'm too close, too emotionally involved to look at her life rationally. That if I follow my instincts, the carry-her-out-under-my-arms ones, then I'm going to mess this thing up big time. The look she gave me today as I started to question why she couldn't keep Darling Dimkins was her full-on don't-you-dare eye, a look that indicates she knows what I'm thinking and isn't having any of it.

And the thing is I know my sister, she's damn stubborn. Pig-headed like a mule, Dad used to say back when she was a toddler and even though there was a definite dearth of mules in the city, I knew exactly what he meant. She used to give us all hell, would pin me to the ground and give me such a whipping, even though she was three and I was nine, with Dad watching on the side, laughing as his son got beat down by a baby and he sprinkled spices into the goat meat simmering for hours on the stove.

But for all her don't-mess-with-me-unless-you-like-the-mortuary attitude, the one ingrained in her very veins, I'm not convinced she is exercising this with Jasmine. I don't recognise my sister in *any* of that relationship, not the Cass I know, the venom-spitting, injustice-fighting, if-you-come-for-the-queen kinda girl I grew up with. The firebrand I know, the one who is all flash and flare, seems to have been doused by Jasmine, a kumbaya type who has not just contained the flame that is my sister but has, I am scared, completely put her out.

When Dad died, Cass was left with only me. I had to be her warrior hero, slay the dragons. I thought I just had to get her to eighteen safely, that then we were home and dry. No one had told me that there is no cut-off date, no one had told me that it's not just protecting her from predatory men when she's young and vulnerable, that there is no age or gender cut-off for abuse.

There is nothing I can do right here and right now. Cassie doesn't appear to be in imminent danger. From the looks she was shooting, I am the one with quicksand beneath my toes. She wants another romantic night in with Jas and me to sod off with her cat.

A myriad thoughts scroll through my head – each one doom-laden – as I drive back home but once I pull up to my house I know the best thing I can do is get in, get the bloody kitten settled and then get myself down to the gym.

I wait for the podcast to wind up, listen to The Love Doctor sign off and give Darling Dimkins a Very Strict Look as I lift his carrier out of the car in the hope that he understands who is feeding him from now on.

Chapter Three

I lie in a foetus curl, all rounded like a snail shell, and wonder whether whimpering out loud is a step too far. It is. But I so want to whimper. The act of making a noise, even just a little-lamb-lost plaintive bleat, is comforting. But I'm not alone in the house so I keep the whimper in.

Everything hurts, every little patch of me, each square millimetre of me is fatigued, and in my heightened emotional state I wonder if this is how it feels to be bleeding out. I know that this is not a rational thought and that this will pass. But my mind does go to dramatic places when I'm like this. My mind is not always my friend and my hormonal mind is very much my worst enemy.

The truth is I have periods so rarely that they are heinous when they arrive. These aren't normal periods, not ones like my mum has or my sister, as horrid as theirs are. These are completely disabling, a minimum-two-pads-and-a-super-max-tampon hideous. Sleeping on two towels whilst my stomach cramps so hard, part of me wants to reach within my skin and rip it out, watch it bounce across the floor, no doubt concertinaing with cramps as it goes. And my back, my back aches so bad and as yet I have found nothing much that touches it. And this is potentially going to go on for seven days.

Seven days.

Still they are better than they used to be. Much better than the days when I used to be dizzy, or would faint in class, or throw up everywhere.

I've had to cancel all my upcoming sessions both at my office and at the uni. And I need to send an apology to Adrian, this man I have been chatting to for the last few days on Bumble. We were going to meet up for meze but I'm not going anywhere right now. I had taken a risk; sometimes I get the ovulation pains – accompanied by the burning searing pain that shoots straight into my coccyx – but then nothing else happens.

This is not one of those times.

Right now I'm almost too scared to move. If I change position just an inch, then I can practically picture raging rivers rushing out of me. It's fair to say I am a seething mass of hormones, self-pity and irrational imagery right now.

In fact, I'm so sad about the thought of another failed date and days spent in bed that I can feel tears pinpricking the corner of my eyes. It would be fine If I'd had a successful date recently, but I've had such an awful run of dating luck, unprecedented, that I really could cry in this moment. It's a miracle that I've not completely healed up but as testified to by the raging rivers of red then that is still open, albeit very definitely not for business. Even Moses would have his work cut out with what's going on down there at the moment. The tears are no longer merely in the corners of my eyes, they're preparing to torrent too.

Because it's not just the pains and the ickiness, it's the emotional turmoil as well.

Normally I can be relied upon to be rational, scientific; everything in the world has its place and I know exactly where that is. Part of my skills in work are being able to cut through the emotion, recognise the feelings but help a person move forward, see what they need to do. I am level-headed, cool. But when I am hormonal all that I usually rely on disappears.

I lose that ability to see things clearly. Instead I become my most emotional self, my most fractured self. Self-belief disappears right out of the window and I am back to being a scared, frightened adolescent that knows she isn't good enough, who will always be the freak.

I feel my eyes well up again and use every ounce of steely self-determination to get myself back to a rational space. A more balanced mindset. The woman I have trained myself to be. I am experienced in this. It is better than it was. I have managed to make changes that take the edge off the worst of it.

And the Adrian thing – bottom line is he's a stranger I'm hoping to have sex with, that's all, and he'll be fine with me postponing. Just because my last two dates were bad doesn't mean I've completely lost my touch. For goodness' sake, I'm the female Hitch, a dating savant for the twenty-first century. I'll get back on my game in no time at all and this feeling sorry for myself over a recent lack of sex is self-indulgent claptrap. Dear God, my sister is happily married and I know for a fact she's not got laid for a good three months!

I remind myself of the girl I was, compared to the woman I have become, and know how grateful I am for all I have achieved. It was far, far from easy but even so, I never dreamed that I would hold the power that I do now and I need to remind myself of that rather than lie here snivelling.

There is a timid knock at my bedroom door and then it opens a few inches and Kevin pops his head around and offers a tentative smile.

'Hey, you,' Kevin says, 'I've brought you treats.' He pops down a tray filled with all my favourite snacks and then takes the hot water bottle in a furry cover he has clamped underneath his chin and waggles it at me.

I swear, best friends are *the* biz. I'd much rather have Kevin than any husband. He has known me since I was eighteen, an apprentice butterfly, and has helped me spread my wings, develop the way I dress and get killer good at eyeliner.

I mean he thought I was some kind of teetotal nutjob when we first met, with an unhealthy relationship with food, but now he recognises that none of that is, ever was, my true self and I was, I am just very, very disciplined. Discipline that has helped me shape my life the way I need it to be for both my physical and mental health.

I smile at him knowing he recognises it's my my-period-sucks-and-right-now-I-hate-my-life smile as he comes and sits on my bed. He leans around me and after putting the hot water bottle by my stomach, gently strokes my back and makes soothing noises as you would to a new-born, then he spears some banana on a fork and tries to feed me.

I rarely eat fruit, too much sugar, but bananas with magnesium for cramping and dark-chocolate-covered popcorn are allowed at this time of the month. I see he has also brought me almonds and pumpkin seeds. For all his own reliance on

MaccieD's I am touched at how he remembers what I need at this time and why.

I take the banana from the fork and pop it in my mouth – feeding me is a step too far – and then, with no fear, he pulls the duvet back a little, squidges up next to me whilst making sure he is careful not to knock me from my position, not one iota, and turns on my TV so we can both cuddle up and rewatch *To Wong Foo*.

Chapter Four

As The Love Doctor I'm here to try and help you solve all your dating worries, your love woes, but when this question came through my DMs this week my interest was piqued. Love is love, it isn't always sexual, and I want to do what I can to help with all relationships. So let's change things up and see how we can help this latest listener.

Never would I have guessed that I would be settling down to deliberately listen to a *Love Doctor* podcast as it streams on a Saturday evening. But then I never thought I'd be a cat owner either and right now I'm sat in my flat, salad bowl from Eat-a-pita to the side of me and one eye on the kitten curled on the other side of the sofa. He's even my social media picture these days, albeit with a little devil-eye adjustment. The very peace of Dim (as I call him now) is an indication that he is merely lulling me into a false sense of security before he unleashes all hell.

I glance at my watch. We've a family Zoom scheduled in an

hour but I need to listen to this first. I utter up a little prayer, please let it be me.

As The Love Doctor starts her introduction, I find myself sitting up dead straight, my whole body paying attention. A bit like when I was a child in assembly and Bristol City had come into the school to give a you-can-do-anything-if-you-try talk. If my ears could prick, they would.

My heart is racing and I feel my breathing quicken, I lean forward as she says she's dealing with a sibling issue today. Is she referring to the DM I sent to her Insta? I had typed my message quickly, almost scared of getting caught, as if Cassie might come across me any second and catch me in the act. The fact that she was miles away across the city as I typed was irrelevant. It felt furtive, sneaky and a little silly. I'd regretted sending the question in the minute I hit send and heard it whoosh. But now I'm keen for an answer.

I had messaged The Love Doctor out of sheer desperation. My concerns for Cassie are so strong that they are threatening to take over every waking hour, and most of the non-waking ones as well. I fret-loop as I lie awake at night until sleep finally comes for me in the early hours and I Technicolor-dream worst-case scenarios. I think about her when I'm on the football pitch, in the gym, all through work, and am praying like I did before Dad passed. Thought and prayer are all very well, but I need to step up more. By messaging the podcast, then at least I'd be doing something. Nowhere near enough but something.

Now the person who messaged this week has done so because he loves his little sister but is worried about her latest choice of partner. We've all been there, haven't we? Whether it be friend or sibling or even parent, what can we do when someone we love chooses someone who we think isn't good enough or, in this case, is potentially downright dangerous?

I hunch forward, my fork pausing on its way from bowl to mouth.

'Arrghhhh!' Something attacks me from behind and my meal shoots straight up in the air, resulting in a flurry of carrots and cabbage and hummus on my carpet. The three falafels landing as eyes and a nose, a chilli pepper making a mouth, and I can't help but grin at the smiley face before a growl escapes my lips as the kitten jumps down from my shoulder into the hummus and starts sniffing the falafels.

'Oh no you don't...' I grab Dim and pause the podcast as I carry him into the kitchen and he mewls, squirms and scratches at me with his hummus-covered kitten claws.

'You're a menace.' I clean him up and return to attack the mess, as he jumps on my back, doing the kneading thing that kittens do. Cass told me this is a sign that a cat has taken to you, feels comfortable, views you as akin to a parent. I do not feel paternal, I feel hungry. I scoop him up and place him on the floor. He defiantly makes eye contact. 'You need to behave yourself, this is important!' I say and waggle my finger. He attacks it.

Of course he does.

I should've anticipated that. I'm beginning to see why Cassie asked me to take him, he's an absolute menace. For all Jasmine's let's-teach-the-world-to-sing mentality, I can imagine there is no way she's putting up with this level of terrorism in her flat. Dim should be pleased she didn't have him skinned. Now I'm thinking about it, I can totally see her as Cruella de

Vil but in a more Bristol hippy way. The two sound incompatible but trust me when I say Jasmine is capable, she is a woman of great juxtapositions.

I give Dim one more firm look, just so he knows the score, and resume the podcast. The Love Doctor's first words do not bring joy to my heart.

The first, slightly pessimistic answer is not much. The more you try and get involved, the more you ram your opinions down your loved one's throat, then the greater the chance of them running to the hills and cutting you out entirely. And this is the last thing you want to happen. What you need to do is stick around, try to be non-judgemental and do all you can to stay in your sister's life. Now that is going to mean biting your tongue and biting it hard. No one needs to be told repeatedly that their choices are bad and it sounds like your sister and you have a great relationship. My guess is she already knows what you think.

I suspected this, of course I did, but hearing it said with authority reinforces it a bit. I've been worrying about whether holding back is the right thing to do, that maybe I should be speaking out more than I am.

The Love Doctor continues to speak sense, states that coercive control is domestic abuse and legally recognised as such and reiterates that I need to recognise Jas is probably trying to isolate Cass, and repeated nagging on my part will make it far easier for Cass to cut me out.

Don't force her to choose between the two of you. The important thing to do is to leave the door open, make it easy for her to communicate with you when she needs to, provide that non-judgemental ear so she has a safe space for the things she needs to say. There's a good chance she is already keeping things from you, so all you can do at this point is to gently boost her self-esteem, make her know how loved she is and that she is not alone or at fault for any of this. And this is often done best in less obvious ways. Show her you care without suffocating her. Just listen.

I know she's right, that I need to be building Cassie up, supporting her rather than dragging at her choices, this needs to be my number one priority now.

Understanding the emotional investment in this relationship will help you to be patient. The truth is people often get caught in these relationships because at the very beginning, in the first romantic flushes, this person was remarkably adept at identifying and meeting your sister's needs and making her feel secure, whether that be emotionally, physically or even financially. With these needs being met then your sister will have invested herself in this relationship and will want to continue to do so...

This bit is important, I'm always asking why Cassie is with Jas, why won't she just leave? It's a simple binary decision as far as I'm concerned, but this woman is breaking it down, making it clear.

...As these relationships deteriorate the victim usually feels they are at fault for the changes, they are somehow displeasing their partner, and they need to get back to that place of security, of feeling loved. They then try to do whatever they can to keep their relationship going, the hope being that it will return any moment to what they were first attracted to. Hope is an amazing thing to have and is very powerful. Normally we should cling to hope but in some cases it can be destructive. The trouble, of course, is that giving up hope in the context of a relationship is hard to do. It means accepting an end to all the hopes and dreams that flourished and got this relationship to the commitment stage in the first place. Not to mention the practical consequences of ending a relationship, moving

out, finding a new place to live and ensuring that you are safe from this person once you do so.

I'm so engrossed that I realise the kitten hasn't attacked me for a good few minutes... where is he? Still listening to the podcast, I scan the room. The Love Doctor starts to talk of the need for self-care and protection for me and the benefits of boundaries to keep myself strong for the day that Cass does reach out for help.

I can't see the cat anywhere. Where is he? Boundaries for self-protection are what I need with Dim, but how do you fix boundaries with a kitten... Oh.

'Hey, what you doing up there, little guy?'

The podcast is still playing as my eye is now on the curtain rail, practically the highest point in the room, where Dim is tentatively balancing. It's the first time I've seen anything relating to fear or uncertainty on the kitten's face and my heart immediately melts.

'Everything's going to be okay,' I say as I head into the kitchen and grab a chair. Climbing up on it I reach over to the kitten and try to coax him across to my hands. The kitten takes a look at them and looks down at the curtain as if weighing up the two options.

One of the biggest things you can do is to try and help raise her self-esteem, make her see that she is good at things and is worthy of love and respect. Are there activities you can do together which can be pleasurable for her? The Love Doctor asks and I pause for a minute to try and have a think, but Dim senses my concentration is broken and lets out a plaintive miaow, I turn back to him as the podcast continues.

If you do, that could strengthen your bond even further and provide opportunities for her to talk to you should she wish to. Create space in your lives where she can have fun, achieve things, feel like herself and not be forced to put her relationship under the microscope when she's with you.

Dim suddenly takes a flying jump at my hands, scratching as he wobbles, and I tilt my hands up to right the angle for him. Then as I try to steady him he scurries down my arm and leaps back at the curtain, and climbs down in a tumbling, I'm-going-so-fast-I'm-not-sure-I-like-it way. It reminds me of that scary hill when you're on a bike as a kid and you're never quite sure if you're going to get to the bottom in one piece but there's no way you can stop without making a tit of yourself so you kind of just give it up to God and see where the speed takes you.

I tumbled a few times, but nowhere near as often as Cassie. I would at least try and put the brakes on whereas she would take her hands off the handlebars and scream with joy as she hurtled down. Dim is, as I've said before, very Cassie.

Meanwhile, I'm left standing on the chair, hands scratched to buggery, and Dim is on the floor looking up at me. He gives me a look, scrambles across to the other curtain and if kittens could laugh, I swear he would as he races up it to the curtain pole again. Seeing as I'm still there I reach out again. No one warns you about the levels of sadism in a kitten, oh no, it's all cute pics and YouTube videos, but I'm beginning to think Dim is here solely to mess with my head. He swipes at my hand and then gleefully begins his tumbledown descent.

I give up. I get down from the chair, reassure myself that the whole cats-have-nine-lives thing is a saying for a reason and turn my attention back to The Love Doctor.

Now I know the temptation is to tell her all about the forms that abusive relationships take, educate her as to why what she is living through is not healthy and not her fault, that just because she's not being knocked into next week with a frying pan every other day does not mean that her relationship is not defined as abusive. But, as I have already made clear, don't! If she opens a conversation about it then by all means use the opportunity to gently point out how these behaviours are not normal, ask her how she would feel if she heard someone was doing this to you, and you'll find she'll probably feel very different about the behaviour when the context is changed and she is not at the centre of it. The Love Doctor continues, talking about how popular culture, soap operas and the like can often open a conversation, and then she moves on to the importance of positive role models, all the things I know from work but have had trouble applying to this situation.

You don't say whether or not you are in a relationship and I can see why this might not be pertinent but if you are or the two of you are close to people who are in healthy functional relationships, expose her to this, use them as examples without directly addressing it.... Okay, this is Malcolm and Sue in a nutshell. They have been role models for a long time. As for my relationship history, not so much.

Cassie is always bitching at me to slow down, be me for a bit. She seems to think I'm on a constant quest to find Miss Perfect so I can start life, and she may have a point. I date a lot and am open about how I want to build a family, maybe foster, give children the best start I can.

I am aware that time is not static. I need to make sure I am with the right person if I want a family and I need to get a move on. I don't want to be parenting teenagers at sixty. She fails to see the sense of this and claims I have a wish-list of qualities that no human on earth can live up to. Surely there is no harm in knowing what you want, knowing it has to be with the right person and not being prepared to settle?

I know the qualities I want my partner to have, things that make good mother material, and if the women I date don't meet them then I move on quickly – it stops everyone wasting their time. Cassie doesn't understand this is a kindness in the long run and thinks I should live in the now, but why would I, if I already know what I want?

I switch my focus back to The Love Doctor. This evening is about Cassie, not me.

...Surround her with love and respect, demonstrate how you value her opinion, how others value what she has to say and what she has to give. Over time she will become increasingly aware of how flawed her relationship is and the more she realises that what she is experiencing isn't normal, isn't healthy and isn't her fault then the greater chance you have of her leaving. This woman hasn't said anything that doesn't make utter sense. I feel relief that I have some guidance from someone who seems to know what they're talking about and has given me a clear action plan. I don't feel quite so adrift. I listen to the end as The Love Doctor reminds listeners of the importance of reporting suspected violence and signposts to organisations that help victims of domestic abuse.

I wish you the best of luck with all of this. I'm grateful that you reached out and gave me the chance to talk about this serious issue on here. My inbox is always open and whilst I can't always respond to every message, I really hope your sister manages to break free soon.

Normally I sign off with a cheery and silly message but after this it doesn't feel appropriate so I shall simply say thank you for listening. This is Doctor Lily Galbraith signing off, be brave, have faith and thank you.

And as she says goodbye, I find myself saying 'thank you'

out loud too, leaving Dim, who has finished desecrating the curtains to move on to some fluffy cushion that Cass bought me last year. I have a map now and am going to call up Malcolm and Sue, get a head start on Cass joining us on Skype and see if they can help me kickstart my plan of action as prescribed by Bristol's one and only Love Doctor.

Chapter Five

I pull myself up on the ledge of the pool and shake myself off. That felt amazing. It was exactly what I needed. I've had a full-on day with Angela as we started to deconstruct what it is that she is looking for and the best way to achieve that.

I am very aware that there are a lot of negative assumptions made about therapy dolls and there is often a belief that the people who have them imagine them to be real. This is not the case at all. Angela knows her dolls are a prop in a role-playing game and she needs a partner who gets that. Her upset over the popcorn was merely disappointment that her date was not that man.

Therapy dolls help lots of people, and they are increasingly used with dementia patients as well as for those with PTSD. They trigger a sense of emotional wellbeing; the act of cuddling and cosseting releases endorphins. Not all doll owners have medical needs and despite them having a bit of a stigma there is absolutely nothing wrong in having and loving these dolls. With Angela, I think the key is to ensure the dolls enhance her life rather than limit it. But right now, her walls are very much up and I have a long way to go in developing a therapeutic relationship with her.

For now my work day is over and I am in the pool at the lido having just finished my mandatory fifty lengths. I'm strict about doing them, because my fitness is important and if I let one day slide... well, I don't dare. And now they are done, I need to warm myself through.

Entering the glass-fronted building at the end of the pool, I grab my towel from the hook and push open the door to the sauna. The wall of heat hits me as I enter, knocking the air out of my lungs. But the familiar smell that I love, of the dry hot air, is tinged with an overwhelming scent of aftershave and whisky.

A lot of aftershave and whisky.

That's new. My nose automatically crinkles.

'I'm sorry about the smell. Really I am. Can you forgive me?' A male voice comes from the top corner of the sauna. It isn't one I recognise and, with the lido largely being members only, that's unusual.

The wooden seating has three stages; the higher the seat, the higher the intensity of the heat. The voice, or at least the man it belongs to, is perched right up the top, in my favourite spot. Which I will forgive, because I am shallow and this man is something else.

Even sat down I can see he is tall and every sleek inch of him ripples, like a racehorse or a big cat. It's hard not to reach out, run a finger down his frame just to see if he's real. He reminds me a little of Trevor Noah – I'm a bit of a fangirl – but has that real-life twinkle that makes him so much hotter than anything beamed through a TV.

'That's fine, really,' I say as I climb to the top, placing myself on the other side as far from him as I can. I've been waiting to get in this sauna all day and I don't want to sit on one of the lower levels. My neck is as knotty as a boy scout's handbook and the heat is the best way I know of relaxing.

'It's not though, I can only apologise –' this man is determined to chat '– I would have stayed at home but a) I was afraid I'd asphyxiate myself and b) I had to be here for a certain time. It's faded a bit. You should have smelt me an hour ago.'

I surprise myself as a burst of laughter shoots from my mouth. This is unusual sauna conversation. Sniffing someone has never come up before. Despite my desire for silence as I came in, I'm here for this chat.

I sit to the side of him and see he has a tattoo on his upper arm, the face of an older man who has the most lively and wise eyes I have ever seen. And I flick a look up to the face of the man sat next to me and although his hair is trimmed short and he lacks the locks of the tattoo man, I see he is the very spit of him.

'It is a little strong,' I concede. Seeing as we've clearly dispensed already with the polite social norms, I follow up with 'Do you normally wear that much?'

'Oh yeah, thirteen-year-old me knows the ladies like it. Or the men. I'm an equal opportunities nasal offender.'

'And do you usually listen to thirteen-year-old you?' I can't help but ask – his silliness is drawing me in. His answering smile reveals dimples and his eyes crinkle, deep conker-brown puddles that promise fun and are framed with the longest lashes I've ever seen. I am bowled over by the physical perfection of this man. He belongs on billboards the length and breadth of the country, not in the sauna, next to me.

'No, never, he was an utter fool. Even more stupid than thirty-year-old me, but you know he was enthusiastic. I'm a little more jaded, and remarkably, way more embarrassed. Teen me would have swaggered to this smell.'

'He would have had some competition from my Impulse Spray.' I note that he is five years younger than I am.

'Aha, see, I am not the only one with a guilty conscience.'

'Mmmm.' I draw out the sound, feeling it vibrate against my lips. I'm enjoying this. 'Didn't feel the compulsion to mix it with a bottle or two of gin though,' I add.

'I feel that I want to explain how I got this particular concoction on me. But really it would definitely be crossing a line to tell you the full story.'

'In that case, it's probably sensible for me not to ask.' I smile. *Cross the line, cross the line*, my inner voice is squealing. I want to know.

'Very.' The man nods and I look up at him, knowing I'm grinning like the Cheshire cat and making sure I hold his eyes. There is no way I'm going to scan the rest of him. I've lost count of the number of times I've had to train clients, male *and* female, to look at the eyes. LOOK AT THE EYES! At this moment the temptation to let my gaze drift just a little bit down is strong.

'But now you know, I'm going to have to ask *why* you smell like a thirteen-year-old boy who has raided his dad's aftershave and then doused himself in a bottle of Glenfiddich as well. Seeing as you're claiming it's not deliberate.'

'How do you know thirteen-year-old me didn't own this aftershave?'

'You might have been an outlier but every thirteen-year-old boy I knew at that age was all about Lynx Africa and Lambrini. I took a gamble.'

'Are you suggesting I'm average?' I carry on holding his eye but flick one of my eyebrows up in answer. He's so cheeky. He's also far from average. He's absolutely gorgeous; and in nothing but trunks. My self-control, and self-respect, is stopping me from full-on perving, but I know what I'll be dreaming about as my head hits the pillow tonight. And if Kevin ever sees this man's eyelashes, he will hunt him down and steal them whilst he sleeps. No compunction. He would very definitely be hissing all sorts of asides into my ear if he was seeing what I am right now.

I deliberately leave a long pause after the eyebrow raise and then say, 'Yeah, I'd say a strong ... five. You know, average.'

The man laughs. A real deep laugh that echoes around the wooden room. It's contagious and I'm now laughing too, less at my joke and more at the genuine sunshine of this man's response.

'You know you need to tell me why you smell like this now, don't you?'

'Hmmm.'

'Oh stop flirting with it, you know you're going to tell me,' I whip back.

'Yeah, I'm tempted. I think you'll find it funny but it's a wildly inappropriate story to tell someone I've never met before whilst we're both in nothing but swimwear. Also it doesn't portray me in a very good light. Strips away this sophisticated vibe I'm clearly throwing out right now and reveals me as ludicrously clumsy, which, honestly, normally I'm not.'

'I'm intrigued. There is no way you can't tell me now.'

'Ah –' he scrunches up his face '– I'll tell you but only on the condition we can never meet again.'

'Deal.'

'Okay, I can't believe this. Right. Okay, so I'm having a shower, and um... taking care of things... no, God, no, I mean...um, grooming. I was grooming.'

'Yeah, already way too much information for a stranger,' I shoot back, deadpan.

'I know.' His voice is steely. 'I warned you.'

'Yeah, you need to continue to the end. You can't stop now, you have intrigued your audience.'

'It kinda gets worse.'

'Okay. Well, I'm sure I've heard worse.'

'Yeah, I bet you haven't.'

I cast my mind back to the clients I've seen this week; yup, I definitely have. 'Come on. You're grooming in the shower, very modern man, and then...'

'Well, then I nick myself and promptly trip over the shower door whilst grabbing some paper to try and staunch the bleeding.'

'Ouch.'

'Oh no, just wait. As I trip I don't just fall down flat on my face, straight out of the shower, oh no. Somehow I manage to contort myself and am all twisty, like a tornado but in human form, and as I'm twisting, bang, I knock some plants over and land straight on ... don't laugh...one of my sister's many cacti. I know, you couldn't write it, people just wouldn't believe you. But my sister feng-shui'd my house recently, at about the same time as she was decluttering hers, funnily enough, and before I knew it I had an entire cacti collection in my bathroom! Apparently, houseplants are very good for you and cacti in the bathroom will bring me great wealth. '

'Really?'

'Right! So she says, but she's just tricked me into having her sodding houseplants, hasn't she? I'm currently looking after her cat as well. The woman has skills. Anyway, I'm getting side-tracked... so I'm all twisty, I've landed on a cactus and as you can imagine, I'm now screaming. What started off as a regular nick has resulted with me on the floor with cactus spikes in my you-know-wheres.'

I'm laughing so much at the thought of this man rolling around on his bathroom floor trying to pull out cacti spikes that I'm gripping on to the wooden seating. Any hope of projecting cool composure has disappeared, this is too funny.

'But still, you ask,' he continues, 'why the smell? Because when you're rolling around the floor with spikes sticking out of your crotch you tend to flail; flail, wail and pull said spikes out and as I did that I knocked over my bottle of aftershave, a stoppered bottle, because you know, obviously I'm as suave as they come, and it went everywhere. Ev-e-ry-where.'

'Oh stop' Tears are pouring down my cheeks. 'I'm sorry, I know we don't know each other, and I shouldn't laugh at your pain, but nicks, spikes and then drenching all that in aftershave. It's too much! I can see why you needed to reach for the whisky.'

'You say we don't know each other but are you sure?

There's something very familiar about your voice. Have we definitely not met before?' The man pauses his story and I gulp. He doesn't look like a listener but then who knows what a listener looks like? And he certainly isn't nor has ever been a client. And I would definitely remember this man if he had been one of my Saturday night dates, *definitely*.

'Yep, absolutely. I have a great memory for faces. You're a complete stranger, I'm afraid.'

'Then I really shouldn't have started this story but now I have, I'll finish it, because strictly speaking I didn't reach for the whisky bottle to soothe my pain. At two p.m. on a Tuesday afternoon.'

'Oh, excellent. There's more.'

'There is. And you're going to think I need locking up for my own safety at this rate. Praise the heavens that I don't have the responsibility of small children or dependent elderly parents.' Hmmm, no children. Is that a hint that he is single and fancy-free? I rather hope so. No man other than Kevin, oh and Dan, has made me laugh like this for ages.

'Okay, so I was aware that I smelt like a teenager on his first date. You know, the one in school you can smell as the aftershave comes around the corner a full five minutes before he does. So after risking life and limb once again with another shower, I was desperate and googled how to minimise the smell of too much aftershave, and it said alcohol. The only thing I have in the house was some whisky I'd been given for Christmas so knowing I was coming here this afternoon, I lost all rationality and started to dab the whisky on, then a bit more, and before you know it I was smelling like the love child of Oliver Reed and Gianni Versace.'

'Oh my God.' I'm gasping for breath now, scared if I laugh more, I may stop breathing.

'Aha, I was desperate, but I absolutely couldn't miss this afternoon – personal reasons which are way too intimate for me to confide in you despite all the hideousness I have just listed, but three showers and I still couldn't get rid of the smell completely. I was terrified I was going to be late for here and thought a swim may help, but it seems the sauna has only intensified it. Still, trust me when I say it's better than it was, and I don't think that it's just that my nose has adjusted to the hideousness of it.'

As I realise I have unwittingly moved closer to this man, leaning in to listen, a young woman pushes the glass door to the sauna open, interrupting the spell that has been cast, intimacy woven around the two of us as his story pulls us together. And boy, do I want to be pulled together with this man. She is another new face and I feel a spike of resentment about her interruption.

'Ah, there you are, Jay. Sorry I'm late. You know I can't do the heat in here, come join me in the hot tub instead.' She motions with her hand at the man I've been talking to and his whole face lights up. You know all those memes about someone looking at you like Elon Musk looks at his rockets or dogs look at food? That is exactly how he looks at her. Pure love. And I immediately see why it was so important to him to be here.

'You made it! Right, coming now.' He bounds down the sauna tiers and throws a quick look up at me as he does so. 'Pleasure to meet you. Hope my stories and my smell haven't scarred you for life.'

'I reckon I'll survive. It's been nice meeting you.' I give him a quick smile, one that doesn't show my flash of envy for what these two have. An envy I am usually *utterly* lacking.

'Glad to hear it and it really has. See you around.' And with that he bounds after the young woman and I watch him comfortably slip his arm around her shoulders as they walk towards the hot tub.

Chapter Six

I follow Cass down the steps and into the hot tub, noticing
that she's carrying her phone with her but concentrating
more on the fact that I have just been talking at length to some
woman, a complete stranger, about my balls.

Oh.

My.

God.

What had I been thinking? My first trip to the lido with the
membership Malcolm and Sue have transferred to me and
Cass, giving us the chance to have access to this bougie bit of
Bristol and as part of my create-lovely-spaces-for-Cass plan,
and I am going to be met at the door by a burly policeman and
a restraining order and politely escorted from the premises.
And rightfully so.

Brilliant way to repay all the care, love and respect they
have shown me and Cass from the very minute they fostered
us all those years ago.

I spend my life at work talking about appropriate

behaviour, respect, boundaries and the consequences of not following such rules and I've just cornered some woman in a small, contained space and banged on about me being naked. What is wrong with me? I'd been so aware that I had a severe case of aftershave overkill after my hideous morning that I'd just started to explain, and before I knew it my mouth ran away with me. I felt so comfortable in her company that I babbled on as if she were an old friend. But I've never met her before, I don't even know her name and she knows more about me than any human ever needs to. All she's done is come into the sauna, presumably for a bit of peace and quiet, and there she was face to face with me and my story.

I am so cross with myself. I am literally heading up a task force for safe spaces for young women at work at the moment as well!

Cass and I sink into the hot tub, Cass carefully placing her phone on the side, and I let out a sigh. The water is warm, the sun shining through a canopy of jasmine and honeysuckle. I need to put my embarrassment from my mind and concentrate on how nice it is to be here with my sister, just the two of us for a change.

'It's lovely to see you...' Cass grins across at me and I'm filled with love for this chaotic, wild little scruffball, a unique combination of feisty and vulnerable. I would set this world on fire for her. 'But you're a little bit pungent. What the hell happened? On family Skype you swore you were going to take a step back from dating so what is this? She scrunches her eyes and inhales deeply, and then sniffs a bit '– is this your way of making sure you put everyone in a two-mile radius right off.' Cassie giggles and I narrow my eyes.

'Rude. I'll have you know that this, this would be very easy to blame on you!'

'Me. Hah. I didn't tip half the counter at Boots on you.'

'No but you did put all those bastard cacti in my bathroom...' I launch into the tale again but with a few choicer words and grin as I watch my little sister cough as she laughs so much, tears streaming from her eyes.

'I'm glad you think it's funny, but unfortunately not only have I had to suffer this indignity this morning, I've also just told some poor woman in the sauna all my woes.'

'No! No, you didn't? That woman you were flirting with in there when I arrived?'

'Um, not flirting. We made a deal on family Skype, remember?' The deal is step two in my Help Cass plan so I really wasn't flirting, although I couldn't help but notice that the woman I have been giggling with *was* attractive. About my age, blonde hair scraped back into a tight bun, cheekbones that models would kill for and a face free from make-up, her eyes blue as the sky above Cass and me right now, shining. She had a little snub nose and a smile that took over her face, you know like that actress in the perfume ads, um ... Julia Roberts.

Her laugh, the way she made you want to talk to her, the way she listened and didn't hold back in her answers, nor flinch at my outrageous over-sharing. There was a warmth to her that was genuine. As I say, very attractive.

Cass's next words remind me why I'm not meant to be thinking these things.

'Yeah, but no one expects you to keep it. You can't help yourself, it's like having the Pied bloody Piper as an older brother, they all want to play your flute.' She dissolves into giggles again.

'Oh, you're on form today, aren't you? Absolutely filthy, Cassie Cooper, you should be ashamed of yourself. And I *was* serious. A change is as good as a rest and I'm going to stop dating for a bit. I made a promise and believe that change is a good thing. That it can open up doors in our lives that would be kept shut if we hadn't dared take a different path.' That had been the real reason behind me swearing on the family call that I was going to give up dating, flirting or any kind of sexual or hopefully sexual engagement with women for six months. I would stop my search for Ms Right and live in the moment as Cass was always nagging me to.

The whole bloody lot of them had laughed for a good five minutes, but after listening to The Love Doctor's podcast I reckoned showing that change wasn't terrifying but achievable was a solid plan. It was a good way of planting a seed in Cassie's brain without being overbearing about the changes I think she should make, and fast.

Which brings me to the phone on the edge of the hot tub. Who brings their phone with them? The whole point is to get away and relax, but I suspect this is an indicator of the bigger picture and every inch of me is itching to refer to it. I hear The Love Doctor's words in my head and hold it all back, but it's not easy.

'You're never gonna manage to last more than a week. I'll believe you can do it when I see it but I think you've just left exhibit A in the sauna.'

'Shhhh!' I furrow my brow. The last thing that poor woman needs if she leaves the sauna traumatised is to hear herself described as exhibit A. I can see myself in the bloody dock now. 'We were chatting, no flirting, I promise. Just chatting. I'm going to prove this to you. You know I like a challenge; you wait and see. I am going to live like a monk for six months and when I do you are going to have to grovel hard. Real hard. That will make it all worthwhile.'

'Brother mine, if you can stay celibate for six *weeks* I shall grovel hard. Six months, and I'll make you a bloody banner announcing to the world that you are a saint and I am a sister of very little faith. How does that sound?'

'Deal.'

'I tell you what, I'm so convinced I've got this one, let's make it really interesting.'

I pause, I had been reaching forward to shake hands to seal the deal. 'Go on.' I never have been able to resist a challenge.

'Bloody hell, did the cacti get your hand as well?' she asks and I twist my hand, all wet and scratched, so she can see it properly.

'Oh no, no, but you know what did?'

'Go on.'

'Darling bloody Dimkins got my hand. And my curtains, every cushion in the house and one of my brand-new Jordans. He's also managed to pull some skirting board off. I don't know how he's done that, he's like The Hulk but in cat form, and then he hides behind the skirting, gets trapped, mews for hours and then does it all again the next night. Three bits of skirting board I've fixed back to the wall so far. Three nights of being woken up at daft o'clock in the morning and having to go search for him!'

'I love that cat. Isn't he the best?'

'No, he's not the best, not by a long shot. Stuffed and in a case he might be better.'

'Ooh, you devil,' Cass responds with mock outrage. She knows me well enough to know that I am joking.

'And what's more, I can't, I won't, call him that stupid name.'

'That's his name, Jay, you can't go messing with that. What if I started calling you something different? You're all about respecting identity, name-changing is definitely a no-go.'

'I'm not called Darling Dimkins and trust me if I were I would have changed that shit by now. The Deed Poll offices would be top of my most recent and frequent calls list and I would be well on my way to having a name that didn't make me look like I should be locked up.'

'Right then, Jack, sorry you feel that way but you can't change her name.'

'Really? Look, if you want me standing on the street calling "Darling" every night, how do you expect me to stay single for six months, huh?' I raise my eyebrows. Hah! Got her.

'With firm resolve, although now you mention it the thought of that is a joy. Will you film yourself and...' Our banter is stopped by her phone vibrating on the side of the hot tub. I watch as her shoulders clench as she reaches for it.

Bloody Jasmine. I want to grab the phone and fling it out of this area and down into the deepest end of the swimming pool just across from us. I know that would make me even worse than my sister's girlfriend but really, need I say it again? *Who brings their phone to a hot tub*, huh?

'Oh, it's just Marcus about a band.' Cass smiles and puts the phone down carefully.

'Okay, is he good? How's work?' I ask. Marcus is one of my oldest friends, I've known him since primary, and Cass works with him at a bar, Mama K's, that we have been going to for as long as I can remember.

'Yeah, um, I meant to tell you about that. I don't, um... I

don't work there anymore. I handed in my notice a month or so ago and asked everyone to keep schtum and last night was my final shift. I know I should have said and Marcus felt bad but, well, you know.' She shrugs her shoulders and I imagine the expression on my face is probably saying what my brain is thinking. 'I want to concentrate on my art. You've always said I'm good.' She continues justifying her decision knowing that I'm going to have something to say about this.

'Yeah, I've always said you should push your art more. You're so talented, but what about bills and stuff?' I try and keep my voice calm, non-judgemental, but what I actually want to scream is *Keep non-Jas bits of your life strong.*

'I know but Jas reckons she earns more than enough to keep the both of us, which she does, and it would be so lovely to be able to concentrate on my art fully, you know. Proper dedicate myself to it for a bit. Jas reckons we could maybe move out of the city, be a bit more rural, get ourselves somewhere with a room I could make my studio.'

Yeah, I bet she does. A little bit further from your family and friends, at home all day, completely dependent. I work hard on keeping my breathing measured and the smile on my face.

'Look, I'm doing it,' Cass continues. 'It's happened. You could just say, "Congratulations, that's a great decision and I'm happy for you."'

'Congratulations, I am happy for you if it's what you want.' I use every muscle in my face to stop my eyes rolling and try and channel the non-judgement The Love Doctor advised.

'Of course it's what I want. Now back to your self-imposed celibacy and making it interesting.'

'But—'

'Nope.' She holds up her hand. 'We're talking about you now.'

'Go on...' I know there is no point fighting this. Let her have this battle and hope common sense wins the war.

'How about if you can keep it in your pants for a full six months, no dating, no apps, no smiling at girls over the top of your beer, casting that bizarre spell you have without saying a word...' She grins, happy to have the subject moved on to something she is much comfier with.

'Woah, hardly,' I protest. She's making me sound like a player and I am the complete opposite of that. The complete opposite! I don't want conquests, I want someone to settle down with, start a family. You couldn't get more different.

'Totally.' She smirks. 'You don't even try and the daft fuckers drop at your feet. It's embarrassing. And quite frankly makes me despair for the sisterhood. Do you know how many women I have had over the years come into work and ask me if I'm your sister and then try and cosy-cosy up to me? So, if you don't date for six months, stop looking for Mrs Cooper, concentrate on living in the present, not the future, then I will not only do the banner thing but I'll... um, what would you really like?'

'Errr...' I cast through my mind quickly and the only obvious answer is for her to leave Jas but that would not be a wise thing to say. It would have her out of this hot tub quicker than a whippet on speed and hurtle me to the top of her shitlist for ever. 'Um...'

'Seriously, you are so golden there is nothing you want in your life?'

I look down at my hands and rack my brains, then inspiration strikes.

'I'd like my flat back.' I wave my tattered hand at her again. 'I'd like you to take back Dim, your spiteful little cacti and the rest of your houseplants, oh –' I'm warming to my topic now '– and all those romance novels that you can't have at your house because you're scared Jas will think less of you but which are fine in boxes in my bedroom. Not to mention that rolled-up poster of Jasmine from Aladdin. It's no wonder I'm not finding marriage material. They come and take one look at my flat and they run for the hills.'

'Except they don't, you do. And let's not forget that Stella really took to that Jasmine poster. It was you that ran from her.'

'She saw that poster and then used to wander around the flat in harem pants and a plait singing "A Whole New World". I mean, seriously? What sort of crazy behaviour is that?'

'I really liked her.'

'Oh I know, you made that quite clear.'

Cass makes an ooh-she-was-gorgeous face. 'Honestly, Jay, taking all that stuff back is a pain in the arse. You know Jas doesn't want any of it in the flat. Her allergies.'

'I'm sure you'll be able to find a creative solution. But you know this isn't necessary. You already have my word that I will not be dating for a full six months. I've promised.'

'Okay then, and if you fail –' she pulls her hands out the warm water and rubs them together '– you have to take over my duties for Sue's choir thing. It's only painting backdrops and things, you don't need any artistic talent. Even *you* can paint a pyramid or whatever they need. And a bit of set shifting. You're far better qualified to do that than me.'

'Woah, I'm the man so I can do heavy stuff? I thought you didn't believe in gender stereotypes?'

'I don't. It's not to do with male or female but with the fact

I'm a creative type and have to treasure these beauties –' she waves her arms around delicately to reinforce her point '– and you bench-press twenty times before breakfast.'

'So what you're saying is that you have no faith in my ability to stay celibate for six months and are going to turn my imminent failure into an opportunity to get out of a promise you've made and really don't want to fulfil?'

'Yup.' Cassie grins.

'In other words, if I shake hands with you on this and just carry on doing what I was doing anyway I have your sworn vow that in six months' time my house will be free from that kitten and all your other clutter?'

'Um... yes.' Cassie sniggers. '*If* you win!'

'Oh, you are so on!' I shake her hand with force. We exchange a grin that has decades of sibling battles, affection and experience all wrapped up in one small muscle movement. 'Want to do a few lengths of the pool whilst it's empty and then if you've got time we can grab some tapas and a coffee and then head back in here.'

'Oh yeah, that does sound good. I thought I was going to miss Malcolm and Sue when they said they were going overseas for six months, but you know what, there are definite bonuses.' She flings her arm out of the warm, bubbling water and waves it to encompass the lido laid out around us. 'And now I won't have to do the set painting either, life is sweet.'

'So optimistic, so foolish.' I say as we start to climb out of the hot tub and head to the pool just at the same time as the woman I had been talking to leaves the sauna. I smile at her sheepishly and hope to God I haven't given her nightmares.

Chapter Seven

I'm doing plank jacks, working my abs to Todrick Hall's latest album. It is perfect as my current HIIT workout music and is blaring through my headphones as I complete my ten seconds, rest and then start a short burst of mountain climbers.

I am trying to focus on my morning workout. The trick is to go so fast there is no space to think but my mind is struggling today to stay on task. I know I'm an 'expert' on psychology but brains are devious creatures and mine seems to enjoy torturing me most days. It's spent the last few nights conjuring up the guy from the sauna doing all manner of not-for-public-places things even though I *know* resisting the subconscious charms of Cacti Guy is a no-brainer, simply because it's quite obvious from the age of the woman who called him into the hot tub that he likes them young. Much younger, and that is a great big red flag. A huge one, one big enough to lay on the ground and carpet the whole of Buckingham Palace. Fantasising about him is wholly inappropriate and my conscious mind – sensible beast that it is – is trying to firmly entrench this view whenever my thoughts tend to slip.

Unfortunately, my unconscious mind has always been a rebellious creature and even my mindfulness practice that I did on waking today was interrupted by my brain taking me to places that left me flushed and not particularly calm.

With my workout finished, I jump into the shower in the hope that the water cascading down my skin may cleanse my mind as well. It's Friday today so I have a lecture to deliver on social cognitive development followed by tutorials this morning and part of the afternoon. I love the fact that I work one day a week in the university; it tethers me to the academic world, keeps me up to date with the latest developments in my field. And it balances out the consulting work I do the rest of the time, the work which is paying the bills and allowing me to squirrel up a nest egg, something that is going to be all kinds of important if I can never have children to help me out as I age.

I run conditioner through my hair and switch my brain off from dwelling on my barrenness as well. On how my knowledge of that has shaped all my life choices as an adult. On my need to remain single so that no one else has to pay the price for my fucked-up ovaries. I recognise where I am going with this – it is a well-trodden path – so I acknowledge the thought, acknowledge its validity and then whack it in a box. I don't need to spend this morning fretting on that one.

I am aware though that spending the afternoon with Angela yesterday is probably why my mind is heading in that direction, and whilst her dolls are no indicator that she has fertility concerns, the lifelike nature of Courtney in particular has been unnerving me and making me think about my inability to have babies.

Fredrico, Courtney, Paisley and Robert had been pushed through the door yesterday for her second appointment this week, in a four-seater stroller that was as unwieldy as a small tank.

She may have originally come to me for dating advice and support but I have got her to the point where she is grudgingly accepting that deeper therapeutic work may be helpful. Her history indicates that there is a strong possibility of PTSD so I did suggest today that I could hand her care over to someone else who is an expert in that field, but Angela was adamant she will only work with me.

I suspect some EMDR, a highly effective psychotherapy that allows people to heal emotional trauma, will be a great starting point. I'm hoping that if we can deal with the causes of her anxiety, help her process trauma she has carried from childhood, she can develop a healthier relationship with Federico et al.

Initially she looked at me as if the therapy I was suggesting was akin to taking a well-known serial killer as a lodger, but by the end of the session she was less resistant and I'm hoping next time we talk she may be willing to tentatively commit.

And whilst Angela's dolls are playing with my mind she is far from my most bizarre client. Early on in my career I'd opened the door to find a fully made-up clown. Then there had been the identical twins dressed in matching outfits who alternated their sentences – trust me, that shit is even spookier than clowns on your doorstep.

I had one client with a marmalade fetish – no joke, marmalade! I haven't been able to see it the same way since.

And then there had been Serena, who could only enjoy sex if the man didn't look at her; in fact she was only ever truly comfortable if he remained blindfolded the entire time. The entire time. From getting undressed to the point of leaving. And whilst most partners don't mind it occasionally, most object to it as a full-time thing. We did a little bit of work on that. I'm all for indulging your sexual pleasures but there has to be a degree of mutuality. To be fair, Serena made massive strides and is now happily married and living in Scotland.

Oh, and I had one client who couldn't bond if the woman didn't call him Mother at the point of orgasm – he was one of my few failures.

However, the majority of the time my clients are remarkably nondescript. Everyday people who have hit a block in their relationships or who are struggling to begin one and suspect that they may be the reason. Whilst my work as a sex and relationship therapist is normally centred around single people who want to find and keep love, I do some more regular work with couples who are struggling as well. I'm a bit like Hitch from that movie with a smidge of the TV show *Sex Education* – throw them together and ta-daa, you have me.

I step out of the shower and wander through to my bedroom, drying myself off as I go, and reach for one of my work outfits, which are all carefully streamlined and colour-coordinated. I like my strict routines – wake up, meditate, HIIT, shower, breakfast. I like order in my life; discipline makes everything so much smoother. My mother comes and gasps at my wardrobe when she visits, unable to marry the child I was years ago to this woman she perceives as ordered and chaos-free.

Perception is a funny thing.

I step into the skirt and zip it up, and as I check myself in the mirror I run my hand down my figure, over my stomach. Fifteen-year-old me would never have believed that this professional-looking woman, this slim, clear-skinned woman standing looking back at her, would be her future. Not believe it even for one second.

If only our younger selves had faith in our older selves to get them through safely to the places we need to be.

Hitting adolescence had me really piling on the pounds, craving carbs and sugar like never before. And before had been bad enough. My periods were a hellscape and at sixteen my mother marched me to our GP, who told me I was fat and lazy and that shifting the weight was the only thing that would help.

Easy to say and – as I learned later – with PCOS and your whole endocrine system working against you, next to impossible to do. It took me a long time, so many tears, years and much frustration, to finally embed a routine that works a little for me. And I am one of the lucky ones. Only now, now I am too scared to deviate from it.

I also know that finding that strength, the determination to change, wasn't down to the healthiest reasons. Should my path ever cross with Scott Oakley and his mates again, it will not be a meek schoolgirl with zero self-esteem that they will be dealing with.

However, that's enough of that.

I grab a pair of heels, slip them on and head to the kitchen for breakfast.

'Hey, morning,' I greet Dan, whom I hadn't expected to see and who is doing yoga next to the futon. I'm used to having the mornings to myself; Kevin's work, and Dan's for that matter, means that they normally keep late hours, and seeing either before noon is a rarity.

'Morning. I'm here early to try and motivate your flatmate,' he says and I quirk my brow – we both know that that will not be an easy sell at this time in the morning. 'He needs help writing a song for Drag Factor.'

'Isn't that in July?'

'Well, yes, but there's no harm in getting him prepared early.'

'Truth! He needs to win this time, I still haven't got over Vivicious' victory last year.'

Dan makes a gesture of pulling a cape around him, stands on tiptoes and proclaims, 'Do not fret! We shall keep him safe from that shrew-tongued harpy. She shall not steal our Jinx's crown for a second year.' He wobbles a bit and then puts his feet flat on the ground again. 'I will sew and sing and play for him and you can motivate him with your bloody good advice.'

'Ooh, I could do with some bloody good advice...' Kevin flings the door open and makes a dramatic entrance, satin eye mask dramatically parked atop his ruffled sticky-up hair. 'My parents are threatening to fly over in July. I don't know how to escape it. I tried telling them there was a chance I was going to be seconded to Papua New Guinea on an exchange, but they didn't believe me.'

'For such a clever person you have the worst excuses ever! Is Papua New Guinea known for its strong financial sector?'

'It was the first thing that came into my head,' he admits and I give him A Look. 'July, Lils, they can't come over then, they can't.'

'Oh God, no!' Drag Factor is important to Kevin, always has been, and last year the regional heats should have been his.

Unfortunately, despite spending a huge chunk of his adult life preparing for them he had failed to prepare for Vivicious tampering with all of the contestants' belongings. This year Kevin has his heart set on winning that tiara – not merely for him but for justice. Or so he says.

I grab his *Glorious* mug from the cupboard in the hope that it may put a smile on his face. We had bonded with the ferocity of No More Nails mixed with a side order of superglue at Freshers' week, where the two little oddballs that we were immediately recognised each other, and made the mugs soon after.

'Right, any month but July. It's so freaking important I'm literally up at dawn. Now. In April! Even Dan is up early, all to make sure my songwriting skills resemble Lennon and McCartney rather than the usual Vengaboys meets The Cheeky Girls mash-up.' He winks Dan a thank-you. 'They can come in June, visit in August, but I need to keep them the fuck away in July!'

I press a cup of coffee into Kevin's hand. 'You never know, this could be a good opportunity to tell them who you actually are. In my experience parents are never quite as shocked as you imagine when truths are revealed.' I use my most placatory tone.

'Oh trust, my parents only have one child and this –' he waves his mug in the air '– is not what they had planned.'

'Maybe they'd be proud, maybe their love for you trumps yours or their expectations. We think you're pretty perfect,' Dan adds.

'We do.'

'Oh yes, the perfect son and the dreamy daughter they

never knew they wanted all in one fabulous if slightly chunky body.'

Dan cackles, and it is hard not to. To be fair I have heard this joke before, every time Kevin mentions his parents, but Dan and he have been friends for a year or so, since Dan started working at the bar, so they don't have the same shared history.

'I read an article recently about how Taiwan is leading the way in LGBTQ+ inclusivity these days. Now may be the time to speak up,' I add but Kevin gives me a look that would shrivel the insides of a far more fertile woman and I recognise that I should shut up.

I open the fridge and pop some yogurt in a bowl and present it as a peace offering to Kevin, who is now draped across a kitchen stool pretending to hyperventilate. He immediately faux slaps it away, a perfect pout on his lips.

'Oh my God, I come in here, my heart in tumult...'

'Tumult eh?' I grin and exchange a look with Dan.

'Tumult,' he reiterates, 'And you offer me yogurt? Good God, girl, this has to be a bacon sandwich situation at the very least. The very least.'

I raise my eyebrows.

'I swear you were put on this earth specifically to make me feel bad.' He sinks his head into his hands.

'Reason for life right there,' I respond. 'Definitely why I keep breathing every day.' I take the spoon from his bowl and pretend I'm going to flip it but instead move in super close to Kevin's face, over fifteen years of friendship giving me permission to do so. 'You literally sobbed at me last weekend when you couldn't do up that dress. You said that I wasn't to let you eat unhealthily on weekdays, that you wanted to be a new disciplined you, you *begged* me,' I remind him. 'You actually said that if I saw you head towards either the frying pan or Deliveroo on weekdays, I was to cut a finger off each time, and remind you that those long silk gloves you invested in so heavily last month would not look the same with missing digits.'

'Friday *is* the weekend!' Kevin protests. 'You're like the ... the Witches of Eastwick –' his current obsession '– if they were health-conscious fascists instead of being all about martinis, female empowerment and beating the devil.'

'You're just cross cos no one has beaten your devil in ages,' Dan observes drily and I let out a sharp burst of laughter.

'Ain't that the truth, and if my parents visit, it is quite likely no one ever will again.' Kevin jumps down from the stool, pulls out the frying pan and glares at me in challenge. 'I'm burning off calories merely through the presence of my emotional drama.'

'In that case, darling, you'll be a size zero by lunchtime,' I shoot back and we all cackle in that way only best friends can.

Chapter Eight

The day has whizzed by and I have got to the lido before it gets too busy. I reckon I can fit my minimum fifty lengths in, have a twenty-minute muscle relax in the sauna, an ice bucket and a little time in the hot tub. Heaven.

I lower my body into the water. There is only one other swimmer in the pool, a couple going into the sauna and the hot tub looks empty. The middle part of the day is always the quietest and that's what I'm seeking. There's a few of us that come at this time; the lido is a small community and it doesn't take long to get to know the other members.

The heat of the day makes the pool seem colder, the sun shimmers on the water and I hold my breath as I submerge my shoulders. A memory of myself and my sister running into the sea in Clacton flits into my mind, squealing with every step as the cold water hit the soles of our feet, our ankles, our knees, our groins – always horrific – our tummies, our shoulders. Our parents watching indulgently, knowing that we loved the shrieking as much as the water.

These days I am a lot hardier, a lot less squealy, and I like feeling the different stages of the water washing over me, shocking my body, and looking like I am oh-so-cool with it as it does so. I like to channel insouciance as I submerge myself. I do not make even the tiniest *ooh* noise or allow a grimace to cross my face. I like the way I show the world that this doesn't touch me.

And yes, I'm a therapist, I know what all that means.

I should just get in the water and be me with it, admit that I'd like to revert to the pleasure of shocked squealing, allow my childhood flamboyance, now buried so deep, to rise to the surface at the same time as my body dips below the waterline. But that was younger me; adult me is not willing to let go of the control I have tightly built, the control that has proved time and time again to be very good for me, the control that got me to here, where I am in my life. Professional, respected, thin.

I turn my mind to swimming, position my body and start my lengths. Five, ten, fifteen. I have my music pumping into my ears – waterproof headphones are the best invention – as I plough through the water. I spot Cacti Guy get out of the pool. I've almost reached the end of my length and could stop now and climb out too. I pull up to the end of the pool and take a second, watching him as he crosses the tiles, up the step and into the building that houses the sauna.

He is as fine as my dreams made out. I've been hoping that they may have exaggerated a bit, that if I ever saw him again, he wouldn't live up to the version in my head.

I was wrong.

He is even more attractive than I remember and with droplets of water trailing down his back, I am in danger of gawping. So not okay.

The Love Experiment

The lido is my refuge; this is where I come for peace. I deliberately don't hit on anyone here. I may be all about the beauty of a forever relationship in my work, and I do believe that being part of a couple can be many people's happy-ever-after, but it isn't my personal preference. I have no desire to be with someone else, to force my inevitable future on another living soul, and here is definitely not the place to scour for hook-ups. No way, no how.

But he has the nicest shoulders; tops of his arms are pretty bang on as well. I remember his eyes as we talked last time, those conker-brown eyes that pull you in, make you want to see into his mind, oh and that smile, those dimples.

No. I turn my filthy mind and lustful body back around and finish off my lengths. I'll be disappointed in myself if I let sexy shoulders and a pretty face sway me. But I swim a little faster than usual and am aware that as I pull myself up the tiles at the end of the pool to get out that I am deliberately making sure the way I hold myself, the way I angle every movement, is as sensual as possible just in case he is watching.

As I open the door to the building that houses the sauna, the couple in there earlier are coming out and my heart leaps. It could just be he and I in there, alone.

Then I remember the woman he was with last week.

I head in, shut the door firmly and climb up the wooden benches to the top. There he is. Just like last time. Just like the start of my dream last night. I smile as we make eye contact and acknowledge him but stay silent until I am seated.

'Hello.' I am friendly, accompany my greeting with a smile and nothing more. My whole saunter-out-of-the-pool-like-Pussy-Galore routine has made me cross with myself. At what

65

age am I going to be secure enough that I don't need to validate myself by being attractive to men?

Probably a little while longer, my inner voice bites back. Bitch.

'Hello.' He grins a welcome across at me and I feel all my feminist angst disappear as I grin back. 'I was hoping to see you again today,' he continues, and my heart pitter-patters.

'Oh yeah?' I try not to bow my head and look through my eyelashes but my body seems determined to channel some Grade A Princess Diana shit. I jerk my head up again. Behave!

'Yes, it's been plaguing me, I really do owe you an apology.' I raise my brow at his words. 'The story I told last week was inapp—'

'Oh woah!' I hold up my hand. It was fine, I can understand why he feels awkward but I hadn't minded the story at all. I appreciate that he wants to acknowledge he stepped over the line, but the truth is his humour was a good fit and Kevin would have giggled as much as I did if he had heard it.

It strikes me as odd that I haven't told him.

'Honestly, no hard feelings, it was a funny story, it's had me giggling all week. You're all good.'

'You've been thinking of me *all week*?' He quirks his eyebrow and a smile crosses his face. We are facing each other and I keep my face straight and allow a long pause. I am not answering that immediately. He is way too confident in himself, and whilst I like this as a quality, he needs to be kept on tenterhooks just for a bit. He strikes me as a bit of a lothario, one of those men that rock the thoroughly charming boy-next-door type, catnip when it comes to the opposite sex. That suits me fine. I like to engage with a man not looking for an emotional connection, one that is all about a quick hook-up, the release of sexual tension with none of the burdensome bullshit that comes from moving that forward and forming a relationship. In fact, I'm going to do a little more digging about the woman he was with before. If he has an explanation that doesn't involve him sleeping with her, then that may make him an acceptable option, *even* in the lido. He'll know the rules and not want awkwardness as much as me. Interesting. But boy, I am not going to make it easy for you.

I run over possible responses in my head, I'm tempted to go with *you're someone who tends to stick in the mind* in a breathy Marilyn Monroe voice. And it's the truth, he did, he does. But no, Marilyn is way too much.

'It was a quiet week,' I say instead and shrug my shoulders nonchalantly. He laughs.

'I don't know why but I very much have the feeling you don't have quiet weeks,' he replies.

'Hmm, then maybe you're reading me wrong. It was generally a week of work and fulfilling my lido obsession.'

'I guess that depends very much on the work. Let me guess, international spy? Olympian synchronised swimmer? Circus acrobat?'

'You're spot on. Yep, I do all those things. I've got to shoot off to China straight after this where I'll be stealing government secrets by crossing a trapeze wire whilst wearing a flowery swim cap. It's going to be risky but I should be okay, I've done it a million times.'

'I knew it, I'm a good judge of character. I can usually call people.'

'Damn near telepathic,' I shoot back and he grins.

'Oh really, is that what you're thinking?' He waggles his

eyebrows and there is a bit of me, a lot of me, that is loving this flirtation. The man is con-fi-dent! Then he sharply changes his tone. 'Mind you, you'd need three jobs just to cover the fees here alone.'

It's true. The lido is a little expensive but so worth it if you are a daily swimmer like me.

'See, I have no choice. If I want to sauna in style, I have to assassinate two or three people a month.'

'Hm, must be tough. I guess I'm ridiculously lucky in that case.'

'Oh yeah, you don't need to kill people to get in?' I'm itching to ask what he does professionally but seeing as it's never a question I answer honestly it seems a bit unfair to enquire.

'No, I mean, again this sounds like something I shouldn't admit to...' he says and I start to giggle. I cannot even begin to imagine what else he may share. 'But seeing as you heard worse last week, I am not ashamed... all right, I'm slightly ashamed... that at the ripe old age of thirty, my parents signed their membership over to my sister and me whilst they are travelling for six months. They're doing a world tour to celebrate their fortieth wedding anniversary and because they've been members for years, they were allowed to transfer membership to us until they get back.'

'Okay,' I nod nonchalantly, but does this mean his *sister* was who he was with last week? What a win.

Just be bold, ask, the door is open.

'So was it your sister you were meeting here last week?' I say, trying not to let my interest shape my tone too much.

'Yep, Cassie, she's a few years younger than me and I don't get to see her as much as I'd like so it was a bit of a treat to spend some time with her. That's why I hot-footed it out the door when she appeared.'

'Ahh, I see. That was kind of the lido to transfer the membership over. I suppose you can bring your partner as a guest?' Outrageous fishing expedition right there but now I knew that he wasn't dating the woman I'd seen him with *and* that he wasn't going to be a member here for life, I am even more interested than before.

Plus we've been sat here talking for a while and at no point yet have I spotted anything scarily off with his personality and, let's face it, I am a professional. So far I have discovered he is a very sexually attractive man, has a sense of humour that is akin to my own and values close family bonds. If my reading is right and he is single and not looking for anything serious, he could be very tempting indeed.

He smirks at me, as if he knows exactly what I am asking.

'Right, I could, I suppose –' he draws out the word, his eyes dancing with mischief, and I find that I can't pull my own eyes away '– but I am very much single, now and um –' he pauses '– for the foreseeable future.'

That's an odd way to finish that sentence, but he is quite clearly letting me know that he is free, available and has no intention of forming a relationship in his immediate future.

This is good. Do I dare break my sacrosanct lido rule here? For the first time ever, it seems safe. I am constantly telling my clients that confidence is attractive, that there is nothing, *nothing* foolish about putting yourself out there and asking for a date. The very worst that can happen is a knock-back but the majority of people are immensely flattered to be asked and often quite relieved that they aren't the ones having to do the asking. I believe in what I say and usually have no problem putting it into action.

But right now, I'm not feeling fully on my game. There's something about sitting in nothing but a swimsuit that strips you back. My hair is scraped into a tight bun for swimming, I am make-up free, my swimsuit is functional, plain black. It gets me through the water efficiently and is the only item in my wardrobe deliberately picked to be as sexless as possible.

I am completely without any of my normal power tools.

I dig down deep. What have I to lose here?

'Well, in that case –' I try and give him my most seductive glance and lean in '– you know I don't even know your name and I do know quite a lot of things about you at this point.'

He leans back and looks at me measuringly. I see a glimmer in his eyes that says he knows what's coming. He doesn't look unreceptive, but I can feel my tummy flipping as if it is full of jumping beans.

'You do. You're right, that seems kind of wrong. I'm Jay.' He leans forward and reaches his hand out and we keep our eyes on each other. I move towards him and shake his hand, and the strength of his grip, the way his sinews ripple, makes me feel a little faint.

'Lily.' I manage to name myself without melting into a lust-caused puddle.

'Pleased to meet you, Lily.'

'The pleasure is all mine, Jay.' Urgghh! I sound like some kind of sleazy Bond Villain, welcoming him to my lair. I may as well steeple my fingers, bouncing them off each other, and crouch over like Mr Burns at his most scheming. I burst out laughing at myself. 'I'm sorry that sounded so sleazy.'

'Haha, it definitely would have if I had said it,' he

admitted. 'You're off the hook though, and honestly I'm interested to see where you go next.'

'Ah well, that I can reveal.' Bollocks to my lido policy, this man is fine with what I am about to suggest, it's oozing out of every pore. Not only was I practically weaned on *Cosmopolitan* articles but I am an expert on this sort of thing, an actual professor. And so far this man has created a bond of intimacy on our first meeting and now assures me he is single and keen to hear what my possibly sleazy suggestion is going to be. I am golden here, all the signs are pointing at go. I take a deep breath, nerves mingling with anticipation. 'I was wondering if you fancied going for a drink one night?'

Chapter Nine

Lily sits across from me at the very top of the sauna, waiting for my answer. She has the most amazing eyes. They spark with a mischief that I find ridiculously attractive, that speak to her character. There is a long-standing lido joke – I didn't recognise you with your clothes on – which Malcolm and Sue say every time they bump into someone outside of the pool. But sitting here with Lily I really like the fact that we are getting to know each other, striking up a friendship without the normal social indicators you would use to prejudge somebody – dress, presentation and so forth. It makes it feel like you are getting to know a person rather than just what they are trying to represent.

Although I can hear Cassie laughing at me in my head. *Another deep emotional connection eh, Jay?*

I'm attracted to Lily, there are no two ways about that. She strikes me as different to the women I usually date. More self-assured, self-contained, and her question proves it.

Would I like to go for a drink with her? I would love that.

I nod my head and am about to accept, knowing I have a broad smile across my face and my eyes are dancing with yes please. I like a confident woman and I am keen to spend more time with Lily. She makes me laugh, appears open and honest and clearly shares the same filthy type of humour as me.

I hear Cassie's voice – *you're never gonna manage to last more than a week*. Argh! Looks like she wasn't far off. There is no way I can fall at this first hurdle. I find Lily attractive; but I *can't* go for a drink with her.

How am I going to phrase this? A no is a no, and that should be fine as it is, and I suspect will be with Lily, I can't see her going all pouty and kicking up a fuss. But a no when you want it to be a yes and somehow want to convey that this isn't a rejection of them as a person but merely a life circumstance… How do you get that in a no?

Honesty, I'll just go for honesty and hope she recognises it as the truth and not just a line, a fabricated escape clause.

'Lily,' I lean forward to show how sincere I am and make firm eye contact, 'I would love to go for a drink with you, really I would. But I can't. I want to explain why but honestly, it's complicated and I know that makes me sound like a lame social media statement. But know that if I could, I would. So, whilst it's a no, it's a reluctant one with sincere regret attached.'

'Jay, it's fine, a no is fine. I would have beaten myself up had I not asked. But now I can fly out to China tonight knowing it's off the table, we're all good.' And she winks at me.

She winks.

'Yes,' I say, grateful that she is good-natured about it. 'I mean honestly, it's a good thing. We wouldn't want you on that trapeze wire without a hundred per cent focus. There's an argument that my very-pissed-off-cos-I-want-to-say-yes no may have saved your life.'

'Seriously?' she asks, placing her hands on her hips and cocking her head to one side, the amusement etched around her eyes showing she isn't really pissed. I flex my muscles and she shakes her head with disbelief and we dissolve into giggles as if we have known each other since we were kids.

Chapter Ten

I am going out tonight – work-related – and have just slipped into my screamingly scarlet I-am-confident-better-be-scared dress and am drawing on eyeliner, giving myself the most perfect flicks before I flutter at myself in the mirror.

I can't stop dwelling on Jay's rejection and even though it is the nicest I have ever received – one of the few, truth be told, since I became an adult – it stings. For all his I-want-to-say-yes speech, the bare facts are he said no. A clear no that's caused all my deeply held insecurities to rise to the fore, floating to the top like oil in water, pulling tiny bits of jetsam – broken, scrambled little bits of nothing that form a tangly, grubby, binding whole – with it as it does so, reminding me of who I used to be.

Jay had sounded genuinely disappointed, but he is adept when it comes to flirtation. On the flip side, the body rarely lies like the mouth does, and his eyes were dilated as he looked at me; I was checking that shit out. But whilst most of us are aware a dilated pupil is a sign of romantic or sexual attraction, it can also be down to fear – very possible – a brain injury – he did say no – or excessive drink or drug use and he was smelling like a distillery the first time I met him.

I reach for my scarlet lippie and mwah my lips at the mirror and then sink down onto my bed. I lie back with my knees raised in a triangle and stare at my ceiling as I take myself back to my schooldays, closing my eyes as I do so and acknowledging the pain that I felt then. The sadness, the embarrassment, the fear and the resignation that came from being the one that was seen as the freak, the ugly girl, the fat girl, the girl no one wanted to be seen even talking to because unpopularity is more contagious than headlice.

I was always chubbier than the other girls at school. Mum used to have to dress me in adult clothes, taking up the hems and the sleeves and saying things like *It's because you're so grown up that you're in a twelve or a fourteen, so much more mature than the other girls*, intimating that women's UK dress sizes were related to age not girth.

She didn't fool me, or at least not for long.

And of course, the more I was aware I was different, the more I would snaffle up snacks to my room. The obvious thing to do was to eat less, but it was a crutch I wasn't prepared to give up. I was a child!

Puberty did not make this better. I was an early starter, final year of primary school; I had the joy of wearing a size sixteen to eighteen at this point – *And you only eleven as well, so mature*. Not only was I dealing with periods but I had spots too, spots all over my face; getting worse as I got older, spreading across my shoulders, my neck, my chest. The thought of wearing a swimsuit back then as I do now would have terrified the bejesus out of me.

By this stage I had stopped jumping in the waves with my sister because I would have landed so hard every sea creature between the English coast and France would have been catapulted up on to the beach. Add in the fact that I was a walking dot to dot and had so many spots and bloody splotches where I'd scratch and pick at them, my body would scare Jackson Pollock. It was a miracle I ever agreed to leave the house. And in truth I didn't much.

My best friend from primary school had left when her parents moved from the area and, seriously lacking social skills, I buried myself in my studies and munched my way through Wotsits, Marshmallow Teacakes, Curly-Wurlies and Freddo frogs. My love for these foods had now turned into serious cravings; it was as if no matter how much I had, my body could not get enough. It wanted more and more and more.

And then there was the hair, no joke. I got hairy. Not beautifully sculpted 90s Rachel hair on my head, oh no. The hair on my head was a mess, but what was worst was the rest of the hair.

All.

Over.

My.

Body.

Kids at school called me Harry, it didn't sound particularly mean, nothing for the teachers to discipline them for like on the rare occasions someone called me Pizza Face or Hairy Maclary, no. Only, every single person in the class under the age of sixteen knew that they were referencing *Harry and the Hendersons*, a show we had all gobbled up in primary school. Yup, they were calling me a Sasquatch and there was nothing I could do about it. And they only knew about the hair that seemed to spring from nowhere on my upper lip, my chin. Dear God, if they had known I had to pluck around my nipples they would have captured me in the night and sold me to the circus. Which is pretty much what happened in bygone days.

I finally got a diagnosis of Polycystic Ovary Syndrome at seventeen and everything made so much more sense to me. Suddenly I wasn't born a freak, there was a reason for this.

I'd been actively trying to lose weight for a year by then, and nothing was working. I starved and starved, I was walking everywhere and I was really doing my best to beat the cravings and still the weight Would Not Shift.

Getting a diagnosis had taken years, with my first doctor kindly informing me – when my mum dragged me there, doubled up with pain – that if I just made more of an effort with my overall diet and fitness my periods would regulate. Fat and lazy then. Thanks.

Once I was diagnosed I learnt that my body was working against me. Producing insulin and storing fat at a rate of knots. The spots, the hair, the weight, it wasn't my fault.

I discovered that women who were hirsute in the past became the Bearded Lady Circus acts we still know about today. These days there is a whole movement of proud women who have hirsutism and they stand by the fact that they are rare and bearded. They are brave and I admire them; but I am a coward and I did not and do not want a beard.

Back in school though, before I understood what was causing these changes in my body, changes that made me feel so different to the other girls, I continued to bury myself in my work. I had always been focused, driven, but as other teens partied, had crushes and broken hearts I kept to myself, ignoring it all. My only crush was Scott Oakley, who was in most of the same classes as me but glided through secondary school with a gilded perfection, smart, good-looking, captain of the football team and popular with all the alpha girls.

We used to catch the same bus to school, and he'd talk to me when it was just him and me after the majority of kids got off several stops before ours. Occasionally we'd walk home together, with him living three streets further out than I did. For these ten minutes of the day, I would be caught up in his golden warmth and feel like the most important person in the world.

I knew my crush was a non-starter, that I had no hope and that my fervid dreams of him declaring his undying love to me under the lilac trees that lined the path as we walked home were exactly that, fever dreams. A burning heat in my body turning my mind quite mad.

Scott never called me Harry or joined in with the other kids when they dug the knife in, not until... No, I'm not going there today, I do not have the time for that. But neither did he seek me out or acknowledge our secret after-school friendship in any way. Like I said, unpopularity is worse than nits.

By the time I'd got my diagnosis and made the move to sixth-form college I had risen to the top of the class and learned my lesson about sighing after boys out of my league. I left with six A-levels, no real friends and a PCOS diagnosis but most importantly I developed a far healthier way of dealing with my symptoms.

I had tried the pill, but that didn't work; it merely gave me migraines and constant bleeding. So instead I learned to change my way of eating. I stopped starving myself, slowly replaced my bad choices with good ones and programmed my brain to resist the cravings. It was not easy but I was a woman obsessed and started to work out like mad. By the time I was ready for uni I looked like a different person. The spots were diminishing, the hair not as hideous. My periods were still hell but I was going to start the next stage of my life with a whole new persona. I was going be the woman I wanted to be, I just had to make her. I was going to take control. In any future interactions, I would be the one who held the power.

———

An hour later and I am sitting sipping a mango mocktail at the bar in a high-end restaurant, watching one of my clients practise his new-found dating skills.

My client's self-confidence is clearly now sky-high, the date looks to be going very well and I know my work with him is done. As I pat myself on the back for a job well done, a well-dressed man saunters over and strikes up conversation. I explain I am not here to flirt but do tap my number into his phone whilst those shallow little butterflies dance in my stomach. He is an orthopaedic surgeon in private practice and I say I am a university lecturer. It's my go-to get-out response – trust me, revealing I am a sex and relationships psychologist does not provoke the reaction one wants when meeting people for the first time. We agree to meet for drinks on Wednesday and it takes all my self-control not to lick my lips as he walks away. Jay may not want to go for drinks but I reckon I can make do with Dr McDishy, my fragile ego reassured that I haven't completely lost my touch.

As I return home and let myself in, I hear the piano being

played. It's a baby grand and the last owners chose to leave the piano rather than take the windows out. Kevin was overjoyed but never plays – claiming to be traumatised by enforced lessons as a child – so either he has suddenly become a Master Pianist or Dan is still here, over twelve hours on. The two of them are increasingly spending time together outside of work, and it's a cute development. I wonder if they're sleeping together and am itching to ask. The Love Doctor in me sees them as a perfect match but I know that Kevin will start some self-destructive bullshit and deliberately sabotage anything if he thinks I have caught wind of a blossoming crush.

I peek my head around the door and there they are, both squidged up tight on the piano stool and Kevin is singing 'The First Time Ever I Saw Your Face' and I know that this is one of the songs he has been saving up for a while, wanting it to be perfect before he performs it. It is not an easy song and Dan is playing the piano whilst looking across at him with an intensity that speaks volumes.

There is no way I am disturbing this little beat of perfection. I quietly withdraw from the door and take myself to bed, a stupid smile on my face.

Chapter Eleven

'And then she like said, Nah, you don't need a new au pair, you need a new husband. Facts.' Chloe is holding court with the girls around her. 'Jay. You listened to it yet?' Chloe asks as I approach them.

They are a tight group of three, the oldest of all the kids that attend the youth club, and have been coming for years. They are exactly who I want to lead as my peer support ambassadors for this latest project as soon as I get it signed off. They always make me smile and Chloe, their self-appointed leader, has a can-do attitude I respect. She is one of those people that will succeed at whatever she puts her mind to, and is a great influence on her friends. A natural born leader and one that comes from a home so broken that it would ensure a dysfunctional trajectory for most.

'Naaah. Shut up!' Ellie scrunches her features up to form her favourite are-you-dumb face. 'He don't listen to podcasts, no offence, but my man's *old*.'

I can't stop the laugh bursting from my lips and I hunch

myself over and pretend to stagger with a cane, stuttering out 'charming' in an old man's voice.

'Serious. you should give her a listen, it's good. They should have her blaring out in the supermarkets and stuff.'

'I did. I gave her a listen a few weeks back, a couple of times.' I say in response. There is nothing that will get me to admit I wrote in to her.

'Wise.' Megan smiled. 'What d'ya think?'

'She spoke sense. I liked her. I could reach out to her if you like, see if she'd come spend some time with us. I could ask if she was interested in volunteering?'

'Could you do that? Like really?' Chloe asks me.

'I'm not making any promises but I can reach out and ask.'

'Slide into her DMs, you mean?' The girls wink and nudge each other.

'No, definitely not. That's not my way. I'll email her office in my professional capacity and see what she says. She chats a lot about how she loves this city, let's see if she's got time to come over.'

'That would be mad.' The girls jump about.

'Don't get your hopes up, she may be crazy busy, but it's always worth an ask or you never know, do you?'

'That's what she says, maybe you're like twin souls.'

'Yeah, and maybe we're both adults who know there's nothing wrong with asking a question. If you don't know, ask. That's how you learn.' I give them my fiercest look but they are too busy shrieking, twirling about and jumping up and down.

I love my job.

Chapter Twelve

My last appointment of the morning was Andrew, who presented me with a bouquet of poppies, clearly whipped from next door's front garden, and the suggestion that I have made it onto his list of top twenty women, in the city of Bristol, in the Clifton area. And then was surprised when I didn't keel over with gratitude and immediately agree to date him. He got a stern talking-to about therapist-client relationships and the adult equivalent of a behaviour plan. Apparently, he had one in school as well and was surprisingly receptive. It is clear I still have a lot of work to do.

But for today, I have no more clients and am free to turn to my emails.

This and Insta are how I select the problems that feature on the podcast and I love this part of my life. The fact that my paid work means I can give a full afternoon a week to answering these problems for free salves my soul. And makes some of the clients that come through the door more bearable.

I flick through my inbox. As ever there are a lot, all of

which deserve answers. It's tricky to strike a balance and so many of the questions are very, very similar, and usually revolve around someone doing things they aren't confident with. I'd started off the podcast largely as sex advice but had been surprised how quickly it changed into a relationship-focused one. Initially, it had been aimed at a millennial audience but the age range has become diverse, with so many people out there fretting about being single, about finding the perfect partner, about keeping the one they have.

As I browse, I see the same old topics come up. I can often guess the age of the person asking simply by the subject matter and whilst I don't believe that assumptions are ever a good idea, there is no denying that there are very distinct generational differences in the questions asked.

Today the usual suspects pop up; there is a message from a woman who loves her husband but is not sexually attracted to him anymore and wants to know how to get that back. This is pretty common and I dealt with it a few weeks ago, so I send her a link to the podcast where it is featured and move onto the next.

There is one from a young man who has a new partner who has kids and knowing her small children are in the house means he isn't comfortable having sex when they are there – should he tell her? Hmm, that's maybe one I can do. I had answered a similar question recently but that had been to do with teenage children. This is quite different. I mark it mentally as a possible.

Ooh, one on different sexual positions, I haven't done that for a while. Truth is there may be many articles and books telling us there are a zillion different positions but they really only boil down to a strong six with the others being mere variations of these. This woman's problem could probably be helped simply by changing position a couple of times during sex rather than sticking to the same one all the way through.

Oop, and a message asking if I'd let someone cum on my face. Always have a few of these. Honestly, men! What is wrong with them that so many think this sort of thing is okay? Truthfully, I don't think men send unsolicited dick pics or this sort of question because they truly believe women like it or find their tiddly little beast a turn-on. They know this shit is not okay. They send it because they like the act of sending.

How do I know if he really likes me? Ahh, this question is cute, it's often from the younger girls and quite frankly a bit of a relief from the 'He says I can't love him if I don't do anal/sleep with his friends/let him post nudes of me in his WhatsApp groups' that I also get from this demographic.

I think a bit. Yes, I'll do this one today. I've had a few from older listeners recently and it's about time I spoke to the younger ones. It's the young girls that got me into this business in the first place; the desire to reassure young women who are going through that heinous time of exploding hormones, navigating social groups and cues and all the turmoil that comes from an adolescent brain. People often want to be young again; me, I'm happy sticking at thirty-five.

How do I know if he really likes me? Whitney bursts into song in my head and I can't help but smile, only to be surprised when the following thought is an image of Jay from the sauna.

I thought that my dinner invitation with Doctor TicksAllTheBoxes McDishy, scheduled for tomorrow, was all I needed to pick my oh-so-bruised ego from the floor but I'm still churning Jay and his rejection over in my mind.

It is hard not to. He is so cute. After he had knocked me back, we had sat and talked for ages. Remarkable in its lack of awkwardness. I had worked hard not to let my ego get in the way, not to spoil the vibe, and we had left the sauna and headed into the hot tub as if we were friends visiting the lido together. He had laughed as I did the ice bucket and point-blank refused to do it himself. I flicked water at him as if I'd known him for twenty years and he actually squealed before threatening to flick me with his towel.

We sat in the hot tub for far longer than we should have. We talked about me as a child and my love for swimming, the charity 5K I had done for the last few years, enjoying the challenge and training leading up to it.

He had talked a lot about his sister, about how despite being the younger one she had once locked him in a rabbit hutch and refused to let him out until he had eaten raw carrots and made snuffling noises. How he was born and bred in Bristol and was devoted to the city. He loved music and was evangelical about the sounds coming out of Bristol.

Every time I think of him, I get a lazy smile spreading across my face, my mind braces itself for pleasure hormones spiking like mad inside and I get ridiculously moony. Only now it's not just about his physique; spending time with him, talking to him, meant we both let each other in a little bit, and that has made my crush even more intense.

But I need to stop, not least because if my mind wanders when I'm around Kevin, he will know in an instant something strange is happening. I have enough of a battle trying to keep that awareness at bay from myself, let alone doing battle with that cackling truth-bringer.

I focus on my laptop and start to make notes for the next

podcast. Some people record theirs spontaneously, claiming it's more natural, but I like the security of knowing exactly what I'm going to say.

I sketch out the obvious points, that asking is the best way, not to be afraid, all the things I now do as an adult. Then I remember how it felt to be fifteen, all the insecurities, the doubts, the cruelty of others at that age. I quickly check the profile of the girl who has sent this question and see she is at uni.

I rarely check the profiles; it feels invasive and those who choose to send in questions deserve their privacy. That is only fair. But in certain cases – and this is one – it's important to pitch it accurately; the advice I offer a fourteen-year-old will differ considerably from what I say to a young woman at university.

My mind scoots back to Jay; I know so much about him and yet so little. I never got around to asking all the questions that you would normally ask when meeting someone. What do you do for a living? Did you go to uni? Have you always lived in Bristol? We had just cut straight to the important shit, our families, our history.

My mind flicks to the doctor I'm meeting for dinner tomorrow. I remember how he looked at me, that once-over that demonstrates he finds me desirable, the up and down in a microsecond that I always find so validating. The one I still seek out to enable me to feel good about myself; to reassure myself that I am now a swan.

I know how shallow this is. The importance of intrinsic validation is a fundamental lesson I work on with clients; that you need to learn to value yourself. But you know what they say about theory and practice; I nail the theory and do a pretty good job of appearing to nail the practice. But only I and Kevin know how firmly that mask is attached. How my physical insecurities are still there, my faux confidence a very thin silken mesh.

I know that those looks of appreciation that are for my body, my arse, my tits, my legs and how I parcel it up are as shallow as shit; they mean nothing about the core of me, the core that I should value above all the superficial nonsense. But it's like a drug, a high I have to keep chasing. Those looks lift me up and make me feel valid, and every time I feel shitty about myself, every time that bullied little girl pops back into my head, then I'm out looking for the validation as sure as an addict will crawl the streets looking for the next hit.

I need to break the cycle. I haven't done all this work for all these years not to be aware of how crazyily unhealthy this is. Jay's face comes flooding back into my head. I know he said no to drinks, but I'm convinced he finds me attractive. All the signs were there.

What was refreshing was at no point did he do that up-and-down once-over, at no point did I catch his eyes slip to my breasts, my legs. The sparks were flying as if someone had set off a ton of dynamite in a diamond mine and it was all based on the rapport we shared.

Is this not the dream I send my clients searching for? Jay seemed genuinely interested in what I had to say and found it amusing. There was no faking that laugh; it reached deep inside and warmed the very core of you, it made me feel proud, accepted, approved of. And all just for me. Nothing to do with my unmade-up face and dull-as-ditchwater swimsuit or sleek sexy dresses and corn-inducing heels. Just me.

That is what I should aim for, I know it. I know that Kevin's bitching about my sexual behaviour is due to his concern that my lack of desire for a relationship is unhealthy. But that sort of rapport leads to love and love leads to commitment and whilst that is the goal for the majority of people on this planet – comfortable companionship, someone you love so much that you want to build a life with them – that is not a luxury I can afford to indulge in. It wouldn't be fair. Not fair to me, not fair to them and certainly not fair to a man as good as Jay, someone who has the importance of family emblazoned all over him.

No, my shallow, sex-seeking, ego-validating wham-bams are the best I can hope for and I cannot let my head get turned by a pretty boy like Jay. The memory of our chat means the thought of my doctor date leaves me cold, and yet that has to continue being my path.

But I liked being stripped-down Lily, I want to keep her for a little while longer. I reach for my phone and reschedule Doctor McDishy. If I cancel I'll regret it but I am not in the mood tonight, and ridiculously it feels like cheating even if it's just cheating myself.

As I hit send, I am distracted by the ping of an email.

Ooh, that looks interesting! And perfectly ties in with my interest in reaching girls who are the age I was when I struggled the most. Little Lily could have done with grown-up Lily then. This looks perfect.

Chapter Thirteen

I approach the building which is sat deep in the heart of Bristol. I have been invited in to meet the kids that attend this youth club and it sounds like the guy in charge, Jacob Cooper, wants to set up a space for the girls that is explicitly for young women, where they can discuss anything they need to. Somewhere he hopes to break down expectations and assumptions that perpetuate in this age group and teach that we must do what we're comfortable with, stay true to what we want to be and try and make our decisions based on our best selves. All of which is manna to my heart. On paper he has managed to encapsulate everything I wanted to do when I got started and somehow got side-tracked by academia, by bills, by life.

It will be hard not to hug Mr Jacob Cooper for this opportunity when I see him but I am very aware I am here because of my professional reputation not my teenage ambitions. I have dressed carefully for today. I obviously need to be Doctor Galbraith but I also have to make sure I don't reek of privilege, so out of touch with the girls that a giant chasm opens between us before I utter a word.

I smooth down the fabric of my jumpsuit and hope I've got it right. I'm in the yard when a girl saunters towards me. She is sassy as hell, I can see it from the way she walks, and I can feel the lift at the corners of my mouth. I would have loved to have had that confidence at her age.

'Hey...' she approaches me and looks me up and down. 'You're The Love Doctor, you came.' Her words are positive but her tone is more reserved. 'I'm Chloe, I'll go let Jay know you're here. We didn't know if you'd show,' she says, turning and heading back to the building, stopping halfway across the yard and shouting over her shoulder, 'You coming then?'

As we enter the building I can see the broad back of a man chatting to a girl on some beanbags. He reaches over to pat her shoulder, effectively screening his face from me, but there is something very familiar about him.

No!

I must be making a mistake.

This is the result of my febrile imaginings and ongoing lust-filled night-time fantasies. It can't be. Am I hallucinating?

Mind you, Jacob, Jay, it's not outside the realms of poss... My train of thought is cut off as he stands up, turns to me and I see him start back, a real jolt of shock on his face.

I can't believe it. The man offering me the chance to work with these girls, do some good in the community, is Jay. Cacti Guy is now standing in front of me with his mouth wide open, looking as shocked as I am, and says, 'I didn't recognise you with your clothes on...'

Chloe swivels her head around at speed, like a horror movie extra.

He doesn't recognise me with my clothes on? *Really?* I feel quite sorry for him; I can imagine how I would feel had I said something as daft in a professional setting. Mind you, talking of clothes, he is beautifully turned out. He is wearing jeans and a T-shirt, but these are not any old jeans and a T-shirt. The cut is sharp, the fabrics are quality and his trainers are so white, they may burn my retinas. The clothes fit him beautifully, the T-shirt sleeves sitting on his upper arm and highlighting their muscular form.

He is clearly a man who takes pride in his appearance.

'Oh my God...' He is fumbling for words now and the embarrassment is written all over his face. 'I... oh my God, I'm so sorry, that phrase is literally programmed in... oh no, that's even worse, I'm so sorry.' He turns to address the small crowd of girls now gathering around. 'I didn't mean it like that.'This is said with much more authority, his voice firm.

'Ha, no worries, I know what you mean.' I smile at him and try to negate any embarrassment he may feel. No one has ever said this to me at work before, and it doesn't do much to enhance my professional standing. But I do know what he means. And that it wasn't meant in any way to be as it sounded.

'You look really different,' he says as he takes a step forward to shake my hand and set things back onto a professional footing. I lean forward to take his hand and somehow he bangs into one of the beanbags, stumbling as he does so and furiously righting himself. The girls are looking at him as if they have never seen him like this before and I feel for him.

'I had no idea it would be—' I say.

'I had no idea—' he starts to say at the same time, and we both laugh.

'Must be meant to be,' I say and then feel like a twat. I meant the work side of things, obviously. What is happening here? This sort of awkward ineptitude from the two of us is ludicrous.

'You two know each other?' Chloe asks.

'Well, yes,' Jake says and we exchange a smile.

This project is going to be so good. It felt right the minute I saw the message, and this has now confirmed it.

'But not dressed?' Chloe purses her lips; her shoulders lifting as she does so, and her head cocks to one side. I have a flash forward to her, years from now, questioning her children. Jake gives her a warning look, but it rolls off her like oil from a spoon.

'It's great that Dr Galbraith has been able to join us. Come on, let's go and join the others,' he says and stumbles on the edge of the beanbag again. 'I'm really not usually this clumsy,' he says.

'Well, apart from that time in the shower—' I stop myself just in time. What is happening to me? A woman who carefully measures every word and yet I'm stood here, speaking without thinking and digging an even bigger hole for the pair of us in front of these girls.

'Nope. No. No!' he says, addressing them. 'That is not what it sounds like either. It's just that Doctor Galbraith has a way of making me clumsy.'

I squawk. 'Woah, don't blame me for your shortcomings, I wasn't anywhere near you, didn't even know you when that shower incident occurred.'

'True,' he answers.

'And as for you taking a beating from that beanbag –' I wave my hand at it '– that's not on me either. Not at all. Not my fault. Don't even try, do not even try –' I repeat for dramatic effect '– to blame me.'

'Yeah, for real. It's all about personal responsibility, Jay,' Chloe adds to a chorus of sniggers. I high-five her.

Jake shakes his head but his eyes are sparkling at me and for some reason I find this man, who I now know spends his work life trying to make things better for young people in the community, even more attractive now he is fully dressed.

Chapter Fourteen

The realisation that Lily is The Love Doctor is huge for me. Revelatory and, on a personal level, mortifying.

I pull myself together, introduce her formally to the girls and go back to my office. I want to give Lily the space, and privacy, to talk to the girls without me hovering over her. I see her lowering herself onto a beanbag, the girls joining her, and hear her say, 'hey, I'm Lily and I know Jay introduced me as someone who has come to talk *to* you but truth is I've come to talk *with* you. You've got as much to teach me as I have you so let's sit down and get to know each other.'

'Okay.' I hear Chloe's voice as I am almost at the office door. She has always been Lily's super-fan so hopefully will be gentle with her, although why I think that after the very non-gentle questioning just now, I don't know.

I pause, just for a second. I have seen this girl tear strips off grown men in the street, I have seen her reduce people to tears time and time again. But I figure Lily is more than capable of looking after herself. She needs to hold her own with these girls or this simply won't work.

'So, I listen to your podcast and I've told all the girls to listen to you too.' There's a chorus of agreement. Chloe continues, 'I like what you do. You're all about being honest about shit, having firm boundaries, with sex particularly. But are you here cos you've slept with our Jay? Cos he claimed he ain't never met you and now we know that ain't true.'

I turn on my heel ready to shoot daggers at Chloe. Here she is meeting the woman she claims to be her idol and she's doing her best to make her feel uncomfortable. I know Chloe, I know how she works, and this is a test, but Lily doesn't know this and more importantly shouldn't be subjected to it.

Lily lets out a burst of laughter. Some of the other girls join in the laughter too, I suspect with relief that an embarrassing situation seems to have been defused.

'Look, we both know there is no need for me to answer that question. You know you've crossed a line asking it. But honestly, I can promise you I have not slept with your guy Jay. I can also tell you, although I shouldn't, that we won't be sleeping together either. Mixing work with pleasure is not something I do.'

'You two have *mad* chemistry and you should know that man is beggin' for a wifey.'

'He's going to love us talking about him like that. He's not here to defend himself but yeah, we've met in a social capacity and we get on well, I think we could be good friends. But the sex thing is off the table. I have my hands full at work so I'm prioritising that rather than anything else at the moment.'

'Well, you better snap him up now if you have any intentions that way. He's never single for long.'

'Ha. I'll bear that in mind, but I think we're all good.' Lily laughs and I sit at my desk knowing there is no need for me to intervene here, although I could easily strangle Chloe. *Beggin' for a wifey*!

Lily shifts the conversation and soon the girls are sharing some of the problems they are encountering in the community in which they live. None of which are easy things to navigate, things that they live alongside in a way that fills me full of admiration daily.

I start to scroll through my emails and become fully aware of who my sauna buddy is. This woman that I have been sitting giggling with, that I have shared some serious stuff with under the guise of a budding new friendship, is the same woman I messaged about my sister. And one I have introduced to my workplace.

On top of which, if our friendship didn't have to be platonic, then I think both of us know that ripping each other's clothes off and pressing up against each other would be hugely tempting. But with the seismic negative ramifications, my vow to Cass and now potentially working together, that is absolutely off the table.

The sexual chemistry between us, as Chloe observed in under five minutes, crackles like an electric storm. Every time I see Lily it does feel like the sky is lighting up and changing colour with forks of lightning flitting between the two of us at all times. I have, I admit, thought myself in love a fair few times in my life. Cassie is right when she says I fall in love easily and quickly. But because I know I tend to fall in love with potential rather than reality I never actually say it, I watch and wait and see how things develop. But I have never experienced an immediate bond like this.

KITTY WILSON

I correct myself, that feels misleading. Obviously in no way am I *in love* with Lily Galbraith, especially now I know that she is The Love Doctor and has read and answered my deepest fear on her podcast. But it feels wrong not telling her that the guy who was worried about his sister was me, as if now it looms as a secret between us.

I also feel kind of trapped, like my hand has been forced. There was safety in saying those things to a stranger, without the fear of mine and Cassie's identities being revealed. But to let Lily know now that I was the one that wrote in to her, then met her in the sauna and have now invited her here feels a bit stalkery. There's an awful lot of coincidences there. What if she thinks I have evil intentions and all this is an elaborate ruse?

I lift my head and see the girls roaring with laughter and I know that the germ of a plan I had, a mere seed – before I knew who Lily was – could well grow into something really positive, really effective for these girls, making my concerns pale into insignificance, I wonder if she would be interested in helping us out a little bit here, beyond today.

In a short space of time this evening she has cut through with these girls – and they are not young women that let their walls down easily. I'm not sure where I'll find the money in a seriously overstretched budget but I will find a way. But first I have to ask Lily if she is prepared to get involved. And admit that I am the one who messaged her about his sister. I don't want to, I really don't want to, but I have a feeling that the thing about Lily and me is that we shouldn't be keeping secrets.

104

Chapter Fifteen

Jay has suggested we grab a drink to talk about the project, and at one of my old haunts so I am excited. I haven't been to Mama K's for years. I love it here. It has a perfect chilled-out vibe, reggae playing in the background if there isn't live music, accompanied by good Caribbean food and a relaxed clientele who are happy just being in their favourite bar. But I haven't been here for ten years or so and I wonder if it's still as I remember, my heart leaping with anticipation.

As I walk through the door with Jay I see that despite a refresh on the decor everything feels exactly the same. It's a bit like coming home and with a happy grin I approach the bar.

This afternoon has been invigorating. These girls aren't easy but they are sparky and engaging and I respect them. I have felt more alive spending time with them today than in my work for a while.

On the walk over, Jay briefly outlined his plans to build up a support system that focuses on sexual health and healthy relationships, the plan being to appoint ambassadors amongst the girls themselves who then go out and spread the message, provide peer-to-peer support and ensure that trusted community spaces, like the youth centre I have just visited, become hubs of learning and support.

And I am intrigued to know what he wants from me with regard to this. I would love to be involved and if there is anything I can do to help, to make just one of these girls have the courage to say no to something that makes them uncomfortable, to walk away from something they know isn't right for them, then that is my life's dream right there. That's why I have studied for years, built up a profile. That's why I do the podcast, in the hope of reaching out to people who can't access me in other ways. And the fact that these girls said they listen to my podcast makes me so proud I feel like bursting. For a second there, professional Lily was all flustered and couldn't find any words.

'Yo, Jay. How you doing?' The barman greets him with a convoluted handshake and pulls him into his chest.

'Marcus,' Jay responds and the two men have a clinch over the bar before Marcus turns to look at me. He looks me up and down and I arch an eyebrow at him.

A slow smile spreads over Marcus's face as he leans across the counter and picks up his phone.

'Ma'am...' He turns to me and holds up the phone.

'Leave her alone!' Jay says, friendly but with a little bit of steel to his voice. A warning.

'Uhhuh,' I say, a little wary but mildly amused.

'I just need to snap a pic—'

'Woah, woah.' Jay lifts his hand in front of my face. 'No, no, no. Stop. You can tell my sister this is a business meeting, *business*. If I were secretly dating, would I bring my date here, huh? Where Cass runs the most efficient underground network of information since the French resistance? Nope. Wouldn't happen.'

Marcus lowers his phone.

'It really is just work,' I add. 'If it helps, you can tell her I did ask him out for a drink a couple of weeks ago but he turned me down.'

'He turned you down?'

'Right?' I say in mock surprise and hope he gets that I'm joking.

'Wow. Jay mate, I didn't think you had it in you. But girl, I tell you, you single then I may be able to help you out.'

I scrunch my face and shake my head in a no-please-don't way and Marcus guffaws.

'No photo then?'

'Nope.'

'No date?'

'Thank you for the flattering offer but no date. I really *am* only here to talk business.' I say and Marcus grins a can't-blame-a-person-for-trying grin and takes our order.

We grab our drinks and decamp outside to one of the tables. The sun is shining, and Jay explains he is hoping I can come on board to help shape the sexual wellness project but he is open about a lack of flexibility in the budget. I reassure him that I'm keen to help, so much so that I don't mind volunteering. And I don't. I make enough money from my consultancy and besides this is what I've been itching to do. He outlines what he has done so far and explains how he hopes the programme will be rolled out initially in this youth group but then across the city, with the idea that the girls will then go on to mentor it themselves. Chloe is his first choice and I can't help but agree. It was clear today that that girl has respect from all her peers and I suspect that she will be remarkably good at spreading the empowerment message. I cast an eye over his proposal so far and we draft some more topic areas. I am keen to get stuck in and promise to do some more once I'm home.

'So now that's done let's talk about you,' I say to Jay, who has just returned from the bar with more drinks.

'Me? Do we have to?'

'Oh yes.' I say. 'Why was that barman going to take my photo to send to your sister? It's a little bit weird.'

'Ha, it's a lot weird,' Jay responds. 'But I've known Marcus for years, he's one of my best friends. The truth is my sister and I have kind of a bet thing going on. It started out with me wanting to show her that it's good to change things up a little. She's always going on about my dating and this mythical list she reckons I have. So I told her I wouldn't date for six months, and she said I could never do it, not even for six weeks, and then it kinda evolved.'

'Evolved? List?' He has lists? *For what?*

'Ha yes, and now if I date or, you know, well, then I have to take over painting the sets for this community choir's musical that our foster mum supports.'

'And if you manage to keep it in your, um?' I gesture in his general trouser direction.

'Then the *most* important thing is she sees that change is possible and, as an added bonus, I get my house back.'

'Eh?'

'I currently have all her houseplants...'

'Ahh, the cacti in the bathroom?'

'Exactly. And boxes and boxes of her clutter that she won't

get rid of but won't store at hers. She has promised she'll deal with it all if I keep my vow.'

'So, you're going to be a monk for six months?'

'Woah, don't say it like that. I'm happy to have a period of celibacy, I'm not some serial seducer.'

'Interesting, cos my sources today said you *are* fond of the women.' I nod my head knowingly as I say this.

'Are you telling me the girls said I was a bit of a ho?' His eyebrows shoot up.

'Whoa. They didn't use that word and had they I would have pulled them up on it. It's misogynistic and shaming.'

He doesn't buy it.

'Tell me they didn't say I was for the streets?' His eyes are wide and I fail to stifle my laughter.

'In a nice way,' I say placatingly and he chokes on his drink.

'There is no nice way. I'm going to kill them. Is that really what they think?'

'They said it in jest and with affection but they did say that you seem to have a different woman on your arm every week. They added you never ever brought that stuff to work, but you know, it's a tight-knit community. Things get around.'

'Yeah. Me by the sounds of it.'

'Ha! Chloe pulled them up, said that wasn't fair cos in your case you're desperate for one to be marriage material.' His eyes are practically out of his head now and once I get my laughter under control I add, 'You're a bit of a local legend apparently. They said they know women who are *so* keen but fail to make the cut.' He visibly winces as I say this.

'Yay, Jay boy!' Someone heads over and, spotting Jay with me, comes and greets him. It's clear the girls are right, there is a lot of love for this man in the community. And I wonder if his promise to his sister is the only reason he rejected me? Or does he have some kind of superpower that makes him know I am never going to be good wife-and-mother material?

'Ouch, those girls are sharp,' he says as his friend heads inside. 'I'd write it off as rubbish but it kind of backs up what Cass has been saying to me, I guess.' He takes a sip of his drink and looks at me over the top of the glass. Those eyes, warm, brown like oozing puddles of melty goodness, are making me suddenly feel squirmy with lust. Nope, that is not going to help me now. I dig deep and switch my work brain back on.

'Okay, so what's your list?'

He widens his eyes at me in a 'please' gesture and takes a gulp of his pint.

'Honestly, Cass is making it way more of a thing than it is. The girls kind of have a point, not that I'm a fuckboy –' he adds that last bit hurriedly '– but that I'm a commitment guy. Yes, I date a lot but because I am looking for someone to settle down with. Someone to have a family with. Not cos I'm into numbers or conquests, the exact opposite in fact.'

'And the list is to do with finding the perfect partner?'

'Exactly that, I need to make sure the woman I decide to spend my life with has all the criteria my kids will need in their mother to make the best of themselves.' His face is serious, and I can see how much this means to him, not in a freaky controlling way but in a determined to do the best for his future family kind of way.

'That's a very fixed way of looking at relationships...' I leave the sentence hanging. How Jay lives his romantic life is none of my business but it's helped me stop thinking about creeping my hand up his thigh, which is what it really had wanted to be doing.

Until this speech.

I move it slightly and sit on it just to make sure.

'Yeah, it was a bit of a shock to discover my sauna buddy was the famous Love Doctor, all wise about everything in relationships.'

I raise an eyebrow; he smiles sheepishly.

'But more than that,' he adds, 'it is kind of coincidental and a bit embarrassing, uncomfortable.'

'Huh, embarrassing why?' Wow! Uncomfortable? If he is going to say something dismissive about my work that means my self-respect will force me to walk away right now. Surely not though, if he wanted me on board with the girls' project? That would make no sense.

I cock my head to one side as I await his response.

'It makes me feel as if I have a secret, and truth is I don't want secrets between us, so now I have to make an admission,' he says, still holding my eyes with his, my lust now replaced by mild anxiety. Although if my heart could understand the word 'mild' and slow down a little, I'd appreciate it.

'Go on,' I say, sure that the trepidation is clear in my tone.

'I...um...' He looks down at his lap and bites the side of his top lip.

Jesus.

'Jacob! You joining us for a kickabout later?' A voice comes booming across the garden and I see his head shoot up and he grins, lifts his hand in a hello gesture, turns it into a thumbs-up and then shakes his head, almost imperceptibly, to indicate that disturbing him at this point is not a good idea. His friend nods in response and goes into Mama K's instead. Meanwhile my heart is now ready to explode out of my chest. A hyperbolic reaction, I'm sure, but there is nothing worse than the unknown.

'You read out a problem a few weeks back on your podcast...' My mind is racing. Um... hated by his mother-in-law? No, can't be, we've established he is single. Weeping willy? Unhealthy crushes on women old enough to be his grandma? I mean, I'm all for talking the good talk and saying each to their own and there is no such thing as unacceptable if it's between consenting adults, but please don't be that last one.

'...about...um...about my fears for my sister in the relationship she was in.'

Ah, the coercive control message. Of course! *That's* why he is showing his sister change is a good thing. That's why staying celibate is important to him. It has nothing to do with him or the women he wants to date, it's his way of having some positive input into a situation he feels so powerless in. A way he can help protect his sister.

His message had got to me, and I made it a special podcast because there was so much to say and it is such a serious issue. I have wondered about that one ever since... so that was Jay. That was Jay about Cassie. Cassie who seems to have every barman at Mama K's under her thumb? That bouncy happy woman who had come and grabbed him from the sauna. Boosh! I know not to judge by appearance, not to make assumptions, of course I do, but still. When we think of coercive control we think of drained-looking women, women who are cowed, fearful of the next verbal blow. We forget that clichés fail to cover the spectrum of experience. It's a powerful reminder.

'That was you about Cassie?' I want to keep it neutral and

not splurge the *no!* in my head. But I ought to check that he doesn't have any other sisters and I'm not mixing things up here.

'Yup.' He scrunches up his face and I pull my hand out from under my leg and touch his arm.

'I had no idea. I'm sorry you're going through this. And that she is. How have things been recently?'

'Yeah, she's still with Jas and she's quit work here.'

'Here in Mama K's?'

'Uh-huh. Jas is "keeping" her. Keeping her in what, is my concern. Quite frankly it feels like it's even more chains she's wrapping around Cass, making it harder for her to leave.' He pauses, and then in a more anxious tone than I have heard him use before, 'I hate to ask this, but I'll beat myself up if I don't. Would you be able to talk to her?'

'Oh Jay, I would love to say yes, bring her to my office and all will be well. But you know as much as I do that any change needs to come from her. If she wants to come see me then obviously I will move heaven and earth to be there for her, but I can't storm in and give her unsolicited advice about her life. That's not going to do anything other than push her closer to this Jas. I'm sorry, Jay. I wish there was a magic wand in cases like this. But there's not, it takes patience, time and trust in the building blocks that were put in place during childhood. Have faith that what made you the man you are also makes Cassie strong enough to break free of this.'

He looks at me and for a second the world feels like it's stopped as I see so much pain in his face. He takes a deep breath. 'That's the thing, those building blocks.'

And as we sit in the sunshine Jay opens up about their childhood, an absent mother, the sudden death of their father, years in the care system before they found security with their foster parents. In a matter of minutes, as this gorgeous, caring, responsible, pained man talks to me, I understand about the man he has become and exactly why he is so worried for his baby sister, and my heart breaks more than a little.

Chapter Sixteen

'That... man's a... terror...terrorist,' Kevin huffs as soon as he gets his breath back, or partially back. It still looks like he is struggling to be honest, as he gasps and flails around on the grass.

Mind you, he's been doing that for the past hour whilst the rest of us did burpees and lunges and side planks. If he'd been a stranger, I would have loosened his clothing and called an ambulance by now. Instead, Dan and I exchange an affectionate look, knowing he's fine, just remarkably out of shape.

The whole millennial obsession with fitness seems to have passed Kevin completely by. Resistant to my offerings of healthy green juices, avocado breakfasts and vitamin-enriched smoothies, he thinks I didn't see the empty box of twinkies (a twelve-pack) in the bin, along with the four Burger King bags and the one Subway delivery, which I know is what he considers the healthy option. Kevin alone is keeping Deliveroo in business. So that, and his fondness for hyperbole, means he is thoroughly enjoying taking this slightly dramatic path, despite all his protestations to the contrary.

'You probably need to hydrate. Here, sit up and take a sip of this.' I shimmy over on my bottom to him and feed him water as if he is a dying bird.

'Thank you,' he says meekly, managing to find a burst of energy and sit up, sip pathetically and then shoot daggers at Joe, the fitness instructor that runs these bootcamps on The Downs, who has just finished packing up his things and is waving as he heads off.

This morning Kevin begged me to let him join this and bring Dan for moral support. He knows I come to this once a week and he claims he is determined to do something about getting a little trimmer. He even ate a carrot in front of me to prove his commitment before calling me an evil hell-spawn diva with a wholly unnatural relationship to exercise as I passed him a sip of my drink. I did mutter something about transference but he merely spat some kombucha at me and added that gaslighting *and* poison are a particularly cruel combination.

However, seeing a photograph taken of him recently at a very unflattering angle – seven chins that I swear do not exist in real life – means that he is newly invigorated with a passion for losing weight. This happens fairly frequently but so far has failed to last. This time he insists that his very soul has been seared with the pain, the shame and the need to change.

He may be shit at push-ups but he is very good with language.

I gently suggested joining my Tuesday night yoga class but Kevin has decided the best way to deal with things is by putting himself up for the brutality and public humiliation of bootcamp.

'So, you on for next week?' Dan asks, the glimmer of mischief clear on his face.

Kevin lies back on the grass and starts to mock hyperventilate again, too traumatised to use words.

'How was your day?' Dan turns to ask me instead. We are adept at this now. We give Kevin a little attention and reassurance and then we get on with what we're doing and he can choose to join in or not. He always joins in.

'Ah, had a client this morning.'

'Ooh, Flowers guy or the doll woman?'

'The doll woman,' I confirm. I maintain confidentiality about my clients, but occasionally I do chat with Kevin and Dan about the absolute basics, no names and no specifics though.

'How's it going?'

'Do you know what, better than I had hoped. We started the preparatory work for EMDR a couple of weeks ago. I think we're taking some serious steps forward.' Dan nods, he's listened to me enough to know what EMDR means. 'I think if we can get to the bottom of her anxiety then she may be able to function and interact a little better, maybe even have healthy relationships and children of her own one day...'

Dan lets out a long, low 'whooooo' and Kevin shoots up into a sitting position, his breathing suddenly normal. He clasps his hand to his chest as he exchanges meaningful looks with Dan.

'Woah,' I say, holding my hand up defensively. 'I know what you're thinking and don't even go there. It's a completely different situation.' I take a deep breath, 'As far as I know my client's anxiety is what is stopping her, *her* medical condition doesn't impact fertility. There's no physical proof that she can't have children.' Kevin's eyebrows have taken on a life of their own and I clench my teeth before continuing the explanation I really shouldn't have to give. 'It's very different to my situation.'

'Yes, it is,' Dan agrees. But I know this man, albeit only for the past year, and his tone is placatory, well-intentioned but not an indicator that he truly believes me. I narrow my eyes.

'Right!' I draw myself upwards. Kevin has had my back ever since the first day we met at university all those years ago, and I'm super fond of Dan as well, but on this one issue they have never comprehended the gravity of it. They look at me as if my potential infertility is all in my head and I don't understand. Why would I make something like this up? I just wouldn't. I avoid ever speaking of it with them, because when it does come up it always gets super uncomfortable, super-fast.

I know it's unreasonable to expect your friends to agree with you on everything, but on this *one* thing, on this I think they should. No one knows your body as well as you do and it hurts that they do that look. The one they are doing right now that makes me want to batter their brains out and spread them all over the downs in some kind of macabre mulching ceremony.

'You know I have Polycystic Ovary Syndrome and the upshot of that is that many women then have problems with fertility. That GP said...' I say, a little aggressively.

'That man was an evil arsehole with no understanding of the female reproductive system or the support you needed. He should have been struck off,' Kevin bites back.

'Yes, he was pretty bloody mean, and he might not have

had any empathy for what he termed "women's problems" but he did have a medical degree and thirty years' experience and he said that the chances of me ever getting pregnant were slim to none.'

'Yes but you can't just—'

I hold up my hand in the universal stop-right-now signal.

'Oooh,' say Kevin and Dan and I kind of give them a half-arsed smile but I've heard this time and time again and I am done with it. Done. 'I can do what I want when it comes to my body. Agreed?'

'Well yes...' they chorus, but both sound reluctant and I know there is more they want to say: *That was then, you should go and get it checked... You did all the research at the start when you wanted to lose weight, why not apply that dedication to your beliefs about whether you can conceive...* And the worst of them all and a favourite of my mother's – *Time is ticking on, you know, why not go and get checked out? Why are you burying your head in the sand?*

People build walls for a reason, I get that. But these aren't just any old walls, this is based on information given by the doctor who diagnosed and treated me; the doctor whose advice, albeit somewhat bad-tempered, has led to all those changes I made from being an obese and unhappy teen to a healthy – well, maybe a little bit obsessive – adult. His advice, harsh as it was, kickstarted me into turning my life around, so why would I dismiss the bits I don't like when the advice I have acted on so far has proven most effective?

And why are my friends determined to try and make me revisit something that breaks my heart – that forces me to face up again to the fact that I can probably never have children – is beyond me and I don't know how to get them to stop.

Chapter Seventeen

I am excited tonight, although by rights I should not be this buzzed up, since I've done a full day's work, played football with the boys and am meant to be having an early night because Henri has booked studio time tomorrow and has asked me to join him. Instead I'm sat waiting to meet Lily at Chrysalis in Old Market.

I've never been here before but when I emailed to say that I have had our plans signed off she said we should celebrate and invited me out to join her and her friends at this place. She adds that she's crazy backed up at work so if I want to discuss the additions that she had emailed back over, she'll be here this evening and I should join her.

That makes it work rather than a date, right?

Bringing the plans with me definitely makes it project-related so I'm not blurring any boundaries or breaking my promise to Cass.

Just to make sure, I've picked out a pair of boxer shorts I have never worn and – before tonight – had no intention of doing so. Cass bought them for me as a joke present last Christmas and they are beyond grim. Plain black with a large photo of her face on them; there are no words to describe how wrong they feel. She thought it was hilarious at the time whereas I grinned feebly, appreciated the mischief of her, and vowed internally there would never be a day on which I wore them.

Seems I was wrong; they are perfect for this evening. Wearing them demonstrates intent. Firm intent not to remove my trousers. And let's face it, a date is an agreement to meet someone socially with the hope of removing your trousers should all go well. This will make that impossible. Impossible.

I'm loving it in here though, even if I was a bit fearful of having an accident that resulted in paramedics having to undress me on the way over. I know Cassie would love it too and wonder if she's ever been. Chrysalis is a kind of pub-cum-theatre in a beautiful old chapel and has a long bar running all along the side filled with every fancy bottle known to man. At the end of the room is a wooden stage complete with plush red curtains and a battered piano to the side. But it is not just the architecture of the place that makes it special. It is positively fizzing in here.

There is a hotch-potch of people, all of whom have got past the intimidating attitude of the tiny elderly woman who looks as if she should be an Aunt in Gilead but instead is fiercely guarding the entrance and welcoming those people she knows with kisses, arm-throwing and effusive love-love whereas those she doesn't – that's me – are greeted with hooded eyes and the feeling that if I don't behave she is going to have the two burly men she sits with grabbing my legs and arms and hurling me onto the pavement. The two of them are older than the majority of the crowd and have shaved heads, huge boots and lots of blue ageing tattoos, and look like they would fit right in at a BNP rally.

I have every intention of behaving.

I'm taking a sip of my drink and hear that diminutive she-wolf shout, 'Darlings!' in a low-pitched shriek, and as I turn to check out who is getting such a rapturous reception I see Lily and her two friends walk in. This must be High Jinx and Dan.

High Jinx looks amazing; she has the prettiest face and her make-up is flawless. She's beautiful. Dan is bouncing up and down and squeezing the woman. I hear him greet her as SyPhyllis and choke on my drink. I must have misheard.

Lily looks over and catches my eye and heads over. I feel my heart quicken in anticipation. She is stunning, in a deep red dress that looks as if she has been poured in to it, her hair flowing gold. As she bends down to kiss my cheek in a hello I catch a waft of her scent, her shampoo. It smells light and summery and I want to breathe it in but stop myself because that would be weird and this is Lily. As in Dr Lily Galbraith, dating expert and Love Doctor extraordinaire, whom I am here to meet because we have some work plans to develop. And because if Cass ever hears, or telepathically senses, that I want to inhale a woman's scent, especially this woman's scent, she's going to be sitting there composing an email to Sue's choir before the evening is out.

However, it doesn't mean I can't appreciate the contact and as Lily draws back I find myself holding her eyes and a silly smile crosses my face.

I'm shit at poker too.

She sits down in one seamless movement. There's something about Lily when she's dressed up. All self-possessed and golden-age-of-Hollywood. Sliding, graceful movements, silky, well-cut clothes and shiny hair.

When Malcom and Sue first fostered us, I pulled the odd sickie from school. But instead of using it to smoke weed, shoplift and outrun police community officers like the majority of my mates, I used to lie on the sofa and watch old musicals with Sue as she sewed. Sue's machine would be going nineteen to the dozen, the volume of the TV on high as she'd sing along, and I would lie there revelling in the domesticity, the normalcy of it, how boring it was.

I'd had my fill of street corners, gaggles of adolescents and drama whilst Cass and I were in the group homes. The novelty and the quiet of Malcolm and Sue's home were new, special to me at that point of my life, something hoped for by both of us for a long time. So, I know my way around a Grace Kelly or Audrey Hepburn movie. And everything about Lily reminds me of those women. A twenty-first-century version, polished, graceful and deliberate but utterly kickass and in charge of her own destiny.

I have seen the way this woman ploughs through water, I have no doubt she could take me out merely by looking at me. She is certainly not a woman who needs a hero to rescue her; that is one of the differences between her and those movies. She'd be more likely to rescue me. Let's face it, for all my gym time, football, healthy eating and fitness, I've been totally bested by a kitten recently.

'Hello.' Her friends come and join us. The man that I assume is Dan – who reminds me a little of a human jack-in-a-box – pulls a chair out next to me as High Jinx stands over me looking me up and down. It's a little unnerving. High Jinx is quite intense. And very tall. I cast a quick glance down. Her heels look like they would break a weaker woman.

I like meeting new people and have been excited about meeting Lily's friends. Over the last couple of weeks, in the lido and again at Mama K's, she has talked about them with so much love I half feel as if I know them already.

'Everyone having the usual?' Dan asks, seamlessly including me in their group and they nod. 'Can I get you another?' he asks, bouncing back to his feet after having spent less than a minute sitting down. Just as I'm about to reassure him that I'm fine, High Jinx who is dressed in a bright turquoise evening gown with so many feathers on she resembles a tropical bird, draws a deep breath and cocking her head to one side, looks straight at me and says, presumably to Lily—

'Another notch, darling? On family night.'

Did I hear her right? I scrunch up my face and wait to see how Lilly responds. I subjected her to Marcus earlier so I should see how this plays out. But another notch, seriously? I have to assume she is talking about me.

'Sit down and behave, you're not funny. I'm so sorry, Jay, Jinxy here can be a twat. I didn't mention that when I was describing her to you earlier, I didn't think I'd have to. But she's demonstrated it herself and in remarkably quick time.'

Jinxy opens her mouth in a perfect O and bats her eyelashes in a surprised manner. They are so long they look a bit like they could jump off her face and scuttle across the floor at any minute.

'No worries,' I say. How else do I respond? Calling me a notch to my face is a pretty weird thing to do. I know what it says about High Jinx, but what does it say about Lily? Hang on, what does it say about me?

'Well, kinda worries. Jinx, this is Jay. Jay is here to talk to me about doing some work with the local youth groups. We're planning on running a programme together about appropriate behaviour and making good choices –' I stifle a smile as she says this '– and I suggested he come along tonight to update me. I didn't expect him to be insulted before you'd even said hello. I should have but I didn't.'

Jinx's expression changes shape the minute Lily mentions the youth groups, and a huge grin breaks out across her face. 'Oh shit, sorry, darling. Huge mouth, absolutely huge. Usually serves a purpose but tonight it's just got me into trouble.' Jinx sits down in the chair vacated by Dan and places her hands on the table, innocence and apology writ large upon her face. 'I'm so sorry. I assumed she was still worried about her Lady's Tuppence sealing shut so she combined coming out tonight with...oops!' Jinx flashes a look of pure mischief at Lily who has one eyebrow raised so high it's almost bouncing off the ceiling, her lips pursed in outrage. I can't hold it in any longer and a burst of laughter at the awkwardness of it all shoots from my mouth and I clasp my hand across my lips to stop any more coming, I don't want Lily to feel embarrassed but High Jinx is a character. Talk about from frying pan to fire.

'I apologise, again, for my wayward tongue.'

I'm not sure I believe her.

She continues, 'it's just that this is meant to be Lily's safe space, this and the lido, so I needed to test your mettle. I did it purely out of love.' She places her hand upon her chest and flutters her eyes again at Lily, who doesn't look like she's buying it, but there's a twist to her mouth that indicates her crossness, which whilst justified, is good-natured.

'What do you need to be kept safe from?' I turn and ask Lily.

'Herself,' Jinx and Dan say in unison and Lily shrugs her shoulders and nods her head as Dan goes to the bar.

High Jinx grins and turns her attention back to Lily. 'Honestly, darling, you've never brought colleagues here before, how was I supposed to know? Especially one this delicious, but if he can't tolerate filth then this may be the wrong venue.'

'Oh, I don't mind a bit of filth,' I say.

However Jinx is paying no attention at all and has turned to the burly men sitting by the entrance and holds her hands up and together as if waiting for cuffs. She bellows across the room, 'Darlings, I have crossed a line again. I think you're going to need to throw me out.'

'I'll throw you out if you don't do what you're paid for!' the tiny woman that Dan called SyPhyllis calls back, gesturing to the two men sat at her side, who stand up and, grinning, approach the table.

'Once again, many apologies. Glad to meet you, Jay, and very glad to hear you like a little bit of filth...' she leans across the table and stage winks at me, her eyelid painted turquoise. The men arrive and pretend to pull her away and she plays along, when with a twinkle in her eye, as sharp as any of her diamantés, she leans back in and asks, 'But do you like the thought of Lily's vagina as well?'

'Jesus Christ,' Lily says. 'I really am sorry, Jay. She can't be trusted anywhere. I'd like to say it's just Jinxy that behaves that way but unfortunately she's a nightmare as Kevin too.'

'This is true,' says Dan who has returned with a tray of cocktails. 'But at least as Kevin she has the grace to look a little shamefaced and occasionally acts remorsefully. As Jinx there is no controlling her. Honestly, at this point, we're not really her friends anymore, we're more like...um...'

'Parole officers,' Lily says drily.

'Bitches!' High Jinx shrieks across at us from the front of the stage where the men have dropped her. Then she turns around, grabs the arse of one of them, waggles her tongue suggestively at the other and then climbs majestically up the steps to the stage where she turns on her heel and as if from nowhere has a mic which she genteelly coughs into.

'I was going to go with carers, but yeah, you're more accurate,' Dan says.

The room, which has been noisy up until now, becomes quiet as if High Jinx has some magic powers of calm. Which frankly I find hard to believe.

'Hello and welcome,' she says into the mic, her voice all breathy as the crowd begin to whoop and holler at her until she waves them down to quiet. 'Now as you know, Thursdays are our open mic night, which is basically just an excuse for all of us to clamour –' she enunciates this word very carefully, somehow making it sensual '– *clamour* for attention and fight over who is the most talented drag queen in the entire city. Something that we all know the actual answer to, don't we?'

Lily and Dan whoop and I find myself joining in.

'And I'm going to prove it to you all now. I'm going to prove it, like for the millionth time, that ... this ... bitch ... can ... sing!'

'She can, you know,' Lily says bending her head towards me whilst Dan is up on his feet hollering.

'You know I need you.' High Jinx says into the mic, beckoning Dan who races over and lifts up the lid of the piano. They whisper at each other and Dan begins to play as High Jinx fills the room with the sound of Minnie Riperton. Not an easy song to cover, but she does, and, most impressively, she does it wonderfully. Every 'la' beautifully hit. She is transformed.

Somehow up on stage in her bright blue, she looks born to be surrounded by lights and adoration and in the short space of one song she has won herself another fan. Her vocal range is astounding. My hands are clapping with as much power as they can when I feel my phone vibrate in my pocket. I pull it out and see immediately it's a message from Cassie.

Hey, I know you know but it's my birthday on Saturday. Jas says we can go out. It seems like forever since I've been anywhere. Any ideas and wanna join?

Jas may be happy for them to go out but that'll change when she realises my sister has invited me.

Nothing could keep me away... I stop typing and look up. High Jinx is speaking into the mic and commanding the attention of all in the room.

'Now in the interests of equal opportunities we do have to open the stage to everyone. This is open mic after all. If you want to just see me, and who wouldn't, then it'll be my drag cabaret Saturday night, finishing up with me spinning you some sweet tunes on the decks. But for now we have to let the others play too. So, it's my pleasure –' she faux gags '– to introduce Vivicious. I'm sure she'll be ... well ... she'll *be*.'

'Everything okay?' Lily asks, my hand still paused mid-air over my phone.

'Yes, it's just Cass. It's her birthday next weekend and I

think she'd love it here,' I answer. She would. She has the filthiest sense of humour and I can see her and High Jinx getting on like a house on fire. Jasmine maybe not so much. Jasmine is trying to make my sister more ladylike. The very word makes me want to be sick. Sensible brogues, afternoon tea and an interest in chamber music. All of which are perfectly acceptable things, they're just not well suited to my sister, who is in her early twenties and more of a cocktails and dance on a table kinda gal. Or at least she was.

'Jinx and Dan will be here on Saturday. Why don't you invite her to come and join them?' Lily says, and her offer seems genuine.

'Are you sure? I don't want to suddenly hijack your social life. Feels a bit much.'

'If she can cope with Jinx then she'll be very welcome.'

'Oh, she would love her.' Especially if she carries on ripping into me. I turn back and complete my message. *I'm in an amazing place at the moment and Saturday night sounds like it's gonna be a good 'un. It's only around the corner from you and you'd love it, love it. Drag cabaret sound fun for your birthday?*

The response is immediate. Jas must be in the loo.

Oh my God, that would be awesome. Followed by love hearts, dancing women emojis, rainbow flags and cocktails. Cass knows exactly what her birthday night is going to bring.

With the message sent I turn back to Lily. 'Will you not be here?'

She looks a little shifty, 'Possible but unlikely. I have other ... um, plans.'

'Okay,' I say. A bit of me dips at the thought she won't be here but on the flip side it will make things a bit easier for me with Cassie. I cannot begin to imagine the teasing should I turn up with the 'lady from the lido' for her birthday.

My eyes switch back to the stage and I see a queen dressed in gold lamé workout gear take the mic as Jinx heads back to our table. She taps it and then addresses us all.

'I'm here to support my sister queens today, by showing you what it's like to be physically perfect, toned in all the right places, and to let you know I have faith in y'all. Know that if I can look this good then I'm sure with a whole lot of effort –' this bit said pointedly, in a tone that undermines *any* claim of sisterhood '– then you can also get yourselves into shape just like the Queen that Olivia was and I am today.'

She nods her head at the man working the sound desk across the bar and 'Let's Get Physical' blasts forth as she starts to gyrate on the stage before dropping down into some side leg lifts.

'The bitch, she did this to get at me, you know.' Jinx slumps into a chair. 'Cow. Listen to her –' she raises her voice '– she can't hold a tune but she sure can move her hips for a living!'

'Don't let her get to you. You slayed it up there,' Lily advises.

'You were pretty amazing,' I agree although my eye has been caught by Dan, who seems to have been trapped by Eighties aerobic moves on his way back from the piano, his high energy a perfect match for the track currently being played. It feels a bit like those scenes in *Glee* that Cassie used to force me to watch. I genuinely expect someone to start handing out bandanas and the whole bar to launch into a choreographed routine.

'You know she's not actually singing.' High Jinx addresses me with earnestness. 'She may be great at lip syncing but she can't hold a tune for toffee. I swear I love every queen on the scene, locally, globally, every one apart from that bitch. She is no sister of mine. Ooh look, there's Adore. Now she *is* lovely.'

'Get off the stage, you bitch, and let Adore Vajayjay up instead,' Jinx hollers, earning herself a look from SyPhyllis. She shrugs and turns back to me. 'She's fab, proper drag queen tradition.'

'Stop it.' Dan is back at the table and sits down. 'You just make yourself look insecure and give her more ammunition. More flies with honey.' He pats Jinx's arm and Lily nods in agreement as Adore approaches the stage.

'Oh wow, She's the spit of Doris Day,' I say. I can't help myself, but it does look as if Calamity Jane herself is here. Lily quirks a brow.

'Are you sure you're not a gay man?' Jinx swivels and asks.

'He never said he wasn't,' Dan adds.

'You can have a knowledge of old movies and not be gay,' Lily says and both her friends raise their eyebrows at her.

'Yep, I'm straight,' I say. 'But I have a strong love of a musical and I can sew a net skirt in an emergency.'

'Oh, you might be my dream man.' Jinx runs a finger along my arm. 'Fit, unattainable and able to sew. How perfect is that? You have done well,' she says to Lily.

'If you could refrain from touching up my *colleague* that would be great. We're here to work,' Lily retorts.

'I haven't seen either of you do much work so far,' Jinx replies. 'Drink, tick, cackle, tick, watch God's own favourite drag queen, tick, but work....hmmmmm.'

'I haven't managed to get a word in yet. You literally haven't stopped since we arrived,' Lily says and then turns to me and I feel a shiver. 'But she does have a point. Do you want to head outside and go over those plans?' Lily indicates towards my laptop and I nod my head; it is what I'm here for after all, not to get absorbed into her friendship group. Although I haven't stopped laughing since they arrived.

'Oh, stay and watch Adore, she does do a good Doris,' Jinx says as she watches her friend. 'But then it's easy for her. She never had the parents I had. I bet hers are all liberal and have a huge house and shop through Ocado and allowed her to express herself however she pleased growing up, sewed Tinkerbell dresses for Book Day.' This seems to have come from nowhere but Dan and Lily exchange knowing glances.

'Well done, you've managed until now,' Dan says. 'You can have five minutes but then that's it, isn't it, Lils? After that we're moving on. It'll be fingers in the ears. If you push to ten minutes, Lily will make you homeless.'

I look at Lily quizzically. 'Oh, Jinx'll explain, don't you worry,' she says with a smile before making the universal gesture for another drink and I nod as she goes to the bar.

High Jinx turns to me and places her arm on mine. Her exquisitely painted face shows a tumult of emotion and I prepare myself to hear something grim. But as I catch a look across at Dan, who looks remarkably unsympathetic, then I wonder if I have misjudged.

'My parents are coming over.' High Jinx sighs. 'Now they're good parents, they want the best for me but they're a product of their culture, their upbringing and they only had the one son. We're all the sum of our experiences and I can't blame them for who they are. But as much as they love Kevin very much and will always want the best for him, I'm not sure they're going to extend High Jinx the same level of understanding.'

'You're not out to them?' I ask and Jinx just replies with a high-pitched screech of laughter. She sounds a little possessed.

'Four minutes,' Dan says. Cold.

'I can't. I just can't. They'd be devastated. Trust me, They still send photos of suitable brides from all over the world. Literally all over the world. I didn't realise quite how many friends of friends with single daughters there were out there. You have no idea how many times I have had to listen to the find a nice bride speech, they're getting so desperate that they've stopped listing ethnic or professional requirements among their demands for my bride-to-be. They haven't quite said anyone will do at this point, but that's what they mean.'

'I'm sorry about that, I just assumed...' and I had. I had assumed Jinx was roughly my age, Lily's age – she said she had gone to uni with Kevin – and had come out years ago.

'Sure, I should have told them by now, and if I was white and middle-class and had beautifully progressive parents then I would have done. If I had parents like she has...' She waggles a finger at Doris Day on stage, who is almost at the end of singing 'Just Blew in from the Windy City' complete with a ukulele, crazed facial expressions and fart jokes. 'But trust me, being this fabulous isn't easy. I know we live in the 2020s and I know the world accepts how hard it was coming out in the Eighties and beforehand when homophobia was at its height and people thought you'd drop down dead if you risked talking to a gay man, but believe me coming out in the late Nineties was also hard, and for someone with parents like mine, with such rigid cultural beliefs, it's still next to impossible even in the twenty-first century, even with Ru Paul making *Drag Race* an international phenomenon. And what's worse is they're coming to the UK in July and I have been waiting for this July all my life! This was going to be my month to make my mark, to make High Jinx famous across the nation.' She flops her head on the table and emits a sigh so loud and forceful that it's in danger of flapping the minuscule skirt of a drag queen who has just walked by, dressed all in white and with a veil on her head that is longer than the dress she's wearing. A sigh loud enough to clear mountain tops, and I work with teenage girls, I know about sighing.

'All my life.' Jinx lifts her head a fraction from the table to repeat this and lets out another sigh.

'One minute,' Dan observes. He hasn't looked up from the phone that he whisked out once Jinx started to talk.

'I have been rehearsing and rehearsing and rehearsing... and I have such a special routine lined up. I know exactly how I'm going to style myself and now they're going to ruin it. Ruin it and there will be posters of my face all over the city, how am I going to explain that, huh? How am I going to explain that their son's face is plastered over every siding, every lamppost, in every *What's On* magazine for the month of July, but the face itself is looking distinctly feminine and plastered in make-up, damn fine make-up, probably the best make-up....'

'They might not recognise you., I say in an attempt to reassure her. 'After all if they don't know you do drag...'

High Jinx gives me a look. 'I look just like my mum in drag....but you know, hotter. They'll recognise me.'

'And time's up!' Lily returns to the table with even more cocktails and as she says this she looks down at her friend still splayed upon the table and smiles gently, but her eyes are steely. She means it. I wouldn't cross her.

Jinx looks up at her through her eyelashes and then her eyes catch something else and she sits bolt upright.

'Oh no. Oh no. Not tonight. That's not happening. Do not dare do your usual stuff tonight. I'm telling you, if you're not doing something new, Phyllis is going to go loopy...' She is directing her words at the latest drag queen to take to the stage. She is the one who was walking past earlier dressed as a bride. High Jinx turns around, shouting over her shoulder, 'Phyllis!'

I watch the tiny woman stand and bring a metal-tipped cane down hard on the floor. Despite the noise at the bar and the low talk from the tables, there is no doubting her intent or authority. The club pauses, silence hangs in the air and everyone waits for her to speak.

'No "All By Myself". No "It's My Party". No "Everybody Hurts". Change it up or I'll throw you out,' she states, loudly and clearly, her voice possessing a strength you wouldn't expect to emanate from her elderly body. The two men sat with her nod to reinforce her message.

'I know. I promised you. Have faith.' The bride nods to the sound man and Etta James's "Stop the Wedding"' floods out. Jinx groans loudly. Dan shrieks with laughter and stands up and throws his arms up in the air and starts to sing along, swaying as he does so. It's the most reserved dance move I have seen him make so far this evening.

'Right,' Lily says as she passes me a glass, her eyes meeting mine with mischief and intent dancing in them.

As she pauses, all I can think of is what I wouldn't give not to have made that promise to Cassie right now. What I wouldn't give to be able to see if I could take Lily up on exploring the attraction between us. Just the way she looks at me is enough to send a frisson of sexual attraction through me.

It's not even just the way she looks at me, it's the way she holds herself, the way her hair bounces by her shoulders, highlighting the curve of her neck. It's the way every step she takes has a fluidity to it that summons to mind the thought of the movements she would make if we undressed each other, as we stroked and kissed and explored.

Then there's the smell of her, the pitch of her voice, the way her laugh warms the whole of me, makes me feel that I've achieved and want to carry on doing so. Every little bit of her appeals to all my senses and brings them into flux, makes me wish we could be together. Makes me wish that my sister and this new project didn't stand in our way.

When I look at her, I am not measuring her up for the future. I am not considering if she has the qualities that would make her the perfect partner for my life going forward, all I am thinking about is far more elemental, far less logical, it's compelling and immediate, right of this moment. I swear I haven't felt desire like this since I was a teen and I'm not entirely sure what to do with it.

I know I can't act on it, but I don't know how to dampen it down, to relegate it to the back of my mind, to rationalise all the ways this won't work, how it would throw a bomb into my life that would cast everything that has been my priority for the last two decades high into the air.

Even if I wasn't as worried about Cass as I am, as determined to show her change is possible and that I'm not some kind of mad dog that can't keep his dick in his pants or cope without a woman by his side, I have spent years building up my skillset in the workplace, and getting to know these girls, getting them to respect me and who I am, and then to shag the famous Love Doctor whom I have brought in to City

Youth to help the girls out would be the quickest, surest way to lose that trust and respect.

But as she hands me my drink, our fingers touch, just for a millisecond, and the jolt that shoots up my arm, across my shoulders and through my whole body is so forceful I wonder how she cannot have felt it too. I am half surprised we are not shooting out blue jaggy lightning as we make eye contact and the whole world around us recedes, leaving only us two.

'Wanna get out of here for a minute?' she asks me, not taking her eyes from mine, and I find myself nodding as if under some sort of spell.

Chapter Eighteen

I return from the bar with a drink for Jay and can see that Jinxy is in full flow and that Havoc is about to take the stage.

Jay joined us this evening because he wants to talk about the practicalities of implementing our plans now that they have been agreed on by City Youth. Instead, he has witnessed a whole lot of Jinx drama and some drag acts, yet not a word has been mentioned about work.

I don't dare take him home to discuss the project, although the thought has crossed my mind. The more time I spend with this man the more I want to take him home, I really do. The fact that he was resolute in his no to me and needs to remain celibate because of his vow to Cass hasn't dampened my desire.

I am not sure I am a good person.

I understand the psychology of wanting what you can't have and there is a bit of that but I'm worried there's more. Up until this evening Jinx and Dan didn't know of Jay's existence and I can imagine the grilling I'm going to get when I get home. There must be a reason I haven't told them about Jay yet and I am not looking forward to defending myself.

I suggested we go out the back earlier, it won't be as noisy as in here and is likely to be deserted whilst the acts are on stage. And even I am not going to try and strip Jay naked in such a public space. I like anonymity for that kind of nonsense.

I accidentally brush his fingers with mine as I pass him his glass and the chemistry shooting through me is insane. I can't ever remember feeling such a connection or an attraction so intense. The pull of the forbidden. Forbidden for now.

'Wanna get out of here for a minute?' I ask – meaning the garden but unable to help myself as the anticipation of what may lie before us infuses my voice. I realise with a shiver that I have never planned my sex life so far ahead in the future.

'For sure,' he says as he rises from his chair in one fluid movement. He leans down to pick up his laptop bag and as I wait for him my eye glances at the breadth of his shoulders, the way his top clings; I can picture exactly what's underneath the light fabric. I have seen it in the sauna, more than once, but there is something extra sensual about his body now it is clothed. I must look like the wolf in Red Riding Hood, and as he straightens up I try my best to compose myself and not look as if I am dribbling. I nod in the direction of the outside space and turn to go; he follows me, so close I can feel his breath on my neck. It takes all of my self-control not to reach my arm back a few inches and clasp his hand.

Outside it is almost empty. There is a couple at a table in the far corner but they are so caught up in each other they do not even notice as we enter. And there are two smokers by the door, smoking quickly before they return inside.

I lead him to a bench and sit down. It will be interesting to see where he sits and whether he thinks about his positioning or whether it's instinctive.

It's the latter, and he sits beside me and opens his laptop. I wriggle a little closer to see it properly and our thighs ping together like magnets. I can feel his warmth against me. Filth begins to spiral through my mind and I make a conscious decision to stop indulging myself, have more respect for his wishes.

We fly through the schedule drawn up and I confirm I can commit to this. His face lights up as he asks if I am sure.

'I am,' I say.

'Then you have made this youth worker very happy. I think you are going to have such a positive impact on the girls. They haven't stopped talking about you since your visit.'

'I enjoyed meeting them. I'm really pleased you asked me to be part of this.' I say and it's true.

'I can't tell you how grateful I was that you responded, although thoroughly freaked out when you turned out to be you.' He laughs.

'Right?' I say. 'I'm never going to get over that. I don't usually believe in coincidences but that was a remarkable one.'

'That or fate.' He says and then immediately looks embarrassed, and I have to admit that for someone who is normally so good with words, who has flirtatious patter fall out of her mouth fully-formed that I don't know how to respond to this.

He closes his laptop, signalling that the work side of the evening is over. I sit back and decide to see what he does now. His reason for being here is done, will he leg it out of the door or will he stay? And if he stays, is he going to keep it just as friends? How committed is he to not dating for six months because from where I'm sitting it is damn nigh impossible to ignore this chemistry?

He turns to me, his movement means our thighs are no longer clamped together and the angled gap between us makes me feel the lack of him.

'You're so at home here,' he says casually. 'Tell me a bit about it. I've driven past lots of times but never been in. It seems to have been here for as long as I can remember.'

'Ahh, yeah. Phyllis is a legend. She started out running a boarding house for gay men in Bristol, back in the Seventies, making sure that they had somewhere safe to live. Life was not easy at that time if you were anything but white and straight and she, well, she hadn't transitioned back then, wanted to create a safe space for others like her. Then the next step was to open Chrysalis, one of the first gay clubs in Bristol. Although with society not being as tolerant as it is now, you had to answer questions on the door to make sure you were part of the community and not coming along to cause harm. Chrysalis was born, Phil became Phyllis and then SyPhyllis when she was on stage belting out Donna Summers and Diana Ross numbers for the punters. She has truly earned her place in Bristol's queer history so when I say she's a legend, I mean it.'

'Wow, that's quite a story.'

'Yep, and Barry and Gary started working the door for her straight out of school, before you and I were born, just. They're as much an institution as Phyllis is. This place is living, breathing history and I love it.'

'I didn't realise it had such a legacy. Dan and Jinx implied this was your safe space too.'

'Uh-huh.' My tone is less enthusiastic.

'Dan said it's the one place you don't get hit on. They said you date a lot, like *a lot*. For all your mocking of me over the things the girls said, are you a bit of a Casanova, Dr Galbraith?'

'Ha!' I splutter and reach for my drink, giving myself time to work out how I'm going to answer. The obvious response is an honest one. Jay isn't some fly-by-night I have no intention of seeing again and I want him to know the truth of me.

'I do,' I say. 'I like dating. I really like dating. I know lots of people get that ennui quickly, the disappointment of another night not having found The One. But I'm not looking for that, I don't want to settle down so I get a real thrill from my dating life.'

'Okay, that sounds like you're pretty committed to keeping things as they are. That's a good thing.'

'I think so although Jinx would giggle that you used the word "commitment". She reckons my phobia of relationships is far from healthy,' I say, regretting the words almost as soon as they're out of my mouth. Part of me wants to explain everything in full, how I was the ugly duckling at school, how that shaped me. I want to admit to him, when I have not even admitted it to my friends, that my fear of commitment may not be entirely healthy despite my protestations. But I am not ready to say those things out loud yet, I'm not sure myself, *I do* like my dating life as it is. I love the buzz I get from one-night stands. And honestly, I'm scared of doing deep soul-bearing at this point, not just to this man but to myself as well.

So instead, I double down rather than backtrack about oversharing. 'There's such preconceptions in our society about dating. We are brought up to assume that women want to settle down and find The One, that that's what we're programmed for –' I take a breath and he nods at me, encouraging me to continue '– but that's not me. I don't want to settle down, get married and have kids. Sure, I can see the appeal of finding the right person, of course I can. I spend most of my working day helping people find, or in some cases keep, the person they want to spend the rest of their life with but for me that's not what I see in my future. I like one-night stands, I like the excitement, the freedom from commitment, that nerve-tingle of first attraction, and I'm really grateful that in today's world we are beginning to grasp that I am not an oddity, I'm not a freak. That I can be enjoying sex for sex's sake, especially as a woman in my thirties. It's about time that the world accepts that women like sex as much as men, that our sexuality, our appetites and our preferences aren't a matter of gender. I have lost count of the amount of women I have had to reassure over the course of my working life that there is not something wrong with them because they have a higher sex drive than their partner. They've been conditioned by society since forever to think that men should want more sex than women do and it's simply not true. It's just not.'

I pause and wonder if I should have stopped before I started. This is not appropriate talk between two new colleagues. But by having Jay in my most relaxed settings, the lido and here, I have become far too comfortable far too quickly with him. It's as if I can't maintain those tidy compartments I keep because he is leaching into all of them. He doesn't seem fazed and is sat watching me with an expression on his face that suggests he is listening rather than plotting how to quickly escape.

'Fair enough,' he says and I wonder again if I have said too much. Have I branded myself with those stupid outdated words like 'slut' and 'slapper' and 'slag' that have no place in a forward-thinking society in the twenty-first century? And why do I care? If Jay judges me this way then I have read him all wrong. Plus, it will mean he loses some of his hotness which may be a good thing.

Which would definitely be a good thing.

Mind you, if he thinks all my viewpoints are off and is working with teenage girls to foster self-esteem then it's kind of important he doesn't hold outdated attitudes about how girls should behave. The very ones that are represented by my small inner voice, that ever-present critic who tries to make me feel bad about my choices whilst my more intellectual, developed and adult self beats her into submission.

He traces his finger down his glass and I feel my breath catch in my throat. I believe in all that I say and yet his silence is giving power to that insecure fourteen-year-old me with the loud voice that never completely goes away.

'But this is me just sharing my frustrations about dating and how it's perceived even by the ones you love the most,' I add. 'It's not an awkward attempt to try and get you into bed. I have heard what you've said about not dating and I would never mess with boundaries so I won't pounce on you like some man-eating Fury, especially as we're going to work together.' And for some godawful unknown reason, I lift my arms into what I imagine to be a Winged Furies sort of pose and let out a caaaawwwww!

I'm so loud that the loved-up couple in the background look up from each other to see what the demented woman on the bench is doing. And truth is I really don't know. If they were to ask, I couldn't answer. Somehow this evening I have literally vomited up a whole heap of anger and a whole heap of self that I wouldn't normally share with anybody.

What has happened to the self-contained woman of the last fifteen years, who holds everything tight to her chest? I'd like her to come back now. I put my wings down and caw again but sedately, a caaww of shame.

My cocktails were mocktails – I rarely drink because it impacts my health – so I can't even blame them.

I look into my lap, hesitant to look up and meet Jay's eyes, imagining he is racking his brain to find a way to leave and thanking the Lord that I haven't actually signed a volunteer agreement yet.

'Caw?' he asks. There is a lightness to his tone, amusement rather than judgement.

'Hmmmm. I was being a Winged Fury. You know, from ancient times. Probably best left in ancient times,' I mumble.

'I can honestly say tonight is an eye-opener. So, tell me more about these ancient furies.'

I look up and see that he is not falling over himself in an attempt to escape. Instead he is looking at me with those deep brown puddles of eyes and making me feel all squirmy again.

'They were, if memory serves me right, goddesses of vengeance rather than sex. I honestly don't know what happened to my body then or what I thought I was doing.'

'Maybe the furies think you should try and get me into bed...' he says.

I scrunch my eyes up and look at him. What *is* his subtext here?

'...I don't know why I said that,' he continues. 'Forgive me. Obviously there's Cass and the work thing. Maybe there is some kind of freaky ancient force making us both say and do things we wouldn't normally.'

'Yes, let's blame that. That works for me.'

'I think Cass would like you. She wants me to be a bit more, um...a bit more Lily.'

I nod but stay silent. I am intrigued.

'I'm the opposite of you,' he continues. 'I find it really interesting what you're saying about the way the world perceives how boys or men should act compared to girls and women. I see a lot of what you're talking about with the kids at work. All this sexual pressure. And whilst it used to shock me as a kid, it's even more alarming now. I think the internet has a lot to answer for – how it shapes these young people and what they think is normal and what should be acceptable sexually.'

'Truth!' I say.

'You're right about how society shapes our attitudes and prescribes our behaviour by gender. Cass thinks time being single, a few one-night stands, would do me the world of good but it's just not me really. I like the security of a relationship, I like the thought of the future I could build with somebody, you know, the whole little house, garden, family thing. I guess that backs up what you are saying about gender preconceptions. It's my dream to build all of that, have some children and devote myself to a happy ever after.'

'See, and yet if we believed the bilge we were brought up on, then you and I would be the other way around.'

'Yep, one-night stands make me feel a bit empty and used. They make me feel sad. I have never really enjoyed them, not even in my late teens and my early twenties.'

'So are you still single because of this list thing you mentioned? You're a good-looking man...'

He grins but in a self-effacing way that is utterly charming.

'The girls at City Youth say women are hurling themselves at you, you want commitment and a good woman to settle down with, so why don't you have it? There must be a reason this list, these qualities are so important or surely it would have happened organically by now,' I continue.

'Isn't that the age-old question? The one no one usually knows the answer to? But in my case, I think I do. I love being in love but I think I put the women I date on a pedestal so high no one can realistically meet it. There's a whole long story there as to why I do that, I'm sure. Fundamentally, I ask for too much and then when I see a crack, when I realise they can't live up to this list of perfect qualities I have in my head, I run for the hills terrified that I've made the wrong choice and I need to get back out there and make a better one. So yes, in summary I guess it's the list thing Cass harks on about.'

'You never stick around and work it out?'

'No, no, I don't. I'm a romantic, but I'm also a bit of a cynic and those two are a hard combination to manage. I want kids, and when I see a flaw in the woman I'm dating I'm immediately thinking how that will translate in the way in which she might parent.'

'Okay, I remember you saying that at Mama K's. That's pretty self-aware. I also remember you told me about you and Cassie being through the care system. That could have had a massive impact on why you want a family and for it to be just right.'

'Yeah. Mum ran off soon after she had Cass, and Dad brought us up. But then he got ill and we nursed him as best we could but he didn't make it. We were put into the system and bounced around from one group home to another, one foster placement to another, and it was all pretty grim. I felt responsible for keeping Cass safe. She was only five years old. Eventually we ended up with Malcolm and Sue, who have been in our lives ever since, and they're amazing. I want to recreate what they gave us I guess.'

'It makes perfect sense, and at the risk of tinpot psychoanalysing here...'

'Hardly tin-pot, is that not exactly what you're qualified to do?'

'Well, yes, but that doesn't mean I can immediately see into people's souls and see why they do the things they do or make the choices they make, but it does mean I can make an educated guess.'

'What does your educated guess say about me?'

'Two things jump out, but I imagine you're already very aware of them.' I had wanted to say this at Mama K's but knew at that time he needed someone to listen not analyse.

'Go on.' He touches my arm, encouraging me to speak.

'I imagine that after losing your dad and going through the care system then the desire to belong is strong but at the same time there's an understandable fear that if you put roots down with the wrong person, you're afraid of history repeating. And once that initial dopamine hit wears off and you start to see flaws then it's only natural that you get scared and want to keep looking for that perfect mate.'

'Do you know what, I hadn't thought of it like that. I know the care thing has impacted me and you're right, on a deep level it makes me want to belong, but the history repeating thing, that explains the fear I have. It makes me feel considerably less stupid if I track it back to that, it really does. It's not having a list that's the issue, it's *why* I have it, and you're saying the answer to that is my past.' He looks at me as if I have presented him with the Holy Grail and the daft thing is it is simple psychology 101: track it back to the trauma that has occurred in childhood and spot how the patterns play out.

'Right,' I agree with him. 'Often, once we are aware of why we are tempted to do the same thing over and over then we can take real steps to stop ourselves. We can train our brain to think rather than react.'

He is still shaking his head and looking at me with an awe that is a little discomforting. 'I don't know why I haven't seen it before. Cassie is the polar opposite of me; she was way too young to remember Mum like I do, or to feel the weight of disappointment when social services tracked her down after Dad's death and Mum couldn't or wouldn't have us. So Cassie wants to belong, will stay for ever, and she sure as hell will do anything to try and get that early flush dopamine high back. So because our memories and understanding of what happened then are different, we act differently. I'm scared to choose the right partner but feel that need to create a strong family unit whereas she doesn't have that fear but is still compelled by the need to belong.'

'Sounds about right to me.'

'Wow, well, in ten minutes you have properly therapised me. Is that a word?'

'I'm not sure.' I giggle.

'It should be. So, so far, you have answered my question on your podcast, you've come and volunteered your time for the girls and now you have given me wisdom that I have been seeking for as long as I can remember. What can I possibly do to pay you back?'

'No payment necessary. Promise.'

'I know...' he says and he winks at me. I know it's old-school but I do love a man who winks. There's something cheeky about it, mischievous and confident. Then he raises his arms high above his head and moves his body so he is standing, his whole torso is stretching out and he is practically on tiptoes. He bends his fingers over to make claws and at the same time makes large flapping motions with his arms.

'Caaaaawwwwww,' he shouts and then repeats it, far louder than I had earlier. 'Caaaaawwwwww!'

As the couple turn around again, I start to laugh, proper deep belly laughs, and I stand up on the bench and join him, both of us cawwing away to our hearts content. I realise that I have unusual combinations of emotions flitting around me; I am warm, I am finding this whole thing hilarious and I am happy. Proper happy and not because I look how I imagine I should, not because I am getting admiring looks from strangers – quite the opposite – but because I am being silly, I am being me and in this moment I don't care what anyone else thinks of us.

Chapter Nineteen

'Stop fucking around and just drink it!'

I enter the kitchen to see Dan waving a frothy-looking glass full of murky green liquid at Kevin. He really is here all the time now.

'You're a demon, a demon. When I asked you to help, I didn't mean you should poison me with this crap.' He looks up as I enter. 'Oh, come and save me, Lily. Be the voice of reason. He has gone old-school and is trying to make me vomit my way to being slim.'

'You asked us to help you retrain your mind and stomach,' I say.

'Right? Right!' Dan says. 'You're a nightmare. This is so good for you, bundles of nutrients that will make your hair and skin glow and will fill you up at the same time. You are not going to be sick!' He spins his attention to me. 'You look nice, very sexy mama. Who are you seeing tonight? Have you finally got your date with that guy?'

'Thank you,' I say, side-stepping the question. I do, or did, have my date with Adrian and have chosen one of my favourite dresses tonight. It's deep purple with a high neck and a deep cowl at the back. However as I came down the stairs just now, I don't know why, I found myself tapping last-minute excuses into my phone and hitting send before I pushed the kitchen door open.

'Make my skin glow?' Kevin queries, looking as if this might be the argument that wins him over.

'Uh-huh and your nails and hair strong.'

'Oh, I do not need to be removing even thicker hair than I do already. Believe.' He raises his hands and starts to rap the opening to Grandmaster Flash and the Furious Five's 'The Message' – giving extra weight to the word jungle – and then slut drops behind the kitchen island, poking his head back over the top to add, 'Seriously, I'm already considering developing my very own bee army to tackle the wax demands my underarms make now.'

'I like your armpits hairy,' Dan says and Kevin flushes and reaches his hand out for the glass.

'Go on then, a sip won't kill me.'

Dan is a Machiavellian mastermind. We exchange a triumphant look.

'I've cooked a coconut, black bean and spinach curry for your dinner so the combination of that and the smoothie should make you full enough to not feel the need to stop at the kebab house on the way home this evening,' Dan adds.

'Nothing will ever make me too full for kebabs,' Kevin says as he finishes the drink without screaming, wincing or shouting blue murder.

'You know the best way to lose weight in time for July –' I pause as his face looks unhealthily eager '– in a way that isn't going to do you any serious long-term harm or damage,' I add, 'is to give up the booze and sugar. Just for a couple of months. If you did that—' I don't get any further as both of them turn to me with looks of abject horror, cup their faces in their hands and perform a version of Munch's *The Scream*.

'Twats, the pair of you,' I say before adding, 'I don't suppose there's a bit of curry going for me?' I'm expecting the nth degree from these two about Jay and need to face it sometime. I have done a pretty good job of avoiding Kevin the last two nights by racing to bed early and spending all of yesterday evening hiding out at the lido before he left to do his Friday night residency at The Candy Counter in Bath.

'Of course,' Dan answers, 'but...Adrian? Are you not off out to see him?'

'Hmmm. Well, yes, he's in Bristol and I'm in Bristol and this one has been simmering for a while so I was all dressed and ready to go but um –' I busy myself taking bowls out of the cupboard so that I don't have to look Kevin in the eyes '– but um... it kinda...errr...I thought... you know what, I'm not feeling it and I'd rather come to Chrysalis with you guys tonight.' I straighten up as I pop the bowls on the side. I don't need to turn to see the looks they'll be exchanging. I'm not unaware that I've ditched Adrian but kept my chi-chi frock on.

'Oh my God. It's that man, it's that man,' Kevin says excitedly, waving his hands. 'When we caught them in the garden playing angry birds or whatever the fuck it was they were doing and she had a smile on her face the size of the suspension bridge, I *told* you something was up, I told you!' He is triumphant and I am tempted to tip curry on him.

'Yeah, cos didn't he ask if we minded him coming along tonight with his sister or something and we said it was fine?'

'Right? Right!' Kevin says in a scary echo of Dan from earlier.

'You didn't sleep with Dr McDishy when you had the chance and now you've ditched Adrian, a guy you have been trying to see for a while now, to come out with us? I'm no detective but –' Dan is popping the curry into the bowls and I grab an avocado and start prepping it as a side '– is something happening here, Lily Galbraith?'

'You said it was work!' Kevin says accusingly but still with childlike triumph dominating his tone.

'And it is,' I say as Dan hands us our bowls, I pop the avocado on and we all head to the table. 'It really is.'

'I was only testing him because I assumed it was a date you believed worthy of bringing to hallowed ground. I was doing you a favour and you made me feel all bad.' Kevin pouts.

'He wasn't a date, only there for work, you know,' Dan tells Kevin, a high-pitched teasing note to his voice, and I can't help but smile. They really are little fuckers.

'I did see them working,' Kevin responds in a similar tone and I sit back and wait for them to get this over.

'Oh yes it was work, work...'

'...and more work.'

'The work was endless.' They're both nodding along at each other like a pair of grandmothers nattering over a fence.

'I saw.'

'She said this about work.'

'He said that about work.' They're enjoying themselves way too much at this point, the words batting between the two of them like a ping-pong ball.

'Then she said, and you'll never believe this, she said... *Work me hard, baby.*' Dan puts on his filthiest voice.

'He said... *Oh, let me do the work.*'

'Okay, okay, the two of you can stop now, I get the picture,' I interrupt. This could go on all evening.

'Weeerrrrrrkkkk me babbbyyyy,' the two of them screech in unison, Kevin laughing so much he's in danger of falling over.

'Okay, yes. Yes, I think he's hot, you saw him, right?' They nod ferociously as they cackle. 'But I asked him out for a drink and he said no. It's all quite complicated but he's not dating at the moment plus he's all about finding The One, so you know, we're hardly a good match. We've agreed it's best we keep anything sexual firmly off the table and just work together.'

'So you say but, Missy, you have kept this one very close to your chest, mighty suspicious.' Kevin holds my eye and I raise both brows at him in unspoken challenge.

'Mighty suspicious,' Dan echoes and I know I should have told these two about Jay the minute I had got home from the lido and certainly after the meeting at the youth centre. But the truth is I had wanted to keep it to myself. I hadn't known how to tell them because the opportunity that Jay was providing was big but it was complex too. I know my thoughts about him cross the colleagues-only line but I do not want to vocalise that, or breathe life into it, and certainly not to the boys.

There is too much dissonance in the way I find myself thinking about this man, thoughts that challenge my rigidly constructed and deliberate boundaries. Talking to Kevin usually helps me figure things out but for some reason I have wanted to keep all this close, hug it to myself and ponder Jay with no judgement. Have his presence in my life a secret.

And that is not something I can remember doing before.

With Jay opening up about his need for a family, how he wants to have children and give them the best possible upbringing, I know a fling between us is never going to roll. We are on completely different, *completely different*, paths so any ideas I may have had about a quickie after we finish working together has to be off the table.

It wouldn't be fair on either of us.

And I am aware that there is something going on inside me regarding Jay. I may be more attracted to him than I realise or attracted to him in a different way to the way I am usually with other men. But with my infertility, with not being able to have children because of my bastard damn menstrual cycle and fucked-up reproductive system, then I know I have to get these feelings, this attraction, under control and keep this relationship entirely platonic and entirely professional.

And the truth is I really like Jay. I think we could be good friends. I respect him, his honesty, the direction in which he's taken his work, the way his sister and the girls at the youth club are important to him. I want to be his friend. And knowing how incompatible we are means that being his friend will be easier. As much as I may fancy sleeping with him, I would not be any good for him either short-term or long-term so that makes the platonic thing a whole heap easier.

I am going to be friends with Jay and nothing more.

And as we sit at our kitchen table, the light of the early summer evening beaming down on us, me in my fancy going-out frock, Kevin in his jeans and hoodie, his hair scraped and taped back, Dan in his regulation boots and black T-shirt, I tell them about how I met Jay, what work we're planning together and why we will only ever be good friends.

Chapter Twenty

Cassie is jumping about with all the excitement of a kitten, in fact she's remarkably like Dim when he brings in whatever half-dead creature has taken his fancy the evening before. Cass even batted me with her paw, albeit affectionally, when I gave her her gift – a new set of brushes and tools for paint – and showed them to Jas, who patronisingly said they were very thoughtful and suggested she put them with the rest of her equipment, canvases, paints, primers, tools, clothes, even a bloody easel, all of which Jas has bought her.

Witch.

Cass deserves these things, she deserves the world and I am grateful that Jas has provided them. I just can't shake the thought that they are less like gifts and more like shackles.

To keep the peace I praise Jasmine's generosity and we swap some entirely true statements about how talented Cass is but Jas and I both know that we are at odds. We are on different teams and tonight it's a bit like Rovers and City pretending they're mates. The trouble is Jas is smart, smarter than me, and I need her convinced that I am not a threat. Tonight must be about me making inroads with that.

Cass, the sweet, naive, and ever-hopeful joy that she is, seems unaware of any underlying tension and keeps bouncing around saying she always knew the two of us would get on famously. The two of us smile agreeably but both know that's not true. That may be the one other thing we can agree on.

However, I can't fault the fact that Jas is trying and so am I and together we grab an Uber and head straight to Chrysalis.

We jump out and head into the door of the beautiful old building but this time when I enter, Phyllis gives me a smile.

A smile!

And a nod, before saying, 'Back again? You're Lily's friend, aren't you? They've just got here.' And she motions towards Lily's table.

Lily, whom I hadn't expected to see tonight.

My heart soars.

I shoot a look over. How can I not? And I am blown away. She looks amazing, next-level a-maz-ing. I met this woman in a sauna, and it was just as well. I'm a confident man but had I first met her as she was when she turned up at the Youth Centre – so polished, sophisticated and put together – then I doubt I would have had the audacity to strike up a friendship.

And I thought she looked fine then, but tonight, tonight she looks like she has stepped off the pages of some glossy magazine; one of those unattainable women that you don't believe really exist and whose images are largely managed through airbrushing and good lighting. But it's Lily, Lily looks like that and it's just her, in real life, no specialist lighting or computer techniques needed. Lily who caws on rooftops. But as perfect as she is, as generous and kind, as funny and relaxed

– even ignoring my agreement with Cassie and with our new working relationship – I know she is way out of this man's league.

'Hmm, Lily, huh? Wanna put your tongue back in your mouth, your eyes back in their sockets and tell me that I was right all along?' Cassie hisses at my side and I see that she is looking across at Lily's table, presumably following Phyllis's nod and my eyeline.

'It may be your birthday, Missy, but don't get ahead of yourself. Yes, that's my *friend and colleague* Lily. We're working on a wellbeing programme for the Youth Club together. Not once, *not once* have I tried to make it anything else,' I say firmly.

It's true.

In actions if not in thoughts.

'She's your *friend*, Lily, is she? You've got a new colleague? You didn't mention it to me. He didn't mention it to us, did he, Jas?' Cassie pulls her partner into the conversation.

Jasmine shrugs because clearly she couldn't give a shit.

'Stop being an arse and come and say hello. She's The Love Doctor, you know, the woman that the girls have been banging on about for some time, and she's going to volunteer at City Youth. And, little sister, you have met her before. At the lido. That day in the sauna.'

'Oh my God, *that's* sauna woman. The woman you met when you reeked of aftershave.'

'Uh-huh.'

'And now she's working with you?'

'A massive coincidence.'

'Uh-huh. But you know what, looking at her now, like in

clothes and make-up – I mean, I love you, bruv, I really do, but yeah, you've got no chance.'

'Hey, hello. You made it, and you must be Cassie.' Dan bounces into us. I'm not entirely sure where he's come from, but he has temporarily saved me. 'Happy birthday!' Dan pulls Cass into an embrace and kisses both cheeks before releasing her and stroking her shoulders as he bounces from one foot to another.

'Thanks, and this is Jasmine, my girlfriend,' Cass says. Jasmine lets out a tight smile and moves closer to Cass.

'Hi, Jasmine, good to meet you, come, come.' And he motions us to follow him. Which isn't exactly my plan for this evening. I hadn't wanted to latch onto Lily's group and whilst I expected to see Jinx and Dan tonight I assumed we would sit separately, but Cass is bounding behind Dan – the two of them are like little twins with their high energy and easy smiles – pulling Jas behind her, their fingers entwined in a message of togetherness.

'Oh, it's okay, we won't crash your table, we can sit over—' I say but my sister interrupts immediately.

'No, I want to sit with your friends.' She puts on a faux pout to remind me she's the birthday girl.

It occurs to me that sitting there will allow Lily to observe Cass and Jas's relationship. Not the original plan but not an entirely unhappy bonus.

Chapter Twenty-One

I sense Jay enter Chrysalis rather than see him and use all my self-control to continue chatting to Adore Vajayjay about her plans for next month. But my body is alert, and it is almost as if it wants to twist away from my mind, separate itself entirely and go and curl around Jay in welcome. And then stay there for a bit. Several hours, maybe longer.

I am not used to this feeling.

But thankfully, as a master of self-control, I finish my conversation before heading back to my table. I smile a welcome at Cassie and the woman whom I assume is her girlfriend, Jasmine. Cassie has the same eyes as Jay, deep melty puddles that warm your soul as they land on you, reassure you that there is nothing that can't be dealt with together.

I slide into the seat next to Jay. Without saying a word, he lifts his arm and I snuggle under. He strokes my hair and I feel myself nestle a bit further into his chest as the conversation continues around us. It all takes about five seconds until I realise what I've done, completely unwittingly, and I sit bolt upright and disentangle myself from him, moving away and putting space between us; but not before I see Cass's eyebrows rise and Jinx and Dan exchange a look.

It all felt so very natural, it was an instinctive action for both of us, and without realising – and certainly without intending – we have shared a moment of intimacy common amongst lifelong friends, long-standing couples.

Colleagues? Um... not so much.

As I unwrap myself from under his shoulder I see the realisation dawn on him too. He lets out a cough and straightens his frame. I don't dare look sideways at him. To have snuggled, for Jesus' sake, and in front of his sister! However, he makes no apology, nor refers to it, merely brings his hands down on the table, 'So, who's drinking what? Let me go and get us all some drinks.'

'We're fine,' Dan says, indicating the drinks already on the table.

'Maybe I need some more Dutch courage,' Jinx insists.

'Yes, cos your shy retiring nature struggles with getting up on those decks knowing all eyes are on you. Get going, you should be starting your set now,' Dan immediately responds.

'Scandalous, but we do need rescuing from that godawful cacophony. Jay, lovely to see you again, and you birthday girl...' Jinx leans over the table and places a kiss on Cassie's cheek. I see Jasmine stiffen but it is almost imperceptible and her smile stays fixed on her face; there is nothing there that I can read for sure. 'I'm going to play tunes that will make your heart beat fast and your pussy weep.'

Jasmine's face certainly changes at that, but to be fair I don't blame her. Cassie however roars with laughter. 'I shall hold you to it,' she says as Jasmine grabs her hand again and intertwines their fingers.

'Drinks?' Jay asks once again.

'Yes, we'll have orange gin and tonics please,' Jasmine replies and Cass nods.

'Really? Cass, do you want Cazcabel too?' her brother asks. 'Birthday shots are tradition,' he adds, shimmying his shoulders.

His sister shoots him daggers and assures him she'd just like the gin.

The evening passes in a flash, there are a lot of cocktails drunk, silly amounts of laughing and even more dancing. Cass is losing herself in the music, her arms above her head, her whole body swaying, Jasmine constantly watching her.

Jay and I have been careful, both embarrassed, I suspect, by the unintentional intimacy earlier, both aware that we are here with people who will notice.

As the lights come on, Cass and Jasmine come off the dance floor. Cassie appears happy although has been far more muted than Jay's descriptions would have had me believe.

'We're off home,' Cassie tells us, Jasmine's arm around her waist. 'I've had the best birthday, thank you. Thank you so much.' She gives Jay a huge cuddle. Jasmine flashes him a smile but its insincerity is obvious.

As they trip out into the street all wrapped up in one another, Jay turns to me, a triumphant grin on his face, so different from that of Jasmine's, so genuine.

'That went well, didn't it? Maybe Jas and her will come out with us – me, sorry, me – more often.'

'Maybe,' I say, I'm not convinced. 'That would be nice. Look, I'm also going to make my way home. I can tell from here that those two –' I point at Jinx still spinning tunes and Dan dancing like he is possessed, even with the lights on full '– are probably going to end up at an afterparty, but I'd rather get home. I know you'd be very welcome to join them.' I turn to go and check with Dan but Jay lays his hand on my arm and I spin back to him, my eyes catching his.

'Thanks, but nah. I feel a good ten years too old for an afterparty. But it'd be nice to... I'd like to...'

I stand rapt; he is stumbling a little. 'How are you getting home?' he finally asks.

'I was gonna walk. I like walking the city in the dark.'

'Uh-huh and what do Jinx and Dan think about that?'

'Yeah, they assume I get an Uber.'

'Because it's not safe to walk across the city at night?'

'I'd argue that. I don't think it's any unsafer here than in the country, say. I've got the streetlights and my phone and—'

'How about I walk you home? I won't come in, I'll just walk you home and then get myself back to mine.'

'You're going to walk back to mine, all the way across the city, and then go back to yours? That's going to take you a good hour.'

'And I wouldn't mind that but I'll probably grab an e-scooter back to mine once I've safely seen you through your door.'

'You really don't have to.' I mean, I don't want to do 'the lady doth protest' stuff but I do quite like the thought of not having to say goodbye to him yet.

'I'd really like to,' he says simply and as he looks at me I believe him. 'It's good to take some time out now and again, walk, look around, look up at the sky, and breathe in the scents of a summer night. It's good for the soul and would make me happy. Are you denying me a chance to be happy?'

'You daft sod,' I say and push him lightly on the shoulder but I know that a walk home with Jay would be the perfect way to finish off our evening.

Chapter Twenty-Two

We have walked all the way from town up to mine. We have seen girls singing at the top of their voices, L-plates attached to them at all angles. We have helped a drunk guy get himself on the night bus home, our feet as quick as Fred and Ginger's as he took time out to express his drunkenness, and his dinner, all over the pavement. We have seen foxes run across the road, marking the city at night as theirs. We have walked next to each other, occasionally bumping into each other and deep in conversation, our heads down as we discuss the night.

And finally we turn the corner close to home and I hear Jay's intake of breath as he catches sight of Clifton Suspension Bridge sparkling ahead of us, the full moon low in the sky.

'It's beautiful, isn't it?' I say as we pause, close to each other.

'I don't think I've ever seen it lit up at night.'

'And you call yourself a Bristolian?'

He smiles and shrugs and an idea pops into my head. I

reach for his hand and squeeze. 'Come on then, I've got something to show you.'

I drag him across the ancient hillfort covered by a blanket of grass around the observatory and as he stops to admire the view again, I impatiently tug him on. My idea has me fired up and I am excited to share it. Although the truth is, it has been many years since I've been down here and my shoes are not made for clambering. I hope the path is still passable, although if it isn't, the strength of my determination alone will flatten any undergrowth that tries to prevent access. Tonight, I am the Prince in *Sleeping Beauty*, nothing is going to stop me.

Jay follows behind me, letting me guide him and chuckling at my impatience. I reach the hidden path and Jay's gentle chuckles turn to a burst of laughter as I start to hack a bit of branch with my high heel. The hi-ya's may be a bit much but it means I am laughing with him as I clear the path.

'You have to be joking me. You want to take me down there in the dark, on the edge of a cliff-face?' I spin around, a hundred filthy jokes springing to mind, and accept he does have a point. Health and Safety Lily would not allow this. But in-the-moment-Lily feels a need to show him this place, to include him in this secret bit of my past. And I have faith in myself to get us there safely. The dangerous bit is fenced off but I can understand why Jay is querying it.

I drop his hand, pop my shoe back on and move towards him, standing so close that you could barely fit a piece of paper between his chest and mine. I feel the sexual pull that I have been working so hard to resist spring up.

Argghhh!

No, Lily, no.

I grab his hand again and consider helter-skeltering over

the grassy banks and back to the street I live on, up my steps and into the privacy of my house. Instead, I lean in, tap him on the nose and watch his eyes close languidly and then pop back open and fix on mine. I hold them whilst trying not to imagine scenarios where I get to watch his eyes do that again.

'This is so worth it. Trust me to keep you safe,' I whisper.

Jay nods and stays silent, his deep conker eyes communicating assent.

We take the path and scrabble through the undergrowth; a bramble catches my dress, causing us both to stop again as Jay untangles it. His hand close to my upper thigh as he gently separates spike from fabric.

I want to encourage him closer, to have him touch me for real there, feel his hand on my skin. Had it been any other man I would lean in and kiss him. In fact, any other man, and I would have leant in and kissed him a long time ago.

Instead, I thank him formally and then grip his hand again, keeping him safe, as we negotiate our way down this treacherous narrow path to the hidden spot that Kevin and I used to come and sit out on, high up and isolated from the rest of the world, staring over the River Avon, the traffic weaving along Parkway and across the bridge, inching towards the city.

Kevin and I had spent one night weaving glass candle holders all through the trees that overhung our hidden ledge as well as dotting them around the edges of the granite ridge where we sat. A fairy ring of lights. I don't expect them to still be there but I'm excited to revisit the special place the two of us had created when we were both at our most bewildered, still trying to work out who *we* thought we were, who *we* wanted to be, instead of being defined by our parents, our schools, our culture.

As Jay and I break through the final bit of undergrowth we come to a halt on the stone ledge. Hewed into the cliff, it is the perfect place to watch the world go by, and high up in the gorge it provides a view that is impossible to find anywhere else in the city. I hear Jay's intake of breath as we stop and he squeezes my hand. I look up at him with pleasure. I knew he would love this. And as he looks out and takes in the view, I catch sight of some of the glass jars still balanced on the stone.

Searching my bag, I find a lighter of Dan's that I had meant to return. I break free of Jay to examine the glass jars. Inside are newish tealights and my heart is glad that someone is carrying on the tradition all these years later. I love Bristol precisely because of this sort of thing. I bend over and light them and, reaching up to the trees hanging over us, I see the glass lanterns still there as well.

With the candles lit, I take a seat next to Jay, who has removed his jacket and set it out on the stone to stop us getting cold as we sit with our backs against the cliff-face.

The candles twinkle at us through a mish-mash of green, yellow, blue, pink, red, orange, purple patterned panes of glass; the light reminiscent of heady Arabian nights. With the moonlight streaming through the trees that stretch overhead and the feel of Jay at my side I am utterly relaxed.

'This place is amazing. You were right. It is worth risking life and limb for.'

I nudge him with indignation. 'Life and limb, my arse. I told you you'd be safe with me.'

'Hmmm,' he says and I nestle into him again as I had earlier this evening but without the self-consciousness. He wraps his arm around me and I feel warm and safe and all sorts of meant-to-be. I am too happy in this moment to deconstruct that, determined to live in this moment, to enjoy these feelings.

'So how did you find this place?'

'Kevin and I were exploring one day soon after Freshers Week. We had just met and become completely inseparable. Two little lost souls.'

'You were a lost soul? I find that hard to believe. You're so polished, so sure of yourself.'

'Oh, believe me, it wasn't always like that,' I say.

'It wasn't? I can picture a little Lily. I see you as one of those girls that always sat at the front and had her hand up?'

'Um, definitely not. I mean I enjoyed infants and I was a bit of a swot but I never minded the rough and tumble with all the boys.'

He jiggles his eyebrows. 'Uh-huh, as Jinx is so fond of telling me.'

'No, no, not like that, you fool.' I bat him lightly on the arm. I don't want him to think of me as one of those precious princessy girls with their perfect hair, uncreased uniform and tendency to be absolute bitches the minute the teachers were out of sight. 'I liked books, I liked learning, but I also liked to kick a ball about, get a bit grubby at playtime. I was a mud pie maker all the way.'

'Mud pies are the best.'

'Oh yes.'

'But after infants, what happened then?'

'Oh...um...' I am not sure how much I want to reveal to Jay. Talking about my insecurities, talking about me as a teen, is not the way I talk to men I'm attracted to. No, they see the shiny version of me, the polished shimmery one that laughs and flirts and falls into bed. The person I present as is not the person I really am. Kevin and I bonded for this reason all those years ago, our need to hide behind carefully constructed identities. Yet here in this moment, I feel like real me, like it *might* be okay to tell Jay the truth of who I am.

'Oh, you know...um...nothing much. Usual adolescent stuff,' I say.

I am not ready after all.

'What about you though? You've talked about being in care, that can't have been easy,' I add and he gives me a look and I know he isn't fooled by me shifting focus.

'It wasn't great.' I know there is a lot that a simple phrase like that covers and my heart goes out to him. 'It's why I'm so protective of Cassie. We were lucky to have had a father like we did but he was taken away from us far too soon and Cassie didn't have the years with him that I did. So I tried to be as much like him as I could, took on that role until finally we found a foster placement and were out of the group homes, you know. Then I was safe to become a teen again.'

'What was your dad like?' I ask but I wonder if I already know, if the attributes I ascribe to Jay are those that his father taught him. That he doesn't just commemorate him with his tattoo but with all his behaviour too.

'He was honourable. Honourable, hardworking and fair. He had a good heart and he lived for those he loved. I've never met a better man.'

That seems about right.

'He sounds like a very special human being. You were lucky to have had him in your life. Is he the man on your arm?'

'He is. I was. I remember –' Jay pauses '– you don't want to hear all this.'

'I do. Tell me about him,' I say, looking up at him, placing

174

my hand on his to reassure him I am genuine. Jay stares out across the expanse of stone and river and road.

'I remember his dominoes evenings. All his friends would come over, it was the only time he would have a drink, whisky...'

'So your love of whisky, that's because of your dad?' I ask.

'That makes me sound like some grizzled old soak,' he splutters. The one thing Jay definitely is not is a grizzled old soak. The moonlight shining in streaks through the trees is highlighting his physique in a way I don't need reminding of. But he is beautiful to me because of *him*, not his arms, his chest, his shoulders. The man he is, the soul he possesses. I have never met a man like him, one that I fancy the pants off as well as respect and admire. I never really believed men like him existed.

'Yes, I guess it reminds me of my father. Not that he was a raving alcoholic, not at all. That couldn't be further from the truth.' He lets out some kind of indecipherable humpf and I stay silent and see if he will fill the gap. 'On dominoes night he would cook up a great big stew and get out the whisky and Cass and I would go to sleep hearing their laughter and know all was right in the world. My dad had the best laugh –' he pauses and I nod for him to continue '– like a silent guffaw, if that makes sense. I don't know how else to describe it. His shoulders would go up and down in these big movements, his mouth would be wide open and yet very little noise would come out. His friends were much louder, one of them had a high-pitched giggle and they would all rib him about it.'

'Those nights sound fun.'

'They really were. And whilst my dad was a stickler for the rules, I would be allowed a seat at the table as soon as Cass was asleep and snoring. And my God, that girl can snore, she's like a herd of wildebeests rampaging, even as a little tot. Anyway, I would creep down the stairs and they would let me have a chair, a special glass like theirs but filled with orange juice, and I would play with them for a full half an hour. I can still conjure up the smells of that room on those nights, the fire in the grate, the smell of the stew Dad would cook, crammed full of hot pepper and garlic, a hint of dark sugar. There'd be the scent of whisky and the mix of all their aftershaves. I still have a bit of a thing for aftershave.'

'I remember.' I grin and he looks across and matches my grin with one of his own. And then I become serious again, 'They're great memories to have.'

'Right, they are. I used to love playing with them. They didn't make it any easier for me to win just because I was a child. No way. If I won, rare but it did happen occasionally, then I knew it was because I had earned it. I respect Dad for doing that. Rules were rules; he didn't mess about. If you wanted something badly enough then your only chance of getting it was to try and try and try until you earned it. That's helped me in life, I think. Dad really pushed the value of hard work. What about you? What about your parents?'

'Good, you know. Dad likes to wash the car and mow the lawn every Saturday without fail and Mum keeps the fridge full, over-worries about the state of her roses, and makes sure she has the time to help anyone that ever needs it, be they close friend or stranger on the street. I'm lucky to have a family that is solid, dependable. An awful lot of people do not have that luck.'

'Truth, but we all have something. Even you, Lily Galbraith.'

'No,' I say and he looks at me as if he knows. 'No trauma like yours,' I clarify.

I have this huge great list running through my head of the reasons I have to leave this man alone, maintain boundaries, but after all he has said about his father, knowing all I know about him and the man he is, the man he aspires to be, I am aching to lean in and kiss him; just gently place my lips on his and let him feel the intensity of what I am feeling for him right now. And this kiss, this kiss is not intended as a precursor to him undressing me, me taking my turn to unhitch his belt, to pull his trousers down and his T-shirt up as we move together, getting closer and more frantic with each movement.

No, my need to kiss him is not that.

It's because I don't know how else to express the intensity with which I like him, like who he is, respect his values and the things that are important to him, how much I care about what he has gone through and where his life has taken him, and how I want to make sure nothing ever hurts him again. I want this kiss to say all that and his lips are just there, right in front of me, I'd barely have to reach forward at all. Strip the sexual attraction away and I know that the reason I want to lean in is built on so much more.

Fuck.

That can't be allowed to happen. I love being single and this man doesn't do one-nighters. So I know anything that happens is going to be way more complicated than a wham, bam!

I love my life as it is, free from meaningful sexual interaction, and in my head I run through the many, many reasons he and I cannot work. Nope. Just can't have this. Can't.

He is looking at me quizzically.

'What?' I say somewhat aggressively but I don't want him to know what has just been flashing through my mind. Not any of it.

'You were saying your shit isn't like mine but you didn't argue that you had none...'

'Ah yes, that.'

'Well, go on.'

Empathy is pouring out of his eyes. Oh no, he thinks I'm all far away and fretting because of some perceived trauma, not because I'm panicking about the fact that my lust seems to come with a side serving of emotion. He's been telling me about his dead dad and I'm sitting here thinking sex. Well, trying to think NO to sex, obviously, but it's still all cantering around the same subject area. He obviously rates me way too highly. I should probably remedy that.

'It was nothing really. I feel like a bit of a twat talking about my stuff when you've just opened up about your dad. Like I said my dad is alive and well, living with my mother in a three-bedroomed house on the outskirts of Clacton. They are really good parents.' That is true. I do feel like it would be wildly disrespectful to continue this thread, when my struggle really was around teenage school stuff, whilst his at the same age centres around becoming orphaned and being thrust into care with the responsibilities he felt to his younger sister.

'You feel you shouldn't tell me about times you've struggled as a young girl because my dad died?'

'Yeah. My stuff is silly.'

He removes his hand from under mine and looks up at me. 'Let's not play top trumps of trauma, it's not a competition. I wouldn't feel better talking to you if you had lost a dad as well. I went through some shit, and I imagine you went through some shit too. I don't know a single person that hasn't but I do know that I don't want you not to tell me your stuff. In fact, I can't tell you how much I want to hear about your stuff.'

'Sadist.'

'Damn right.'

'Really. Oh God. I guess what I was trying to say –' and I take my eyes from him because suddenly I feel a bit shy, and regardless of what he says I do feel a bit of a dick '– was that my adolescence was pretty easy compared to what so many girls go through, but the emotions I felt, they were intense. They led me to some really dark places and I felt so bloody alone. Even with my next-to-perfect family. My parents didn't have a clue what was going on; both of them just saw me as their absolute treasure who was so golden that her life must be golden as well. It would be beyond their comprehension that I was having such a rough time in school. Such a rough time.'

'Go on'

'I don't know that I want to...' I say and then I realise maybe I do. I haven't told anyone the details about what happened at school, not even Kevin. Conjuring that lost girl to the surface of my memories again is making me hurt so much for her.

I use the methods I am forever encouraging clients to use and immediately visualise adult me standing over teenage me and wrapping her up in her arms, resting my head on the top of hers and telling her she is good enough, she is safe and everything works out okay.

'Everything is okay now,' I say out loud, and it's true, it is. 'But when I became adolescent and all the hormones kicked in, I developed a condition known as PCOS. The side effects at that time were that I got fat, fat and really hairy.'

His eyes widen.

'That's wild,' he says and I'm not sure how I feel about that. 'I mean I would never have guessed,' he adds hurriedly, 'and I know that stuff shouldn't matter but I also understand that at that age particularly, it really does. Kids are harsh over that stupid superficial shit. Did they give you a rough time?'

I nod. 'Yeah, they were pretty grim, but you know it was just teasing, we all have to put up with teasing.' And another image flashes into my head, one that often revisits me at night. One that I have never had the courage to tackle, arguing with myself that I don't need to; that I am safe now and no one can hurt me again. I carry that memory a lot and as I look across at Jay I wonder if I'm going to tell him about it.

'I think we label a lot of things teasing which are actually way more than that, and it can, and often does, have a massive impact on our adult lives, the way we perceive ourselves, the way we interact with others. So you know, and I know you do, that the throwaway we-all-have-to-put-up-with-teasing doesn't really do it. I have heard so much from my girls that they write off as bantz, or boys being boys, or even the catty shit that goes on from other girls, and rarely, very rarely does it deserve such a minimising approach.'

He's right, of course he is. I close my eyes and before I know what I am doing I let the words spill out. I tell him all about the time the boy I spoke to on the bus – the boy I thought of as my sort-of-friend even though he didn't talk to me inside the school gates – sent me a note asking me to meet him in the science labs at lunchtime.

Jay is holding me tight and stroking my hair as I speak to him about what happened next, my eyes closed because I don't want to see any of the things that may be flitting across his face: disdain, pity, revulsion at my stupidity. I can feel the tears rolling down my cheeks as I speak of how those boys, Scott Oakley and a group of his friends, six of them in total, pushed me to the ground and, using a skipping rope, hogtied me on the floor behind the chemistry bench. How I didn't know what was going to happen next, how I had no power to move, the rope stretching my arms and legs out and making me unable to do anything other than wobble from side to side. How they shoved a football sock in my mouth to stop me from screaming, and how I was too terrified in that moment of what was coming next, of how I was powerless to stop it as they danced around me making pig noises, as Scott Oakley knelt beside me and started undoing the buttons on my shirt.

'God, Lily' is all he says as I gulp and open my eyes. I can hear the horror in his voice, and the empathy. He has tensed and is holding me even tighter now, my head on his chest as he strokes my hair. 'I am so sorry you had to go through that, I am so, so sorry.'

'It's okay,' I say. 'One of the popular girls came in, I can't remember why, something trivial, and Scott and his mates ran out, laughing as if they had done nothing worse than tied my shoelaces together. She sat next to me, removed the sock, untied me, gently buttoned me up. They didn't *hurt* me. I skipped out for the afternoon, went and sat in the park until it was time to go home. I was always so grateful to her. She stopped it getting worse and she never said a word to anyone. I could have become the laughing stock of the school but she kept my secret. I don't know what they planned, if anything. All I know is I spent the rest of the year making sure I got a different bus home.'

'That's not teasing, you know. That's assault. They did hurt you, so don't do that, don't dismiss that.'

'I know. I know what it is. I think it's part of the reason I do what I do, you know? I wanted to protect every young girl I could, I wanted to be there, give them the tools to get over the sorts of things girls are subjected to on a daily basis, the things that society constantly says are dreadful but that never change.' I move away from Jay. I could be happy having my hair stroked for ever but I want him to understand why the opportunity he has brought to me is so important.

I turn and look directly at him, amazed that after the telling of my story, I do not feel ashamed or dirty, I feel angry and I feel safe and those two things are a surprise to me. 'I've got lost somewhere along the way. Somehow I've become this Love Doctor persona, and that's worthwhile, but it's not what I got into psychology for. What I got into psychology for is what you are doing, so asking me to be part of this wellbeing project means a lot. That type of work has always been my goal. Girls as young teens, they're why I've been working so hard, gathering the expertise and the knowledge to be able to do something with it, to support them at what can be the most challenging and confusing time of their lives. It was tough enough being a Nineties kid but to grow up in this world of social media, of never being allowed to switch off that unrelenting pressure of images being thrown at you, of needing to make them, post them, the insane sexual pressure alongside it – that's such a lot. The opportunity you're offering, to show these girls that it is okay to be them, to say no to what they don't want to do, to take charge of their bodies, to embrace their autonomy, to treat themselves as they wish others treated them; all of that means the world and I am so grateful you have come into my life and guided me back to that path. Thank you. You have allowed me to stop, recalibrate and adjust myself so I'm back on the course I wanted to be on.'

'Lily, you don't need to thank me.'

'I do. And thank you for listening too. That's not a story I ever tell and I don't know why I overshared with you. I'm sorry.'

He leans up onto his knees and plants a gentle kiss on my head.

'Lily, you are one of the bravest, strongest women I know, and I know lots. You don't need to thank me. You certainly don't need to apologise to me, or anyone. You have no idea how glad I am that I sent that email and asked you to get involved.'

I shiver a little, because of the care in his kiss, I think, and because being this honest with someone is refreshing, liberating. As I do so one of the candles starts to flicker and then dims, and another does the same.

'I reckon they're telling us it's time to get you home. It's getting cold,' he says and I nod and agree and whilst I'm not sure what I am feeling, I'm fairly sure it's not the cold.

Chapter Twenty-Three

W hilst I fumble for the key in my bag, I know I do not want Jay to go yet. The awkwardness I was terrified would appear after opening up to him has not materialised as we giggle our way home. I put the key in the door but before I unlock it, I turn. I don't think I can wait a minute longer to see what his plans are.

'Do you want to come in?' I ask and then quickly add, 'Not for sex, genuinely just for a drink, a coffee, you know. But definitely not for sex.'

'Well, I'm glad you made that clear.' He laughs, startling a cat that is perching on a fence and which then skitters down scritch-scratching all the way to the pavement.

'I thought it best,' I say, smirking, and turning back to the keyhole. He hasn't answered but now the question has been asked I can relax. I push the door open and take a step inside, turning again as I do so and motioning that he is welcome in.

'Come and have a tour.'

'A tour, a coffee *and* a promise that my chastity is to be

respected. Who could ask for more?' he answers and I lead him through the narrow hallway into the kitchen, aware of his breath on the back of my neck, of his presence, the whole width of him, standing behind me.

We enter the kitchen and I feel the air between us as we separate a little and I wave my hand around. I suddenly feel nervous and start to gabble.

'So, this is the kitchen. We knocked it all through and now have this one massive room. There's a piano for Kevin over there, although he claims he can't actually play but Dan practises a lot.'

'It's huge.'

'Yeah, we're really lucky.'

'So do the three of you rent together?'

'No, it's just me and Kevin, but Dan is here all the time. I'm hoping there is a little romance brewing but don't dare ask in case I jinx, ooh no pun intended, it.'

'So The Love Doctor is always looking out for love for others, even when she's off the clock.'

'Love makes the world go around. Oh, but not for me,' I add hurriedly in case he thinks I'm hitting on him again.

He doesn't say a word, just looks at me inquisitively, in a way that reminds me of that wise old owl that always features in the storybooks of children. I wonder if I look at my clients like that. I hope not. It's a little disconcerting, as if he can read my mind and predict my thoughts and behaviour. I wonder if he's drawing conclusions between being bullied at school and my need for control, my antipathy to a relationship for myself. Kevin certainly bangs on about it and he doesn't know the details of it, whereas Jay very definitely does now.

'What would you like to drink? Did you want a coffee?'

'I should probably aim for some sleep tonight,' he says so I open the fridge and offer him a cold beer. He smiles and I open it and pass it to him.

'So, your podcast, do you record it here?' He gesticulates at the big table in front of us. 'I can picture you here with one of those old-fashioned fluffy mikes as you share your wisdom.' I arch my eyebrow. He knows me well enough now, surely, to know wisdom is something I may aspire to but very definitely don't have yet. Maybe when I'm eighty.

'No, not here. Although I'd love one of those mikes. Mind you, what's the betting that Kevin would find some way to feature it on a dress or turn it into some kind of fascinator?'

'High, I'd say.'

'Uh-huh. Although it is thanks to him that I have the most perfect place. I learned early on that a small space is best for the sound quality, preferably with soft things like curtains and coats that absorb sound and stop too much echoing. Here, come see.' And I lead him into the hallway and up the stairs to Kevin's wardrobe room.

I am not unaware of the tension between us as I place my first foot on the step. Heading up the stairs with someone who makes me feel all the flutters the way this man does usually has a different purpose and it's one I am struggling to shift from my mind. I wonder if Jay is thinking the same. I had thought it hard controlling my thoughts towards him outside on the ledge but here, in the intimacy of the house, it is even tougher.

And then, as if he can read minds, Jay pauses and says, 'Is this just a ploy to get me upstairs, Madam?'

I know he is joking but there is no getting away from the fact that it is very tempting indeed.

'No, if I were bringing you upstairs for nefarious nocturnal goings-on, you'd know it, Mr Cooper,' I say in that ridiculously breathy Marilyn tone that I had the good sense not to use the first time I met him in the sauna. Good sense and I are normally on very close terms, but somehow after midnight that fucker always proves to be a fair-weather friend and has now clearly disappeared for the evening.

His eyes widen and my foot hits the top step. I stumble a little and try to right myself but not before he has reached out to steady me, his fingers splayed on my coccyx. To downplay the charge swooshing through me from my tip to my toes, I stand as a circus ringmaster does when he is announcing his finest acts and fling the door to the dressing room open.

'Ta-daaaa!'

'Wow,' he says as he sees the room where Kevin has all his costumes.

It's a fair response.

The heads and the wigs are there, creepy as hell, and I get a vicarious little thrill at watching Jay's facial expression as his eyes walk along the top row, looking at head after head after head.

'I know I've met Jinx, and I'm a fan, but are we sure she's not a serial killer?' he asks.

'Ooh, my mother taught me to never make a promise I couldn't keep so I'm afraid I can't promise you that. It's entirely possible. She could easily fit at least two bodies under her Scarlett O'Hara Southern Belle gown, one taped to each leg. So, who knows.' I shrug my shoulders.

'You're alarming me with how possible that sounds.'

'Hmmm,' I say, 'perhaps we should check through the rails for clues, cos you know...now you've said it...' I grab a trilby and a cerise feather boa. The hat I plonk on Jay's head, the boa I wrap around his neck and he twirls for me as I do so.

'There, now you look the part,' I say and he takes another twirl in front of the mirror and laughs.

'This is not how I expected Cassie's birthday evening to pan out.'

'I bet it's not what Cassie had in mind either. Take a selfie and show her,' I say.

He doesn't.

'This is a work of art.' He holds out a floor-length sequinned dress, lime green, and I jump up.

'This is one of my absolute faves. Isn't it something? It looks awful on the hanger but is drop-dead on. Now Jinxy always pairs this one with this,' and I pull down a wig of gorgeous titian tresses and remove his trilby and pop the wig on him, taking the dress and holding it up against his frame. 'What do you think?'

'That it's not really my colour?' He laughs. 'Will she not mind us going through her stuff?'

'Oh God, no. She's always encouraging me to play. Sometimes a whole group of us come back and do dress-up. She loves people getting pleasure from the things she loves, it's that simple. She won't mind at all, promise.' And she won't. She might get a bit hot and bothered at the thought of Jay being in her closet but that's only because I caught her checking out his abs earlier this evening. To be fair, she made no secret of it.

'Well, in that case –' Jay picks up a sexy red Jessica Rabbit dress and with it still on the hanger drapes it over my neck and then grabs a curly brunette wig and plops it on my head '–

tonight, Matthew, coming through those curtains we have...um...er...I know...we have Sinitta!'

He makes a drum-roll noise and mimes it with his hands as I grab a brush and sing, 'Boys, boys boys...looking for a good time' and then pop the brush by his mouth so he can sing. Still with his wig perched atop his head, he pulls strongman arms and starts to sing 'So Macho'. Then he grabs my free hand and twirls me around as we both sing along. In the tiny narrow space between the desk and the rails we jive and spin and bump hips and it is so much fun.

I drop the brush.

We both bend to pick it up and the atmosphere changes as we start to straighten up.

The room is buzzing with energy.

I know I am not alone in sensing the chemistry here and somehow being in this space heightens it, the knowledge that my bedroom is but a few steps away raises the pressure. The room is so quiet and I feel my heart is booming so loudly that he must be able to hear it.

Our eyes are locked as we both straighten, our bodies in tandem. I can feel goosebumps popping all over my body and in this moment nothing matters to me like this man does.

My breathing is becoming ragged as we both stand tall, staring at each other. His pupils are huge and I note his chest is rising and falling as fast as mine.

He is feeling exactly as I am. He is as lost in this moment as me.

I put my foot forward a little, not all the way to his but close enough. I don't take my eyes from him as I do so. Prickles of lust are shooting through me and I'm using all of my self-restraint not to push him back into the rails of clothes, lean into the furs, the sequins, the feathers, feel every inch of him up against every inch of me.

I have never been this turned on in my life. I know it will take the merest touch to make me explode.

I move my other foot forward.

My mouth opens and I bite my bottom lip. Jay lets out a ragged breath and then moves his foot so the point of his shoe is now touching mine.

He moves his other foot forward.

I reach up to touch his face but his hand shoots outs and grabs mine with such force that the very strength of him makes me even wetter.

'We can't,' he says.

We very definitely can.

'I want to,' he adds, his fingers still around my wrist, his touch, that action, making my blood pump through me ferociously. I nod slowly and raise my free hand to trace a finger down his chest. He shakes his head at me and I take my hand away from him in apology, flexing it as a gesture to suggest he may want to grab this one too.

He smiles and shakes his head again but he does reach down and take it, holding my hand in his, his fingers weaving through, one side of him showing tenderness, the other side of him resolute.

'If you want to, and I want to – and I really do – then...'

'Oh, I want to,' he whispers, ' but tonight, I don't know... It feels...' These words are falling from his lips yet his hand in mine is tracing patterns on my palm, stroking, pressing. His body is saying something very different and I know what he is asking. He is scared that this is a response to earlier, that I am doing this as a result of opening up to him, that this desire has arisen from gratitude or relief.

'I have wanted you from the first time we met,' I say very clearly. And as he looks at me I hope he knows this is the truth of it. The way I am looking at him, the way my body is arching to him all back this up. I lift the hand he is holding and place a gentle kiss on the inside of his wrist. He groans lightly and I hear myself emitting a similar noise.

This man turns me upside down, inside out. I have told him things I have never told anyone else. The ledge tonight was the most intimate moment of my life. I haven't suddenly wanted him because of that; I have been dreaming of him, thinking about his hands on me, mine on him, for so long now. I have always wanted him to touch me, stroke me, fill the whole of me. I have visualised the way I buck against him as he moves in me and all tonight has done has made me realise this is the next natural step. The things that were holding me back before are insignificant, they don't matter anymore, this is bigger than all of that.

I need him, my body craves him, I just need to know if his reasons hold. I need his consent. I continue, 'I have spent days and nights dreaming of this. This is not just a tonight thing, I promise. You have no idea how much I wan—'

His lips are on mine, he has released my hands and has curled one behind me, fitting into the small of my back as his tongue explores my mouth, his other hand in my hair, cupping me and bringing me into him. I am leaning back over the table, my bottom resting against it as he presses into me and I pull him in as far as I can.

I can feel how hard he is through his trousers and my heart is hammering as I reach down and pull at his top, thrusting it over his head. We have to break our kiss to do so and he stares at me with such intensity, such need that I don't think I can wait much longer. I reach behind me for the zipper on this dress. But he bats my arms away and reaches out and pulls me up from the table and turns me slowly.

I let him guide me around and suck in my breath as I feel him undo the zipper, his hands deliberately slow as he does so. I want to turn back around and capture his mouth again, welcome him into me, but I also want to see where he takes this next, what he is doing. As the zipper reaches its end, he moves the dress off one shoulder and then the other and it puddles to the floor, rather as my stomach feels right now. He traces a line down my spine and starts to kiss the top of my shoulders, working his way across and down. His lips are like feathers on my skin and I am both impatient for more and lost in the dizzying pleasure of this sensation. He lowers himself and reaches my coccyx with his mouth and then with both hands on my hips switches me around again so we are facing each other and from his kneeling position he looks up at me. I clamp one hand on the table to steady myself while his hands lift my bottom onto it so I am perching, and then with the most ridiculous look of mischief, and intent, he lowers his head and kisses me in between my legs.

My breath is coming hard and fast now. He is utterly in control and I seem to be losing it. He is using his tongue in deep circular motions, teasing me, not quite hitting the sweet spot but letting me know it is coming.

My back arches and I start to moan as his circles get closer and closer to the central point. It doesn't take much longer and I am lost, my body exploding, my mind all dizzy and I don't know if I have the strength in my legs to stand but I do know I need him inside me, I need more.

I pull him up and latch my mouth onto his, and catching sight of Jinx's terrifying polystyrene heads, I push myself off the table and, my mouth glued to his, my hands exploring his body much as he has been mine, I push him back. Entwined and animalistic, I manage to get him out of this room and push the door to my bedroom open. Never have I felt more like this is how things are supposed to be.

Chapter Twenty-Four

'Oh my God, we've done it!' Cass shouts with triumph as, after quite a lot of 'to me, to you... this angle... let's try this...', we manage to get the biggest wardrobe known to man around the corner of the stairs. There is a possibility that my back may break or at the very least my knees will snap and I will spend the rest of my life crawling from one place to another. But despite this nothing is going to diminish my smile today.

When I woke up this morning, I woke tangled up in Lily's sheet, her leg splayed across my body, my face buried in her shoulder. We had slept late but to be fair we had stayed up late, exploring each other, revelling in each other, cramming in as much loving as was possible in one night. This was like nothing I have ever experienced. It was instinctive, primal, it felt right, as if I had been waiting for this night my entire life without ever realising it.

As I lay there upon waking, watching her sleep, she opened

one eye, and then the other and jumped so high she practically lifted off the bed.

Shit!

I had woken up happy and contented and ready to see where we go from here. I had forgotten all about Lily's fear of intimacy, of mornings after. In the moment, I had forgotten all Lily told me, and she has frequently, about how she only does one-night stands, how she avoids anything that could lead to commitment.

Last night we were in tandem, we were together as if we were made to be that way. It hadn't occurred to me that her reaction would be different to mine come morning, that she didn't automatically believe we may have a future, that we now *need* to be an us.

After her initial shock, she had rolled over, given me a long languorous kiss and told me she was late for work. Very late. Then, as if she had remembered it was Sunday, apologised and said she meant brunch, she had a brunch with some of the women from the university. I did the gentlemanly thing, returned the kiss and left, damping down my desire to jump in the shower with her as she hurriedly prepared herself to leave.

She clearly needs space and whilst I know what I want, Lily needs time to work out where we go from here. She needs to take the lead and I understand her desire to be in control, to make the decisions herself, especially after what I heard last night. I understand now why Dr Lily Galbraith presents herself as having such a polished suit of armour. I also understand how lucky I was to have removed the armour, if only for a little while.

But man, it was hard leaving without declaring my heart, exiting merely with a cheerful grin and a discreet acknowledgement that we won't let this affect the work we have to do together.

I also know that I need to talk to my sister, admit that I have broken my vow. But even the thought of that, even that cannot keep the beam from my face today as my mind flashes back to snippets of our evening, to the intimacy shared.

'Stop a minute, I need a break for a sec,' Cass shouts from the other side of the wardrobe, bringing me back to the present. I balance my end on the stair. 'Oh my God, whose idea was this?' she pants.

'Umm....yours?' I state.

'No need to be clever about it,' she snaps from behind the walnut panels.

'We're doing well, we've just got it around that corner,' I say, 'and I really wasn't sure we were going to manage that without resulting in a call to 999.'

'That may still happen.'

'Are you indirectly threatening me with violence?'

'Not so much indirectly.'

'What have I done?

'You're being annoyingly perky this morning and I don't like it. I have a head that feels like someone has squeezed it in a vice and then stamped on it.'

'Did you have a great birthday though?'

'Yeah, yeah, I did. It was cool.' Her voice trails off a bit and like a terrier on the hunt my ears prick up a little.

'You don't sound so sure.'

'No, it really was.' Her tone peps itself up again. 'And it was interesting to see you there, clearly a regular...'

'Hardly,' I say. 'I'd only been there once before.' I peek around the side of the wardrobe as I say this and she peeks back. I stick my tongue out. It doesn't matter how old you get, your siblings are your siblings and that is acceptable behaviour until one of us hits the grave, and quite possibly after.

Cassie sticks her tongue out as well and I see she is managing to shape her hand into the finger gesture on both sides of the wardrobe. Charming.

'Clearly a regular and, most interestingly, with the woman you *weren't* flirting with in the sauna,' she continues.

'Uuuhhhhhh...' I issue a long growl.

'Oh, you can make all the growly noises you want, I saw the way you looked at each other last night. I'm not blind. The sparks between the two of you could have lit up an entire town. In fact, if the electricity ever fails, I'll just get you and Lily round and plug the two of you into some sort of generator.'

'Are you feeling rested fully now? Shall we do the last bit?' I suggest, changing the direction of the conversation. 'One, two, three, hup.'

'Kzzzkzkkkzzzzz.' Cassie makes some bizarre sort of crackle noise as she lifts again and I ignore her. We finally get the wardrobe down the rest of the stairs, with a little wall bashing, and hoist it into the van we borrowed from Marcus, Cass shrieking that her womb is going to drop out if I make her do any more lifting. I resist pointing out that whilst I know very little about wombs, that seems biologically unlikely, and it is her poxy wardrobe in the first place.

Sitting on the short wall in the front of the flat, Cass is still huffing and puffing as if she has just run twenty-five miles, and I pass her my water bottle.

'It's kinda sad saying goodbye to this baby.'

'Baby? It's got to be about two hundred years old and is the size of four grown men.'

'I know, but still. The choir will be able to make good use of her. I look at her and I see so many imaginary worlds. It's a real Narnia wardrobe, one that once you push past the old furs and smell of mothballs you get lured into hidden worlds from children's storybooks from years gone by.'

'Do you have fur coats?

'Fake ones, yes, I do. I was wearing one last night, you fool,' Cass says and I shrug. She gives me a withering look and continues, 'I just liked the idea of opening the door and seeing them and imagining what might happen if I stepped in.'

'Did you ever step in? Were you lured into magical worlds?'

'Nah. I'm still a bit claustrophobic so it was one of those things that seemed like a good idea but you know... Anyway the community choir are very happy to take it on.' I am not unaware that Cass had wanted a wardrobe like this all her life and now is getting rid of it. I am willing to bet Jas is behind this.

'Yeah, and you can see it when you're up there painting the scenery for this year's production.' I squidge her shoulder sympathetically as I speak, knowing that will be my job now but unable to resist teasing her a little longer.

'Oh honey, I told you, I saw you two last night. I don't think it's me that's going to be painting the backdrops for *Joseph And The Amazing Technicolor Dreamcoat* this year, oh no.'

'Ha! Shut up.'

'For all my teasing, the two of you do look cute together. You seem to create a world that exists only for the two of you, you know.'

'No, we don't!'

'You may not be aware of it but you definitely do, I can't help but comp—' She pauses; her face has changed and as she speaks these words it is not filled with the joy of teasing me as it normally is. She looks down at her lap and fidgets with her top, scrunching it up into a tight ball and letting it go again before putting a big smile back on her face.

All of this occurs in a microsecond but I know Cass, and I know this means there is something not right, something she's not prepared to talk about just yet but is in the back of her mind. Can't help comp— Complain, compete...err, compare? Compare, is that what she means? Is she comparing me and Lily to her and Jasmine's relationship? I don't want to get too excited so I keep my face as composed as it can be, reaching to grab my water back so I can take a pull as she continues to speak. 'You look like you should be together, you know? There's something about the two of you together that just sort of fits.'

'Hey, slow your roll, that's not going to happen,' I say, although I couldn't agree with her more. But I am not 'fessing up just yet, I want a little bit of time to process myself, find out what is going to happen before I unburden myself to my sister. I cast around for a flippant get-out that is not a lie.

Aha! 'I have my hands full with bloody Dimkins as it is...' It is true – by the time I got back home this morning, he had shredded yet another cushion and emptied the washing basket. I considered googling demonic possession. 'And you're forgetting, Lily is a self-confessed workaholic who loves her single life and has no desire to settle down and build something.' All true, but I don't like having to say it; which indicates I probably should remind myself of this frequently. I brace myself and name another truth. 'Plus, we have very different life goals. Where she wants to be at forty and at fifty is a whole world away from what I want.'

'You're a workaholic too,' Cass retorts.

'No, if I was then would I not be there now rather than helping you?'

'It's a Sunday.'

'And work stops on a Sunday?' I ask. I'm fairly sure that people have been working on Sundays for quite some time now. My girls' problems don't disappear because it's the weekend.

'Yours does. You don't have to be in until this evening.'

'You're undermining your own argument, you know,' I say. Cass squishes her face up into her I-don't-care expression and I can't help but smile. She has been doing that since birth.

'Okay,' Cassie nods. I am surprised that she is not mounting more of a campaign to prove me wrong, but if she's happy to leave it then I very definitely am.

Though some self-sabotaging bit in me feels the need to add, 'And also, whilst I know we don't believe in leagues...'

'No, we don't,' my sister retorts firmly, 'They're reductive judgemental bullshit.'

'Yep, all of that. Still, she is kind of outta mine.' I don't know why I'm saying this, what response I'm hoping for.

That mischief-laden grin slips back on to Cass's face. 'Yeah, she is.'

'Thanks.'

'Well, what do you want me to say? I think you're the best man in the world but you know, she's very glam, she lives in a different world to you and me. She doesn't live on frozen pizza and oven chips...'

'Oi, I don't live on frozen pizza!'

'Yeah, fair point, you are very health conscious. And I don't either since Jas banned junk food. But I bet she doesn't have to hoik wardrobes down two flights of stairs, she pays someone to do that.'

I want to tell Cass that I was at Lily's house last night, that I think she's being a bit harsh. But I know that she'll miss the point and is merely going to punch the air in joy at the thought of me with a paintbrush in my hand whilst the sound of 'Any Dream Will Do' is being repeatedly rehearsed.

'Come on, let's get this thing delivered,' I say instead and usher her towards the van. The hope that she is beginning to spot flaws in her and Jas' relationship remains strong in me. I remember what Lily said on the podcast before I knew she was Lily, that being around other couples may reveal to Cass what is different about hers. It had never occurred to me that The Love Doctor herself and I might become her example.

'You know, Jay...' Cass starts to say and I flick my head to look at her. We are in the van now, almost at the community choir's base. 'I know I giggled when you said you were out of Lily's league but actually I want to say something about that.'

Oh bloody hell, does she have to? I brace myself for whatever may be coming next.

'The truth is I've always admired and respected the way you treat the women in your life, Jay. I know I complain, and I'm right, about the way you want them to meet point a, b, c and all the way through to bloody zee before you will consider rushing them down the aisle and making babies. That is *not* healthy...'

'Hey, I agree, I've conceded that point. Am I not actually

living the very rules you want me to right now?' I feel myself flush at my own audacity.

'Yes, you are. Let me finish what I'm saying.' She punches me on the leg and I make a pinching motion with my fingers like we used to as kids. Obviously, I'm not going to do it now; we're full-grown adults. But I do rub my leg and pop a pained expression on my face nonetheless. And then I remember something I meant to bring up from yesterday.

'Talking of what you've been *saying*, missy! I would really prefer it if you stopped telling everyone – telling Lily and *all* her friends – that I am like a honeypot with bees swarming around everywhere I go. Firstly, not true...'

'True.' Cassie coughs out the word, as if we were still at school.

'Secondly, it makes me sound like some sort of fuckboy, which I most definitely am not.'

'Hmmm'

'Oi!'

'Yes, okay, you're not a fuckboy. Which, if you let me finish what I was saying instead of butting in with your nonsense about bees, you would have heard me already. What I am trying to say, big brother of mine, is that I really respect the way you treat people, but particularly the women in your life, because, and actually especially because, you've got them all swarming around you like bees at dusk. You are respectful and supportive, kind and thoughtful. You don't try to take charge or control or push. You message when you say you will, you make time for the things that are important to them instead of just expecting them to sit watching you at the gym or on a football field... Don't make that face, some men do, they want an adoring fan at their side...'

'Good God, I can't think of anything worse.'

'Right? And two things should be said here. One, I have watched you with countless –' she pauses and rolls her eyes for comic effect '– countless women and I have seen them look at you. Some of them even dribble. The point is I have never seen you look at a woman like you looked at that girl last night, and I have to say she was shooting out all the love pheromones back. It's as if the two of you are in a bubble and the outside world can't even begin to dip inside. Real soulmate shit. But the second thing, and this is the most important, is that for all the things I've said about this Lily woman – how she may be polished, she may seem posh, all of that – at the end of the day that doesn't count for much and you are not only *not* out of her league, or anyone's for that matter, but she would be bloody lucky to have you.'

Chapter Twenty-Five

I have swum length after length, the cold water of the lido not cold enough for me this evening. I reckon I have done a good sixty lengths and stood under the ice bucket twice and I am fairly sure it's not the blazing heat of the day that is making me crave cold water but the fact that I woke up this morning with Jay.

Woke up with!

As in slept with, spent the night with...cuddled!

I never spend the night anywhere, and if someone is coming back to mine then I have their exit route planned before they even walk through the door. I am the queen of exits; they are seamless, they are quick and they are necessary. But it didn't even occur to me to plan an exit strategy with Jay. Didn't pop into my head once. I had fallen asleep in his arms after a night of sex like I have never had before.

Sex with intimacy, of *knowing* the person I was sleeping with, liking, respecting them. And yes, I know what that means and it alarms me even more.

Two more lengths and I need to get home and hope I can escape the markers of him that will now be all over the house, each room holding a memory. I may have to burn the table I do my podcast from.

When I woke this morning I had turned to see him there, watching me in a this-is-how-people-look-at-each-other-after-they've-made-love-in-a-movie kind of way. I think I would have been less terrified if he was there sharpening a knife with a pair of tights over his head. And yet the core of me wanted to roll myself into him even further, lift my lips up and meet his, begin this morning in the same way we had ended last night.

And then the realisation of who I am, how I am flawed, hit home. I cannot follow a path of natural progression; I cannot give this man what he deserves so I made excuses to get him out. The whole thing became worse as I claimed I had work and then realised it was Sunday.

Jay was the perfect gentleman; saw I was flustered, gave me the sweetest kiss and then left me to it. *It* being hiding in my office and then sneaking into the lido to try and swim my fears out and stop me looking at my phone like an anxious teen.

It has always been super-easy for me to compartmentalise my life, to keep home at home, fun at the bar at the bar, my sex life firmly private and anonymous and my work at work. Jay is the first person that has successfully straddled *all* areas of my life and I don't know what to do.

Neither am I unaware that, despite hiding out all day and only coming to the lido this evening when I know he has a shift, that I have looked for him at the end of every length, popping my head out of the water to see if he is here whilst trying to pretend it is just the natural taking of a breath. I have been swimming long enough to know that scanning the outside changing room floors for feet I may recognise is not a normal part of my routine. Neither is scanning the water from the sauna – which looks out through one huge floor-to-ceiling window over the pool – to see if he is here. He is not. And something in me dips in disappointment.

I towel myself off extra hard, self-flagellating punishment. I was feeling rough this morning and haven't really picked up all day. My head is banging and I am weak all over. But then I had explosive, mind-fucking sex three times last night and barely got four hours' sleep. It is no surprise that my stamina is flagging and my body is craving the comfort of a bed.

I sit in the boudoir, pick up the hairdryer and line up the straighteners. It takes a lot of effort to get my hair as I like. Kevin reckons if I applied the discipline to people as harshly as I did my natural state – frizzy, hairy and spotty – then I could have made a fortune as a dominatrix. I think I'll stick with the career I've got, although with the session after Angela tomorrow being Andrew-the-dashing-flower-thief, maybe I should reconsider; flicking a whip around could well be the making of him.

Angela has been doing so well, making great strides with EMDR. It turns out that her traumas in childhood have led to all sorts of issues, one of which explains this need to mother, but to mother without any risk. I'm hoping that as she processes the traumas then it will decrease her anxiety and she may be able to start changing the behaviours she has in place to help her manage it. I don't want to push but I'm hopeful at the end of this she may be able to engage in social settings without the dolls, even if just for very brief moments.

As I turn the dryer on, I suddenly am bent double, my

uterus concertinaing in on itself and forcing my body to go with it.

Oh Jesus, not again. I really am not prepared for this, I thought I'd have a bit longer.

I uncurl my body and knowing another one will hit in a minute I start to do some box breathing to calm myself. And oof, there we go again. I grab the dressing table feeling like a paper fan, those ones you make in school, my insides pulling together in tight folds, stabs of pain as each fold lies on the next.

I reach for the Naproxen kept in my bag and knock some back with a quick glug of the water. It won't take the pain away, but it should stop me bending double. I wonder if it was hormones that made me feel like crying this morning when I kicked Jay out?

I'll be okay, I just need to head off to bed and cocoon myself there for the rest of the night and pray that this month is a gentle one.

Chapter Twenty-Six

'So what do you think? Anything to add?' I ask Chloe, Ellie and Megan. They have stayed behind to talk about two sessions I have delivered, one yesterday and one just now, modelling the roles Lily and I are asking them to take on as peer support.

'You were a bit too quiet like. Shouldn't your job be to push the message that what that girl is putting up with ain't right?'

'Nah, he needs to build trust, make a relationship first, that's what this is about. You can't just come at someone like that if they don't know you. They won't listen to nothin'.'

'Chloe's right, you need to read the room. If I had just met you and then told you what to do, where you were going wrong in life, would you react positively?'

I laugh as Ellie mimes how she would respond to that and we carry on chatting over the plans and good practice. As the girls leave I hear my phone bing. This wellness project is going well so far, the girls have been super responsive, but it is not my work that needs sorting out right now. They say you can't have everything in life, and right now my work life is a big old tick, my health is good, but my love life, let's just say my high has faded slightly.

I've never been one of these people that follow the don't-message-until-Wednesday rules. I believe that if you like someone, you tell them so. But not wanting to push Lily I thought I should wait for her to message me, give her some space. I know this woman and I know the surest way to scare the living breath out of her is to go too hard, too fast.

At the risk of sounding like a twat, once we had met it was as if our souls recognised each other, as if we have been living our lives waiting for this moment. As if we simply had to wait for our brains and our bodies to catch up to this. And our bodies definitely caught up on Saturday night. I have never known a night like it. Our bodies recognised each other then too, I know they did, and now I am waiting to see if Lily's brain has caught up to this at all.

Or at least I waited the whole of Sunday, and then hearing nothing sent her a text this morning. Nothing scary. Just a hello and a hope-you're-okay message.

Friendly.

I have heard nothing.

So now as my phone beeps I grab it, the butterflies rising up in my stomach. This has to be her surely? But my phone has been beeping all day and not once has it been a response from Lily.

Hey Jay, hope you don't mind me reaching out. It's Kevin and I hate to ask but I wondered if you were free and could do me a favour?

Of course, I type back immediately. Odd, but I finish here in a bit and then my evening is more or less free. My only plans are the gym and to see what chaos Dim has caused in my absence. He is furious that I stayed out the other night and has stopped bringing me presents – thank God – and is very definitely sulking. He didn't even bother to feign gratitude as I opened up the super posh tray of cat food I had bought by way of an apology, stalking past me once he had wolfed it down and then shooting me looks of fury from a distance.

Brilliant, thanks. Lily is sick and I promised I'd pick up her click-and-collect grocery order. But there's been an emergency at work. Any chance you can pick it up instead? I'll shoot you the email you need and then if you could drop it round to her that would be crazy helpful.

If she's sick does that explain her not answering? I don't like the thought of her being ill. I can pick up some fizzy vitamin C and echinacea whilst I'm grabbing her groceries, the two things that Sue used to pump into Cassie and me like they were the elixir of life.

And if she wants, I could cook for her. I run through the possibilities in my head of how I can best help as I shoot back a message to Kevin.

No worries at all, send it over and I'll get it sorted.

Thanks, darling. The spare key is under the recycling boxes to the side. If you could let yourself in quietly – she might be sleeping – and then maybe, and I don't want to take the piss, but could you take her up some water and the almonds so they're there?

Okay. Will do. I send the message back and hurl myself into action. As long as I stay silent and don't disturb her, Kevin has given me an opportunity to show how much I care.

Chapter Twenty-Seven

I have had to cancel work and reschedule my clients for next week. I am not even up for getting my hair brushed and clothes on to sit in front of the laptop and zoom them. Currently my top half is a dead ringer for Oscar the Grouch, and down below... well, Carrie at prom springs to mind. On top of which, I can barely move, everything aches and I keep bursting into tears.

I have just sobbed my way through *The Repair Shop* on catch-up and am considering a shower but I simply can't be arsed. I have plates piled up that need seeing to but have not got the energy or inclination to do anything about it.

What's the point? I feel disgusting and I hate everything about my life.

I hate my stupid body.

I hate the fact that everyone thinks I'm so fucking polished and no one really sees me.

I hate the fact that I am so weird that I have never had a

circle of girlfriends from school to stay by my side throughout life.

I hate the fact I *have* to be disciplined when all I want is a fountain of chocolate topped off with a tin of condensed milk and old-fashioned sugar cubes.

Arggghhhhhhh!

I roll over and decide I may as well have a nap, it's easier than a shower and may provide some respite from my stupid self-loathing, self-pitying brain, even if only for ten minutes.

I am just snuggling into my pillows when I hear Kevin coming into the house. Glancing at the clock I realise he is here a good hour earlier than I expected him and before I know it I am sobbing again, this time with gratitude that I have such a good friend. I would kill for some chocolate-covered almonds right now.

I hear him coming up the stairs and manage to gulp some of the tears away, mopping myself up on my duvet cover, gross thing that I am. And then I hurl the covers off (down to my waist) and play dead – it's one of our favourite games – lying there in my full grotty glory. I see the door handle turn very slowly and I close my eyes so I look as lifeless as can be.

The door creaks open and I ready myself for his shrieks of laughter. We've been doing this for so many years but today my room really does look like a crime scene. He's going to love it.

'Lily?'

Shit!

My eyes open immediately.

That is not Kevin's voice, that is Jay's!

What the hell is he doing here?

I grab at my duvet and pull the covers back up and over

me, head included. This man may have seen me in the most intimate way any person can, but this, this is levels above that. I have yesterday's make-up on and I'm wearing an old, stained T-shirt along with my period pants, which are big enough to propel a sailboat across the ocean. This is not lacy, slightly breathless, sexy Lily, this is Lily as no one, NO ONE, is ever allowed to see her bar Kevin.

'Oh wow, you scared me. Are you okay? Kevin asked me to bring these up.' Jay addresses me under my bedding.

Kevin did? I'm going to kill him. I may hang, draw and quarter him first though.

'Okay, thank you,' I squeak from underneath the duvet, whilst rubbing rapidly at my eyes.

'Can I see your face?' he asks as he approaches the bed, sitting down at the end of it, amusement in his voice. I'm glad he finds this funny.

'No.' My answer is short but pertinent.

'Kevin said you were sick, and he's sorry but he had an emergency at work. I've brought your almonds upstairs and some water, what else can I do?'

'Nothing,' I say, still under the duvet, and I remember my knickers on the floor. 'Close your eyes, close them now!'

'Really?'

'Do it!' I sneak a look from under the duvet and I see him there at the end of my bed, eyes scrunched shut and my heart warms for a millisecond. But only a millisecond. As if this man wasn't all over my life as it was, now this is the icing on the cake. I don't have time to dwell on my embarrassment though. 'Keep them like that,' I say as I grab my knickers, wriggle back and shove them under my pillow.

'Right, thank you for the shopping. I am fine. You can go

now,' I say, safely back under my duvet. I have been feeling guilty about not answering his message earlier but now a whole new tumult of embarrassment washes over me.

'Are you sure? Lily, I have a sister, there is nothing I haven't already seen. I could cook you something or we could watch TV or play cards. I'm a whizz with dominoes as you know. Should I go pick some up and come back? I can keep you company for a bit.'

'No, NO! NOOO!!!!' I squeak like a frenzied giant mouse. 'No, just go, please.'

'But...' I don't need to peek to see the confusion on his face, I can hear the hurt in his voice.

'Jay, please. I don't know how else to say it, you shouldn't be here, please just go!' And I hear him get up. I feel him hover over my head, buried as it is under 3 togs of feather, as if he is considering dropping a kiss, and then I hear him walk away and the door shut behind him, and again I cry.

Chapter Twenty-Eight

A piece of paper slides under my door as I turn my hairdryer off and shake my hair out. Normally, having finished my Saturday morning yoga class, I feel pretty zen but today I am still caught up in incandescent fury.

It's lasted quite a long time – over a week and counting.

I scowl as I reach to pick up the note, unfolding it to see an invitation to lunch in the kitchen from Kevin and Dan.

And whilst it may be cute that he is trying to make up for sending Jay over when I was my least polished and most private self, a sandwich is not going to cut it. Frankly he could do all my chores for a year and do so dressed as Patrick Swayze – as Vida Boheme, obviously – and it would not be enough.

I am pondering my rage, my current favourite activity, when my phone bings and I see another message from Jay.

Sorry I can't join you all today, #MakeSureJinxWins! Catch up soon? x

I grimace and scroll up through his other messages since the night we spent together.

All unanswered.

I'm sorry if I upset you. Get well soon and shout if you need anything x

My sister is an actual demon x

Thank you, I had a really special weekend. Hope you are smiling as much as I am xxx

These messages don't help my fury die. They make me panic, feel guilty, confused. Three things I am not fond of. So I go downstairs instead to see what culinary delight awaits me.

'Oh you're going to be so proud of me. We're going to be properly civilised. I went to The Deli and bought food, like healthy food. Look!' Kevin is swooping around the impressively laden table and gestures at some beetroot hummus and a yellow-looking puree. There are three different types of salad and some beautiful pastries, patinaed with sesame seeds. I suck my bad temper in and sit as he pulls me out a chair. He is trying after all.

'Healthy food?'

'I knew you'd be impressed.'

'I am, I never thought I'd see the day you'd willingly buy salad. Never!'

'I would have agreed about Kevin and salad but you know, never say never, always wise to be flexible,' Dan says with a smile.

'Oh and you are very flexible,' Kevin says but not with his usual flirtatious attitude. This is more as if he has to say it because he can't help himself but can't quite make eye contact as he does so.

A shy Kevin? Are my secret hopes for these two true? I want to punch the air, my bad temper momentarily allayed. Kevin *is* crushing on Dan. I am here for this! Now I have to find out if Dan feels the same. I think he reciprocates – why else is he suddenly spending every possible waking moment with Kevin practising romantic duets over the piano, helping him to design and make his outfits? – this could have legs.

'I am.' Dan nods matter-of-factly but *he* doesn't mutter it, *he* holds Kevin's eyes as he speaks. Flirtation alongside statement of fact? Oh, I hope so.

I know I am smirking but I can't help it. I start to scheme to see if I can push these two together more than they already are.

Whilst plotting, I pile my plate with salad and scoop a tortilla chip into some of the beetroot dip.

'Thank you for this,' I say and Kevin beams. 'So what's the plan? Let's sort out what you want to do with regards to your parents. Although I have to say I didn't expect apology lunch first.' I take a bite of the chorizo-and-goat's-cheese-filled pastry and hope Kevin's deli habit overtakes his Deliveroo one.

'Apology lunch?' Kevin snorts, actually snorts, and Dan's eyes grow wide. 'For you? Oh, this is not that. You do not need an apology lunch. A wake-up call, some hard truths maybe, but not an apology lunch.'

'Woah, what do you mean?' I'm fully taken aback. 'You completely overstepped the other day. I felt so humiliated. I always thought I could rely on you to have my back but by sending Jay around you were completely insensitive.'

'Insensitive?' Kevin's eyebrows rise so high they virtually disappear into his hairline.

'Yes, insensitive. You should have found a better solution

than just choosing the most convenient.' I can't believe I'm having to explain this. But instead of nodding in comprehension Kevin's nostrils flare and his eyes bulge, like an over-stimulated horse.

'You needed shopping the other day and I couldn't do it.' His tone is firm; he is calm but speaking through gritted teeth. 'Dan couldn't do it so I arranged for someone else, deliberately chosen because they're someone you seem pretty damn comfortable with. And yes, I did see him leave the other weekend. And yes, whilst you were up there in your Pity Palace I got your food delivered, water and snacks brought to your room, so the way I see it you should be thanking me, not stropping around the house dwelling on how wronged you feel because someone saw you looking human. If anyone deserves an Apology Lunch right now, then it's me.'

Pity Palace? Stropping!

I drop the pastry back on the plate, my mouth open at this unexpected assault. This is unlike Kevin, and I don't understand why he is being like this. I want to challenge this but don't want a full-scale battle.

I limit myself to raised eyebrows and mutter 'unbelievable' at the salad.

It is enough, it seems.

'*Me* unbelievable?' he responds quickly, angrily. I have never heard Kevin this angry before. Ranty, yes, daily, but there is real force to his tone here. I flick a look across to Dan who shrugs his shoulders and gives me a sympathetic smile but isn't lining up behind me. 'Me unbelievable?' he repeats. 'No, not me. Normally yes, but not in this instance. This is on you. You bitch me out for being insensitive but when I messaged Jay earlier to invite him to this Let's-support-Jinx-when-her-parents-are-here meeting, the one we were all doing together, remember? When I texted him, he apologised because he already had plans, added he was happy to still be involved *and* asked how you were. Now Jay is not a man who struggles to communicate so it seems pretty obvious to me if he needs *me* to tell him how *you* are then that man has been texting you, probably ever since he kindly came across town to deliver your shopping...'

I feel my mouth form a mutinous pout. Kevin *never* tells me off. My mind is a whirl and I'm not entirely sure what to say, where to look, how to respond. But that's okay because he clearly has no intention of letting me get a word in.

'So in therapist-speak, Lily, I guess my 'insensitivity' could be what you guys call transference. And, even though I should be focusing on Drag Factor, you need a friend who is not afraid to speak up when you start indulging in your usual bullshit. Ghosting this man is beyond destructive. Jay and you have something special... Don't make that face. I know you're keen or you would never have let him get so close, nor would you have secreted him away from us in the first place. Ghosting...and I notice you don't deny it –' I don't but I do train my eyes down and stab my salad pointedly with my fork so I don't have to see Dan nodding gently '– ghosting a man you respect and trust and don't forget that has *always* been your holy trifecta...' He's right, I have lost count the amount of times I have told clients that love cannot be enough; without trust and without respect the relationship will not flourish.

Before I can consider this revelation, Kevin is bowling a new one at me. 'But even more importantly, a man who is linked to work you have always wanted to do. And Lily, I have known you before you were *Dr* Galbraith and I have watched you flourish and develop through several incarnations, but I have *never*, never seen you make an emotional decision that could negatively impact your work, your clients or your professional reputation.'

Shit.

He's right.

I've been ignoring Jay because I have been so upset about the fact he saw me when I was all grotty and in bed, and because... and I know it's true, I've been feeling vulnerable because we slept together when we probably shouldn't have and I don't know what to do with that now other than ignore it. Okay, I do know, I just don't seem to be able to behave like a healthy adult in this situation.

But I do not look up at Kevin and admit this.

I do not look up and apologise.

Instead, I try and change the conversation.

'Message received.' I try not to look like a truculent teenager at this point but my chin is probably sticking out so far it's about to bang into Dan. 'So, seeing this lunch is meant to be about working out a plan for Drag Factor, maybe we should concentrate on that.' There, nice diversion. Slightly shitty tone but nice diversion.

Then I go and sabotage myself further and launch an attack.

'Although, do you not think that now you're over thirty, well over thirty, and the whole world is familiar with Drag thanks to Ru Paul *and* Taiwan has a reputation for being pretty liberal these days, maybe now would be a good time to tell your parents rather than hiding the truth of who you are from them?' I feel my eyebrows raise as I fix him with a look.

Kevin arches an eyebrow. I know I'm supposed to offer succour and comfort but he started this by saying best friends have a duty to speak straight, to highlight things that need to be said.

'Seriously, you are suggesting to me that my experience with my parents is false, my concerns and fears that I have carried for years are nothing to worry about and that I should turn and face my demons.'

'I'm sure they're not that demonic... Mind you they have given birth to you so maybe...' I do a weighing up movement with my hands, aware that I am being combative, and what would normally have been taken as a joke now has a darker underbelly.

Dan reaches across to Kevin and strokes his arm, a gesture of support that amplifies the fact that I have crossed a line.

Kevin pauses and takes a breath. 'And you are suggesting that I am making a fuss about something, allowing it to shape my life. Constantly running from myself because I am too scared to turn and face a truth from my childhood that may not be true after all? Is that what you're saying, Lily?' Kevin tilts his head to one side, a definite note of challenge in his tone.

I can't blame him. I have deliberately gone in on an uncomfortable issue.

'Woah, woah, let's not get into this now.' Dan removes his hand from Kevin's arm and does the whole lowering hand movement to try and calm us down.

I look across at my best friend and resent his implication here. I know what he is saying. That I shouldn't dare judge him for his reluctance to talk to his parents about his sexuality, his chosen profession, when I myself have never faced my fertility concerns. About the fact that I accepted as a teen that I can't have children and have gone no further with it.

But why would I? Why would I open myself up to the confirmation of the things that give me pain? Hearing when I was eighteen that I would struggle to conceive wasn't easy but it wasn't exactly all-consuming. I hadn't given thought to having children as part of my future life at that point. I was obsessed instead with no longer having thighs that chafed and the fact I had developed rather pretty ankles. I had no idea of how my attitude towards children would change as I aged and now, here in my mid-thirties, it's an issue that I know I should get checked out.

But I don't know if I'm brave enough to dredge all that up again. If I address this successfully, will I be raising my hopes? I don't know if I could handle the disappointment.

Does Kevin think that I don't want to watch children of mine run screeching into the sea as my sister and I did? Does he think I don't want to face the things that I am most scared by? That I have never gone and found out more about my chances of conception because I don't care rather than perhaps caring too much? I don't know myself how many of the choices I make are self-protection or honest desires. And I don't know if I am strong enough to delve into all that yet.

I do know fighting with my best friend isn't the answer though.

I don't know how I have allowed this to escalate.

Kevin is lashing out because I was attacking. It's not up to Dan to defuse this. I reach out for Kevin's hand and whilst he twats about pretending I'm not allowed to hold it, eventually I manage to wind my fingers through his.

'I know what you're saying, I know why, and I'll concede I may need to look at that. As to what I said, I'm sorry. I was being an arse, I got defensive. Of course, you have to do things for you when it is right for you, and it is none of my business. But I guess what I'm saying is that your parents may not be as disappointed or as outraged as you think, and, truth is, the only way you are going to know for sure how they will react is if you have the conversation. They haven't sent you bridal considerations for a while now, they may be more switched on than you realise.'

'She could have a point,' Dan adds gently.

'Hmmm...' It is more of a growl and he untangles his fingers from my hand so that he can bury his face in them. 'I know. I understand what you're saying but the truth is I do not have the bandwidth to cope with the emotional tumult of that conversation, not at the same time as Drag Factor.' He says this through his fingers and then lifts his head and addresses us directly. 'I need to win the regional heat this year. I cannot let Vivicious have her chance in the spotlight again. No way. I want to show how the drag community represents the best of us, not that cheating bitch with no morals. So, can I talk to my parents about who I really am at the same time as facing my insecurities and taking to that stage and showing the whole world that I have got what it takes? No, just no. This lunch –' he waves his hands at the food on the table '– this lunch is not to discuss how I can get my parents to accept me as I am...' He pauses and takes a breath. Normally this would be massively over-dramatised but it's quite clear to both of us that Kevin is genuinely feeling all tangled up right now because of this. I reach across the table again to reassure him he is loved but before I can do so,

Dan has leaned over and pulled him into his chest. I withdraw my hand and watch as Dan holds my oldest and best friend tight and as Kevin takes a deep breath before looking up at Dan and nodding.

'Shall we go back and make a plan to help you with Drag Factor week? Like we were meant to? Ignore everything I said. I was lashing out because I didn't like what you had to say. I'm sorry. I was reacting rather than thinking and I am grateful for all the help you give when I'm feeling like shit. Tell me how I can help.'

Kevin purses his mouth and fixes me with a severe look.

'You do exactly what I say and you won't ever question how I handle my coming out again?'

I nod solemnly.

'Ever?' he reiterates.

'Ever,' I state. And I mean it.

'In all seriousness, this is the plan so far... I'll pick them up from the airport on the Friday and give them dinner super early on Friday night and play adoring son for a bit,' Kevin says.

'You *are* an adoring son. You are a very good son. This visit is an outlier – had it been any other week they would have had your full attention.' It's true, no one else sees that Kevin calls his parents every week and chats to them at length, finding out all about their lives whilst somehow managing not to give anything away about his own. I see the effort he goes to to get the most perfect present for them, every birthday and each Christmas. And each year he takes time to make them something. I am not convinced either of them know that the beautiful hand-crafted gifts they get each year have been made by their son and showcase his prowess on the sewing machine.

'Okay, so we'll feed them and remind them that I can't see them on Saturday and that you and Jay will...'

'Woah.'

'You do exactly what I say,' Kevin reminds me.

It's my turn to growl.

'Pick them up from the hotel on the Saturday, wear them out and then tie them up – not literally, obviously, I have enough drama in my life without having to picture that image – tie them up with things to do, and in time for you to sprint back to Chrysalis. I know Dan is helping me with the practical side of things...'

'Music, costume, staging, choreography...' Dan ticks off things on his fingers and they exchange another sweet little side smile.

'Yes, all that. But Lily, then you get yourself back to the club so you can help hype me on stage. I can't do this without you there. You're like my lucky pants but in ... you know ... lady form.'

I grin across at him, my ill-feeling towards him assuaged by the fact he needs me there. We've been friends too long for me to continue to hold a grudge about his interfering.

'It's a deal.'

'Good!' Kevin replies. 'Now whether Jay is involved or not is up to you. It is not my job to rebuild your burned bridges. But you need to get over yourself, smooth out any awkwardness and make sure you and he have a decent working relationship. So I am going to text him and tell him I'm keen for him to be there.'

I wince, I can't help it. Kevin picks up his phone and sends a message. There is still a large chunk of me that wants to rip it out of his hand and scream no... but he is right, I have been a nightmare this last week and usually, even with crazy hormones shooting around, I have a much better grasp, much more self-control. Plus, I do need to work with Jay, so I need to grow up pretty damn quick.

Kevin finishes tapping on the screen, shoots me a very satisfied-looking smile and says, 'You're welcome!'

God help me.

Chapter Twenty-Nine

I flick open the cap of my bottle and take a long glug of water before passing it to Henri who nods in thanks and takes a long draught. We are all sat splayed across the grass and breathing fast, bar Mo who sits grinning at us and looking as fresh as dawn.

We've been playing football together since secondary school, but Mo has been playing professionally for ten plus years now and when he can join us he makes us work hard!

Today was one of those days.

My legs may burst into flame at any minute.

I stretch my hamstrings out and see that Marcus is doing the same, whilst Luke and Keith are both just lying on the grass, knees raised, their breathing indicating they may be giving birth. Luke is holding his side and Henri is sitting up rubbing his calf. All of us work out but none of us are as fit as we used to be.

'Yo, Jay. So I saw Jess out the other night, she's single again,' Mo says. Everyone laughs.

'Uh-huh.' I nod. I dated Jess a few years ago and she's pretty awesome, strong, independent, kind.

'She said to say hi.' Mo winks. 'Even said she wouldn't mind giving it another go. Said I'd pass it on.'

'All respect to her, she's a good woman, but no, she's not for me.'

'Haven't you heard, Mo,' shouts Marcus, 'our boy ain't dating at the moment.'

Another burst of laughter, from everyone, greets this. I look around at them all. 'Thanks, boys, thanks a lot.' More laughter.

'Seriously? You not got anyone? I don't think that's been a thing since we were twelve. Was it twelve?' Henri says.

'Nah, ten at least, I reckon. This man ain't never not had a girlfriend. He had started whilst we were still swapping Digimon cards,' Luke added.

'Thanks. Thanks for that.' I nod, place my hand on my chest and do a faux bow before lifting an imaginary cup.

'Cassie's got him on a short leash. She's stepped in and told him he needs to stop searching for a wifey and spend some time on his own,' Marcus tells everyone.

'Not exactly what's going on,' I answer quickly, scrunching up my nose to reinforce the point that Marcus, as ever, is chatting shit.

'Yeah, what have I got wrong then?' Marcus sits up and looks across at me. I shrug, I share most things with the boys but I'm not going to start talking to them about Cass and Jas. Cass would never forgive me. Especially if she goes back to work at Mama K's. I love Marcus like a brother but discretion is not one of his qualities. Neither is silence. He likes an audience and has the filter of an overactive seven-year-old.

'Not much.' I decide that rolling over has to be the easiest way after all.

'So you're not dating at all? How long has that been?' Luke asks.

I shrug again. 'Been a while.' I cast my mind back to the family zoom when I had made the initial promise. That has to have been two months ago at least.

'No women at all?' Luke asks. I don't know why they're having so much difficulty understanding this.

'He's not saying no women, *Cass* is saying no women –' I shoot lasers at Marcus and he laughs and carries on '– but you should have seen the gal he came into Mama's with a few weeks ago. She was fine. Like Hollywood, no-filter-needed fine.'

'That was work,' I say brusquely.

'Yeah, so you both said, but I'm telling you the chemistry these two had was lighting up the place.'

I roll my eyes and let out a sigh. I might not be able to talk to them about Cass but I really could do with speaking about Lily. I still haven't told my sister about it all yet and there is so much shit spinning around in my head with this I could do with talking it out. I have spent the last week convinced I have ruined everything, and it hasn't been helped by getting a message from Jinx earlier inviting me to a planning lunch. I was more than slightly relieved that I had footy and a ready-made excuse not to force myself into yet another situation with Lily. Jinx's last invite didn't exactly pan out well.

I've given my word I'll help with the #MakeSureJinxWins plan and I will but I really don't need things to take an even worse turn with Lily. I knew she needed space after our night together but there's space and then there's silent, never-ending depths of far-out galaxies, and with her not even returning my messages now, that's where I feel she's banished me to.

I miss her.

I miss the sparky, slightly flirty banter we used to have and I've spent the best part of the last fortnight working out how to get it back.

But it may never happen.

This woman has so many sides to her and she'd been softening around the edges the more and more time I spent with her. Having her talk to me so frankly about her past felt like a bit of an honour to be honest. I believed her when she said she had never told anyone else about what that bastard had done to her in school. And it made me want to wrap her up and chip away at all the insecurities that she still carries.

After telling me about her PCOS, I went away and read about it, learned that her periods have always been a nightmare, and yet I hadn't joined up all the dots until I stood in her room.

I have seen so many sides of Lily now and it's hard to believe that the Lily with her head on my chest on the night of the ledge was once intimidating to me.

It's also hard to deal with the fact that it was a one-off.

'Yo, Jay!'

'Eh?' I say, turning my attention back to the boys.

'You were absent there for a bit. You okay?'

'He's thinking of that girl, I'm telling you. *I'm* thinking of that girl and I don't even know her.'

'That's cos you're perverted man,' Mo shoots back quick as a flash, shaking his head.

'Unnecessarily harsh,' Marcus responds.

'Hmmm,' we all say in unison. Keith scratches his chin, taking us back to the playground.

'Cheeky fuckers. But... am I right?' Marcus asks.

'Mmm, kind of,' I grudgingly admit.

Luke has shot up into a seated position and says, 'I've never seen you look so down over a girl before, and we remember Shani in Year Seven. What's going on?'

'Honestly, I'm not sure. She's not...er...she's not answering my messages.'

'You've been ghosted, oh maaaann! Nah. Can you believe it, someone's ghosted our boy. Never thought I'd see the day.' Marcus slaps his thigh.

'Yeah, thanks for that.'

'Happens to the best of us.' It doesn't. It just happens to Marcus more than most.

'Come on, let's go grab a pint. That'll sort you out. Who's coming?' Everyone bar Mo and me jump to their feet at Marcus' suggestion.

'Nah, I'll catch you in a bit though,' I say and they all drift off, leaving me and Mo on the pitch.

'So what's actually going on?' Mo says. He has always been the most insightful of my friends.

'Mate, I don't know.'

'You like her?'

'I really do, like really do.' I take another sip of water.

'And is that because she's not falling into your arms, making you fight for her? Is this a basic psychology thing, man?'

'I've thought about that, I have. I really don't think it's that. I think I've just found my person. There's something about her. And yes, she looks great but it's more than that, she could have

233

three heads and five noses, but I don't think it would change how I feel when I'm with her.'

'And how's that?'

'At peace. Or at least I did. It feels right. It's intangible, I can't put it into words. I just know that I want to spend every waking moment with her and all the asleep ones too.'

'I've never heard you say that before.'

'I've never said it, I don't think. I can't see why I would, I've never felt like this before. Sure, I've been in love but I think I've always been caught up with the practicalities, you know. The belief that I could make a life with someone and want to go and do that...until I don't. You know what I'm like. But this, this is completely different. This is a feeling, something I know to be true, and all the things I worried about before, none of that matters because with Lily that need to be together trumps anything else I've ever felt. I'd do anything for her. What I want comes second place. Seriously, man, all I care about is making her life better.'

'You've got it bad. She's not returning your calls?'

'She's not returning my messages. I haven't called because I know her, Mo, and if she doesn't want to return my messages then how is me bounding in with direct calls going to do anything but alienate her?'

'Fair. So what are you going to do? Just suck it up and not say anything?'

'Honestly, I don't know. We're meant to be working together on some projects, one for the youth club and one helping out her best mate, so I'm thinking I just need to bide my time, coax her out in those situations. If I push, I'll scare her more than she's scared already.'

'And what does your sister say?'

'Hmmm, I haven't actually properly told her yet. We're catching up tomorrow so I thought I'd speak to her then. I need to speak to her before I do anything else. I have no idea what she's going to say. As much as the boys are joking, I did promise her I'd stay single for six months and it's important to do that. I really can't go into the whys...'

Mo nods. He understands the need not to share every last thing, and that's one of the reasons I have always respected him.

'So, you're going speak to Cass, you're speaking to me, but the only person you're not chatting to about this is Lily? And she's the only person who can help you resolve it. Is that about right?'

'Yeah, I guess so.'

'Look, man, I don't know the full situation and I admire you respecting her need for space. In the crazy world we live in everyone is all about speaking your truth and honestly, sometimes I think your truth should take a back seat and respect the needs of those around you, but in this case, in this case I think you need to speak out. You need to say how you feel and see what happens, and it may not pan out your way and that's gonna sting but you'll be all right. The one thing I do know is that Lily is entitled to have all the information and that includes you being honest about how you feel and see where she takes it. And if she wants to carry on blocking you out, so be it. But at least you know you've done your best and know that you couldn't have done any more. Cos the one thing you don't want hanging over your head is that if-I-had-only feeling. Yeah, she's ignoring you and normally I would say leave it. That in itself is a screaming loud message but if your work overlaps with hers, then it needs sorting. You need to speak to her, knowing that you can't control how she responds but you can take charge of what you say.'

'It's not that simple.'

'Mate, it's *always* that simple. Anything other than honesty, empathetic honesty, is fear-based. You and I, we've always felt the same about shit and I don't think this is any different. You've never been a coward, Jay, and you've never been frightened to veer from the pack. I get that you're scared but if you feel this strongly, you need resolution. Talk to Cass first if you really need to and then take some action, mate, because you're going to eat yourself up from the inside out else. I was terrified when I put it on the line for Sara, terrified. It's part of the process. Love is never easy, and you've always had it easy in that arena, now you need to step up and take the hard knocks.'

Mo stands up and shakes himself out. I get up too.

'You don't think it's selfish of me, if I know she doesn't want to talk, to go and push myself in?'

'I know you, you ain't never going to push yourself in insensitively. So yeah, talk to her and then if her answer is a hard no, then back the fuck off. As long as you don't get weird or stalky then asking once? I reckon that's the right thing to do. For the both of you. Let's go get that drink!'

Chapter Thirty

'Thank you so much for this,' Cass turns to me and says as I kneel next to her, painting backdrops in the local community centre. She has a little dollop of paint on the side of her face and I can't help myself as I grin at her words and then lunge forward and add a quick dollop of sand-coloured paint on her other cheek. 'Oi!'

'Just evening you up,' I say with as much innocence as I can muster. She scowls and I raise my hands in a 'stop' gesture as she looks at me, devilment in her eyes.

I brace myself for war.

She takes her brush and prepares to flick it at me, only pausing as we hear Olive, the woman who runs the community choir, enter the hall. She is wearing red leather trousers and the loudest neon yellow T-shirt I have ever seen, with a picture of the community centre on. It's not exactly an outstanding architectural beauty, more reminiscent of several old portakabins glued together with a flour and water mix.

'Hello, you two.' She approaches us and Cassie lowers her

paintbrush and shoots me an I'm-going-to-get-you-later look. I have had millions of these in my time. All of them terrifying. She's probably going to try and pin me down and pour buckets of paint over my head but to be fair I knew this before I turned up.

Truth is it's a welcome distraction. I must confess today about breaking my word and I'm dreading it. The knowledge has been hovering like a thundercloud on Carnival Day and I need to get it done. I had wanted to clarify things with Lily so they were straight in my head before I said anything to Cass, but Lily's prolonged silence means I can guess where she stands – as far away from me as possible – and I want to own up to Cass. Get it out of the way and accept any punishment she metes out.

I can't regret my night with Lily.

Although Mo's words from the other day have been spiralling around my head too, and he may be right, maybe for my own sanity I need to talk to Lily properly before I give up – but either way the first thing to do is tell Cass the truth. I can still demonstrate change is good and she may have some helpful insight. At this point I'm willing to listen to any and all advice. I'm biding my time for the right moment, even though I'm convinced she is going to crow triumphantly, leave me to paint the scenery and sprint to Gretna Green with Jasmine.

'What a picture you two make. You've always been so close.' Olive drops a kiss on my head and then Cass's and we both smile up at her as if butter wouldn't melt. Cass even makes her eyes extra wide and bats her lashes. I don't know how she manages to do that and how it fools people but she's been doing it successfully for years now.

'I wish my two were more like you,' Olive says warmly.

Her two are forty-year-old twins that both still live at home and count the cornflakes she pours for them every morning just in case one has more than the other. How she has put up with them for so long I do not know. But with those two she has the patience of a saint. A saint in dire need of two strongly worded eviction notices.

'Oh, you don't, Olive. Honestly my brother is a monster. Look, look!' Cass gestures to her paint-smeared cheek and shakes her head as if there is nothing to be done about me.

'You little ratbag,' Olive says to me before turning back to Cass. 'Mind you, look at him coming and helping you.' It's my turn to nod and smile as if I have been escorted to earth by winged angels.

Their heavenly chorus interrupted as Cass snorts.

Olive doesn't seem to notice and continues to speak and pat both of us on the shoulder. 'Now you must think of some way in which we can help you for doing this. You always make our scenery look so great, it has such an effect on morale. Oh, look there's Eric.' Olive darts off to welcome the caretaker and the cast members filing in behind him, all in the same T-shirt as hers.

I am safe from Cass's revenge for a little while. She's no fool, she won't attack me in front of an audience, and I settle back to paint in a clay jar as she is detailing a pyramid in the background.

I need to broach the broken vow, but Olive has her cast doing star jumps at the end of the hall and I don't really want to discuss the fact I have had sex recently in front of them.

I have learned that the older generations are adept at being unable to hear almost anything apart from gossip. At which point their ears suddenly develop the hearing capability of a bat. Of a cauldron of bats. And I know if I start talking about my recent sexploits that knowledge will be beamed straight to Malcolm and Sue's phone, no doubt with added graphic hyperbole. Eric the caretaker already looks like he's about to have a heart attack from the five star jumps Olive has just made him do. I don't want to push him over the edge.

Ever psychic, Cass wiggles her eyebrows and very lightly gestures towards Eric. I am not the only one afraid for the man's life. I nod and grimace.

Olive looks like a tiny mouse but one with soft, soft white hair, a crochet bag on her arm and a selection of clothes that would put Dame Edna to shame. She may have no control whatsoever over her overgrown twin babies but marshals this lot in here as if she were running the KGB at the height of the Cold War.

'Hup two hup two.' The star-jumps have stopped and now they are following her as she does some kind of high knees up run, straight out of the hall door and out onto the large playing field out the back. This may be my chance to tell Cass, get it over and done with and face the consequences.

'They are funny. I do love Olive but promise me now, Jay, *promise* me you will never let me sign up for that madness.' She jerks her paintbrush in the direction of the cast whom we can now see through the window stretching up and then touching their toes at an alarming speed. It's a justified fear. Olive has been trying to recruit us from the minute we wandered into Malcolm and Sue's house, trepidatious about what this new foster placement would bring.

'I promise but um... that does bring me onto something that I need to talk to you about, Cass.' She can tell from my tone that I am serious and carefully places her paintbrush across the pot and swivels to face me, crossing her legs once she is in place. I put my paintbrush down too and adopt the same position.

'I don't know how to even begin to say this.' Weak but honest. I take a deep breath. 'I genuinely can't believe I'm saying this, but that vow I made, that promise... Umm... l feel dreadful because I have reneged on it and I really, truly didn't think there was any way that was going to happen.'

Cass shrugs her shoulders and scrunches her face up into that triumphant I-told-you-so expression that she was born knowing how to do. Then a quick flash of panic crosses her face 'Oh my God, you haven't got back together with Teresa, have you?'

'No!'

'Or Juniper? Ani?

'As if!' I say.

'Okay then, oh, or Beth?'

'Seriously? She married that Nathan three months ago. Have there been any of my girlfriends you've liked?'

'Stella was okay,' she smirks. 'I had forgotten about Nathan though. Beth would have dragged anything up the aisle.'

'Thanks.'

Cass giggles. 'Well then have you...?' She pauses. 'Oh. My. God. You and Lily. You and The Love Doctor. Be still, my heart. Are you dating Lily now? Has that happened?' She starts punching her arms up in the air one at a time and the triumph on her face now is tenfold what it was a second or two ago.

'Um...' I hadn't expected this reaction. 'We're not dating, we're just staying friends but you know, your birthday night...and I promised I'd remain celibate for six months and I barely made two and ah shit, Cass, I just..'

My speech is interrupted as we hear Olive bellow outside, 'No slacking, come on. Twenty more!'

'I wanted to show you change is possible and not something to be scared of and I've fucked that up pretty badly.'

'I know that change is possible, you daft sod, and often necessary. Seriously! I'm not four. The main thing here is that you may have fucked your plan badly but you know as long as you didn't you-know-what Lily badly, we're all good. That, I can't be having.'

'You're so gross!'

'And yet you love me.' She leans over, putting both her hands on the floor and sticks her tongue out at me like a rabid puppy before sitting up again.

'I do. And I completely understand that you have crowing rights for millennia over this.'

She grins and shuffles forward to get closer to me. 'Yup, but skip all that. I want more details...'

I fix her with a no-way-in-hell look and it's her turn to make oh-gross noises.

'I didn't mean like that,' she says, after a highly exaggerated faux-gag. 'You said you're not dating. That, I want to know more about that.'

'Nah. It's embarrassing but full disclosure –' I hold up my hands '– she's not responding to my messages. So I'm guessing that's a clear sign that she does not want to know. So it just has to be a one-night thing.'

'I don't really know what to say about that. I mean, rude, but also shout out for the gal who knows her own mind. Bet that's never happened before.'

'Seriously, is that all anyone is thinking?'

'Why, who else knows?'

'I had footy the other day.'

'And you told that bunch of morons before you told me?'

'Nah, not strictly. I chatted to Mo a bit.'

'Ah, that's okay. Mo speaks sense. What did he have to say?'

'Yeah, he said normally if someone's not answering your messages then you should leave them be but because we're scheduled to work together and because I feel pretty strongly about her then I need to step up and try and talk it out, just once, but talk it out. '

'See, like I said, the man has wisdom. But back to the vow thing, it was you that pushed the staying celibate for six months thing, I never said you had to be celibate. All I said was that you had to avoid a relationship and that I didn't believe you'd be able to maintain celibacy.'

'Yeah, I failed at that. I did try.'

'Look, you're not understanding, although I'm relieved I don't have to make a banner. You're sitting there with a hangdog face as if you've just emptied my fridge, sold my house and killed my kitten...'

'A nuclear bomb couldn't kill your kitten,' I say, 'although it would do considerably less damage.'

She rolls her eyes. 'But actually you haven't done anything to upset me. If I'm hearing right you've just had a one-night stand, which I believe I recommended.'

'Well, yes, if you're going to look at it that way. Does that mean I'm off the hook for this...?' I swing my arm around at all the painting we need to do. I may as well push it a little bit. She's been very reasonable so far, and whilst we may have almost finished Potiphar's house, there is the prison scenery to be started yet.

'Not a chance in hell. Oh no, brother of mine, you have to do *all* of this now without a word of complaint but –' she holds her hand up before I can say a word '– but because I am a good and loving sister, I shall help you. It can be a joint project.'

'I don't have to do it all alone?'

'We want them to have recognisable scenery, don't we?' she teases.

I chance my arm. 'Is everything all right at home?' I ask. She's been moaning about doing this from the minute Sue asked her so whilst I'm relieved I've not been stuck with it all I'm wondering what has prompted this sudden sibling generosity. Regardless of what she says, she could now be skipping out of here and leaving it all to me.

Her eyes cloud over just for a minute, and she tugs at the bottom of her sleeves for a bit before looking up and meeting my eye. 'Yeah, all good, but I don't want to talk about me. Let's talk about you.'

'Please let's not.'

'Oh, oh, I think you owe me that at least. Let's talk about Lily and about how my initial one-nighters-only recommendation is about to change. I enjoyed getting to know her at the bar, she's not what I imagined at all.'

'Why were you imagining her in the first place?'

'Well, you know, I've been listening to the podcast. You did tell me to. More than once.' She tugs at her sleeves again.

'You have?'

'Yup'

'Okay.'

'Uhhuh.'

'And?'

'Yeah, I really like her. She covers a wide range of topics, doesn't she?'

'Right?'

'Last night alone I listened to *How do I choose between two men*, *I hate my wife's son*, and *Food Play and the importance of a big bath or wet room*. You didn't cover her with lard and roll her in pistachios, did you? I mean she's an open-minded kinda girl.'

'You're gross.'

'Oh my God! You did.'

'No, I didn't, you tit. We didn't. Obviously not.'

'So just like regular sex?'

'Do other people's sisters ask them for this much detail? I'm fairly sure they don't.'

'Answer the question!'

'Freak!'

'Me or you?'

'Oh, for God's sake. Regular sex as in nothing kinky but at the same time...' I pause.

'Oh my God, let me guess, it was magical.'

'Why are you taking the piss? I didn't say that. That's not something I say.'

'True, but I had a feeling. So you've had a one-night stand? Tick. You've also fallen in love, haven't you? Not so tick.'

'Not so tick? What's that even... You know what, I can take that. That's better than a giant cross or big black mark.'

'Ah well, the only reason you haven't got that just yet is because I like Lily. I *really* like Lily and I would have been furious if you had broken the rules and got all cow-eyed over some other girl but with Lily I can only approve. So much so, that I will help you convince her that she needs you romantically in her life. Women know women.' She waggles her eyebrows.

'Hmmm, I don't think anyone is going to manage to do that. Can't even get her to pick up her phone right now. But listen to this, Cass – when I'm with Lily I'm not sitting there making plans for the perfect future, working out how we can get a house here, have kids at such and such a point and then maybe move to a bigger house. I'm not doing any of that because honestly, for the first time ever in my life, it doesn't feel important.'

'Oh yes. Oh yes. Okay, so what do you think about when you're with Lily?'

'I don't know if I think, to be honest...'

'Hahahaha.'

'Oh stop it. I just feel...'

'Hahahahaha.'

'Nope, listen.'

'Okay, I will.' She rocks forward from the leant-back position she had taken as she laughed.

'What I'm trying to say is when I'm with Lily I don't think, I just feel. I just feel that everything's right, that that is where I am meant to be, that we work together. You know. I don't want to be some hideous cliché but she gets me, I get her. We have all these differences and none of that matters, we fit. We fit right. And honestly, I don't know that I have ever, ever felt that before, that sense of belonging, you know?' Cass smiles at me, but a silent smile and I guess that's her way of saying she understands.

'So yep, right now, I am a little bit lost. It's clear she doesn't want to speak to me so I think it's unlikely we're ever going to be a thing. If all I can be is her friend, then I'll take that. I even... I told her about Dad, you know.'

Cass lays her hand on my arm and I know with that sentence alone I have managed to convey the strength of my feelings towards Lily.

'So yes, Lily and I slept together...' I am looking out of the window aware that Olive's enforced exercises seem to be winding down so I had better get a move on. I can sense that Cass is moving slightly to the side of me but I am caught in a flash of memory of that Saturday night when Lily and I slept together and she lay her head on me and gently moved her lips to mine; and the feeling I had, that feeling that the world had stopped and nothing else had mattered.

'...but I can't see it going any further. Although I should warn you I'm going to do what Mo says and give it one last go. And I do feel like shit for not quite keeping my vow but am very grateful you've called exceptional circumstances and have let me off having a very, very black mark.'

I turn my head again and refocus on Cass, who is suddenly very close to my face, hands behind her back and a look of glee on her face that is alarming.

Then quick as a flash her arms shoot out and before I can move she has painted a cross all across my face and is laughing like a hyena.

'Not a black mark but a very definite sandy-coloured one,' she shrieks as Olive and her worn-out cast re-enter the hall.

I sit alongside Cass finding it hard to believe that has just happened. Not the giant paint mark slashed across my face, that was inevitable, but the fact she is not fussed in the slightest about me breaking my word. Instead, she seems pretty happy that Lily and I have had a moment. Several moments, a fair few hours and possibly the most romantic night of my life. She didn't even dissuade me from trying to talk to Lily about maybe moving things forward. In fact, she is humming 'Love Is in the Air' and keeps throwing me cheeky grins as we return to our painting.

Olive is back in the hall, congratulating her troops on their physical prowess and telling them that now they have warmed their bodies up they need to do the same for their voices but are allowed a sip or two of water each first. A queue forms near the tap and there is an awful lot of good-natured huffing and puffing as I brace myself for Joseph tunes.

Cass's phone rings and it is a new ringtone, 'Love The Way You Lie'. Cass's ringtones are always Rihanna. Queen RiRi is her absolute idol, was her crush from the age of ten and her life coach. I wonder about the change of ringtone from 'Only Girl' and watch as she grimaces when she hears the tune. I've never seen her grimace at RiRi before.

'Hello, love,' she says brightly into the mouthpiece. 'Aha... uhuh.... Yep, all day...why? I've got so much to do.'

Olive starts shouting at her little gang, making them do a warm-up exercise that sounds like they're murdering frogs.

'Yup, who? Jay's helping me out. And the cast are here rehearsing. What? Of course it is. ...right.' She turns and snaps a photo of me on her phone and then taps at the screen.

'What the?' I mouth.

She shakes her head and carries on speaking to the mouthpiece. 'Yes....yes...I promise. I said I would. Yes, I will. Of course I will. I gave you my word, okay, then. Okay. Love you too.' She hangs up the call and looks at me and pastes a fake smile on her face and rolls her eyes.

'Honestly, can't live with them, can't live without them.' I move towards her to give her a cuddle but she shrugs me off. 'Come on, let's get this done. I need to be home in a bit.'

'Okay,' I say. I don't push her. I don't need to. I can sense she's getting closer to confiding in me and if nothing else listening to Lily's podcast is a real step forward. Changing Jas's ringtone seems like a mini revolution, a step towards the Cass I have always known.

I pick up the paintbrush again, aware that Olive has marshalled her troops into neat lines and is gesturing at Ellen to take her position at the piano in the corner of the room.

'Okay and at the ready, let's warm up those vocal cords.' Olive is standing in front of the lines barking like a sergeant-at-arms. I brace myself for 'Any Dream Will Do' and am shocked to hear the strains of 'Sexual Revolution' filling the room.

Bloody hell. I pause my painting and look out across the room to the group of thirty-odd men and women all in their matching T-shirts, bellowing the hell out of it. They are giving it their all and it is contagious, I shoot a look across at Cass and see she too is dancing as she paints.

I grab my phone, hit record and then send the video to Lily. This not only works as an ice-breaker but genuinely could be exactly what Jinx is looking for!

Chapter Thirty-One

I'm scrolling through my phone after seeing Angela when it pings with a message from Jay and my heart does some kind of weird pitter-patter of excitement. It's either that or a minor myocardial infarction.

No! This is not supposed to happen. I should be feeling guilt not heart-flips.

I was ignoring him resolutely but my fight with Kevin made me step back and look at myself.

And I have been a bitch.

Jay has been honest, open and done nothing other than try and help. I've allowed my vulnerabilities to dictate behaviour and completely overreacted. Me ignoring Jay has not been adult me, it has been damaged panicked child me and she is not in charge any more.

At least I didn't think she was.

I understand that emotional armour has a role to play and is there as a conditioned response. But my behaviour shows that my armour hasn't softened over time but is battle-ready and sharpened, harming people that I really don't want to hurt.

And the bewildering thing is that with Jay, if I strip out my emotionally damaged muscle memory, I am not one hundred per cent sure of *what* I want.

My excitement over receiving this text is disconcerting.

I was hoping after the sex – and the immediate post-coitus high – my excitement when I see Jay's name, when I think of him, picture his face, his arms...oh shit...see, point proven... I *was* hoping all of that would diminish once we had sex.

Diminish. Dissipate. Disappear, ideally. The itch having been scratched. That is usually what happens to me. The act of the act means the sexual tension burns out, curiosity (and everything else) sated.

But the truth is, I have never really had sex like that before.

Don't get me wrong. I am The Love Doctor. I dole out sexual advice on a daily basis and have experienced some truly amazing, wall-banging, bed-rocking, scream-inducing sex in the past.

Jay and I are something completely different and instead of it allowing me to smile and move on, it feels a little bit like I am caught up, that walking away is hard to do now. He is constantly in my head, has been really since we met, and instead of getting rid of him, sleeping with him has led to some kind of invisible string pulling at me, tying me even tighter to Jay.

That is the exact opposite of what I need to happen.

And me flailing about, lashing out like a powerless child, has been a demonstration of how out of control I feel.

I would like to speak to Kevin more. He blindsided me the other day. But now I've thought about it, can acknowledge he was right and that I shouldn't be ignoring Jay, I need him to say something that will stop me getting the jitters every time my phone beeps and I am hurtled back to a night of tangled sheets, sweaty limbs and whispered words.

Talking of which, what *has* Jay sent me? It appears to be a group of people, most of them of retirement age dressed in the most garish T-shirts I have ever seen. One has customised hers and it is dripping with added feathers, and she is wearing a cork hat – I kid you not – and gyrating her hips like Elvis.

Why is he send— Oh wow! I turn up the volume of my phone and it all becomes clear. Do you know what, this is indeed a rare find. This could actually work. The man is a genius. I need to hunt Kevin down. He has been missing recently, off with Dan all hours and often not coming home at all, and I haven't seen him since our fight. But I know he feels strongly that his Drag Factor entry is lacking something, needs more.

I'm happy that he has found someone who understands all of his foibles and has the practical skills to help him in the run-up to Drag Factor. My lack of dressmaking skills and inability to play or read music have been a frequent cause of distress to Kevin so to find someone passionate about both has been a huge bit of luck. And saves me from having Kevin hurl insults at me because I don't know anything about seam allowances or the correct way to pin. I shall hunt him down tonight and show him this video. This could be exactly what he needs to 'lift' his entry.

My buzzer goes and startles me; I have no more clients scheduled. What if it's Jay? What if he has come to tell me in person that ignoring him is Grade-A shitty behaviour? What if I let him in and lose all self-control and before we know it we are sinking onto the sofa, the two of us entwined and...Oh God! What if I let him in and he tells me I am a loathsome human being who should be ashamed of herself and he doesn't want anything further to do with me? I find myself putting my phone on the table, the screen facedown. Then I pick the phone up and put it behind a cushion.

What am I doing? I pop it back on my desk and go to answer the door. It'll just be a parcel or something, a wrong address, it's not going to be Jay. He has clearly just sent me this video so he must be at... I go back for my phone and bring the video up again. He's at a community centre that's over the other side of the city.

The buzzer goes again but this time it's not one polite buzz but lots of quick, staccato buzzes, insistent. Whoever it is, they're impatient.

Heading to the door, I glance in the mirror to check my outward appearance is no reflection of the flustering I feel inside.

I take a deep breath and pull the door open. Another quick fantasy plays though my mind. Jay is on the other side of the door in nothing but his swimming trunks and has come to tell me that he can't stop thinking about me and then as I see his eyes, his face, his chest, I pull him into the building, drag him up the stairs and... Oh, stop now! Stop!

I pull open the door, half of me keen to re-enact this fantasy, half of me terrified in case it really is him and I'm either going to have to use all my powers of restraint or defend the indefensible.

'Oh my God, what were you doing in there?' Kevin pants as I open the door and he pushes his way in. Relief soars through me followed by a stab of disappointment. No lurid office-based fantasy for the end of my working day after all.

But he is a picture all by himself. He is dressed in the most amazing gown, although it's not a gown, more a half-sewn sheath, made of a gold, sort of bronze, fabric that shimmers and changes shade with every movement. Not that movement is advised, because it has a central slit so high that if he moves a millimetre there is a chance I'll get to see all the way up to his navel. It is very tight and one arm is flapping open, not having been sewn yet.

'I was coming,' I answer. 'There's no need to ring the buzzer like—'

'Like, like, like. Don't talk to me about liking anything right now. My world is falling apart.'

I am trying not to stare but besides the beautiful gown, Kevin has on a blonde Dolly Parton wig that he clearly hasn't fixed in place with his usual adhesive, it is more than a little lopsided and he hasn't made his face up. Neither is he sporting glamazon heels; instead he is in a pair of old trainers that I thought he had thrown out months ago. I have seen Kevin in many, many states over the years but I have *never* known him to set foot out of the house in such a fabulous gown without putting the whole package together. I try and distract him...

'You're looking amazing. I've not seen that dress before. Have you and Dan...'

At the mention of Dan Kevin starts to wail, managing to choke out, 'My world is falling apart and you want to talk fashion?'

'Your world can't be falling apart. I've got you. Come, tell me what has happened.'

'Dan has run off and left me.'

255

'I'm sure that's not the case.'

'It is. It is.' He flaps his arms in an attempt to make me realise how serious it is. 'Owww. Oww.' He starts pulling at his dress and then lets out an exclamation of triumph and waves a pin in the air at me. 'See, first he pierces my body and now he is trashing my heart. I knew I shouldn't have let this happen. I knew it.'

'Tell me what's happened. What is Dan doing? Shh shh.' I can't imagine Dan ever doing anyone any harm but Kevin is truly in a state. I take the pins, sit him on the sofa and then cradle his head against my tummy as I stand there, stroking his hair.

Kevin starts to sob into my belly and I hold him there for a bit until his sobbing dissipates, when I move to the side and sit down next to him on the couch.

'Now, now, tell me what's happening. Let me help you if I can.'

'We were having what was meant to be the final fitting.'

'And it looks beautiful.'

'It may look beautiful but I am full of pins, stuck left right and centre, a walking talking pincushion.'

'You've always liked a lot of pricks,' I say trying to lighten the mood but instead of giggling and agreeing he scowls at me, shouts 'Oww' again and pulls out another pin before giving me a mournful look.

'I used to, I used to, but finally I realise there is only the one for me...'

'Bloody hell.' It falls out of my mouth without thinking. 'Do you mean Dan?' I make my tone softer but my head and my heart are doing victory jumps.

'Dan,' he repeats, nodding. 'And now I have been brave

and given my heart...' He looks at me like a mournful puppy and I feel myself scrunch up my lips in support, all my irritation towards him evaporated. 'Now, I've stuck my head over the parapet, taken a chance on life and I have been shot down, shot down, and into a million tiny pieces.

All of this is so heartfelt but it's not giving me any facts. The one thing I am sure of is that there has to be a rational explanation.

'And I have Drag Factor coming up, Dan has literally abandoned me in the middle of this fitting. I am still not sure about the first song, we were supposed to be making a final decision today, and now he has fucked off to go and flaunt himself all over The Downs with his lover.'

'Dan has a lover?'

'He has an ex.'

'We all have exes!'

'You don't.' A mini grin shoots across his face. Clearly, broken hearts don't impact sarcasm.

I shoot him a *behave* look.

'Yes, okay.' He accepts it. 'We all have exes but neither you or I are bonking them up by the Suspension Bridge right at this moment.'

'I doubt Dan is either,' I counter.

'Well, that is where you are wrong. One minute he was just checking me for fit, and the next his phone went and he flew out the door leaving me head to toe in pins, with no bloody way to get this dress off on my own – I literally cannot pull it over my head without help – and no real explanation other than he has to go. Well, that's it, isn't it? I have Drag Factor next week and the one person I'm relying on to get me through has flaming well stolen my heart and then upped and disappeared.'

'I'm sure he'll be back soon. Can I help with the final song choice? What is it between?' Normally I would know all of this.

'How can I concentrate on a song choice when my heart has been broken into two?' Kevin snaps, clearly cross that I am not grasping the severity of the situation.

I catch sight of my phone on the table. 'Does this help?' I ask. 'Look what Jay has sent me.' I play the video and Kevin stops sobbing and sits up straight, his attention captured from about halfway in.

'Go on, play that again,' he says, tears dry now for a moment. 'And who are these people?'

'A choir who do a bit of am-dram that Jay is helping out with'

'Oh my God! My cutting edge Drag Act makes him think of a practice song by pensioners in a community centre!' Kevin places his head in his hands.

I give him a minute.

He peers at me through his fingers and we hold eye contact whilst I wait for his thought process to complete. 'They'll come and help me sing?'

'I don't know for sure but I imagine so, otherwise why would Jay send it?'

'Right, I don't have time for your petty protestations,' he says and I wince, 'Ring him, ring him now and find out.'

I don't want to ring him. I'm not ready to speak to him yet. I have apologies to make, but I'm still constantly repeating the night we had as a thread of clips so familiar they autoplay. I shake my head to get rid of the explicit replays spooling around in there now.

'Don't shake your head at me. This is desperate!' Kevin says quick as a whip. 'What are you waiting for?'

'Um, what do you want me to say?' My heart is now about to launch into full-on failure.

'Tell him that we need those pensioners, especially that one in the feathers. She is camp! And we need them for Drag Factor and I need him here now too. He can help us on our search. In fact, just message him and tell him to meet us at the observatory. Oh and to bring a coat, a long coat. And binoculars. Quick, quick, quick!'

Chapter Thirty-Two

Somehow I am now lying on the grass by the observatory with Kevin in his so-tight-it squeaks metallic sheath, covered up by Jay's paint-splodged overalls, with bits of fabric squeezing out all over the place and his wig still very much at an angle. And I am still breathing.

From what I can tell my outside is showing no real evidence of the mayhem that is going on inside. All the feelings that surfaced as I waited for, and then watched, Jay park and walk across the road to meet us.

He was as good as gold when I called, He didn't make any mention of the fact that I have fallen off the face of the earth since our night together. Merely saying that he had finished helping Cass out for the day with painting so was heading home to have a shower. Neither did he seem at all fazed by Kevin shrieking into the phone that 'Now is not the time to get washed, for God's sake, this is a life or death emergency.'

He had duly arrived on The Downs – we weren't exactly hard to spot – and gave me a big grin in hello, which kind of made me feel reassured, safe and that all was right in the world. It also made me feel guilty that I have been *such* an arse. I should just have talked to him. Been as honest with him as he was with me in that very first text he had sent.

Thank you, I had a really special weekend. Hope you are smiling as much as I am xxx

I can't forget it. The minute I had seen it I had gone into insane panic but now, with reflection, how is this anything other than perfect? He hadn't put any pressure on me. He wasn't asking for anything; he was merely telling me how he felt and hoping I was happy too.

Which I guess I was, in those off-guard moments when I forgot to be petrified about what it all meant.

However, these thoughts were banished, just for a second or two, on his arrival as, not having a coat on him, he stripped out of his overalls and handed them to Kevin to try and get himself into without causing damage to the gown. Remarkably Jay had way more paint on his face than he had on his overalls.

However, it wasn't his face I was looking at as he was unzipping his overalls, shaking them off his shoulders, down his arms, pulling his hand through and then wriggling his hips, peeling them further down his legs until he stepped out of them and handed them to Kevin.

Kevin is as transfixed as I am and it's only as Jay laughed at us and quirked his eyebrow that both of us had the grace to turn back to the task in hand. Which at that point was to cross The Downs as discreetly as possible – so easy with Kevin bewigged, with earrings to his knees and in overalls – and take up a watchful position by the observatory. Kevin made us crawl in a line – formation as he called it – from the woods that had provided cover as we snuck up from The Downs and then he made us lie flat behind the tiniest slope whilst shouting, 'Quick, quick, before we're spotted!'

The best we can hope for is that Bristol is known as a city jam packed full of quirky creatives and people think this is a performance art piece, all of us lying on the grass looking through the zoom feature on my phone screen.

'That's him, that's him,' Kevin hisses so loudly that it alarms a group of schoolgirls walking past us in their blazers, who immediately follow the direction of his gaze to see who he is making the fuss about.

'Don't look. Don't look! Do you know nothing about being discreet?' Kevin hisses, making them scurry away from the madman in the park as Jay and I cackle like demons.

'Is it him?' I manage to splutter out and then zoom in on my screen. 'No, it's not.' That man is twice his size. I show Jay and we both start to laugh again and I have to admit I am loving having him by my side, sniggering together as we used to.

'I can't see clearly. These contacts make my eyes beautiful but even more blurry than usual.' I've got the giggles now – trust Kevin to bring us on a spying mission when he can't actually see. Our reaction is winding him up further. 'Will you two stop dicking about? You wouldn't laugh at someone if they truly couldn't see, so you should be more supportive of me.'

'Kevin, you have actively chosen to have gold eyes rather than good vision. Of course we're going to mock you. Just take them out.'

'Don't be ridiculous, I'll lose them and they cost a bloody fortune,' he responds. Jay and I are still laughing, Jay is banging the ground with his arm, and I can only assume it's hysterics born from desperation.

'Will you stop it! I'm bereft of the man I love and you're just laughing.'

That makes us stop in a second and we exchange glances. This is a first. Far rarer than crawling around Bristol in some ridiculous get up with Kevin and doubting my decision-making prowess.

'Love?' I say, adjusting the phone camera and scouring the land ahead of us, trying to be relaxed in my posture so I don't scare Kevin off by repeating the L word.

'Yes, I have lost the man I love and you are not taking it at all seriously.'

'I am. We are. Have you told him?' I ask.

'He knows,' sniffs Kevin

'Have you told him?' I ask again. If there's one man in the world more reluctant to become emotionally involved with someone than I am, it's Kevin.

He nods and a whole cluster of emotions flit over his face. He is happy, buoyant and proud – and all of it is chased away in a millisecond by sadness and concern.

'Is he definitely coming here?' Jay asks

'It's the most probable place. Jack and Dan met here at some event in the observatory itself that Dan was working at.' Kevin turns to us, purses his lips with displeasure that this is even a fact. 'And then they were inseparable for years and would come back here for every anniversary. I am not happy about this. Not at all. But yes, it is the obvious place for them to come.'

'Is there any chance they've been and gone?' This is a possibility and whilst I'm happy to support my friend, I really can't spend the next few hours up here lying on the grass waiting for something that may not even be happening here.

Kevin shrugs. 'We got here as quick as we could,' he says, shooting a look at Jay, who holds his hands up as if agreeing that somehow it's his fault we may have missed Dan by daring to be over the other side of the city when we called him.

'What exactly happened before Dan ran off? What has made you think he has come here to meet Jack?'

'His phone rang – rang, not a message. Who does that anymore? It was clear that it was Jack. His caller id speaks so as it rings it was saying Jack, Jack, Jack. Like some freaky Nineties dance track. Anyway he pounced on the phone and turned his back to me – turned his back, Lily. What more do you need to hear?'

'What was said on his phone call?'

'Not much, it lasted seconds. I heard him say, "*Now? This minute? I'll be there...oh my God, I love you.*" Then he turned to me, didn't meet my eyes, said he had to go out and dashed out of the front door. He didn't even stop and kiss me.' Kevin pulls a sad face. 'What more do you need to know? I'd say all that is fairly conclusive. He said he loved him, *loved him*, and in front of me too.'

'Okay, that is something. We'll find out what's going on. What does this Jack look like?'

'Tall, dark and meddlesome.'

'Ooh, hang on. Look. There.' Jay is cocking his hand against his forehead as he looks over at the observatory. Then he leans into me, my whole body fizzing as he does so, and points at my phone screen, tapping it to zoom in. 'There, there, is that them?'

'Oh my God, they're kissing.' Kevin is wrinkling his eyes up as he peers at the screen.

'They are not kissing,' I say.

'Lips just touched skin,' Kevin half screams. A whisper scream where the intent and emotion are fully there but the volume isn't. It is most restrained, considering.

'Yes, but lips didn't touch lips,' I qualify.

'Do they or do they not have their arms around each other?'

'Well yes...but...'

'They are cuddling and they just kissed. That's sexual contact right there!'

'No, no, it's not.'

'Pah and what makes you the expert?' Both Jay and I lift our eyes from the screen at this point and stare him down.

'Oh, okay, fair enough. You're The Love Doctor. But the thing is, you have sex with people and don't feel an emotional connection so I don't think you can actually advise me right now on love.'

Ouch. I don't dare look at Jay.

'Oh my God, look! look! He's taken his arm and they're... no, they're not... yes, they are! They're walking to the woods. Oh my God!' Kevin uses one hand to push his wig up a bit. It would appear that sheer emotion is enough to make it topple even further.

Jay and I do exchange another look at this point. That doesn't bode well.

'Look, Jack has a bag with him, a huge bag.'

'He does. What's wrong with that? You don't think he's planning to chop him up in the forest, do you?'

'Pah! He's not a serial killer! Honestly, you have such a

vivid imagination at times,' Kevin spits. 'That bag is rammed full of sex toys!' he adds with utter conviction.

'Really?' asks Jay.

'No,' I say, although my curiosity is piqued; I haven't done sex toys for a while on the podcast. A whole huge bag of them – now that is something.

'I am not having this,' Kevin screeches and jumps to his feet – the whisper part of his scream very much over now – and starts to race to the woods; the comedy of trying to do so in such a tight frock and overalls drawing curious looks from the people clustered up here, taking a walk or admiring the scenery.

I leap to my feet to follow him, scared of what he might find, and Jay is but a millisecond behind me. In no time at all we are at the woods on the other side of the observatory and as the three of us stand there clustered together and listening for clues, we hear them.

'Oh no, it's not going to work like that.' Then there is some laboured breathing before the voice speaks again. 'You need to pull it harder. A lot harder.'

'I am pulling as hard as I can.' This is definitely Dan's voice.

Kevin takes a deep breath and barrels off through the undergrowth. His, or rather Jay's, overalls get caught on a branch and he pauses to hoik them off and then continues running full pelt towards the voices.

'What on earth...?' We all break through into a clearing where, sure enough, Dan and someone tall and dark and – I can't testify to the meddlesome but he is very definitely handsome – are pulling at a branch. Or at least Dan is whilst the man, who I have to assume is Jack, is pulling at a bough. Kevin almost falls over himself as he comes to a screeching halt and as he stumbles, Jay and I bash into him. All of us are panting and have made enough noise to wake the dead. We are like a pack of crashing wildebeest and both Dan and Jack turn to look at us with amazement on their faces.

'Oh my God! What are you doing here?' Dan asks, tree in hand.

'What are we doing? What are we doing? What are you doing? I love you. Pull harder! Seriously. I don't know what to say to you. I hope you don't expect me to believe anything you say right now.'

'I haven't said anything yet,' Dan retorts.

'Semantics,' huffs Kevin.

'Mmm, not really,' I whisper. 'Let him speak. They do appear fully dressed.'

'Oh trust me, that means nothing.'

Jack looks perturbed but has the good sense not to comment.

'Well, go on, then.' Kevin says, his arms folded as he nods towards Dan and shoots a filthy glare at Jack, strong enough to kill a viper at a thousand paces.

'Hello, I'm Jack.' Jack steps up and holds out his hand for Kevin to shake. Kevin looks at it, raises an eyebrow and crosses his arms. Jay steps forward instead and introduces himself.

'Nice to meet you. I'm Jay.' I am struck once again how good his manners are in every situation but before I introduce myself to Jack I can't help but glance across at the large bag he was carrying. There are an awful lot of tools and implements in there and honestly not one of them looks like I would want it anywhere near my body. I'm not convinced Dan would either. I really do think that Kevin has the wrong end of the stick here.

'Hi, I'm Lily.'

'Oi. You two are meant to be on my side. Show a bit of loyalty,' Kevin says and we both nod at him, step back and cross our arms to mirror his pose. I try not to think about how ridiculous the three of us must look.

'I'm so pleased to meet you all. I am literally just helping Dan get some wood to help with the props for Jinx's –' he nods in Kevin's direction '– Drag Factor entry. I saw you in Cardiff a couple of years ago and I thought you were crazy talented. I was quite jealous when Dan told me he was seeing...um –' he stops and shoots a panicked look at Dan '– um...working together.'

'We *are* seeing each other and we're very happy,' Kevin says a lot less petulantly. It would appear that having Jack as a fan does a great deal to mollify him. That and the lack of a single butt plug in the open bag. 'Was that the one where I sang "Rolling In the Deep" and was wearing my cerise catsuit? I lived and died in that catsuit for a while.' Kevin removes his hands from his hips, which both Jay and I take as unspoken permission to stand like normal human beings again.

'Yes, you were and you did. I will remember it for ever. I'm really looking forward to coming along to your regional finals. I can't see that you won't win.'

'You were really just helping...'

'Of course he was, you silly fool.' Dan has dropped the bit of tree now and has come to Kevin's side. 'There's no finer craftsman in Bristol, and he's only just got back to the UK after doing some aid work overseas and I couldn't believe my luck. The timing was perfect. We were just trying to build a surprise for you on stage. You did say I was in charge of stagecraft. And that you needed me to work harder on making it unique.'

'I did. And I suppose you do have a wedding ring on.'

Kevin says, directing his latter statement at Jack. 'Presumably you're not married to Dan.'

'No.' Jack smiles.

'So we're seeing each other and are very happy?' Dan asks directly.

'We are.' As Kevin replies, there is a grin so big on Dan's face that it takes up all the space. His beam is so bright they can undoubtably see it from the observatory.

'Is that formal now? No more shilly-shallying, flippity-flopping about?' He clasps Kevin by his forearms and stares into his eyes.

'I have never been floppy near you,' Kevin says and leans in for a kiss.

'Eewwwwwwww' is the chorus from Jay, Jack and myself. Soon turning into an 'ahhhh'.

'Shall we make a move?' Jay whispers in my ear and I turn and smile. That is a very good idea indeed.

Chapter Thirty-Three

'So what do you think they're planning on doing with their stolen wood?' Jay asks as we wander across The Downs. I hear him but I am not really paying attention. I am finding it hard not to think about the last time we were here. I can see the track that leads to our spot, where we sat and looked out over at the gorge. The place I had told Jay the worst of the bullying I had suffered before I became new, streamlined Lily.

'Lily. Are you okay?' he asks gently.

I smile, nod that I'm fine and answer him. 'Um... I have no idea but I'm sure it will look amazing. Now tell me more about the video you sent.'

'Aren't they great?' His face becomes animated and his eyes shine. 'I've known most of them for years and I was up there helping Cass with the painting...'

'That explains the mess on your face. Cassie?'

'Yup,' he grins and I wonder if he has told her we slept together. The thing with my anonymous hookups is that we have no friends in common, if we do we don't reveal it. Things are separate, tidy. I like Jay. I want to carry on being his friend. I do. And Cassie has verve and spunk and flair. But I do not like the thought of sitting with her at Chrysalis knowing she knows I've had sex with her brother, that they may have discussed it. And if he's helping her paint – I distinctly remember painting being part of his punishment for breaking his vow – then he has already mentioned it.

Cassie probably won't be fussed, vow or not, but it's the idea of people talking about me behind their hands and weighing me up, sniggering. I know it goes back to school. But it still makes me feel uncomfortable.

'Shall we grab an ice-cream?' He interrupts my thoughts as he nods at a little wooden truck selling all sorts of posh flavours.

An ice-cream is a precursor. Once we have that, the next thing is to chat.

I feel the pressure in my chest, tightening like an evil puppeteer has placed iron bands around me and is now pulling them as hard as he can.

I know Jay and I need to talk. Kevin was right; I need to apologise and ensure the Youth Club project is something we can still work on together. But I am scared of what he may say. I'm scared of anything that upsets the equilibrium of my life, and this man has been doing that ever since we met.

I breathe out slowly, trying to calm myself, remind myself that I am in control.

'Ice-cream?' Jay asks again.

'Oh, um...yes...' I want to say no, run and hide but that is not the sensible option. Sorbet. Sorbet is the sensible option.

'I'll have a mango sorbet please.'

What if Jay is about to ask me for a relationship. He is a

man who needs commitment and children. I can't provide that. I'm a thrill-of-the-chase girl not a sleeping-with-the-same-person-every-night woman.

But the truth is this man hasn't asked me for any of this. He may just want an amicable working relationship. I need to get myself in check.

'Lily, are you okay? You're a bit of a funny colour. Maybe we should sit down.'

I smile wanly at him as a couple walk past, all hand-holdy and loved up. Beyond them is a heavily pregnant woman. She is one of those glowy types, the ones with the tight bump and no additional fat. I bet that wouldn't be my experience, I wouldn't be blooming, I'd be wilting. Hormones have never been my friend whereas this woman has earth-goddess-and-bringer-of-life written all over her.

I watch as Jay grins at her and she beams back.

This man wants children. What if he's planning on sitting me on some grassy knoll and lining me up to churn out offspring?

This is ridiculous. I need to get out of my head.

Jay finishes beaming at Mrs Walking-talking-fecund, flourishes his hand and suggests we sit.

Okay, sitting is good. This is going to be a quick, honest conversation on a summer's day, between two adults who both want a good working relationship. We both knew we shouldn't have slept together, we knew it at the time. I'm the idiot that has been rude recently, I'll apologise for that and then this is easily fixed.

I nod and take a bite of my sorbet and lower myself to the grass. The sun is beaming down on us and this could actually be a nice afternoon. It's the first time we've seen each other since he came to my room, and we have already broken the ice nicely with all that Jinx and Dan madness in the woods.

I turn to Jay and we shyly smile at each other. He could be as nervous as I am. He's the one who's been rebuffed and ignored. And by the one who's meant to be a bloody expert on sex and relationships.

I feel a wave of affection for him. He hasn't really done anything wrong, it's me that's triggered myself into peak madness, and he looks so daft with that paint on his face. I don't want to hurt this man.

'So, the paint, the video. Is that the community choir? And they're happy to be involved with Drag Factor?' I start with some non-threatening subject matter.

'Yes, Olive is very keen. And what Olive says, the choir does.'

'Looks like Kevin is keen to have them involved as well.'

'Yes, hopefully...'

A *plink plink plink* noise interrupts us and I turn and see that we have plopped down a few metres from a harpist.

Of course we have.

Because who doesn't want to be serenaded by a harp when they're trying to keep it together and have a grown-up conversation with a man they would like to sleep with again, whilst *knowing* that cannot happen? I hope to hell that Jay hasn't organised this as some kind of big romantic gesture.

I stare in horror at the harpist when I realise he couldn't have. He's covered in paint. He had no idea he'd be here at this time today.

I feel myself relaxing when, boom, Jay blindsides me.

'...Look, Lily, I want to be straight here. I think you and me, what we have is extraordinary. I think for the first time ever in my life I am falling in love, proper love, not potential, not possibilities, pure proper love. I don't want to scare you but I do want to be honest and I think we should give it a go.'

I've just told Lily that I love her and it was terrifying. My hands are clammy and my tongue snakes out and tastes sweat on my upper lip. Nice. Then the bloody harpist that I had not even *noticed* as I sat down, because I was working and reworking how to say what I need to say, has started to play 'Make You Feel My Love' by Adele.

Kind of relevant for me but, by the look on Lily's face, absolutely terrifying to her.

I know I have to hold my nerve, but I have *never* declared myself this way before and am suddenly cold despite the heat of the June sun beating down.

Lily on the other hand looks even worse. She has gone pale and is looking down in her lap, her breathing is laboured, and I can see her lips moving as she counts her breath. I need to know I've given this my best shot but the initial signs are that this is not going to go the way I had hoped.

And there is so much more I want to say. I want to talk about how I want to be more than a friend to Lily, I want to tell her how the night we spent together was so special for me, that I'm not suddenly looking at her to make all my future dreams come true. In fact when I look at her my plans for the future disappear into thin air. Being with her in the moment feels so right and that is all that matters. I want the moments to continue.

'The other night was pretty special for me,' I add. I don't

want Lily and me to be some stupid movie where no one is brave enough to speak the truth and both the hero and the heroine are left with feelings of attraction, love even, but are too scared to say anything. I'm not going to mess about at the edges here. Mo's advice was good, I can't go wrong with honesty... Can I?

She looks up at me and alarm is all over her face. She looks petrified. Actually frozen in stone and ready to splinter into tiny shards.

That's not good.

'Ah,' she says. And then pauses.

What the hell does 'ah' mean? Getting to know Lily has been nothing short of amazing for me. Like nothing I have ever experienced in my life. I don't just mean that the sex was red hot – it was – but there was so much more than that. There was a serious connection. That's how it feels to me: sleeping with her wasn't mere physical release but a meeting of two souls.

'Ah?' I repeat back. Mentioning the soul thing will send her running into the bushes.

'Yes, um...' Lily is looking at the ground and has pulled up a bit of grass and is fiddling with it. It is the most awkward I have ever seen her, even more than when she did the caww thing on the rooftop of the bar, even more than when she made me close my eyes before throwing me out of her room.

'I know you don't usually do commitment,' I say, 'but I'm not asking for that from you. I understand all you have said about not wanting that. I'm just saying if you would like to keep doing what we did the other night –' she flushes at this and I am reminded of her face, flushed for a wholly different reason as I had moved inside her, as she had clung to me '– if you would like to keep doing that then I would like to too.

With you and me something just seems to fit. I want you to know that I am keen to explore this, to take little steps. I'm not racing ahead and asking you to marry me or have my babies.' At this point she goes white and starts to aggressively pull up pieces of the grass we are sat on.

I'm not trying to make this worse, I'm trying to reassure her.

'Honestly, I am just trying to live in the moment, not make plans. I really am not thinking that way. What happened between us meant something to me and I wondered if it was the same for you. But you went quiet and now I'm getting the distinct impression that it didn't.' My words are calm but I feel I'm on the border of begging for a clear answer.

She is shredding the pile of grass she has collected in her lap. Any hope of her face turning to mine, her lips gently meeting mine as we agree that we feel the same, has disappeared. But there are still things that need to be said. I'm not letting my personal life mess up the opportunities Lily can give the girls.

'Look, Jay, this is not what I need right now.' Her eyes are still downcast and her tone is not friendly, more bear-forced-into-a-corner than oh-wow-I-think-I-love-you-too. Half an acre of ripped-up grass currently sat in her skirt backs that up.

'For me, that whole evening was one of the best nights of my life. We were perfect together. We had adventures, didn't we?' I say. I can't believe she did not enjoy the evening as I did. She *seemed* to be fully on board at the time. I remember her telling me *This is not just a tonight thing*, she promised.

I thought she meant it.

Have I completely misunderstood? I thought from the things she said that we were in this together. That her silence afterwards was her vulnerabilities coming to the fore and could be worked through. Today is showing none of that is the case.

'We did.' Her answer was slow to come.

I persevere. 'We sat under the stars until the wee hours, telling each other things we hadn't told anyone else.'

'We did.'

'And then we made love.'

She winces.

'Yes,' she says curtly, 'and we never should have done. It was a mistake. Unprofessional of both of us. We knew it at the time. We stayed up silly late and then we had sex and it was great, it really was...'

I do not need her to reassure my fragile male ego that my penis works properly. That is not what this is about. For me it's about more than the sex, it's the way Lily and I feel together, as if I have found my missing half, my one. I want to get that across, make her realise that what we have is unusual, has differed from anything I have ever felt before. I need to give this my best shot.

'But—' I say.

'But we are not some rosy-glow romance story,' she interrupts, her firmness unmistakable, and I can feel all the hopes I had, all the hope that has carried through me to this point, shrivel. 'You and I do not have a Happy Ever After. Ever. I am sorry that I have ignored your messages, that was rude of me and I do want to work with you on the Youth project but it can only be—'

'Yo, yo yo....look at this. Ice-cream, chilling in the sunshine, that's where it all starts, eh?' Some random bloke, drunk, has jumped behind us and is making weird leery noises and doing a pretty crass motion with his hands and mouth. I realise he is attached to a wedding party who have appeared from nowhere and are hovering around the harp, and us, and looking like they are getting ready to take pictures with the Suspension Bridge in the background

Great.

If I wasn't doing a great job of sabotaging things, then Drunken Wedding Uncle is here to help me finish it off.

I just need the bride to offer to lend Lily her dress and I'll have a hat-trick of disaster.

'Look, mate, congratulations to your friends and everything, but we're trying to have a talk here.' I smile but my tone makes it clear I'm politely saying Fuck Off.

'Oh, you're a pretty one, ain't you?' He is dancing around – all kinds of messy for a Tuesday afternoon, wedding or not – and comes in up close to Lily's face. I lean forward between the two of them and say, 'Seriously, back up.'

'Yeah, yeah.' He raises his hands and stumbles back and I turn to Lily and make a grimace.

She just looks at me.

I can't decode it but it isn't friendly. There seems to be a whole mish-mash of things there.

'Sorry about him.' Great, now we're being approached by the buzzed-up best man. 'He just loves love. Don't we all love love? Isn't love the best?' He beams at us and sweeps his hands at the Bridal Party.

'Jesus Christ. Really, Universe?' Lily shouts into the air.

'Oh sorry, you're having a moment. Sorry, guys – hey, everyone, give these guys some space.' He backs away, hands raised in the air.

Lily's jaw is clenched tight, a vein pulsing at her temple.

'Lily...' I lean across and rest my hand on her arm and she flinches. Flinches! I already know at this point I have no chance of us running off laughing into the sunset but I didn't expect to be repulsive to her. 'Go on, what were you saying?' I say, even more concerned as she folds herself down, her hands clasped in an arc around her knees, which are pulled up tight to her chin.

'I was trying to say sorry about ignoring your messages.' She makes direct eye contact as she says this, and I sense it's deliberate, to reinforce how strongly she feels despite her discomfort at having to do so. 'I knew I shouldn't have slept with you and I was trying to work out how we move past that when you turned up and saw me, well... I wasn't okay with that. I felt invad— Look, it wasn't okay. I do want to carry on working with you on the project but I don't know how easy that's going to be, especially if you're going to be lovelorn and clingy.' As she says the last sentence she moves her eyes back to the floor, where my heart, and pride, currently lie, both in smithereens.

Ouch!

I swallow hard and feel myself biting my lip.

'Okay, I want that too. We can be adults, we can make it work through timetabling if you don't want to have to see me.' I pause. I have managed to keep my tone even but she doesn't rebut my suggestion. She just stays silent, her mouth pursed up.

'Look, I gave my word to Jinx I was going to be involved in Drag Factor. I've enjoyed being part of it, but obviously if it makes you uncomfortable...' I feel completely humiliated but am trying to keep things functional.

'Kevin wants you there, and you've got the choir involved now.'

My mouth drops open. She is saying it as if I am being deliberately manipulative, trying to force my way in. 'I did that to help.'

'You're everywhere. You've been in my life a couple of months and you're everywhere...' She doesn't sound angry, she sounds trapped, resigned. That I'm all over her life, suffocating her.

Is this what she thinks? How she feels?

Part of me is becoming angry at the injustice. Not wanting to be with me, that's fine, that's personal choice, but I have *never* tried to crowd her. I have tried to give her space. I am only here now because according to the bloody Love Doctor the healthiest relationships are the ones where there is honesty as well as respect. I'm trying to be honest, at no point have I been mean or lashed out, because I *do* respect her. Clearly that respect isn't returned.

And the thing is Lily knows me, she knows my story. And this cuts deep. I pride myself on not being needy, on protecting myself, protecting those I love. My mind throws up a picture of Cass's face at 'Open Days' when prospective parents would walk right by us or talk for a minute or two and then awkwardly make excuses to move on when my sister made it clear she wasn't going anywhere without me. I see the set of my shoulders, the jut of my chin, adolescent me trying to be adult, soak up all the hurt.

I broke a vow to Cass for this woman.

'Look, I wasn't trying to rush you down the aisle. I've taken on board the things that Cass and the girls said, I'm committed to

281

my promise to live in the moment. But you and me, I would've gambled on that, I thought we had a chance; I was never lining you up for some mythical future where I take over your life. I'm sad that you think I'm trying to do that, that I would do that. I'll sort out the timetables for the youth centre so you can do your mentoring sessions when I'm either not on or elsewhere.'

She unfurls herself and yet again I cannot read what is going on with her, what her eyes, her face are actually saying to me. But honestly, right now I'm not sure I care. I have felt so many things for this woman but now my heart is aching for her, not in a romantic way – trust – but because I suspect her vulnerabilities are dictating her choices. From the periphery of my emotion, I recognise that the harpist has switched to Beyonce's 'All The Single Ladies' and I could curse her. Is she literally soundtracking our conversation?

I start to stand up. I don't know what else is left to say. Lily hasn't replied to my last comment but as she too stands she turns to me and places her hand on my arm. She gulps, and I see a tear pricking in the corner of her eye but I do not know why. I'm not sure I have the energy to work it out. I am suddenly exhausted. Exhuasted and I just need to get out of here. Get home.

'Jay... I...' Lily has started to speak and I take a deep breath and brace myself for one last insult, one last attack when from nowhere a bouquet of flowers comes flying through the air and bounces off Lily's shoulders.

'Oh no, you are joking me. Seriously?' She spits the words and grabs the bouquet, spinning on her heel to face the bridal party, who are giggling and muttering apologies when, with the force of a Olympic shot-putter, Lily hurls the bouquet back, the force of it lifting her back foot from the ground. It seems as if all her frustration, all her emotion is condensed in that throw and I watch, the world now in slow motion, as the bouquet hits the bride square in the eye. I hear Lily's sharp intake of breath and see the bride bend double, fall to her knees and let out a shriek that causes everyone on The Downs to swivel their heads.

Her new husband is panicking, and I run over to see if I can help. It's quickly clear that no real damage has been done, no cuts, no bleeding and nothing broken, the shock of the impact being the biggest side-effect. The bride's husband and I help her to her feet as she steadies herself, laughing that she now has an awesome wedding story, and prepares to throw her bouquet again.

I turn to leave them to it and cast around for Lily. I can't see her anywhere and then spot her, tiny on the horizon, running, running away from me as fast as she can.

Chapter Thirty-Four

I'm at work, and relieved to be so, with my day off yesterday going so badly I'm not sure I want to have one again. I had gone straight home and scrubbed all the paint off my face and then headed out to the gym, not sure that I could be by myself and process all the things that had gone so terribly wrong on The Downs.

I can make my peace with the fact that Lily doesn't want to be with me. Her ignoring me before we met that afternoon was pretty indicative of the fact that she wouldn't fall into my arms, but some of the things she said were hurtful, and I can't believe this woman who I thought was quite literally my soulmate has judged me so harshly.

It's hard for anyone to hear that they're a mistake, and certainly the phrase is not leaving me alone, but it's the injustice that really bites. I really don't think I have been crowding her. At no point do I think that I have been pathetic and lovelorn like some heartbroken adolescent, and to suggest that I would behave so in my place of work is beyond insulting.

Running on the treadmill in the gym, the speed set high to see if I could run off some of my emotion, rather as Lily clearly did after battering that poor bride, meant that I was able to get the phrase *Lily Galbraith can just fuck off* satisfyingly coursing through my head as my feet and my heart did the hard work.

But in the wee hours of the night, that sentiment was not the one filling my mind. Instead, I felt bereft, as if I had lost my best friend, Christmas had been cancelled and the whole world had seen me walking the streets naked and had laughed and pointed.

Part of me had spent the night lying there, making excuses for Lily. I had known her vulnerabilities and had gone too hard and too fast. I should never have used the word 'love'. I should have gone gently, gone back to shared friendship and worked from there.

But that seems manipulative – am I not allowed to feel the way I do? Why should my feelings be forced to take the backseat? Should I not be able to hope that if I want to spend my life with a partner they would not want me to be hiding things, being dishonest or playing games, albeit a long one?

Part of me last night told myself I was allowed not to be understanding, not to be such a pushover. She had been rude, bloody rude and hurtful. She bears responsibility here too and I can't see how we can come back from this. It's obvious that there is no way back, that Lily is not going to apologise or try and make me see why she has acted as she has. And that's because she doesn't care. That is the one thing that yesterday had made abundantly clear.

And that was the main thing that had me lying awake as

anger spiralled around in my mind. I knew despite my internal ranting that it was only there as a superficial forcefield covering up my hurt. And the hurt is a wound that does not need further prodding right now.

But the joy of work means I do not have the time or space to dwell on my wounds, that these girls have far bigger problems than mere romantic rejection.

'Jay, Jay!' Ellie comes bowling through the door as I am playing a quick game of table football with Shireen, one of the younger girls. 'Man, I can't believe it, like literally cannot believe it. Your mate messaged and has offered me studio time. He can fit me in a week on Wednesday at four. So pumped, man, so pumped. I'm gonna be a star!' and she twirls and then bumps hips with me, making me miss the goal.

'Oi, I would have won that!'

'Not a chance,' Shireen snips back before high-fiving Ellie. 'Winner stays on.' She nudges me out of the way and beckons her mate over to play.

'That studio time comes with conditions, Ellie.'

'Yeah, yeah, I know. I gotta get myself to school. Your boy says any absence and the slot is cancelled.'

'Right. And he will cancel it too. You think I'm tough on you, believe when I say Henri is going to be more so. The man don't take no shit. He's doing this as a favour to me and I'm doing it to blackmail your arse into going to school. You maintain, I'll maintain. And I'm gonna be checking in with your school on the Tuesday, believe it. So, no more absences from tomorrow on, you got me?'

'Yeah, yeah. For sure.' Ellie says with ennui that even the most jaded celebrity would admire.

'So, Jay, you going to that Drag thing next week, the one

Lily's friend is in?' My back stiffens. That is the one name I do not need to hear today, the words 'lovelorn' and 'clingy' in my head again, cutting deep.

'How do you know about that?' I ask and Chloe lifts her eyebrows and fixes me with a look that is nothing short of terrifying.

'We keep in touch,' she says enigmatically. 'That first meeting, we asked what sort of thing she does when she's not working and she told us about this bar she goes to.'

'Yeah and we looked it up and saw there was all this stuff on and when we spoke again she told us her best mate was in like this competition. And my brother can get tickets for anything, anything...' Ellie adds.

'Yep, I remember.' She has told me about her brother's ticket-securing skills before. 'But even with tickets, you guys are underage.'

'I'm not,' Chloe states. It's true. 'Anyway, tickets say you have to be over sixteen. We're gonna behave. It's Lily's patch.' She shrugs her shoulders and if it had been anyone but Chloe I wouldn't have believed her.

Mind you, how Lily is going to react when she sees the girls there is anyone's call. I figure she'll stay professional and be pleased to see them but the one thing I have learned about Lily is that I cannot predict her reactions.

Chapter Thirty-Five

I am so ashamed of myself I am not sure what to do other than bury myself in work. One minute we were back to our old selves with Kevin and his ridiculous lovestruck antics and within half an hour I was a bouquet-hurling banshee who should be charged with ABH.

The embarrassment and shame have been haunting me now for three whole days.

It hadn't started like that. It started with Jay and me in the sunshine, sharing moments; you know, those sideways glances where you're both thinking the same thing, that secret mutual smile and a quick bashful look away because you don't want everyone around you to know you're having these intimate shared moments with no verbal communication necessary.

I had been guilty of perving over him a bit as well, taking me back to that night, the way he made me *feel*. And as we lay on that bank of grass scanning The Downs for Dan, I resolved to try and concentrate on that, the way *he* made me feel rather than the way my head makes me feel.

And for that moment it was pretty bloody lovely.

And then it was just the two of us getting closer and closer to the fact that we were going to have a conversation where I was planning to apologise but make it clear that I was in no place to move on with Jay. When he went and threw the L word at me.

The L word.

After one night.

And whilst I had been in a bit of a panic spiral before that, the minute he said what he said, I lost it.

Totally lost it.

I'm not entirely sure I was in my own body. It felt as if I was above myself, screaming at myself to stop but not being able to control it.

And the thing is, I pride myself on my control. I have spent years, decades, mastering it. Control of my diet, my exercise, the way I look, the way I interact, the way I shape how I want to be perceived – and then bosh! It deserts me.

I can't remember any time before, as an adult, when I have felt so lost, so out of control. The fear was real; I had heart palpitations, I was sweating, fluctuating between feeling sick and feeling faint, and was about to escalate into full-blown panic attack. None of which was helped by having some poxy wedding celebration unfold right next to us, as if the universe was deliberately tormenting me. And before I even knew what I was doing I was lashing out at a man who probably didn't deserve it. Who definitely didn't deserve it.

And I ran.

Sprinted.

Managed to catch my breath well enough for that.

I mean, who runs away from this sort of thing? Like

literally runs as if her shoes were aflame, little fork-tongued demons lighting her soles. Romantic films and books, all the things, show us running towards the hero.

Then there's me.

I have lain awake into the wee hours playing the scene over and over in my head, remorse and embarrassment more effective than the strongest caffeine. I had reached for my phone a few times to apologise, send a message. But each time I put it back again. I have hurt that man enough. I can't offer him what he deserves so I'm best leaving him be.

But even with all my navel-gazing, I have cleared my backlog of paperwork, prepped and double-checked my course teachings for next term and for the girls at City Youth, and will be driven to polish my houseplants and skirting boards shortly.

I've also had a run of clients; Angela has just left. Her EMDR sessions have gone quickly and have been much more positive than I had dared hope. I'm seeing a more relaxed woman in front of me, lighter.

We are not going to sort all the things pouring around in swirls in this complex woman's head but we are very definitely making a dent. This is the fifth or sixth session in a row where her attention to the dolls has been fleeting. Today she was able to speak to me without having one on her lap as a distraction, and she has joined MeetUp and is talking about maybe going out one evening. She even mentioned that she may do so sans dolls.

However Angela was my last client of the day and now I need a new focus. I have filled the last few days with swimming and working and swimming and working. I even had a complete blowout at the bar the other night – minus

Kevin and Dan but plus booze, which I rarely, rarely succumb to – and danced way more than you would have thought possible for a Wednesday night, but that still hasn't shifted the thoughts whirling around, engorging my head.

I reach for my phone, but I'm not sure if Tinder and Bumble have a pull on me now. I haven't logged in properly for a while, but I tap on the little fire icon and find myself swiping it up and closing it before it even opens.

I force myself to face the truth.

Since Jay has entered my life I have been displaying out-of-character behaviours. Repeatedly. I would suggest to a client that a new person proving the catalyst for such changes may indicate they are not a healthy influence. But I *know* none of this is on Jay; my reactions to Jay are down to me. And if I dig real deep, scrunch shut my eyes so tight it hurts my jaw, only then can I acknowledge that I'm feeling a little out of control here because I've been developing feelings.

Feelings.

FEELINGS!

I know.

The fear that I have fallen for the popular boy again has not escaped me.

The fear that I have fallen for a man who deserves children in his life plagues me.

The knowledge that I have actively sabotaged something that I never thought was possible, that maybe could have worked, makes me even more self-loathing than I was before.

The knowledge that I have hurt a man I respect, trust and have spent large chunks of my days, weeks, moony-eyed dreaming about his very goodness, destroys me. The snippets of sleep time are sweaty and tangled, filled with the memory of him.

I know I've never felt like this about anyone.

And I am floundering.

I need to take control back. Forge a path forward without Jay.

Freshly aware of my flaws, I am not going to let *anything* limit me anymore. I'm going to do something for myself that I should have done a long time ago. Decades ago. I didn't have the confidence then, I was scared of the answer. But I like my life now. I am secure in it. I can explore my options with the giant safety net that I have successfully created.

The people around me have been instrumental in this. Everyone seems to be making positive change. Kevin is now officially seeing Dan and that makes my heart so happy. Since their announcement in the woods the two have been playing dreamy starry-eyed lovers all over the house and it is so cute. But his change in relationship status is all because Kevin stopped being fearful; he took the gamble and risked everything I know he is deep-down scared of. I know how squishy and tender his heart is, I also know how easily it is damaged. Like so many of us, I guess. How hard it is for him to open up and take a chance.

And for all his outrageous hyperbole, ridiculous drama and peacock feathers I know how deeply he fears his parents finding out who he is, who he is most comfortable being. So by staying the course and doing Drag Factor when his parents are in the same city as him is huge. It's showing a strength, a determination of purpose and a desire to live life the way that suits him. That I really admire.

Then of course there's Angela. The strides forward she has

been making have been inspirational. Angela and Kevin are making determined steps towards the future they want. The session material I have been writing for the girls at Jay's youth group has further woken me up, made me realise I'm not really living my life with the courage and power I promote.

Everything Kevin has been saying to me for years has been right. That doctor I saw as a teen was probably just a miserable old misogynistic wanker and I need to go and find out more about my health. It is great that I have been able to lose the weight – I know the majority can't, through no fault of their own – that I am fit, that I eat well, and it is horrid that I have a shitty intermittent cycle that incapacitates me when it turns up and affects my potential fertility.

I have always been genuinely happy in my fulfilled life, without children or the thought of children. But the last few weeks have reminded me that people can change, that exploring new options doesn't mean you're unhappy with your old ones. It's just that sometimes we change our views, our desires, and that's okay. In fact, *not* changing as we grow is the concern.

So maybe it's time to see if my lifestyle choices are based on fact and desire rather than fear and misinformation. I *am* secure enough to properly examine what my options are. It can do no harm to know for sure one way or another. Am I not always banging on about educating yourself, that fact-checking and making informed choices are all good things to do?

The time I got my diagnosis may have been a day of relief and understanding, that I wasn't a freak that didn't fit in for no reason. At eighteen I was a bit celebratory about the news that I couldn't have children, that there was no danger of unplanned offspring if I went out in the world, explored my sexuality.

What I hadn't realised was all my old beliefs about not being worthy weren't resolved but had burrowed their way under my heart like a little mole digging and digging, heading determinedly to my core.

I have made decisions the whole of my adult life based on this belief that I can't have kids and never once have I questioned it, researched further. I am a well-educated woman and am more than aware there are a myriad ways women can conceive outside of the norm.

Instead, I was happy accepting the word of some bitter arsehole and I failed to explore it further. But now I am ready to take a look at this. To check it out, find out what my options are for my future. Checking now before I am too old for the chance for children. Just find out for sure, see how I feel if I learn it's not an impossibility.

I click on a website for a clinic only three streets away from my practice and begin to look at booking an initial consultation.

One of the things I do know is if there is ever a man out there for me, a man that I can see myself committing to, he needs to be there for me and me alone. Whether I can have children or not needs to be something he is happy to deal with. That he can live without the promise of biological children in his life.

Jay needs children, and I care too much to force him into a future where that compromise is a possibility.

I know and understand how important it is for people to have children, I do. It's hard not to link the idea of sex equating childbirth when you have had a head teacher shriek in assembly – beard and spittle quivering with the fervour of his emotion as he screams across the hall – that fornication is solely for procreation. I reckon that's why I'm an exponent of fornication for recreation.

But I also know the importance of valuing myself for who I am, how I am, and learning not to feel guilt that I may not be equipped the same way other women are. I'm also beginning to realise that a relationship might work for me. It's worked for my mum and dad. It works for my sister and right now is working for Kevin. I have known and loved that man for ever and yet never have I seen him as happy as he is now.

Maybe I am worthy, maybe cuddling up with someone in my pyjamas, with no make-up on, high heels kicked off at the door and left there – you know, unless a certain mood strikes me – is something I might really like.

It is something I might really like with Jay. But I know even if I did decide I was up for – and able to have – kids, I am way too cowardy-custard to ever say that out loud. To anybody. A girl can't get rid of all her insecurities in one fell swoop. And besides, I have messed that man around too much. If my bridges weren't already smouldering beforehand, then my meltdown the other day has guaranteed they are thoroughly torched and now ashen. And even if I hadn't, I can't say no, change my mind and say yes, maybe, and then keep chopping and changing; which is more than probable.

Baby steps.

If I am considering breaking my binds to single girl life then I need to allow myself a little bit of slack. An acceptance that I may fall off the wagon a couple of times. I am not having Jay be that wagon.

Chapter Thirty-Six

There is the sound of laughter, of Keith's kids playing, of glasses being carried across the garden. Everything smells of summer and normally this is the good life. Shirts are off, music is on, I'm surrounded by people that I love but I am still struggling to shake off the blues.

Images of Lily and me constantly scroll through my mind. The day she first came to the youth centre and I made a fool of myself stumbling all over the place. The sight of her when she walked into Chrysalis and I was wearing my no-sex pants. The way she made me laugh up on the roof, the way she made me feel safe out on the ledge, the way she looked at me time after time after time. The way we created our very own bubble where we were just us.

But as I lay my head on my pillow at night, it is her scrunched up on The Downs, upwards foetal, I know it from the homes. Her skin pale as she bites her lip. *It was a mistake. I knew I shouldn't have slept with you.* The tear in the corner of her eye at the very end.

'Jay, Jay, man. Come on, come help.' Luke has left Keith on the barbecue and is beckoning us up to help get food out from the kitchen.

I follow him through, behind Mo, who, on reaching the kitchen first, turns and passes me a bowl of slaw and some bread rolls.

'So, did you get to talk to your girl?' he asks, his voice low.

'Yeah, we talked. She's not my girl.' It is the first time I have said it out loud but I think I've needed to. She's not, it's just the truth.

'Shit, sorry, man. At least you said your piece.'

'Yeah, it was... It felt brutal. But, you know, it's done.' I say as Marcus joins us.

'For sure, but you know what this man would say,' Mo states gesturing at Marcus who has just joined us.

I grin and say, 'I do. And nothing that man says is sense.'

Marcus shakes his head in disbelief, a grin across his face. Marcus is a fool but the man brings the sunshine. 'If you're talking about me then you *must be* talking women.'

'Donkeys, mate. We were talking donkeys.' We move back outside.

'Now I know that ain't true. You've been looking down, Jay. You should be smiling, look.' He points to the sun. 'Ah...ah!' He shakes his hand at me and then clicks his fingers. 'It's that girl. Has she knocked you back again? She did tell you it was work only. She's obviously seen a finer man.' He runs his hand down his torso, stippling his fingers and beaming. From the corner of my eye I see Mo shake his head. Marcus stops. 'I'm sorry, but you know there's a whole world of p—'

'We've got kids here,' Mo says forcefully.

Luke joins us, having heard the conversation and dangling

a pack of Red Stripe. 'Did you guys not have like work and some event thing happening?'

'Yeah. Is that sorting itself?' Mo adds.

'Work's fine. I'm going to structure her sessions so they are when I'm out-of-office, it'll still run fine. The event thing? Oh, you mean Drag Factor. Yeah, I don't know what to do about that. I gave my word. I've got the choir involved, all that means I should go. Some of my young ones from work are going but you know, I'm not feeling it. I can't. It would be weird, right? It would be weird.' I nod, convincing myself.

'Yeah, yeah. You can't be doing that,' Marcus says firmly as he takes a can from Luke and pops it open. 'Nah. Have some pride. You don't need to be in her life anymore, not outside like professional commitments. Bin it.'

I look over at Mo. He shrugs. 'He's right. You have no obligation to go. Don't feel bad if you don't.' He wiggles his head and says ultra-casually, 'But if you're not sure, then see how you feel in the moment. You'll know what's right then.'

'Nah, he's talking bollocks, mate, it's weird, it's stalky and you should have more respect for yourself.'

'Sometimes things aren't black and white, sometimes there's nuance,' Mo chips in.

'Nah, you see, no, there's not. Sometimes things are clear, clear, clear. And I'm not on shift that Saturday, so you and me, we're going to have a night. Have. A. Night.' He slaps me on my back and I decide he is right. What am I even thinking? Lily is out of my life. There is no way I am going to Drag Factor.

Chapter Thirty-Seven

I decide to drop in quickly on Cass on my way home from the barbecue. It seemed like a good idea when I had it; she's been MIA for a good few days now and I want to actually physically check in. But as I ring Cassie's doorbell I'm feeling nervous. My stomach is a pit of knots and fear at what I may find. My mind seems to naturally shoot to worst case scenario. Best case in this situation is that Cass answers the door and tears a strip off me for interfering.

Because what I really need this week is someone else I care for deeply shouting at me.

The thing with Cass is she does love painting and has a strong sense of responsibility, so not showing up this week to help finish off the scenery is a huge red flag. I have called and messaged and she has always responded in normal Cass words, i.e. full of swearing and telling me to back the hell up, let her live her life her way, but no real explanation for her absence.

Seeing as I've been spending a fair amount of my spare

time this week going to the community centre as Dan puts everyone through their paces for their choral back-up to Jinx, I have managed to finish the majority of the scenery. Most of it had been drawn freehand by Cass so I just had to fill in the gaps with the colours, all of which were pretty obvious. But it's been weird working alongside Dan and yet no longer feeling part of Team #MakeSureJinxWins. Neither of us has said anything about it, but it is more than clear that I am not welcome in Lily's life.

'Hello.' Cass's voice comes through the intercom.

'Hey, Cass, it's me, can you buzz me in?'

'Seriously? What are you doing here, Jay?

'Checking in.'

'I'm fine.'

'Can you just come downstairs?'. I'm not prepared to go until I can see her in person. Check she has a face and all her limbs. Jas has never been violent as far as I'm aware but I don't trust her an inch and I need to see Cass for myself so I can relax a bit. I need to know something is going okay.

'For fuck's sake, Jay.' I hear Cass slam the intercom down and soon the thud, thud of her feet hammers down the stairs like a very pissed-off baby elephant.

Definitely not chained up then.

She wrenches the door open and there she is, not a whisper of a bruise or even a tiny plaster. There is no outward sign of injury at all although she looks like she hasn't slept for days and there's a pallor to her skin which doesn't indicate someone in the prime of her life.

'What?'

'Hey, I was worried.' I pause and then add, 'It's not like you not to show up. I've done the best I can with what was left at the community centre. You can always paint over it if my amateur attempts affront your artistic soul but...'

'Show me.'

I pull my phone out my pocket. 'Here, pull up and swipe through the photos of the backdrops.'

'Oh, wow, they actually look really good. We'll make an artist out of you yet.' Her tone softens further. 'Was Olive all right about me not being there?'

'Yeah, I covered for you plus she's super excited about being involved in the Drag Factor thing. She has been piling the pressure on to make sure I go. But enough of that, I wanted to see you in person, make sure you're all right.'

She doesn't answer straightaway but swipes the screen on my phone again. 'Oh, look at everyone. Is that guy they're all singing around Dan that we met the other night?'

'Yeah, he's been putting them through their paces. Dan wants them to all stand and do a little choreographed routine when Jinx takes to the stage, a flash mob in the audience.'

'Wow. They look great. Will they be um wearing...um...?'

'The T-shirts, yup. They insisted. Dan's asked them to make any extra touches as flamboyant as possible.'

'Ha. Does he know what he's asking? Has he met Olive?'

'Oh yes. She is now officially his second mother.'

'Sweet.'

'He may not think that when she turns up next Saturday dressed in nothing but a pair of neon coconut shells, the T-shirt tied in her hair. He may well regret giving her free rein on the word "flamboyant".'

'Oh, I'd love to see it.'

'Well, go down. The more people cheering for Jinx the better. And you have a very loud cheer.'

'I do. When is it? And why "go down", why not "come down with me"? Does that mean you're not planning on going?'

'It's tomorrow night. Will you make it?'

'Um...I don't know. Things are...um....' She shakes her head and then meets my eyes. 'But I'll try. I really will. Again, are you not going?'

'It's kinda...um...probably not.'

'If you're not going, then I'm not going! And I actually really want to go. What's happening?'

I shrug. If I tell Cass she's either going to bawl me out for being an arse or screech mean things about Lily and I am not really willing to deal with either option.

'Wow, so you want to be all up in my shit but you're not going to tell me yours? Whatever it is I suggest you get over it. Olive will be gutted if we don't support her guys in their moment of glory. You know it. You're going to disappoint Olive, are you? And Eric?'

'Cass...' I try and mimic the puppy-dog eyes she does so well.

'Don't even try. Is this Lily-related?'

I wince.

'Has she filed a restraining order?' She giggles at this, but it's a little bit too raw for me to smile back. 'Oh, Jay. Right, well, whatever it is, that needs to be sorted out. Do you not think Drag Factor would be a good place? The two of you could talk whatever needs to be talked out on the rooftop. It's her territory so she'll feel secure. It's not like you to leave things in a bad place.'

I lower my eyes and shake my head. I don't want to be pathetic but I still don't have words. When I got home after our talk on The Downs even Dimkins came and sat on me and tried to give comfort. I nearly suffocated but he tried.

'Oh, bro, we'll get this sorted. We will.' She gets a wan smile and she does a sympathetic thing with her lips, tilts her head. 'Promise, but I need to get on so can you sod off and we'll deal with this later?'

'Yes, but only if we do real talk now? Just for like thirty seconds.'

'Go on,' she says resignedly. It's the quickest way to get me to leave quietly.

'Are you all right? Like actually all right? I'm worried about you. And is there anything I can do? Me, the car, Darling Dimkins, we are always at your disposal.'

'I know you are. And I know you're fretting about me. You're always fretting about me.'

'Not always.'

'No, sometimes you're giving me a big old bollocking.'

'I do not do that.'

'You did the time I ripped up some of your Yu-Gi-Oh! cards!' We both smile and before I can retort that she's lucky she can still walk, the smiles fade on our faces and she reaches out and takes my hand.

'I'm all right. I am. Things are a bit up in the air at the moment and I'm not going to pretend to you right now that my life is easy but the podcasts have been helping. I'm just about to listen to the *Safety tips for anal* one. Should be a hoot. Or terrifying, could easily be terrifying. But, look, I'm getting there. I've got a plan. I need you to give me space, let me do things my own way. I've got to live my life for me, big brother, and not you. And that means me sorting my shit out myself.'

'Okay.'

'Okay, and then I'm going to sort your shit out, but for now will you fuck off?'

'Okay.'

'And see you at Drag Factor next week?' she asks and I shake my head. 'We'll see', she says, 'now sod off,' and I leave my baby sister to be an adult.

Chapter Thirty-Eight

'So, that's it. That's the tour.' Kevin closes the door to his bedroom and grins at his parents. 'And now you've seen every room in the house, what do you think?'

'It's a very fine house, son,' Chih-hao says. 'Very fine indeed. It makes me happy that you have a piano. I was so pleased you took it back up again at uni, we had despaired when at eight years old your teacher advised we let you focus on something else. Maybe you can play us a tune later?'

Kevin shoots me a look; we both know that he can't play for toffee. He can bang out 'Silent Night' at a push when filled with enough mulled wine and can do a damn fine 'Twinkle Twinkle Little Star' if he has to but he has never had the heart to admit to his parents that the money they sent him throughout uni to help with 'his music lessons' actually went on glue sticks, medical tape and tucking panties. The fact that he has a piano is because it is beautiful and he offered to keep it when the previous owners couldn't get it out of the flat. Its presence in our life is no indication of his musical expertise, merely of his kind heart.

His mother, Shu-feng, who I suspect is far wiser to her son's machinations, tries to create a diversion as Kevin smiles wanly at his father.

'We haven't seen this room, what's in here?' It is unusual for her to speak such a sentence; she is a woman who says very little.

'Aha,' says Kevin, standing outside his dressing room. If his parents spot those wigs atop those terrifying heads they may well send him for a psychiatric assessment. At Broadmoor.

I give him a nod because I know what he is telepathically asking me and he flings the door open wide.

'This is Lily's dressing room. She has such an extensive wardrobe because you know she is so... well, um... successful.'

'Oh, I know,' says Chih-hao, 'I read an article only the other day about how her podcast is highly recommended. I am sorry we haven't listened.' He pinches my cheek with pride but I am very relieved. The thought of them clustered around a laptop listening to the sex-toys-are-our-friends talk scheduled for this weekend is enough to ensure I never record another episode. 'But I have to ask, the article mentioned your sign-off and I am curious. I understand *Be brave, have faith and be true*, all of that is good advice, but why do you say *Don't lick their faces*? Do I understand right? No one would do that.'

He looks genuinely perturbed.

'I know, Uncle Chih-hao,' I say using the affectionate address both Kevin's parents requested I use many years ago. 'It does sound silly but it was because when it all began at uni, way before the podcast or I became the Love Doctor officially, I was getting a reputation for blunt but good advice, and friends – and sometimes complete strangers – would come and ask me about problems in their personal lives and so on, that sort of thing. Kev and I were inseparable but every time he was with me as someone was leaving, I'd tend to reiterate the key message, for example, *Be brave*, and your son would always, *always* add, *But don't lick their face*. It started off as something stupid that made us giggle and it kind of became a thing. When that whole aspect of my life turned into a career, I kept it. Partly because it had become normalised and partly for the nostalgia.'

'So, it's our son's fault?' Chih-hao says and I shrug and smirk.

'Right, well, this is the room where she records her podcast that you and your friends are planning to listen to all those thousands of miles away,' Kevin says, giving me an evil look.

'Yep, all happens in there,' I say. Shu-feng stands on tiptoes to look past her son and see inside the room and lets out an audible gasp.

'She really likes cosplay,' Kevin says completely out of the blue. He shoots me a plea with his eyes, so I nod to try and help him. I am currently wearing one of my knitted dresses from Reiss, in navy. I don't look like I enjoy dressing up as characters at the weekend. I'm sure I could, and I have done a little role play in my time, but he is digging a hole here.

'Oh, but isn't cos play –' Chih-hao takes a look at the room laid before us and says slightly more wanly '– um... anime and superheroes and things?'

Kevin's eyes bulge and I'm not sure if it's because his dad is more au fait with cosplay than he suspected, or if it's just the terror that they may explore this room more fully. 'No, Dad, cosplay is anything you want it to be and, as you can see, Lily here has a penchant for sequins and feathers.'

'Lily has?' Shu-feng queries.

I feel compelled to help him out and walk into the room and reach for his Marie Antoinette dress. 'I really like French historical costume and, you know, it seems a shame not to celebrate the beauty of some bygone eras.'

Kevin's fears begin to be realised as Shu-feng moves inside and starts touching the clothes. She pauses after a couple of minutes whilst Chih-hao talks about the importance of costume and its emblematic role during the French Revolution. As he pauses for breath, Shu-feng looks at the clothes I am wearing, which are very like the clothes she has always seen me wearing, tight- fitting and fairly neutral. She raises an eyebrow and looks directly at me. That woman is the boss of the direct stare and I find myself examining the carpet.

'Right, right, come on, that's the house tour done.' Kevin practically grabs his mother and hurls her back out of the room and towards the stairs. 'We don't want to miss dinner.'

'Ah no, good point. What are we doing for dinner, son?'

'Lily is cooking.'

I nod and wave my hand to the stairs in an attempt to get Chih-hao down them and away from the dressing room.

'Hmmmm,' says Shu-feng knowingly. It's her usual verbal response and why her question earlier was such a surprise.

'Then why will we miss...?'

'She's very fussy. She likes to start at um.... 6.23 on the dot, isn't that right, Lils?' Both his mum and dad look at him as if he is a small child trying to bluster his way out of a situation.

Kevin shrugs, knowing he's been caught talking nonsense. 'We thought it would be nice to have a night in as tomorrow is going to be such a busy day.'

We wander through to the kitchen and I get out a block of tofu and start to cut it up, roll it in flour to give it a crispy edge and fry it as Chih-hao chatters away about the way tofu is made from soy beans, with particular attention given to the way it's strained and how the curds form. I try and eat it at least once a week but he is putting me off it a little.

'So your piano, it fits the room nicely. I can picture the piano being played as Lily cooks. I assume you do most of the cooking.' I look up and smile and nod as I put the tofu into bowls of rice and vegetables. The piano does get played if Dan is here whilst I cook, it's just that Kevin likes to vogue all over the room as it's played rather than sitting on a stool and bashing the keys. Although I know that despite his panicked look earlier, Dan has been teaching him to play again recently.

'That's about right,' says Kevin, cheerily grinning at me, safe in the knowledge I'm not going to rat him out as I bring the steaming bowls over to the table.

'Ah, Lily, thank you. This looks delicious...'

'Hmmm,' Shu-feng murmurs. I know that Kevin and his mother share a similar taste in food and suspect she was secretly hoping for something cream- and butter-based, maybe sprinkled with half a bag of sugar and topped with a squirt or two of golden syrup.

'...and you're looking well too. Still swimming every day?'

'I've been doing bootcamp.' Kevin speaks before I get a chance to, so I nod and smile and try to hide the smirk as I picture Kevin's continued bootcamp participation. He has told the trainer, Joe, that he has a medical condition so needs to sit out certain sections. A medical condition that has him lying on the ground making daisy chains most weeks unless Dan happens to join us. His presence has healing powers.

'Hmmmm.' Shu-feng spears a piece of carrot and looks across at me before she puts it in her mouth. Her face suggests I am trying to feed her rocks but I know full well that Shu-feng will eat anything put in front of her.

'Ah, I read an interesting article the other day about fitness...' And Chih-hao begins one of his speeches – honestly, they can go on for a good fifteen minutes without him seeming to draw breath. He would have made a great athlete. As ever, it's Shu-feng's cue to dive into her meal.

I have always been fascinated by Kevin's mother. She is a tiny woman and has always reminded me of a sparrow. Her mind is as sharp as a pin, her face inquisitive and cheery, her head frequently cocked to one side. She looks like she has the tiniest appetite and probably does no more than peck at three peas and a rocket leaf but that is so far from the truth it's laughable. The woman can eat. And all once her husband is speaking. She waits for him, head cocked politely, nodding at the conversation and making *hmmm* noises the meaning of which can be inferred from the pitch of her response. But when he launches into yet another monologue about something she unclasps her hands and fixes her full concentration on the food in front of her. I don't know how she stays so tiny. I do know when I first witnessed it I sat so agog that Kevin tapped me under the chin to indicate I should probably close my mouth. But by the time Chih-hao is saying he heard a fascinating thing about boats the other day, Shu-feng has eaten three bowls of food and is casting glances at the kitchen to see if there might be extra floating around.

Knowing her as I do I have picked up a large squidgy cake from the deli on the corner. Seeing mother and son's faces as I take it from the fridge and carefully place the three-tier creation on the side is a picture. Kevin shoots around the table at speed to clear away the dishes, making room for cake. As I am cutting slices for them Kevin knows both his parents may be distracted enough for him to remind them that they couldn't spend the day together tomorrow.

'Mum and Dad, before you came over I mentioned I had a full day of work scheduled for this weekend that I simply can't get out of, and I'm so sorry but I still can't. Any other date and I would. Instead, Lily will take you out tomorrow and we can catch up on Sunday. I'll be completely tied up at work.' I hand him an extra big slice, partly because I know how uncomfortable he is saying this to his parents but also because he has managed to utter that last sentence without accompanying it with a wink and a smirk.

'And, Uncle and Auntie, I have got the best day lined up,' I say to try and mitigate the blow. 'We're going to be so busy. I remember, Chih-hao, last time you were over you were fascinated by the thought of caves under the city and—'

'Ooh,' said Chih-hao, 'that sounds good. I would like to see the caves. But Shu-feng and I noticed lots of posters all over the city as the taxi brought us in. Your Pride week? We saw lots of activities advertised. Did you know Taipei's Prides are the biggest in Asia? We thought we may see how Bristol compares?'

'Um...more fascinating than the caves is the fact that Lily's friend may be doing all that with you as well,' Kevin interrupts, so determined to halt the direction of conversation that his voice is positively burbling. Like a brook. One I wish I could dam.

'Hmmm?' Shu-feng's eyes widen. I have known them for over ten years and never have they yet met a 'friend' of mine. I could kill him.

'Um... Sorry, that's not happening now,' I say firmly whilst shooting daggers at Kevin.

'We used to think you might end up marrying Kevin,' Chih-hao smiles and both Kevin and I cringe. In fact, Kevin lets out a disgusted squeal at the same time and I shoot him a filthy look. 'But I'd be excited to meet your friend. Tell me, what does his father do?'

Jesus! He's worse than my own parents would be.

'There's been a misunderstanding, it's just me.'

'Ah, that is a shame. Is he marriage material?' Chih-hao winks and I petrify. I'm trying to think of a way to say I am not likely to see him any time soon whilst paying respect to Jay and acknowledging that yes, he is, just not for me.

The doorbell goes and I breathe again. A distraction. Hallelujah! Kevin jumps up, a flash of something indecipherable on his face but it certainly doesn't look like he is relaxing as I am beginning to.

He does a big-eyed *help* look at me as Dan enters the room with a large bottle of single malt whisky, wearing his very neatest clothes, and my heart wants to melt. There isn't a skull or a chain in sight and the four of us sit swilling Chih-hao's favourite spirit in large-bottomed glasses as the sun sets and Dan and Kevin sing, and play, a variety of duets on the piano and I realise why they have been spending so much time on the piano recently. All the prep hasn't just been for Drag

Factor; Dan has been tutoring him so he can play for his parents. The knowledge of that melts my soul as the liquor coats my throat and warms my body and I look around the room watching Chih-hao tap along with the music on his glass with real pleasure, while Shu-feng's *hmmm*s are reminiscent of a blissed-out cat.

Chapter Thirty-Nine

I have taken Chih-hao and Shu-feng to Redcliffe Caves and listened whilst Chih-hao talked and talked. I also watched Shu-feng ram at least six caramel bars in her mouth – sideways and whole – whilst he did so. It's been pleasant enough but all I have been able to think about is Jay, and how he could have been here with us had I not been such a twat. How he would have giggled at Shu-feng's stealth snacking, and chatted away with Chih-hao about things this city is famed for.

I have spent the day watching the way these two work together, how Chih-hao wordlessly guides her over the uneven bits of floor in the caves, how Shu-feng nods as he speaks, never once growing tired of it, stroking his arm when he gets excited. Their love for each other shines through all that they do and it reinforces the pangs I am feeling. I could have had this, and the more I see it, the more I recognise I might be happy with this life. Happy waking up every morning with a man who turns my insides out.

Watching them makes me think I'd like to give it my best try.

How I fretted that the sex would ever become boring I don't know. This couple in front of me build each other up all the time and I wonder if my work focusing on couples who have been tearing each other apart has impacted what I think relationships are.

Chih-hao and Shu-feng are a very timely reminder that finding your one can be pretty special.

As we drove through the city they have excitedly pointed out every Pride poster in the city. I swear they have not missed one and I'm feeling bad as I drive them to the Hippodrome for an evening show that Kevin bought them tickets for.

I'm not convinced it's where they want to be. But regardless of my Sherlock-like belief that these two want to be involved in the very sort of event that their son is competing in this evening, I am not going to force this one tonight.

Tonight has to be about Jinx and what makes her secure.

I let them out of the car, assure Chih-hao that this is the same show as the one their friends saw in London's West End and remind them a taxi will meet them outside afterwards to take them on to a restaurant for a post-show tasting menu.

I race back to the house to shimmy myself into my dress for tonight, gallop up the steps and let myself in.

'Arggggh, my eyes! They burn. I hope to God that's not what you're wearing tonight. Who are you? Where's my real flatmate?' Kevin is in the hallway about to leave and I let out a laugh. I'm so pleased I have caught him. Although I don't blame him for the revulsion.

I had left the house today in a bodycon dress and heels before I realised that I don't need to dress like this all the time.

That yes, it makes me feel good but the last thing I want right now is approving glances from random men. The man whose eyes I want to see light up with approval, with desire, is the very man whose heart I torched but two weeks ago. Only his.

Bumbling around caves with my best friends' parents didn't need me to be peek-sleek and it was more sensible not to wear kitten heels to a place with uneven flooring. Especially as my feet have a lot of dancing to do tonight.

So, very proud that this was ushering in a more mature Lily, a more confident, intrinsically motivated Lily, I had run back into the house and changed into jeans, a T-shirt and flats. And not for a fitness class.

It would seem my flatmate does not approve.

'Be proud. I am new, streamlined, doesn't-give-a-shit-about-shallow-bollocks-Lily.'

'Did aliens kidnap you in the night?'

'Something like that.' I smile in reply, if intermittent and fevered dreams or long periods of wakeful self-flagellation are aliens. 'Anyway, enough about me, I have a dress you're going to love. Fear not, new doesn't-give-a-fuck me is getting left at home for this evening. You will have glam Lily, in a dress so short it flashes her cervix, shouting her support tonight.'

'Glad to hear it.' He purses his lips in the hallway mirror and turns his face from side to side, chin up.

'Is there anything I can do?'

'You can lend me that lipstick I love. I'm having second thoughts about mine and yours could be perfect. I'm gonna need to try it with my outfit.'

'Consider it yours.' I rummage in my handbag and present it with a flourish. 'Anything else?'

'Have you spoken to Jay?'

'No, I can't, you know. Can't.'

'But you want to?'

'I've cocked it up.' I shrug my shoulders. Kevin knows how I feel, he's been subjected to torrents of emotion about how I've been a twat, hurt a man I should have cherished, listing the reasons he is the *only* man I could consider breaking all my old behaviours for, and so on. And on and on and on and on.

'Are you ready, love?' I hear Dan shouting through the front door.

'Go, I'm going to get changed and I'll be right behind you. You've got this,' I tell him.

'I know,' he says. 'I hope so, anyway.' He says that more falteringly. He heads to the door and kisses Dan hello and then turns back to me.

'You better decide what you want to do about Jay because Dan and I love him even if you don't.'

'The thing is I do. You know I really do. But there's nothing I can do now.' I shrug my shoulders and wish we were talking about anything other than this.

'Well then, it's a good thing I messaged him earlier and told him it wouldn't be the same without him. I don't crawl across grass with just anyone, you know.'

'What have I told you about interfering!' This time though I am not knocked sideways by a wave of dread; instead it is a little puddle in my tummy, mingled with something else I don't recognise. Hope?

'What have I told you about how you *need* me to interfere in this case? I know you. I know you're wrong about this, you've just admitted it and I don't think it has all played out just yet. And I know about true love.' He motions his head towards Dan, who is waiting patiently on the steps.

'Did he answer? What did he say?' My stomach is flip-flopping. Am I going to have a chance to apologise? I don't think I have the words to show how much I regret my behaviour the other week. What if I mess it up, again? Anyway, surely he's said thanks but no thanks. 'What did he say?' I repeat, trying to stay nonchalant.

Kevin scrunches his face. Oh shit, I knew it, I knew it! It's better if he doesn't come.

'He took some persuading and honestly, I'm not sure if he will make it but...'

Dan stands on tiptoe and shouts from behind him. 'The man is no fool.' He winks and grabs Kevin's hand. 'Come on, gorgeous, we need to get you there so you can run through one last time fussing, panicking, and driving us all crazy. And you –' he tiptoes again '– *you* can thank us later!'

Chapter Forty

I have made up for my dialled-down outfit from earlier and I'm now all-out flamboyant in the dress I bought especially for tonight, and especially for Jinx. She is going to love it. I have kept it a secret simply because I know the mere sight of a sequin sends her into a tailspin of happiness and this little beauty is made entirely of sequins, creating a peacock effect. It is the most bling outfit I have ever owned. Ever. It is also so short and tight, the hem mere centimetres from my groin. And I love it. It makes me feel super confident and I am going to whip up *all* the dancing and happiness tonight to help secure Jinxy's rightful place on her throne.

I arrive at the bar with my heart beating in anticipation. My heart has felt frantic ever since Kevin said he has been messaging Jay. What if Jay is already here? I have been running through things in my head, practice conversations, but nothing I can think of is enough to apologise for the she-demon I was the last couple of times I have seen him.

I step out of the Uber and take a deep breath, looking at the rainbow flags fluttering by Chrysalis. He won't turn up. Why would he?

As I am about to enter, I have one of those shivers-up-your-back moments and I shudder. My nan used to say that someone had just walked over her grave. That. I know it's just nerves, it must be nerves, but at the same time something makes me take a step back and look up and down the street.

I spot Jay. Is it Jay? Can it be? I recognise the way he holds his body, the way he moves with each step. I have been thinking of him every waking moment – and the non-waking ones too – for weeks now – is this wishful thinking? The man is walking purposefully towards the bar and is in black tie. Each footstep brings him closer until I can see it is him. It really is. He's come!

I bite my lip and start to fidget with my dress, pull down the hem, and then, worried I'm misshaping it, pinch it up at my shoulders. I try to run through some of the things I had prepped on the way over but my mind is blank.

Blank! Completely blank. Like black. Dark. Nothing.

I let out a deep breath, and then need another. He seems to be slowing down and I will him to speed up, get here, get this over with. My stomach feels empty, my legs feel hollow and I am lightheaded. I dig my feet into my shoes, pushing the heels into the pavement. Tethering myself.

He's here. It can't go that badly, can it? If he's here that *has* to be a show of willing. Oh, but what if he is here for some kind of humiliating public revenge? The thought barrels into my brain and it takes a huge effort to push it out again.

No, Jay is here because he's a good man who keeps his word, he is here *despite* me, not because of me.

I watch his face as he approaches. What is he thinking? Is

he pleased to see me? I watch as he realises I am standing waiting for him and I'm relieved to see a smile creep across his face as he tries hard to contain it, to keep his cool.

That has to bode well, doesn't it? I don't expect him to forgive me, but I know that smile: that is the smile of a thousand teenage crushes. If he is pleased to see me, that is great, even if we never get back onto a romantic footing.

He would be right not to want to date me any more – I mean, *I'd* advise him against it – and I'm fairly sure rudeness, insensitivity and physical assault are not qualities high on his mythical mother-to-be list. But if we could be friends again, work alongside each other with a smidge of camaraderie, then that would give me something to build on, allow me to prove myself over time.

He's getting closer and I'm panicking again about what I'm going to say.

Sorry. It just needs to be as simple as sorry. For now, sorry is a start.

He reaches me and stops, I stand on the pavement, facing him, waiting for him, and I'm reminded of how I moved my foot to his in Jinx's dressing room, how he reciprocated.

I manage to give him a smile, a timid smile. The fear must be written all over my face. I open my mouth to start my apology and nothing comes out. I give him another shy smile and try again. Nada.

But it seems okay; he is sliding me a little shy smile hello too. Mine would quite like to morph into a *would-you-look-at-us-both-so-attuned-we-are-arriving-at-the-same-time-maybe-we-should-get-married* grin but I rein it in.

I'm not convinced his is saying the same. It's hard to

decode and my confidence that he had been fighting a smile from the minute he saw me has disappeared.

Seconds pass as we look at each other but they feel like aeons. If he could only be telepathic, that would definitely help. I try and channel all my apologies through my eyes.

'You look beautiful.' His first words are simple as he looks at me. Suddenly I feel ten foot tall. This man finds me beautiful! Even after having seen me at my most horrific, emotionally and physically. That has to be a good thing, surely? I feel myself blushing. I hardly ever blush!

'You look pretty amazing yourself,' I say. And it's true. He has gone full on dapper tonight and looks very James Bond. It is at complete odds with his usual garb but seems utterly fitting for today. He looks like every romantic hero ever and I may well become a dribbling wreck before we've even got through the door. Although I suppose I should be grateful my voice seems to be working again.

'Thank you.' He says it simply and then waves his hand towards the entrance, when suddenly we hear a piercing whistle and turn in unison to see Chloe, Megan and Ellie teetering along the street.

I know I still need to say sorry, explain myself, maybe hurl myself at his feet and beg a bit, but none of that seems appropriate in front of the girls. I'm not sure whether to feel grateful or resentful about their arrival.

We wait for them to reach us, our hands dangling by our sides, every bit of me wanting to reach out and curl my fingers into his. I find myself having to pull my hand away as my fingers edge towards his, independently of my brain.

'A'ight,' they all nod as they approach. 'Thought we'd come down here and see this for ourselves. Gotta love drag.

If your mate wins this she might be on next season's Ru Paul.'

'Maybe.' I smile. 'Good to see you girls.'

'And yeah, we know, we promise not to drink,' Chloe says to Jay, aware that their presence may make things a little awkward for him.

'You best believe it, we know the bar staff,' he retorts. 'Come on then.' He waves again and we all enter the room together.

It is already packed and Dan is on the decks playing tunes to get everyone pumped. I have *never* seen it this busy before; the whole place is alive. There are all the regulars dressed in their absolute best and I can spot the neon T-shirts of the community centre's choir cast.

Phyllis is up on stage with the three judges for this evening, all gathered by the gold-painted mdf judging panel that they will be sitting behind. One is a journalist from the local news, one of those women who is so lovely and smiley that everyone wants to be her friend. Then there is Urethra Shankin, a drag queen with a similar story to Phyllis's but based in London. She adores playing the villain and has been judging Drag Factor since its inception. Finally, there is James St-John Aubyn, an actor who rose to prominence as a teenager in the *Carry On* films and has been a vocal ally of the LGBTQ community ever since. The four of them are cackling evilly, the newsreader doubled over, she is laughing so much. I watch as she grabs hold of the mdf to support herself and it wobbles dramatically, which sets them all off again.

As Jay and I head towards the bar, Olive whizzes past us – on rollerskates – in a pair of black velvet hotpants with different coloured velvet hearts patched onto her bottom, and fishnets on underneath. She is carrying a tray of cocktails and stops to kiss Jay on the lips and asks him something about Cass. I don't hear his answer but it reminds me that I haven't asked directly about his sister. That's the trouble with overwhelming lust, endless introspection and an overwhelming need to apologise, they can make you a little bit selfish.

We grin as she zooms off, freezing as she sees Phyllis from her position on stage catch sight of her. Eek, roller-skates surely have to be a no. But instead of waving her cane in fury, Phyllis beams across and blows a kiss. Of course, she and Olive are friends. I would never have put the two together before but now I have, it makes perfect sense.

'I owe you so many apologies but first, how is Cass, is she okay?' I ask.

'Something is going on and I've promised to back off and trust her but it's not really easy. Then she messaged earlier and told me she needed me to meet her down here later.'

'It'll be great to see her. I hope everything is okay though.' He flashes a half smile at my words and I know he has all sorts of emotion resting on her turning up. I also know now why he has turned up this evening. I resolve to make sure I am not just here to scream for Jinx but to keep a watchful eye on Jay as well, in case Cass doesn't manage to make it and he immediately imagines the worst-case scenario.

We head to the bar together and get our drinks. He turns to me. 'I'd best be getting on. It was nice to see you though, Lily.'

Argh, of course he doesn't want to spend time with me. I shouted at him for leaching into all of my life, for a start. I still haven't managed a proper 'sorry' and I'm not sure it's a conversation that should be shouted over music. I want him to be able to hear every word – once I've worked out exactly what they are.

'Okay, but I'm about to go find Jinxy, I know she'd love to see you. Come with me?' Before he can answer we hear shouting, even with the tunes playing.

'No! Just no! I'm not having it.'

I exchange a look with Jay, who scrunches his face up in alarm and shrugs his shoulders and follows me as I prepare to head backstage to see what is going on.

Just as I turn though, I feel before I see Jay break out into a massive grin as Cass enters the club. She is weighed down by three huge, huge bags that look like they hold a lifetime in them and a big grin is on her face. She ambles towards us, deliberately going slowly, lifting each leg in turn and placing them down as if she is in slow motion. I can see Jay arching his brow wryly whilst working really hard not to run towards her.

She looks as if she has just been let loose in a candy store, such is the grin on her face once she reaches us, although she does flick me a little bit of side-eye before turning back to her brother. 'So you know that whole I'll-do-anything-for-you-little-sister thing?' she says, her bags swinging and looking like they may knock her over any minute.

'Yes,' says Jay. His tone is a little Herman Munster but joy is dancing out of his face.

'Can I move in then?'

'Can you take charge of your blasted cat and have all the cacti, every single one of the buggers, in your room?'

'Oh. My. God.' Cass draws out each word like a stroppy teenager and Jay breaks and wraps her up into the biggest of bear hugs. Then he lets go, takes each bag off her shoulders, carefully placing them on the – slightly sticky – floor, and wraps her up again, this time spinning her round.

'I'm taking that as a yes!' Cass shrieks as her hair spins out like a windmill and she beams as much joy as he does, despite the red rims of her eyes. It is impossible not to watch this scene and be reminded of the goodness of Jay, of all the love he has, of all the love he gives.

Jay drops her to her feet and then grabs the bags. 'Let's go put these somewhere safe and out of the way.'

We head backstage again, raised voices still audible.

'I'm going to drag you out by your thirsty-ass wig and shake you so hard that every last bit of filler in you is rolling across the floor.'

'Ooh, drama,' squeals Cass. 'Not sure that it's safe.' She cocks her head in the direction of the arguing.

'I'll take a look,' I say.

Whatever is going on, I hope Jinxy isn't in the middle of it but then what sounds like very much her voice rises and I hear her say, 'I will pull this shit off and make you bleed, you shady bitch!'

As Jay, Cass and I turn the corner we see chaos in front of us. There are eight queens getting ready out the back, all of whom are familiar faces from the West Country drag scene. They are all in various states of undress, some have their wigs fixed already, some are still just in wig caps and tape. Most have their make-up fully done but Jinx still has a fair way to go; her eyebrows and sideburns are glued down but she hasn't made a start on her foundation yet. With only a little while until kick-off, this is alarming.

More alarming still, she is standing next to Vivicious and is holding her by her long pony-tailed weave, which I am fairly sure is an absolute no.

'Put her down, Jinxy, you know she's all kind of fucked cos she were never loved as a child,' Meryl Strip calls across the room as she is rummaging through the staging cupboard whilst wearing tucking panties and prosthetic breasts and very little else.

'Yep and she isn't loved as an adult either.' Jinx kicks Viv in the ankles and I step forward to try and de-escalate.

'Ooh, I think these are yours, Twinks,' shouts Lickety Split, a female drag queen who has come up from Cornwall and is dressed in a floor-length gown made out of little tin squares, all featuring a different Cornish image taped on to them and linked like chainmail. She has her make-up half done, one eyelid painted as the Cornish flag, and is waving a pair of diamanté stockings.

'And might this be something to do with you, Ann?' calls Meryl, who is pulling out a huge piece of fabric like a magician pulls scarves. I try not to laugh. Meryl is making the most ridiculous faces as she pulls and pulls.

'Right!' Phyllis storms in, marches past us and up to Jinx and Vivicious. 'What in the name of Grace Jones and all that is holy is going on? Let go of her now!'

Jinx arches her brow and then drops the ponytail as if she were doing a mic drop, her eyes fixed on Phyllis rather than Vivicious, who is rubbing her head and shooting lasers of hate across at my very best friend in the world.

A chorus of fury greets the older woman as the girls explain that Vivicious has been messing with their things.

Again.

It's a repeat of last year's antics, when the whole thing

descended into chaos as they all – bar Vivicious – lost key pieces of their acts leaving everyone only partially ready, totally flustered and Viv the clear winner.

This time Adore has lost her ukulele, Jinx's borrowed lipstick – mine! – has gone walkies and OestreGem is only wearing one earring and is sitting in front of a mirror letting out a long piercing shriek, her face resembling the movie poster for *Scream*.

'How do you know it was her?' Phyllis demands, 'And that you're not all a bunch of careless wenches who can't be trusted on the biggest night of the motherfucking year to keep your shit together?'

'Adore Vajayjay saw her,' Ann Tagonism answers.

'Is that true?'

Adore nods. And sings, 'Caught her red-handed' whilst miming strumming the ukulele.

Phyllis taps her cane three times and the room is immediately silent. Even OestreGem stops mid-scream and Meryl ceases her rifling and stands up straight.

'We do not behave this way,' Phyllis pronounces, and the two burly men behind her nod and cross their arms. 'For decades we have had to put up with disrespect and all the bullshit that comes with it from society and yet we have always been a sisterhood. When I started my first house back in the Eighties, when I bought this club, this was all to create a space for us to come, meet, breathe in safety knowing that we were secure. We support each other. We are here to lift each other up. To help each other reach our goals and live our dreams. This is not on.' She looks slowly around the room and makes sure she makes eye contact with everyone present.

I love Phyllis but she could scare the bejesus out of the devil himself.

Everyone nods in subdued agreement.

She taps her cane three more times whilst looking Viv straight in the eye. 'I notice you are not denying this. Have you anything to say?'

'Each girl for herself. This is business, it ain't personal.' Vivicious shrugs.

'All I need to hear. Barry, Gary, get her out of here. Get her out for good and I will go and explain to the judges why she won't be performing tonight.' Jinx nods smugly at Viv as Gary and Barry each take an arm.

'I'll pack your things and leave them in the gutter,' Lickety says as her fellow contestant is dragged out. 'Right next to you.'

'Oh, wait. No!' Jinx shouts. 'She's my most serious competition.' Cass bursts out laughing.

'Well, thank you very much.' Meryl purses her lips.

'Shit, bitch,' Oestregem cackles and slams her hand down so hard on her thigh the dressing table she is sat at jiggles.

'I need to beat her. Phyllis, please. I need to win because I'm the best, not have it hanging over me that I only won because I didn't compete against Vivicious.'

'Really?' Phyllis looks at Jinx's face. 'This *is* your year –'she turns to Ann, who is making a *seriously?* face '– and you know it.' Turning back to Jinx, she continues, 'It was always going to be. You have come so far this last year. You are the stand-out best, whether she's here or not.' The room fills with murmurs of agreement and I love this place for exactly that. Phyllis is right, this is a place to raise people up, support them, and everyone in this room was doing exactly that, knowing how much this year means to Jinxy and how much work she has put in.

'Please.'

'Right, Barry, Gary, bring her back!' Phyllis hurls the words over her shoulder and the two men march backwards with their arms still under Vivicious' armpits, stopping and gently dropping her into the chair she had been assigned for make-up.

Phyllis bends down, gets very close to her face. 'Do your very best to win. Do you understand me? Do your very best. But first you can help everyone find their shit. Everything. Clear?'

'Yes. Although I don't need to try that hard, look at them...'
'Them' all start to hiss.

'And you're on first so you've got seven minutes, seven, to find everything and sort that out.' Phyllis uses the tip of her cane to point to the ponytail, which is more than a little messy now. 'Um... Ann, I'll move you to second to last cos it looks like you still have a lot to do. Is that all right, everyone?'

Ann, who is in a bodysuit with a basket-weave structure around her torso and not much else, looks around to check everyone is happy and then gives Phyllis a great big hug – or as much as the basket will allow. Phyllis bats her off as if she is an insect and the room erupts in laughter.

'Are you okay?' I ask Jinx as the commotion dissipates and Vivicious has handed back some earrings, three lipsticks, the ukulele and a bottle of Hennessy.

'Darling I am fine and dandy.' She grins at me as she takes my lipstick back from Viv and tuts at her loudly. 'Now get out the front there and get that crowd ready!'

Chapter Forty-One

The three of us have stood and watched Viv, who is going to take some beating. She starts with 'Young Hearts Run Free' and then segues into 'I Want You Back', finishing with 'Good Times'. She is an absolute assassin when it comes to lip-syncing and her dance skills are off the scale. She is flipping herself here, there and everywhere, can power-slide like a rockstar, and the way she flips her long, long legs around a pole is terrifying. She knows exactly what tracks to choose to please an audience and get them participating. She is hugely impressive and the judges think so too, with her scoring a 9, an 8 and an 8. A daunting first act and not one I'd want to follow. However, despite Phyllis clapping by the side of the stage, Vivicious still shot daggers at her as she sashayed back down the steps.

She is followed by TwinkiBelle, dressed as a record to pay testament to the rich musical tradition of Bristol. OestreGem is a drag queen in the old tradition and belts out a Tina Turner medley with incredibly strong vocals and a whole lot of comedy in her delivery. Next up is Adore, who sings a song with her ukulele that I haven't heard before and misses the mark a little bit. Cass looks at me and grimaces but in a sympathetic kind of a way. I nod and give Adore a congratulatory hug as she comes down the stage steps. It takes courage to perform, whatever the outcome.

During a break for everyone to grab some drinks, Cass looks across at me. 'So, I think I need a wee.'

Jay looks at her slightly askance, but I smirk.

'So do I, strangely,' I reply. Jay looks at both of us and shakes his head.

'What? You want us to wee on the floor?' Cass says combatively in that way that only siblings can.

'Fine. See you in a bit.' Jay turns to go and speak to some of the members of the community choir and I follow Cass to the ladies. I am flattered that maybe she wants to talk to me about Jasmine and slightly terrified that she may instead want to speak about her brother.

'So...' Cassie calls through the stall. I giggle – I can't help it. I never really had that whole hanging out and chatting in the loos at school thing.

'So, I know your brother is made up that you're here tonight and by the look of those bags you brought in, you'll be staying with him for a bit.' I finish the sentence for her.

'Yeah, I think so,' she says as I hear the pull of the loo roll. 'Not for ever but for the foreseeable.'

'How you feeling about that?' I ask. It kind of just slips out and I am glad that the wall is separating us otherwise this would feel a bit like a session.

'Strong, good, hopeful. You helped, you know? You and Jay. Obviously, Jay has always done his best to help but he's a little cack-handed and sometimes, despite his best intentions, I find it a bit overwhelming. But he's a protective big brother and I know how lucky I am to have him. I've known for a while that things weren't right with Jasmine. I loved the attention at first, she made me feel so safe and so goddam loved, but as time went by it was clear that something was off. Her loving became oppressive in the end, suffocating, frightening at times. I would catch her just staring at me, and it wouldn't be a gaze full of love, it would be unnerving.'

'It's hard to accept that the thing you've invested in so heavily emotionally may not be working. Leaving is a process and it needs to be done in our own time,' I say.

'Yeah, I needed to be sure and then I needed a plan. And I didn't dare confide any of that to Jay because I didn't want Jas seeing anything that might give her a heads-up. Jay is not as subtle as he thinks he is. She'd been due to go to a conference this weekend and I'd been worried because in the past this causes tension. It's fine if I go with her but if I don't she's been known to cancel them and stay at home, saying I can't be trusted to look after myself. In fact, she's so convinced of this she once screamed, like really screamed at me for hours, refused to let me out of the bedroom, jammed the door shut and screeched about how I couldn't be trusted, and yet nothing she was saying or doing represented the way I have acted in this relationship. I know how important this weekend's conference is so I was hopeful, but it seems like she has some kind of psychic sense for knowing what I'm up to, as if she is somehow monitoring the house. I've been so paranoid that I've been checking the light fittings, the furniture, all in the dark to see if she has some freaky camera installed, but I never found anything.' We are both at the basins now, washing our hands and I reach out and rub her shoulder. I can imagine how frightening that must be, how trapped and desperate Cassie must have felt.

'But I did my best, I assumed she had some way of watching me, and I have been so obedient, so meek. Even when she's not home I'm following all these rules she has for us to ensure we live peaceably even though none of them made sense to me. I've not fulfilled my promise to do the scenery for the community choir and that stung but it meant I "proved" my trustworthiness. Leaving the house is always evidence of a crime.' She sighs and rolls her eyes but I know this goes deeper than the throwaway reaction she is communicating. 'But it worked. She trusted me, she's gone away and I am out, out! I'm gonna block her number and then hide for a bit. I've left her a letter saying it's over and to leave me be.'

Four girls stream into the loos and Cass becomes quiet and then flicks me a look of mischief before leading me to the two shabby high-backed velvet chairs sat at the end of the bathroom. 'I know that it isn't fully over, she's going to make things difficult for a bit, but I'll be safe at Jay's. I just have to ride it out. Look, I was determined not to talk about this. I want to move on, not revisit. I didn't drag you in here to talk about all that.'

'You didn't? We're not here to talk about Jasmine?' Oh shit. My heart starts to boom again.

'Pfft! As if! No, I have far more interesting things to talk to you about. Namely you and my brother. What is going on there?'

'I don't know what you mean,' I say, somewhat mendaciously.

'You know exactly what I mean. You're going to make me spell it out? My brother is practically perfect but has spent so long trying to race to the finish line that he forgets to enjoy the present, so... we had a bet.'

'Ahhh,' I say, 'I know about the bet.'

'I wondered if you did. I wasn't sure if he'd tell you. He needed to spend some time living in the present and not actively seeking out Mrs Right, the perfect baby maker. He needs to live in the moment for a bit.'

I gulp.

'We're not dating, I'm not a baby maker.'

'Oh, I *know* you're not dating,' she says, gliding right past the important bit of that sentence. 'And that's what I'm talking about. From what I've heard, you were refusing to answer his calls, his messages, and I don't know what else happened recently but he was weird about it the other day, said there was no way, no how, the two of you would work... and now you seem to be here together. I was worried that it might be me holding you two back, now I'm worried that you're both mentalists who are determined to fuck it up,' she says and I shrug. I mean, that is kind of me in a nutshell.

'It's not you,' I say carefully.

'Oh, trust, I know.' Cassie is a steamroller, with all the verve and energy of someone in her early twenties who powers on through without always slowing down to pick up on cues and clues. 'I know the thought behind the vow idea, the let's-show-Cass-that-change-is-possible as if I'm some four-year-old that needs to be shown something to be able to copy it. I know what he was doing. And then you came along and are all perfect and everything... I'm not being sarcastic, you really are.'

'I really am not. I cannot begin to tell you how imperfect, flawed and fucked-up I am.'

'Oh, I'll give you a chance, don't worry. But you're not letting me get to the good bit,' she says petulantly and I can't help but smile. 'The good bit is that he did manage, whilst deliberately trying not to, to get caught up in the moment. To do so with you. And I know you've been clear on how you're um... not looking for a relationship and we both know how important that vow was to him but despite all of that the two of you had a magical night, the most magical night apparently.'

I open my mouth to speak but she holds up her hand. 'Nope, no. I'm his sister, I don't need to hear details of this magical evening, plus, you know, lesbian, so that whole thing, just yuk. I really don't want to hear about it. But I do know that I released him from the vow, because he has lived in the moment without fretting about the future. I've practically given him permission to march you down the aisle, even though that's not my place, but there's been no movement forward. So I'm at the point where I know it's not me stopping him, and I know Jay – I have seen him in relationships, I have seen him at the height of a crush, but this, this is something else...'

'Cass...' I try and interrupt. She is so on the wrong path here but she holds her hand up and cuts me off. 'My brother is very much in love with you, deeply, genuinely and unlike any of his other short-lived infatuations. So the only thing stopping the two of you from having a wonderful relationship must be you, sweet pea. I get that you like being single and yet I've seen you with him. And relationships are your job, I know you *know* they're not some oppressive life sentence. Not all of them.

The two of you together, the way you interact, treat each other, all of that has had a lot to do with me realising that is what I want in my life, that that was not what I had with Jasmine. But it is what *you* have now, or had until whatever has happened between you to mess it up. You've had me so intrigued I've listened to every episode of your podcast and heard that Jay was so concerned that he reached out to you. All your advice, that fact, all of that has made a huge difference to me ending my relationship, sorting out my life, so now it's my turn to meddle in his. And I have to ask you, bearing in mind all I have seen, what is it about my brother that is not good enough for you?'

Chapter Forty-Two

C ass and Lily have disappeared to the loos and have been gone for ages. We are four acts and the interval down and I cannot see them anywhere.

I turn and have a good scout around the club when I see a couple that, from the photos on display at Lily's house, look very much like Jinx's parents.

No! Jinx's messages said they were meant to be having a post-show tasting menu that should take them three hours, but instead they are standing in the doorway looking wide-eyed.

Dan is on the decks, Lily is off with Cass and I need to do something quick. However, why ever they are here, I can't risk Jinx seeing them before she goes on stage. As I push through the throng of people, I see Chloe and the girls. I make frantic waving motions at them as I approach.

'Hello, hello. Mr and Mrs—' Oh, sod it, I don't know their surnames. I hope to God I've got the right people. 'Um... I'm Lily and Kevin's friend. What a pleasure to see you both.'

'Ah, you're Lily's *friend*.' The man leans forward and

emphasises the last word. It *is* them then. I stop my signalling and reach out to shake their hands.

'Yes. Lovely to meet you. Was something wrong with...um...never mind. Can I get you both a drink?'

They both nod and mouth the word Scotch at me. I need to keep them as far away from the stage as possible. My freaky-ass semaphore seems to have worked and Chloe, Megan and Ellie sidle up to me like perfect little homing pigeons and I am crazy thankful.

'You good, Jay?' Chloe asks.

'Could you do me a favour and take Mr and Mrs um...Kevin's parents up to the roof terrace whilst I grab some drinks?' I say to her, hoping my eyes are conveying the desperate nature of the situation. 'Keep them there,' I mouth slowly, just to make sure she understands.

'Yeah, of course. Everything okay?'

'Yup, yup!' I say, my mind already racing ahead. I need to get Lily. There is no point texting her, she won't check her phone for hours. And, let's face it, she has form for not responding to me immediately.

Meryl has taken to the stage and her special talent appears to be a striptease. This is most definitely not the act with which to break Jinx's parents' drag cherry.

'It's very noisy down here. If you follow Chloe –' I gesture at her '– she'll find you somewhere quieter to sit and I'll be with you the minute I have your drinks.'

As I'm queuing at the bar I realise that once I get to the rooftop terrace I can ask Chloe to go and find Lily. As soon as I'm served I gallop up the stairs two at a time, whisky slopping over the sides of the glasses. I like and respect Chloe but she could say just about anything to Jinx's parents.

As I reach the door to the terrace, I see all the twinkly white lights and am reminded of Lily having her cawww moment. That had been the first time I saw any vulnerability in her and now I know that she has coffers full of it, just like the rest of us. I am about to turn the corner when I hear an ominous conversation.

'I think you've got that bang on, Mrs Huang.' Ah, that's the surname, thank you, Chloe. I freeze as I hear her add, 'They would be well sorted if they were together. They both told us that they don't mix business with pleasure and that they're working together. Actually, because of that Lily has offered me a job to help me through uni. I need to stay in Bristol for my family and she's said I can run her social media, do some admin, manage her appointments and all that. She's sound and we've always loved Jay.'

I didn't know Lily had set this up for Chloe.

'She's a very impressive young woman, always has been,' says Mrs Huang.

'Right, and me and the girls have chatted and we think loads of people work together all the time. Look at Rochelle and Marvin, Rihanna and A$AP Rocky,' Chloe says and then mischief sneaks into her tone. 'I would tell Jay but you know, boundaries. That's not my business.'

Then she winks straight at me. She knew I was here all along. It doesn't stop her though. 'Life's too short, ain't it? The two of them should be together.'

'They should.' Mrs Huang says.

'Couldn't agree more,' her husband adds.

'Hi, you lot, I've got your drinks here, sorry, spilled a bit. Thanks, Chloe, um...' How to phrase this so as not to show the Huangs I need Lily now?

'I'll get back to my mates then, but I'm just going to the loo. Do you know where it is, Jay?' There's a glimmer in her eyes and it makes me wonder if she has been keeping her eye on me and Lily since she got here.

Jinx's dad starts chuntering on about the bar's architecture and I mouth 'get Lily' three times at Chloe whilst pointing in the direction of the loo. As she heads off, I use the break given by Mr Huang's monologue to escape into my own thoughts.

The girls are right, I want to be with Lily. I really do. But I've made it clear enough. On The Downs she showed clearly how she is far from interested, but the way she greeted me when I arrived tonight, the way she's been by my side all evening, did I give up too easily? Has she changed her mind? I'm so confused but know that if there is still a slim chance that I have a shot I have to get over my hurt, my pride, and leave the door open for her.

Cass thinks it's a good idea, the girls think it's a good idea, even Mr and Mrs Huang whom I hadn't met before now think it's a good idea. So now, tonight, is the last shot, tonight I have to hope and pray that Lily has begun to agree with them and finds the courage to let me know.

Chapter Forty-Three

'What is it about my brother that is not good enough for you?' Cass says and I don't know what to do with myself. Is this what she thinks? That I'm some snotty cow that believes I am too good for Jay? It's so ridiculous I could laugh but my heart is hammering in my chest, in fear not amusement. I need to make this right.

I lean forward from my chair and grab Cass's hand and look her directly in the eyes.

'There is nothing wrong with your brother. Nothing at all. You have it all wrong.' She arches an eyebrow and I know I'm going to have to explain this properly to her. Make her see the truth of all that has been holding me back.

'It's because I *love* your brother, I really do, and as a fully-fledged human, not some kind of sex toy...'

'I heard that episode tonight, whilst I was packing up to come here. I'm glad you know there's more to my brother than his, I don't know... six inches?'

I smirk but need to carry on with what I have to say. 'He is

347

not the one who is flawed, it's me. Your brother is an amazing man, completely different from any man I have met before, from any of the men I have spent time with before. From our very first meeting he wanted to get to know *me*, even when he had seen me at what I thought was my very worst. But when he told me how he felt, well, we all carry stuff and he's been forcing me to look at mine. And...' I squeeze her hand tightly to reinforce how much this means.

'And?' She still has an eyebrow arched and she has a right to be pretty shitty with me. But I'm grateful she's listening and I need to say this out loud for myself as well.

'And I know that when I lashed out at him, I was scared...'

'You lashed out at him? What? When?' She is suddenly furious, full mother hen, and I realise she doesn't know about The Downs.

'He told me he loved me and I...well, I lost all sense of him and who he was and went a bit crazy.'

'He told you he loved you? Wow. That takes a lot for Jay to say. In all his past relationships, he's never dropped those words. They come with a lot of meaning. And you...' She shakes her head.

I feel shit. I know all this but Cass's words bring it home all the more. 'I got scared, I was frightened of deviating from all I have been using to keep myself safe for so many years,' I say.

'Safe? Safe from what?'

'From being hurt. But when I realised I had lost Jay, completely fucked it, that's when I knew that he was *the* man I had to take the leap with. That the thought of my life without him is actually way scarier than any of the things I thought I was terrified of. That closeness, the intimacy, the sharing of who I am and wanting him to share himself with me, that is what matters.' My words are falling over themselves, their speed showing how much I mean them.

'So you hurt my brother because you were scared of being hurt?' The disdain in her voice couldn't be clearer and I know how basic I sound. I need to explain better.

'I love your brother. The way he cares for you, his integrity, his honour, his lack of superficiality, they all add up to one very rare person and that's not something I ever expected to find in a partner. And then when I did...well, Jay wants kids, he's made no secret of it, and I don't know if I can have them. Fertility-wise, not choice-wise. I am taking steps to find out and if it turns out I've been carrying this belief that I'm infertile all my life and I'm not, then I need to look at *if* I want to be a mum. Up until recently I wasn't sure if I did. I've told myself for years that motherhood is not for me. But to have children and have children with Jay, little mini hims, well, that doesn't just not panic me anymore, it makes me actively want that dream to come true. But there's a whole lot of steps to get there and I didn't think it was fair for Jay to have to travel that path alongside me. I thought... I thought he deserved better.'

'You should've talked to him about this. I know Jay, I know how grateful he is to Malcom and Sue. If he says he loves you then he really, *really* does and if he can't have children of his own with you that wouldn't necessarily put him off.'

'It might,' I say dryly.

'Honestly, the Jay before he met you, yeah, probably. But I also know he has been open to fostering as well. You can do that short-term or as respite for other families. There are all kinds of solutions. It would make him so happy to give kids like him and me a chance.'

'You're right, I owed him that. I was so caught up in my

own head with this whole list of reasons why I wanted to be single, but Jay has blown all of them out of the water. He has shown me that being with him is more meaningful than any of the reasons I have for remaining on my own. He has shown me that I could have a different future, that it's possible for me to have a relationship without losing any of my identity, and that life would be brighter and richer for it. And he is the only person I can see that with. My fear of ending up in a relationship has now changed to a fear that I've jeopardised any chance of one with the man I respect, admire and love so very much.'

'Oh my God!' Cass flaps her hands at me in frustration, which is not the reaction I had expected. 'You two are the same. The both of you need a goddam bloody ass-whipping. You and Jay, him with his wish-lists and you with your reasons. What I'm hearing is you love him, he loves you. No one is saying the two of you will be together for ever but you have to give it a goddam try. It sounds like he has tried to, so now it's down to you. You need to shake yourself up a bit, take a risk and do it tonight. That man has had enough hurt in his life to last a lifetime, if you don't sort this soon, then the hurt you've caused is going to snowball inside him and there will be no way back for you.'

I gulp at the severity of her words, but she's right, I know she is. I need to remedy the pain I have caused and I need to do it as soon as I can. I need to open up to him as he did me and show that my fear of that is considerably less than the fear of losing him for ever. But how?

The bathroom door opens and Chloe comes in. 'Ah, found you, I've been...' She pauses and takes in the two of us, the atmosphere clearly emotional and heightened. 'You good?'

'Fine,' says Cassie. 'I've just been putting a bomb up this one's arse, she needs it.'

'Ah, I can't say, she's gonna be my boss.'

'In that case you're off the hook. But someone needs to tell this girl to take things with my brother to the next level and stop twatting about.'

'Your brother? Jay?' Chloe asks Cassie and I sigh.

'Uh-huh,' Cass confirms.

'Oh well, in that case, hallelujah and thank God for you. Cos someone needs to make this dippy bitch listen!'

Chapter Forty-Four

I'm back in the main room of Chrysalis now, Chloe's and Cass's words whirling around my head. Cass is right. I have made a huge mistake that needs rectifying as soon as possible.

We have pushed through to the front of the stage and despite my racing mind, I want to give Jinx my full focus. I've missed Meryl Strip but Lickety Split is amazing, and Ann Tagonism's hot air balloon costume is nothing short of art. The crowd are hyped and we are more than ready for Jinx's final act.

Suddenly there is a billowing puff of theatrical smoke and Jinx appears in the centre of the stage. She is wearing a huge frou-frou ballgown, the bottom half resembling a bird cage, with the hem decorated with the old paper Bristol Pounds. Her dress is an homage to all the green spaces in Bristol. She has her French Revolution wig on but it has been added to with birds and flowers and is so detailed that it could be examined for ages and still new things would reveal themselves. My heart swells with pride for my clever, clever friend.

As the smoke clears, Todrick Hall's 'Fabulosity' starts to play out. The beat is fierce and fast and Jinx launches herself fully into the song and hi-energy choreography. The choir join in, backing her on the Chaka Khan vocals, and they dance with everything they have, a joyful exuberant flash mob sprinkled through the audience. They are perfect, taking it to a level not seen in here tonight – as hard as that is to believe – and the room explodes. Olive is throwing herself into it as if she has ants in her pants. I catch sight of Jack and someone I presume is his husband springing about next to him. Cass is dancing like a speeded-up Jack-in-a-box and I am alongside her giving it my all.

Dan has created a small forest on stage, including a hanging bough, and Jinx is incorporating it all as she pouts, struts and twirls through this first song. As the track ends, I am exhilarated and my heart fills full of love for my best friend, who is standing there in the most amazing frock and punching the air with such high energy. She sings the final 'fabulosity' of the track, her pitch perfect, and then, boom, a death drop.

The crowd screams and she grins, rolls over on to her side and as the music changes, she starts to sing the song she wrote about Bristol's different parks; it's tongue-in-cheek and very funny. Her humour is sharp but definitely not family-friendly as she homes in on all the city's distinct areas. The crowd has gone from whoops and cheers and high-energy bouncing to cackling loudly. She is still using the wooden props to contort herself into the craziest positions as she sings and with each new verse she pulls off an item of her dress.

I had no idea she was such a whizz with velcro.

First go the sleeves, then the skirt and then the bodice. The dress underneath is sheer bronze-gold mesh that shows the most remarkable shape and is the most sensual outfit to have been worn on stage tonight, even more so than Vivicious' leather Grace-Jones-on-meth outfit and TwinkiBelle's porntastic red latex body suit. As the song ends on a filthy joke about Tog Hill, she pulls off her wig to reveal a smaller, sleek dark brunette wig that flutters down her back and gold mesh that falls down over her face.

The audience lets out a collective long slow 'woah', the lights go down, smoke rises from the stage again and a spotlight picks out Dan on the piano. There is silence on the stage, matched by the audience, who are now open-mouthed waiting for the final part of her act. Dan starts to play 'The First Time Ever I Saw Your Face' and I am standing there holding my breath as Jinx begins the song, on a stage now darkened and free from frills, her voice so pure that I could cry.

I hear a sigh similar in intensity to mine and as I turn my head I see the Huangs standing there. She is stood in front of him, him with his hand on her shoulder – a small but meaningful gesture from this man – and they both watch their son at his most fabulous, most camp best.

I should have known from their determination to be involved with Pride that they would have found a way to this event tonight. Flyers were everywhere.

I'm not sure if they are aware it is their son but they would have to be blind not to. For me Jinx and Kevin are inseparable; it is no different seeing him as Jinx than it is for me to change from a blue dress to a green dress – I am still me and Kevin is always Kevin – so surely they recognise their child?

Whether they know or not is not of huge importance to me

in this moment, I am far more worried that Jinx will catch sight of them and it will throw her off balance. I consider escorting them out but can't bear to miss Jinx's finale. She'll never forgive me. There is very little I can do but stand here and smile and pray they don't suddenly explode as they recognise their son. In which case I *will* miss Jinx's finale and be kidnapping the pair of them, wrapping them both up in gaffer tape and leaving them in the loos. As charming as the little velvet seats, the perfumes and the mints are, that is not a place they would want to be for long. I know some of the things that happen there.

Shu-feng asks Chih-hao a question, he smiles and nods and she turns to me.

'Is Kevin singing this for Dan?' My legs wobble and I let out a gasp before asking her to repeat the question.

She does so and I have not misheard. My relief is overwhelming and a huge breath releases across my lips. She knows and seems fine with it; they both seem fine with it. I don't really know what to say, other than the truth.

'I hope so. I think so.'

They exchange a look, their eyes gleaming, and look as proud as proud can be.

Under the spotlight, Jinx hits the end of the song, singing 'your face' and holding the note perfectly as she looks across at Dan. Then she turns back, makes eye contact with the audience and pats the side of her wig and raises her brows.

Jinx walks across the stage, the spotlight seconds behind her, clearly unaware that she was going to do this, and she gives Dan the biggest smacker on the lips.

Scanning the crowd, she nods her thanks to the choir, gives them a side clap and then freezes for a millisecond as she takes in all of us bouncing in excitement in front of her. Her eyes find me in the crowd as we move up and down in waves, chanting her name. Jay and Cass are next to me jumping up and down and screaming. Jinx looks happier than I have ever seen her but then she sees her parents on the other side of me and her eyes widen in horror and she looks as if her world has collapsed. Then they both stretch out their arms and give their child a double thumbs-up. Jinx still looks confused, as if she can't fully compute what she is seeing, but after the thumbs-up her mother shapes her fingers into a heart and the love shining from her face can't be mistaken. I see Jinx's lips wobble but meanwhile Phyllis steps up the stairs onto the stage, walks to the mic stand and addresses the crowd, calming them down with her hands before she asks, 'And the judge's scores for our very own High Jinx?'

The whole bar watches, rapt, as the judges hold up scores of ten, ten and nine and Jinx bursts into tears, trying to stop them by batting her eyes rapidly and holding her fingers just below her lower lids, almost forcing the tears back inside her eyes.

'I can't let all this run,' she says, sniffling and laughing all at the same time. 'I'm never going to manage to create these cheekbones again.'

'That gives us a clear winner tonight. Thank you, judges.' Phyllis nods at them. 'And I am as proud as proud can be that our wonderful, most audacious, truly original High Jinx is the Official Queen of the Southwest.' She raps her cane on the floor and Barry and Gary march on with the most preposterous crown covered in cherubim and apples and trumpets, along with a sceptre which looks suspiciously like Phyllis' old cane with lots of diamanté glued to it.

Phyllis takes the crown and motions to High Jinx to kneel in front of her, and then, as she bends one knee, Phyllis crowns my best friend in the world and the crowd roars.

Phyllis motions at the mic and leaves the stage and Jinx, still sniffing and trying hard to force back the tears, takes a deep breath and then fixes us all with the smile I know she has been perfecting in front of the mirror for years.

And boy, is it worth it.

She opens her mouth to speak... and pauses, keeping her audience in the palm of her hand. The whooping starts again and she waves her hand to get everyone to shut up.

'Right, I want to keep this brief because I know even in my moment of shining glory that you all want to get back to the bar and knock back at least one bottle of voddy to celebrate my very –' she pauses again, playing with us all '– *very* well-deserved victory. But before you do that, I do have to say a few thank yous. A thank you of course goes to Phyllis, for being a haven as well as a maven when I was looking to find my people. You supplied me with a safe space that allowed me to develop my wings, made of diamanté and tulle obviously, and to learn to fly. Phyllis, you are like a second mother to me and to practically every girl here with us tonight, certainly those of us who have been here up on the stage. So thank you.' She clasps her hands and bows her head and Phyllis twitches her cane to suggest that High Jinx gets a move on, but everyone standing close can see the tears pricking in the corner of her eyes.

Jinx takes another deep breath. 'And that brings me to my real mother, who is standing down there with my father at what I imagine may be their very first drag show, watching their son be the most exquisite, talented woman that they could ever have imagined. I have been worried about telling them the truth of the whole of me for a long time and yet by the look of them now, and their presence tonight, I realise that I have made assumptions that were false and forgot to remind myself that they have always been there for me. They even bought me my very first Kylie album when I was not much more than yay-high.' She holds her hand down low, toddler height. 'I am sorry for doubting you, for allowing my insecurities to shape my fears. Having you here tonight is really special and I cannot thank you enough.' Jinx blows kisses at them with a double-handed gesture and then angles herself to take in the piano.

'Then there's Dan. Dan helped me with everything that came together tonight. He has spent days and days, no, weeks and weeks, helping me train my voice and get pitch perfect. He and our friend Jay are responsible for the inclusion of this fabulous community choir –' she sweeps her hand at the choir in the audience '– and he helped sew these costumes and gather and build my mini-forest-on-a-stage here. Dan, I think you may be the love of my life.' Jinx blows him a kiss to rapturous applause.

'There is one outstanding thing left to do before I let you all go back to the bar, and the love-of-my-life takes his place behind the decks to make sure this evening continues being fabulous. But first I must do this, because this is going to be the best way to say thank you to my oldest...not oldest, ouch, longest-standing friend.'

She grins at me and I grin back. What has she planned?

'As I am now officially Queen of the Southwest, I believe my word is law now, so you, yes, you, madam, get your sassy arse up here with me.' She marches over to the steps and reaches out her finger and beckons me.

'I think she means you,' I say to Shu-feng hopefully.

'No, she means you,' Jay, Cassie, Chih-hao and Shu-feng say in tandem.

'Yep. No, I'm not coming up there. This is your day,' I shout up at the stage.

'I decree it.' She stamps her cane in the floor in the same way Phyllis does and waves her hand at Barry and Gary at the same time as Mr and Mrs Huang push me from behind towards the stage. I mount the steps reluctantly and go and stand next to her. I should have known she would milk her moment of glory for all it was worth, and I'm proud of her for doing so. I just wish it wasn't resulting in me standing on the stage wondering what hell she is planning.

'Right, and who are you?' She shoves the microphone under my nose and I glare at her.

'I don't want....'

'I will actually have your head chopped off,' she declares confidently. 'Who are you?'

'Really? This is what you're using your glory for?' I question.

'Who are you?'

'Okay then. Hello, everyone, I'm Lily Galbraith.' I do a little curtsy to the audience and the choir, every single one of them, bob back.

'And...and who else are you?'

'Um...do you mean the Love Doctoring?' I hiss out the side of my mouth at my friend.

'Oh yes.'

'Okay, I'm Lily Galbraith and I am The Love Doctor. It's

possible that I'm going to kill my best friend this evening. Maybe on stage.'

'Yeah, yeah. So repeat after me, I'm Lily Galbraith, The Love Doctor, and I have many issues,' Jinx says with a smirk, 'the worst one being—' She pauses and hands the mic back to me. What exactly does she want me to say?

'My worst issue would be ...um... that my best friend from the age of eighteen is now a bossy-arse crowned queen clearly not afraid to abuse her powers.'

'No, no, we know that's not it, don't we? That is a blessing not an issue.' She gives me a hard stare. The sort that would frighten even Paddington Bear.

'I am The Love Doctor and I am a commitment-phobe,' I say loudly to the crowd in a resigned-and-at-a-meeting voice.

'Hallelujah. Yes, she is, ladies and –' Jinx sweeps her eye over the crowd, who miraculously are very engaged with what is happening, even though I rather wish they weren't '– ladies. And I am here for all Lily's choices. For years she has been prowling amongst the unsuspecting of Bristol, advising by day and being very... um... active at night....' Naturally she accompanies this with a stage wink.

Oh my God, I'm going to kill her. I don't dare look at Jay. This is not what he needs to hear right now, a confirmation of my love of the single life. What the hell is she doing?

'...but now we have to ask, is this what she wants in life? Why still single, Lily?'

'Because it made me happy and because I have self-determination and because that was my choice...and because I had never met anyone who was enough to make me want to give up my single life.'

'But?' Jinx asks and suddenly I have a moment of clarity. I

know what she is trying to do. She is trying to get me to 'fess up to the very thing I was discussing in the loos with Cass earlier. That it is fine to be happy in your life and make your choices but we also need to know when to make adjustments, when to shake things up a bit and not just carry on living as we always have been, just because we are scared of change. It is very easy to become constricted by our choices and the only thing I want to be right now is honest about the changes I want to make, the changes I want to make with Jay. And that is what she is trying to make me admit, here tonight, in my safe place with an audience of largely familiar and entirely friendly faces. I need to do this, I need to do this for me and I need to show Jay how my love for him is so important I will face very public, very possible, rejection to make sure he knows it. And my best friend is giving up her minute in the spotlight for me to do this.

'But...um...' Jinx queries, motioning for me to continue.

'But when the time is right you will meet the perfect person. Just remember the golden rules,' Cass shouts up to the stage and Jay spins his head to look at his sister.

She has some voice.

It's possible that people in the bar across the road heard. The golden rules; she really has listened to the podcast. And Jay *is* the perfect person, he is the only person I have ever felt like this about, the only person whom I can see sharing my life that would improve it, make it more.

'Be brave!' Chloe shouts.

'Have faith!' Ellie adds.

'Be true to yourself!' comes from Megan.

'But don't lick their faces!' the teens and Cass shout in unison, hands around their mouths with High Jinx next to me on stage pumping her arms in the air. I begin to feel the tears, but more importantly I feel the strength, the support of the people in this room. My friends, my chosen family, these women Jay has brought into my life – and Jay himself. The man I was never looking for, but the man that found me anyway. The man that accepts me exactly as I am, the man not interested in the superficiality I have cloaked myself in for my whole adult life. The person I want to wake up to every day, the person I want to build a life with, the person I want to make decisions with, decisions that will go on to shape the two of us and the people we are and the people we want to become.

Suddenly I find all the strength in the world. I know what I want and I know I have the courage to give it a shot.

'But I have been a fool,' I say, my voice strong and empowered and projecting across the whole of the bar, the conviction clear in my voice. 'I have been too scared to recognise that a change has occurred in my life and that I've been hiding behind my past rather than facing my future.'

The crowd all nod empathetically and I see Cass grab Jay by the hand. She looks as if she is preparing to pull him onto the stage. My mortification has utterly vanished now. This makes sense, I know what I have to do, *I have to* or I will regret it for ever, and I am relieved to see Jay hold Cass's hand willingly. He doesn't look as if he needs to be pulled, he doesn't look like he wants to run screaming for the door, instead he is allowing her to walk him to the steps, where she flaps him up.

He takes the steps and it is a miracle he doesn't fall because his eyes are locked onto mine the whole time from the second he places his foot upon the first step. I feel a warmth, a fluster and a tingle all at the same time. Images flash through my head – the very first time we met, and how his twinkle and ridiculous story drew me in, the night he lifted me onto my podcast table, oh my God, the day he came and saw me at my most vulnerable and wanted to do nothing but care for me – and I am grinning at him and extending my hands.

'You like what you see, huh?' Jinx drawls into the microphone in a very dirty voice.

'I do.'

'And once more for those at the back.'

'I do,' I shout.

Jay is opposite me now. We are standing about a foot apart and he reaches for my hands and twines his fingers in mine and this feels ridiculous, I have literally just said 'I do' to this man in front of me, on a stage, in an old chapel, and yet at the same time it feels so right. Not that I'm actually marrying Jay, or plan to. A girl can't change overnight. But he is here with me and his eyes are full of mischief and affection, and promise.

'So are you announcing in this very public place that you have a serious crush...'

'Serious!' Chloe, Megan and Ellie call out and Jay grins and gives them a look.

'A serious –' Jinx mimics the girls' way of saying the word, dragging out the final syllable '– crush on this man here?'

'I fancy him a little bit, yeah.'

'A little bit?'

'Quite a lot.'

'And yet up until tonight is it safe to say you have neglected to mention this to him?'

The whole room is silent now. Even the judges, still in their seats, are looking at me.

'Is there anything else you'd like to say to him before we let these fine folk here get to the bar and resume some dancing?'

'Jay, I am really sorry I have messed you around and behaved so badly. I would like it very much, very much –' I look at him so intensely, trying to create a world for just the two of us here, make him realise how much I mean these words and that, as madly public as this is right now, this is what I would say to him privately as well, and that maybe I should have done so a lot sooner '– *very* much if you and I could make a go of it, if you're still willing to. I love you so very much, so very, very much. Let's live one day at a time with each other and see where it takes us. And do it without lists, without fear, without expectations putting pressure on us. Let's just live a day at a time, love a day at a time and really enjoy each other without letting our heads get in the way. What do you think?'

The room is still and it feels like hours before Jay, who is grinning from ear to ear and looking like all his dreams are coming true, whispers to me – a message from him to me, the audience now irrelevant – 'Doctor Lily Galbraith, Love Doctor extraordinaire, I would really, really like that.' And he pulls me to him, my feet skip over themselves until we are pressed up against each other and he bends his head and kisses me with a fervour that shows me how much loving the two of us have in our future, and the room explodes, the crowd roars and when I open my eyes a minute or so later I see the judges holding up cards that say ten, ten, ten.

Acknowledgments

I have had so much fun writing this book, it was one in which my characters truly came to life and took over in telling their own story. However, I do have an awful lot of real-life people to thank for their support and input along the way.

The first is my agent, Hayley Steed from the Madeleine Milburn Literary, TV and Film Agency, who helped me develop the concept for this book and cheered me on all the way through. She and I always seem to be on the same page with things and I can't imagine what it would be like writing without having her in my corner. And a thank you to Elinor Davies, whose emails always make me smile.

Next is my editor, Charlotte Ledger at One More Chapter, she is so open, collaborative and supportive that I feel truly blessed working alongside her. Her edits are insightful, encouraging and make the book so much stronger. Some of the things she has said to me as I wrote this book will remain engraved on my heart forever and I cannot thank her enough for the way she has helped me to develop as a writer.

The whole team at One More Chapter are wonderful but a special shout out must go to the authenticity and sensitivity reader, who managed to dispel any concerns I had about writing certain parts that are outside of my own lived experience. Their report made me shed a happy tear and meant I could really enjoy the run up to publication.

Another thank you has to go to Tony Russell, whose eagle-eyed copy-edits picked up those little details that are hard for me to see, I really appreciate your diligence. And to Eleanor Goymer, who is remarkably skilled at finding the exact words needed when they eluded me.

This book was meant to be solely about Lily and Jay and is very much their story, but High Jinx was so dominant throughout that I had to write her romance too – she made me. But I was very aware that watching TV shows and attending drag events was not enough research to make sure that I could write her as authentically and empathetically as possible; so I enlisted the help of Jolene Dover – the absolute Queen of Wales – who was not only unwavering in her patience as I fired daft question after daft question at her but who makes me screech with laughter every day on Instagram. Do give her a follow, and I guarantee her stories will make you giggle too. I am officially a super-fan. I also have to send a big thank you to Alke, a Bristol-based drag artist who patiently went over some of my scenes and made sure that everything was exactly as it should be.

With the girls from City Youth, I needed someone far younger than me to help with their dialogue and was helped by the gorgeous Alea Robleh. A lot of what she suggested has been sanitised along the way but there are certain phrases in my head now that will never stop making me giggle.

As ever, I have to shout out to Jane Cable and Cass Grafton, who keep me sane as I write. Their check-ins, wisdom and encouragement mean the world. These are the two women I will shoot a message to when I need instant guidance or reassurance and they will be on my screen in a second, helping me solve all my plot niggles and worries.

Talking of role models and people that mean the world to me, I've dedicated this book to Norma and her son, my friend Matthew. I have known these two since I was sixteen and I swear there are no kinder people on the planet. They have been by my side as I grew from teen to the person I am now and through all my adventures have never been anything but non-judgemental and supportive. I think Matthew may well buy more copies of each of my books than anyone else on this planet. They will always have my heart.

Then there is Cindy White, another school friend, who taught me so much about Taiwan, its customs, traditions and way of life. Any mistakes are entirely my own, but she certainly stopped me from making many, many more.

And finally, my family – there is no one that makes me cackle as they do. Namdi brings me happiness every single day and my children make me so proud; Jack is such a skilled writer and his current project has me reeling with its brilliance, and Katharine came with me to all the drag events I attended as I researched this book. She lit up every room we were in, made me dance on tables and live my best life all in the name of research. This book simply wouldn't have happened if it were not for her.

ONE MORE CHAPTER

One More Chapter is an
award-winning global
division of HarperCollins.

Sign up to our newsletter to get our
latest eBook deals and stay up to date
with our weekly Book Club!
<u>Subscribe here.</u>

Meet the team at
<u>www.onemorechapter.com</u>

Follow us!
 <u>@OneMoreChapter_</u>
<u>@OneMoreChapter</u>
<u>@onemorechapterhc</u>

Do you write unputdownable fiction?
We love to hear from new voices.
Find out how to submit your novel at
<u>www.onemorechapter.com/submissions</u>